NELSON

Breaking the Line

David Donachie

ORION

First published in Great Britain in 2002
by Orion Books
an imprint of The Orion Publishing Group
Orion House, 5 Upper St Martin's Lane,
London WC2H 9EA

A CIP catalogue record for this book
is available, from the British Library

ISBN 0 75282 474 0 (hardback)
ISBN 0 75284 681 7 (trade paperback)

Typeset at The Spartan Press Ltd,
Lymington, Hants
Printed and bound in Great Britain by
Clays Ltd, St Ives plc

To my beautiful daughter Charlotte
who has never once let me win an argument

GLOSSARY

Aft:	The rear of the ship.
Afterguard:	Sailors who worked on the quarterdeck and poop.
Bilge:	Foul-smelling water collecting in the bottom of the ship.
Binnacle:	Glass cabinet holding ship's compass: visible from the wheel.
Bowsprit:	Heavy spar projecting from the front of the ship.
Broadside:	The firing of all the ship's cannon in one salvo.
Bulkhead:	Moveable wooden partitions i.e. walls of captain's cabin.
Cathead:	Heavy joist that keeps anchor clear of ship's side.
Capstan:	Central lifting tackle for all heavy tasks on the ship.
Chase:	Enemy ship being pursued.
Crank:	A vessel that won't answer properly to the helm.
Forecastle:	Short raised deck at ship's bows. (Fo'c's'le)
Fish:	To secure and lash the raised anchor to the ship.
Frigate:	Small fast warship; the 'eyes of the fleet'.
Larboard:	Old term for 'port': left looking towards the bows.
Leeward:	The direction in which the wind is blowing.
Letter of Marque:	Private-armed ship licensed to attack enemy. (Privateer)
Log:	Ship's diary, detailing course, speed, punishments etc.
Logline:	Knotted rope affixed to heavy wood to show ship's speed.
Mast:	Solid vertical poles holding yards.°(see below).
Mizzen:	Rear mast.
Muster:	List of ship's personnel.
Ordinary:	Ship laid up in reserve.
Orlop:	Lowest deck on the ship, often below waterline.
Quarterdeck:	Above maindeck, from which command was exercised.
Rate:	Class of ship 1–6 depending on number of guns.
Rating:	Seaman's level of skill.
Reef:	To reduce the area of a sail by bundling and tying.

Scurvy:	Disease caused by lack of vitamins, especially C.
Scuppers:	Openings in ship's side to allow escape of excess water.
Sheet:	Ropes used to control sails.
Sheet-home:	To tie off said ropes.
Ship of the Line:	A capital ship large enough to withstand in line combat
Sloop:	Small warship-not rated. A Lieutenant's command.
Spar:	Length of timber used to spread sails.
Starboard:	Right side of ship facing bows.
Tack:	To turn the head of the ship into the wind.
Topman:	Sailor who worked high in the rigging.
Wardroom:	Home to ship's officers, commissioned and warrant.
Watch:	A division of the ship's crew × 2. A portion of the day.
Wear:	To turn the head of the ship away from the wind.
Windward:	The side of the ship facing the wind.
Yard:	Horizontal pole holding sail. Loosely attached to mast.
Yardarm:	Outer end of yard.

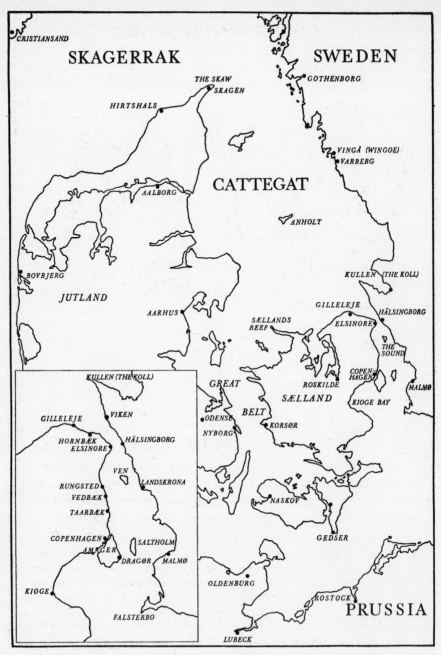

The approach from the North Sea to Copenhagen and the Baltic showing (inset) the direct route past Elsinore, and the alternative, through the Great Belt.

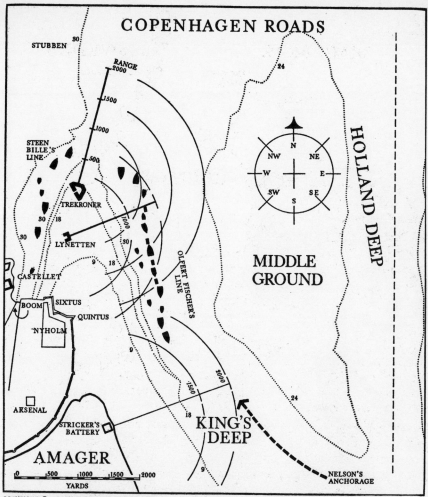

COPENHAGEN ROADS

STUBBEN
RANGE 2000
STEEN BILLE'S LINE
TREKRONER
LYNETTEN
CASTELLET
BOOM
SIXTUS
QUINTUS
NYHOLM
ARSENAL
STRICKER'S BATTERY
AMAGER

HOLLAND DEEP

MIDDLE GROUND

OLFERT FISCHER'S LINE

KING'S DEEP

NELSON'S ANCHORAGE

N NE E SE S SW W NW

0 500 1000 1500 2000
YARDS

Copenhagen Roads, showing the positions of the Danish ships and Nelson's course (broken line) southward down the Holland Deep to the night anchorage south of the Middle Ground. Depths are shown in feet and ranges are in yards. The precise positions of the shoals will never be known for certain. The standard drawing of the Battle (by Bundesen in 1901) was based on a chart of 1840, but documentary evidence and a chart from a survey made a few months after the Battle (and not seen by Bundesen) shows it to be wrong in certain respects. The above chart, by the author, relies mostly on cross-checking. Although drawn independently and before the existence of the 1801 chart was known, it subsequently proved to be nearer the 1801 chart in showing the position of shoals than the previous charts – by Andreas Lous in 1763 and 1775 – which were probably in use at the time of the Battle. The experience gained in the Battle and in replacing the buoys probably led to the new survey in 1801 – it was begun in August and completed in November.

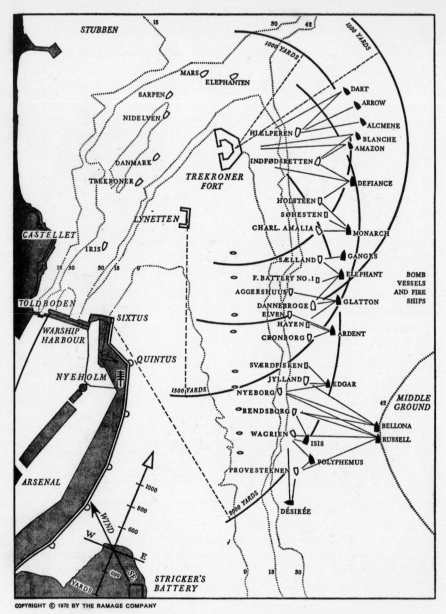

This chart by the author is based entirely on the reports of Danish and British officers and the logs of their ships, which agreed with each other to a remarkable degree. They allowed the position of *Russell* and *Bellona*, for example, to be established with some precision, and this in turn located the edge of the Middle Ground shoal. Depths are in feet and ranges in yards.

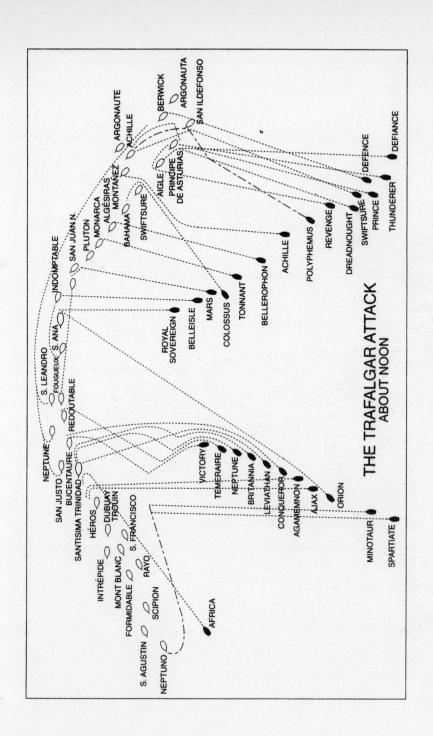

THE TRAFALGAR ATTACK
ABOUT NOON

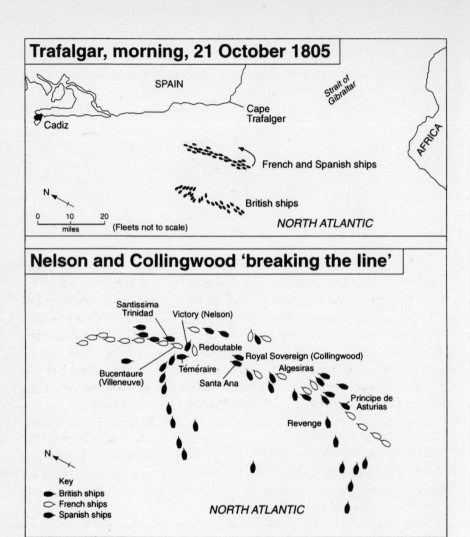

Trafalgar, morning, 21 October 1805

SPAIN

Strait of Gibraltar

Cape Trafalger

Cadiz

AFRICA

French and Spanish ships

British ships

N

0   10   20
miles

(Fleets not to scale)

NORTH ATLANTIC

Nelson and Collingwood 'breaking the line'

Santissima Trinidad

Victory (Nelson)

Redoutable

Royal Sovereign (Collingwood)

Bucentaure (Villeneuve)

Téméraire

Algesiras

Santa Ana

Principe de Asturias

Revenge

N

Key
British ships
French ships
Spanish ships

NORTH ATLANTIC

Prologue

~

1798

Alarm was not an emotion often expressed in the Admiralty building, sat squarely at the top of Whitehall. The working centre of Britain's global maritime reach, everyone who occupied it, from doormen and servants to clerks, secretaries, civilian officials and admirals, prided themselves on their ability to take bad news with the same air of equanimity with which they received the good. All worked hard to comport themselves in wartime with no more application than they did during the short periods when Britannia was at peace.

Such an attitude was seen as a measure of their professionalism. That this did not extend to the First Lord of the Admiralty, who was a civilian and a political appointee – and thus a temporary controller of the nation's maritime power – was hardly surprising. To his oft repeated interrogation, 'Damn it, where is Nelson?' the more experienced could only advise patience.

Lord Spencer, the present incumbent of the office, openly admitted that his responsibilities often interfered with his sleep. That he should be so affected was met by his more experienced colleagues with a mixture of sympathy and understanding, tinged with mirth. Yet even the most sanguine had to admit that the circumstances of the moment were exceptionally grave. The Royal Navy might control the seas on which they sailed, but on land the enemy, France, was everywhere victorious.

Austria, greatest of the nations to partake of the First Coalition against the French Revolution, had put five armies into the field in as many years and had seen them crushed. All of Northern Italy down to Rome was in enemy hands, a series of gimcrack republics set up on the Parisian model by the fearsome General Bonaparte.

The present French regime was less extreme than its predecessor,

1

which had lopped off the heads of King Louis and Queen Marie Antoinette. Known as the Directory, the current five-man government contained some of those regicides in its ranks. These men, naturally suspicious and tainted by greed, had created a policy that substituted theft abroad for terror at home and shipped Bonaparte and his army into the Mediterranean in search of further conquest.

Here was a golden chance for Britain to take on this menace, for the sea suited her more than it suited France. Catch that fleet and transports at sea and they might sink the ambitions of the Corsican, as well as those of his political masters. Lord Spencer, against opposition, had agreed to send Sir Horatio Nelson, the Navy's most aggressive junior admiral, after Bonaparte.

Nelson was undoubtedly a fighter, and a few admirals who had commanded him saw the genius admired by the public – none more than John Jervis, Earl St Vincent, stationed off the main Spanish naval base of Cadiz, who had recommended his appointment. Others, though, including many of a more elevated rank, observed in Nelson only an insubordinate risk-taker, a man who had enjoyed a degree of success, but who was bound to overreach himself. Now, having sailed into the Mediterranean nearly two months before, the man seemed to have disappeared off the face of the earth.

'Damn it, where is Nelson?' echoed in the corridors of power, the coffee houses, and the salons of the powerful, repeated by serving officers, ministers and courtiers all the way up to King George himself. The sovereign was known to dislike the admiral and disapprove of his appointment.

The Prime Minister, William Pitt, wanted peace, but knew that would only come once France had been humbled. Nelson had been sent to stop Bonaparte, and clearly he had failed. He might have suffered a catastrophic defeat, losing ships and men that the Navy could not do without. Rumours abounded of a great battle fought in Egyptian waters, of a fleet destroyed, Nelson dead, most of his captains prisoners of the French, and Bonaparte triumphant again.

Those admirals senior to Nelson who felt the task should have been entrusted to them had ceased merely to question the wisdom of the decision. The looks cast at Lord Spencer now were not of pique from those who felt they had been overlooked, but said 'I told you so'. They knew what the First Lord did not: that Horatio Nelson might be as brave as a lion, but he was also an upstart and a chancer.

The weather did nothing to help: it was a cold November of high winds and slanting rain that rattled windows, and on nights when clouds raced across the moon, the First Lord would stand by his bedroom window, repeating, to the annoyance and pity of his wife, 'Damn it, where is Nelson?'

Fanny Nelson quelled her anxiety about her husband in strict adherence to her daily routine. She dealt with her correspondence, supervised her household, made calls on her friends and received them in return, all interspersed with sessions of embroidery. She tried not to think of what would happen to her husband should he prove too impetuous.

Certainly, his life was at risk, which Nelson's father, the Reverend Edmund Nelson, never ceased to mention on his frequent visits. He reminded Fanny that his son had been mischievous as a boy, that his behaviour at school had resulted in several letters from his head-master. Midshipman Horatio Nelson had been troublesome too, a fact which the Reverend Nelson had discovered from the boy's uncle and first captain.

In the Mediterranean, Nelson's history of endless single-ship actions, cutting out expeditions, sudden landings and hard won sieges, was seen by his tall, beetle-browed father as stemming not from zeal but impatience. That he had taken two ships in one attack at the battle of Cape St Vincent, a feat never before achieved by any naval officer, the Reverend saw bleakly as foolhardy rather than brave.

Yet Fanny was cheered by letters from men high and low singing her husband's praises, naming him a hero fit to stand in the same pantheon as Francis Drake. Some were indecipherable scrawls from those barely able to read and write; others beautifully crafted epistles from professional scribes employed by the wholly illiterate. The ones that pleased her most came from people of some station – noblemen, city merchants, land owners, ambassadors and their wives at foreign courts, all those who wanted to record their gratitude to Rear Admiral Sir Horatio Nelson KB for their peace and security.

She had also a stack of letters from men with whom her husband had served; soldiers, sailors, political envoys and even exiled Britons, either temporary travellers or those domiciled abroad. Many were kind enough to mention her son Josiah too, and to note that, as a young naval officer, he was on the way to making both his mother and his stepfather proud.

Then she had Nelson's own letters, full of affectionate sentiment as well as advice on everything from her dealings with his family to how she should disburse their new found security. It grated on her somewhat that her husband felt able to recommend to her a house when he was a thousand miles from the location and she just a few.

3

But he had always been prepared to expound on any matter that he felt came within his province.

There were other letters that Fanny read out of a sense of duty, scurrilous anonymous drafts that sought to inform her, more in sorrow than in anger, that if her husband was a true British hero, he was no saint. If they were to be believed, there was no venality to which Horatio Nelson would not stoop: corrupt misuse of government monies, grovelling to foreign potentates, and a concubine in every port. These she dismissed as the natural products of jealous natures. Her husband had achieved so much that envy was inevitable. He spent Admiralty money on his sailors' comfort. He flattered kings and queens in the interests of his country. As for the last accusation, Horatio had needs, all men did, but they were those of a mature husband and stepfather: he was not a callow young rake.

But sometimes, as she looked at her reflection, she was aware that the looks he had once admired had faded. Gone was the glow of a skin once warmed by Caribbean sun, and in its place a pallor brought on by northern weather and age, with lines now that no amount of powder could disguise, around the eyes, the mouth and even her lips.

In such moments, when she contemplated the difficulties of a naval wife, it took a stern mind to allay her fears. She was a good and dutiful spouse, an accomplished social hostess; she treated supplicants at her door, especially wounded ex-sailors, with the proper measure of kindness, even sat listening to the ramblings of Captain William Locker, one of Nelson's former commanders whom her husband called his 'sea daddy'. Fanny wrote continually to her husband to report her actions, meetings and tender feelings, and was reassured by his replies – naturally infrequent from a man on active service – which never failed to remind her that she was the companion of his heart.

She prayed that he was safe and well, that he would be successful in his duties, and that he would come home one day to rest on his well-earned laurels in a scene of harmonious domestic tranquillity which she would create for him.

1

How can you continue to fight with a cutlass blade through your heart? Horatio Nelson knew it was there, just as he knew that it caused him no pain, and did nothing to impede him in the assault on the enemy frigate. The approach had been made in silence; guns run out, lower sails taken in and boarding nets rigged, the usual rush of clearing for action – bulkheads knocked out, furniture broken down, delicate plate and glassware packed into boxes, the gunner filling charges that the ship's boys raced to deliver to the gun captains. He had seen mouths move, understood requests made and orders given, but had heard no sound.

Even the enemy cannon, eighteen-pounders firing off the first salvo, had belched smoke but no noise. It lasted throughout the long gunnery duel. Wooden bulwarks were smashed on both vessels, guns dismounted, masts wounded and rigging ripped asunder until the ships closed for the final act of boarding. Jumping from one bulwark to the next Nelson felt as though he was floating. But cleaving with the sword that had belonged to his naval ancestor Captain Gadifrus Walpole, he cut down those who appeared before him with heavy blows.

Somehow, instead of landing on the enemy quarterdeck, he had slid through the scantlings on to the maindeck as if the great timbers that made up the side of the ship did not exist. That meant he had to fight his way up the companionway towards the daylight of the quarterdeck, just as he had at the battle of Cape St Vincent. Familiar faces surrounded him, swimming in and out of focus, but he could not recall a single name. The fight to remember began to seem more important than keeping himself alive or taking the enemy ship. Yet ahead of him, drawing him onwards and upwards,

5

was a light so blinding it seemed the sun itself was at the head of those open stairs.

Nelson felt fear then; the terror that something not human lay beyond that light, whose heat penetrated the heavy cutlass blade that protruded from his upper body. Suddenly pain seared through him and shapes formed in the radiance ahead. Faces appeared, but this time he could identify them: his father, his brothers, William, Edmund, Suckling and young George; his sisters Susanna, Ann and Catherine, all waving, as if in farewell.

Those images dissolved into another. The next face to appear was that of his dead mother, which melted into a *tableau vivant* he had seen as a child, a representation of the death of his hero, General James Wolfe. Only this time it was Nelson lying in the arms of a fellow officer. The image was shattered by a great explosion, which halted his intended flight, as the French ship *L'Orient*, a mass of orange and red light against the night sky, blew up in Aboukir Bay. Darkness turned to daylight, to reveal behind the falling debris not an Egyptian shore but a calm, sandy Norfolk beach dotted with the red brick houses of the North Sea coast. And behind that the green undulating slopes that led to his home at Burnham Thorpe.

He swooped in like a seagull over All Saints, his father's church, still showing an open damaged face to the world at the south nave, still chilly inside even on a summer's day. The trees that shaded the passage down to the Parsonage were in full leaf, reflected in the still waters of the reed-fringed pond that lay foursquare in front of the house. From inside he heard pealing laughter, and knew that he was its object, but try as he might he could not enter to share in the happiness that lay inside.

His eyes opened, one good, the other opaque, and he was faced with a blank expanse of white linen. Someone, probably his servant Tom Allen, had opened both shutters to flood the room with light. He registered that he was lying on his side, the stump of his right arm trapped and numb beneath him. The bed in which he lay was wider than his cot and there was none of the normal swaying motion, nor the creaking of timbers and cables, the smell of pitch, wood and corruption that went with sleeping aboard ship. Instead a familiar perfume, mingled with the smell of his own warm body, rose from under the heavy coverlet.

The vivid dream was still with him; the faces of long-dead shipmates, the family he had not seen for years and the mother who had died when he was seven. The action he recalled was that with the Spanish frigate the *Santa Sabina*, a bloody affair, in which the Dons

6

had lost over a hundred and fifty men dead and wounded, their ship left with not a mast standing.

He recalled the name and dignity with which the captain had surrendered. Nelson had taken in his hands the sword of Don Jacobo Stuart, great grandson of King James II, who claimed to be the rightful king of England and Scotland. Nelson glanced at the mantel above the fireplace, over which hung a portrait of his own sovereign: heavy jowls, hooded eyes and the thick, disapproving Hanoverian lips of King George III. In Nelson's memory the Stuart pretender had looked so much more princely than his King.

His head sank back to the pillow and again the scent filled his nostrils. It had all begun last night under that portrait. He had spent the night with his benign host Sir William Hamilton, King George's ambassador at the court of Naples, and his wife, the beautiful and accomplished Lady Emma. She had sat by his right hand, wafting that scent, while she led the plaudits at the banquet held to celebrate his victory at the Nile.

Later she had flitted into his room and Nelson recalled the passionate, lascivious creature who had introduced him to a depth of passion and accomplishment he had never before experienced. He felt as if, for the first time in his life, he had truly made love to a woman. He could still feel every touch of her hand as she helped him to remove his clothes; he had an ache in his groin as he remembered their frenzied and prolonged love-making and blushed when he thought of the way he had sinned.

Worse, he had dishonoured a man he considered a friend and supporter. How could he face Sir William Hamilton after he had, under the man's own roof, made love to his wife?

Emma threw the umpteenth draft of the letter she was trying to write at the basket. It missed its target. She and Sir William often wrote to each other, even though they were man and wife and shared the same establishment. But Emma was more than his spouse: she had become the British Ambassador's helpmate at the Neapolitan court. A close friend of Queen Maria Carolina, Emma had proved invaluable at communicating to the queen her husband's ideas, thus easing his task.

At times their letter writing was a way of clarifying their thoughts, at others a record that would show, should an action be questioned at some future date, proof of proper intentions, and sometimes a way to resolve a disagreement, or express affection.

This letter was of a type that Emma had never penned before. In all the years she had lived with Sir William, both as mistress and wife, she had never strayed in her fidelity, although she had received innumerable offers from potential lovers, including King Ferdinand of Naples. The list of dukes, counts, earls, lords and knights, artists, writers, wits – English, German, Austrian and Italian – who had tried to bed her was endless. Sir William had taken as much pleasure from observing them fail as Emma did from their flattering attentions.

Emma put her quill to another piece of paper to try again. What to write? That she had always held him in the highest esteem, that they had a bargain which, though unspoken, was obvious to both, that if an attraction proved potent enough, neither party was debarred from the pursuit of pleasure? That she had not exercised such a right did nothing to dent its potency. Emma knew that Sir William was no prude: now in his sixty-eighth year, he had grown to manhood in an age when the present British predilection to rectitude was deemed unseemly in a gentleman. That was why Naples, with its hot sunshine, warm waters and febrile sensuality, suited him better than gloomy Georgian London.

Part of Emma wanted to pretend that last night had not happened. How could she be sure her husband knew the truth? Her mother, guardian of her bedchamber, who had alerted her, might have been wrong. Sir William might have left the house to go to their seaside villa at Posillipo for any number of reasons – he had done so before. A bilious feeling after the banquet, to fish perhaps, a pursuit he loved, the need for some solitude or a desire to bathe in the warm waters of the Bay of Naples.

The door creaked, and Emma fixed her eyes on the paper. She knew who it was: only two people would enter this room unannounced – her maid, Francesca, and Emma's mother. However, if it had been Francesca, Emma would have heard her since she never stopped singing. Her mother, with a key to every room in the palazzo at her hip, moved silently.

Mary Cadogan examined the back of her daughter's bent head. Her hair, which good Sir William called 'Titian', had not been combed and the loose strands picked up the light from the open windows overlooking the bay, making it seem golden. The furious scratching of the quill, she knew, was intended to shut her out. But Mary Cadogan had interfered often in her daughter's life, always – in her own mind – to the good.

'Is that a letter to Sir William?' she asked.

'It is,' Emma replied, her voice far from welcoming.

'What will you be telling him, girl? That your time spent in the

8

Admiral's bedchamber was all innocence, or that you gave your Nile hero a fitting reward for thumping the French?'

'I think, Mother, that what I write to my husband is my business.'

'That be true, Emma,' Mary Cadogan replied, easing herself into a chair beside her daughter. 'But I wondered if you might want to speak of it first, seeing as how in the past, you have done yourself more harm than good by flying off the handle.'

'Don't you mean you have, Mother?'

There was venom in that, since both women knew that Emma was in Naples due to her mother's influence. It was she who had seen first that her daughter's liaison with Sir William's nephew, Charles Greville, was over; that after six years as his mistress, the man Emma claimed to love had traded her off to secure his inheritance from an uncle he knew to be besotted with her. Maternal persuasion, aided by deliberate coldness from her previous keeper, had convinced Emma that her love for Greville was wasted; that security lay with a man over thirty years her senior.

Mary Cadogan had one overriding concern; that after a life of ups and downs, of widowhood, being a kept woman so that her family would not starve, and a near descent into prostitution, the only thing that mattered was the comfort of a good roof over both their heads. She thought her daughter too romantic to be sensible, too fanciful to see where danger lurked or advantage lay. She had done everything she could to prevent Emma falling into the same traps in which she herself had been snared, only to fall short too often.

There was a child, now grown to womanhood, who had no idea that Emma was her mother. Any number of folk could recall that the present Lady Hamilton had once been a lowly housemaid named Lyons, and as Emma Hart that she had been at best a lady of easy virtue, at worst a whore. She might be at the top of the social pile in Naples, but back in England her title brought mockery not respect. Received at court here, she was debarred from audience with the King and Queen of England and shunned by those who took from them their social cue.

'If you are thinking of penning a confession, girl, I feel I am bound to advise against it,' she said.

'I'm old enough to make my own decisions, Mother.'

'Old enough, for certain, and you've been that for many a year. But I hazard if you look back and examine some of the decisions you have made, and how I've aided you from being foolish, you might see fit to pass by me what it is you're planning to do.'

Emma turned to face her mother, her curling uncombed hair

framing what was still a beautiful face. In shadow Mary Cadogan could not see the green eyes and the flawless skin, but she knew them well – indeed the twelve years they had spent in Naples were hardly reflected in Emma's features, certainly not the miserable look of the first year. Good fortune, some hard maternal truths and Sir William's ease of manner had combined to turn her first into his mistress, then into his wife, gifting them both that life of ease Mary Cadogan so desired. That Emma did not love her husband was of no account: to Mary Cadogan's way of thinking, more attachments survived through mutual respect than ever endured on a diet of connubial bliss.

She could not believe that Sir William would respond to Emma's first lapse by sending her and her daughter packing. Emma was his wife: he would respect that – and not just to avoid public embarrassment. But he was getting on in years and for a woman who prided herself on being longsighted that was a consideration. Old men were as prey to jealousy as the young, sometimes more so. And Mary Cadogan knew that they were entirely dependent on Sir William, even after he was dead and buried. Starting hares that might affect the future was a bad idea if you had no idea to where they would run, so silence was likely to be a better option than confession.

For the tenth time since she'd woken up, Emma was examining her own actions, which seemed to her to have been caused by some force of nature. But to say so to a woman as practical as her mother was impossible.

'All Naples,' she insisted, 'indeed the whole of Europe, fêtes Nelson as a great hero, a saviour, the man who has finally checked the French abomination. He is the most famous man in the world. Am I to be immune from such . . .' Emma was unable to find the concluding word. 'I'm sure Sir William will understand the nature of what has happened.' She could not say that the attraction she felt for Horatio Nelson was one that had been with her ever since their first meeting five years previously. He had been a captain then, and whole, with both arms and two good eyes. She had written numerous letters to him from this very desk, never once allowing her feelings to surface in her correspondence.

But then he had returned a hero. Instead of the bright-eyed man she remembered, Emma had encountered a wounded, weary one in need of comfort. At the sight of him her repressed feelings had burst out, multiplied tenfold by tenderness. Every time she touched Nelson she felt an electric charge run through her. She could not tell her mother that what had happened between them last night was no mere fancy. It had been inevitable, and right now she would rather be back in Nelson's suite of rooms than here.

'Then you don't fear that Sir William will be agitated?' Mary asked.

'Why should he be?' Emma replied with an assurance she did not feel. 'My husband has hinted often enough that he considers it impolite to enquire into such matters.'

'Then why alert him to it?'

'How can you say that, Mother?' Emma snapped. 'It was you who told me last night that he . . .'

'Knew you bedded the Admiral? Well, that's as maybe, Emma, but I can't see what good it will do to go rubbing it in. From what I know of Sir William you're right. He won't say a peep. Nor will you know by his face what he's thinking. Being deep is what he's good at. Let him be I say.'

She was tempted to add that Nelson would sail off soon, as all sailors did, ending something that her daughter should never have started, and that once that happened, provided a discreet silence was observed by all, life could return to normal.

Naked and without his wig, Sir William Hamilton lay in the warm shallow waters of the Bay of Naples, one had gently fondling the loose wrinkled skin of his scrotum, ruminating on past scrapes. Like any young aristocrat he had whored his way around London and Europe in the company of like minded individuals, including the present King George, a riotous prince then, a dull-as-ditchwater prude now. Hamilton's first marriage, a sensible match, had been made more to secure his wife's income than for any notions of love – as a younger son of a ducal family he had had little in the way of an inheritance.

He could hardly say that the same sentiments applied to Emma. He had been smitten by her the first time he had seen her at his nephew's house in London; her beauty, her vivacity, her innate kindness and natural wit. As the past lover of many women he had seen every facet of their behaviour: false affection, outrageous infatuation that could not last, naked greed for a man who had a good post, a reasonable unearned income, a palazzo, servants, carriages and access to the highest society. Emma loved these things, as any sensible woman would, but her enthusiasm was based on innocent enjoyment not calculation.

It was enlightening to compare his first marriage to his second, his Lady Charlotte to his Lady Emma. The former had been refined, reserved, dutiful, the very epitome of the English rose abroad, a companion of the mind more than the body. The latter, over thirty years his junior, was more Italian than the Italians, high spirited, often gauche, intelligent, instinctive and an unrestrained delight in the bedchamber.

It was hard to recall the *ingénue* who had arrived here all those years ago, with her comparative lack of refinement. Yet even then Emma had charmed Naples: the peasants hailed her as the living embodiment of the Madonna, while the aristocracy admired her as akin to a Greek goddess, more so when she learned, in four years, to speak Italian, French and German. Emma sang with gusto if not refinement, while her beauty and theatricality attracted the admiration of every visitor who called upon Sir William at the Palazzo Sessa. An invitation to watch her perform her 'Attitudes' was much sought after: her renderings of classical poses were sensual and greeted with much applause. But in the privacy of the bedchamber, he was gifted with attitudes that owed much to pagan rites. And yet, for all the abandon of which Emma was capable, she had been faithful.

Greville, the nephew who had exchanged Emma for a promise of being made Sir William's heir, had on occasion complained about her spirited behaviour. He had also shown an unattractive possessiveness whenever some gallant flattered her, even though Emma had never once caused him to feel he might be cuckolded. At least Sir William could pride himself on never showing jealousy, though he could not deny that now he felt it.

'Why Nelson?' he asked himself, softly. Looking down at his bony chest he knew that his age was a factor; that he was no longer potent enough to keep satisfied a creature like Emma. For some time he had considered it inevitable that Emma would succumb to the blandishments of the kind of man she would have rejected in the past.

The Admiral was a hero, and for Emma that would outweigh wit, wealth or any common accomplishment. She considered herself part of his victory at the Nile, which had seen, for Britain, an enemy fleet destroyed for the first time since the Spanish Armada. Had it not been her efforts and close connection with the Queen of Naples that had kept the British fleet at sea? Her intercession had ensured that supplies had been forthcoming from a kingdom that was nominally at peace with France, a nation that should, for neutrality's sake, have turned Nelson away. Without Emma, would Nelson have won his battle?

'Once a conqueror, how easy it is to be a seducer.'

Sir William tried to imagine the scene. Nelson would not have

forced matters, he was sure. For someone so at home in his professional milieu, the man was a sad case in a social setting. Quick to
blush, more forthright than was polite, and utterly lacking in that
ready wit and *sang froid* required in the circles in which the
Hamiltons moved, Nelson seemed always to hover on the edge of
embarrassment.

Yet Sir William liked and admired him for many things; his
honesty, ironic in the present circumstances, his zealous attention to
the needs of his sailors, and that he was prepared to offend anyone,
kings, princes, dukes and sea lords, if he felt it necessary. Sir William
had seen him in different guises: the timid social creature who
seemed to be a battleground of all the available medical disorders,
and the outspoken advocate of any policy he held to be right, which
gave a hint of the man he must be in a fight. According to his officers,
when danger threatened, afflictions dropped away to reveal an *enfant
terrible*. Sir William knew those officers adored Nelson, just as he
knew that Nelson doubted he was fit to lead them.

Nelson had been famous and a hero to his profession since his
actions at the battle of Cape St Vincent, where, disobeying standing
orders, he had accomplished a previously unheard of feat in capturing one Spanish ship from the deck of another already taken. Even
his failure at Tenerife, where he had lost both a battle and his arm,
had enhanced rather than damaged his reputation. His appointment
to the Mediterranean command, with the express task of stopping
Bonaparte had caused, according to Sir William's correspondence,
much disquiet in the breasts of more senior admirals who felt the
duty should have fallen to them. Sir William could easily imagine
that while many were anxious about Nelson's failure to beard the
Corsican menace, those same senior admirals would have been crowing about how right they had been.

They wouldn't be crowing when news of the Nile reached London.
Nelson had done the impossible: he had not only destroyed a French
fleet and French ambitions in that region. He had saved the Turkish
Sultan, the route to India, secured a breathing space for Italy and
imposed the first check on the insidious Revolution that had made
every European nation tremble for fear of France. And then he had
come back to Naples and bedded Sir William's wife.

Closing his eyes, Sir William placed himself once more in the dimly
lit corridor outside Nelson's rooms. That he had gone to see to the
well-being of his guest forced a reluctant smile to his lips. But then
there had been the sight of his wife slipping into Nelson's room, and
minutes later the grating sound of the key turning in the lock. He had

pictured what was taking place behind those double doors: his wife, her hero, both naked and writhing.

Still fondling his groin, Sir William was aware of an increasing and now rare tumescence as the thoughts he harboured flitted through his mind. He knew how unrestrained his wife was: she knew how to arouse a man, and how to tease that arousal until passion could no longer be contained.

He signalled and his valet stepped forward, first to pour fresh water over him to wash off the sea salt, then to wrap a towel round him as he stood up, a trifle unsteady on legs that had grown thin with the onset of age.

'My carriage in twenty minutes,' Sir William said. 'I shall be returning to the Palazzo Sessa.'

'Maestro,' his valet replied.

2

Tom Allen knew he was not the brightest of men, nor the best of sailor servants. He hung on to his job because he was quiet and unassuming and his master was benign. This morning, though, as he helped his admiral to wash, dress and comb his hair, he had the sense to realise that something was not quite as it should be.

First, his master had not asked where Tom had been the night before, or why he had been left to undress himself. All the excuses Tom had rehearsed to cover the truth: that he had drunk too much wine, then spent the night with one of Sir William's female servants had remained unspoken.

From fearful silence, Tom graduated slowly to talking about the ball and the banquet, how splendid they had been, a fitting tribute to such a justly famous man. None of this had produced a smile or even a nod. But when he had told him that Sir William was not at home, that he had departed an hour after the last of the guests to spend the night at his seaside villa, Nelson shuddered.

As he cut up Nelson's breakfast Tom watched him closely, seeing the frown on his master's brow. The Admiral was troubled, and Tom didn't know why. He had beaten the French wholesale, so he could not be fretting about that, especially with the praise he so loved being heaped on him by the bucket load ever since. Happen it was that head wound he'd got at the Nile, still paining him, though he hadn't said anything when Tom combed his hair over it to hide the ferocious red scar. Tom felt it was his duty to know what was upsetting his master. It was also a way of protecting his position: Old Nellie might be kind and gentle, but he had got shot of one servant, and Tom had no desire that the same fate should befall him.

In his mind Nelson was running over a dozen scenarios, none of which brought on a sense of happy anticipation. First he would have to face Lady Hamilton; that in itself would be not be easy – it never had been, given that he could never act rationally in her presence – but now there was the added complication of what had happened between them. A worse prospect was Sir William. That he had left the palazzo to sleep elsewhere might have an innocent explanation, but only a fool would think so. He must have found out, either through his own observations or from his servants, where Lady Hamilton had spent the night.

Thinking back to the banquet Nelson realised that he must have been wrong. He had assumed at the time that Sir William had not noticed the attention his wife was paying him as the principal guest. With the Austrian born Queen on one side of him, Lady Hamilton on the other had been called upon to translate their exchanges. As she had leaned across him to hear the Queen over the buzz of three hundred other guests, the physical contact between her and Nelson had been constant, intense, and for him physically uncomfortable.

That, of course, had been the precursor of what had followed. Could he have stopped it? The fact that he should have done was not in question; he was married and so was she. Looking at his image now in the glass he was torn between knowledge of the sin he had committed and the pleasure he had taken from it. To a man who believed in an all-seeing God it was troubling that he could not decide how much his Maker would have observed. Would He have perceived the depth of the impulse that had led to their coupling? Would He weigh that in the balance against the offence?

The real horror was that he would probably have to face husband and wife together, in a three-sided exchange in which Sir William would be wounded, Lady Hamilton possibly remorseful and himself unable to be open. This would compound his sin for he would have to add lies to the other broken commandments. Even less attractive was a scene of mutual recrimination in which he would be branded a poltroon, a man who could smile at his host one minute and cuckold him the next. What Sir William would say to his wife scarcely mattered, since Nelson would be obliged for her sake to take upon himself entire responsibility for what had occurred.

That there could be no repetition of last night went without saying. His marriage to Fanny might have withered in the face of a cold English climate, but she was still his wife. He felt another stab of guilt when he recalled the nights he had spent two years before in the amorous embrace of a Genoese opera singer. Yet that had been brought about by loneliness added to the desire, after many comfortless years with his wife, to once more prove himself a man.

Carla d'Ambrosio had been a rather overblown and foolish creature, heavily powdered, plump and given to giggling. He was well known in the states bordering the Ligurian Sea for the way in which he had harassed the French armies invading northern Italy. As the senior officer of a fast-sailing squadron of romantic heroes he was fêted whenever he entered port, and it was inevitable that ladies of a certain type had set their caps at him.

Carla had been just one, and if Nelson had been taxed to admit why he succumbed to her charms when he had refused so many others, he would have been hard put to give an honest answer. He had drunk more than normal, so that her foolishness melted, glass by glass, into attraction. But he could also remember a feeling of stubbornness: in his mind's eye he could see again the faces of his officers as he dined the lady aboard his ship, HMS *Agamemnon*. They would never know how their disapproval had driven him on where he might naturally have stopped. He didn't want to be the paragon they supposed him to be: he just wanted to be a man like any other, with red blood in his veins, salacious thoughts in his head and the comfort of a hot-blooded creature in his cot. And Carla had been warm and eager, where his wife Fanny was obliging but cold. For a week he had behaved as he supposed a normal man would when separated by a thousand miles from fear of discovery. Whatever remorse he had felt then at the breaking of his marriage vows had been assuaged by the certain knowledge that time and distance would erase the affair. That would happen here too: he had told everyone when he arrived of his intention to sail on to Cadiz within two weeks to report to his commander in chief, Earl St Vincent. Yet that thought brought with it a stab of regret.

'This 'ere victuals'll have to go back to the kitchens to be warmed if'n you don't set to 'em,' said Tom.

Nelson shook himself and glanced at the food on the table, a beefsteak, quails and a glass of red wine. For someone who normally took a light repast with the rising of the sun, this was a late and hearty breakfast indeed, yet he could not contemplate eating it. His stomach rebelled and he jerked his head to indicate that Tom might take it away.

That earned Nelson a frown. 'It's not for me to tell the man I serve that he's wrong, your honour.'

'But you're going to tell me anyway, Tom,' Nelson replied wearily.

Frank Lepée, Tom's predecessor, had been just as bad, with the added burden that he drank like a fish and in his drunken ramblings could not hold his tongue. At least Tom was sober. Clearly this was a morning for unwelcome memories. Carla d'Ambrosio had done for Lepée, who could never stop referring to it, in private and before others, as if he was his master's conscience. Nelson had pensioned him off, making it clear that his stipend was dependent upon silence.

'I am that, sir,' Tom insisted, 'since you need to be telt. I knows you fret, 'cause I've seen you at it, and I do say that it does no good. What's going to happen will happen, and starving yourself won't aid matters one whit.'

Nelson could have told him to be quiet, and he knew that most men given unwanted advice by a servant would have done just that. Instead he stood up, tugged at his dress coat, smiled weakly at Tom and left the room.

Nelson had spent no more than a few nights in the Palazzo Sessa, several years previously, so the layout of Sir William's abode was still a mystery to him. It was a warren of corridors, staircases and passages, some sunlit, others in near Stygian gloom even in the middle of the day. The building had that air of decay which seemed to go with warm climates, as if the elements combined with the lassitude of the inhabitants to render frayed what should have been noble. In places the marble floors were cracked, as were the walls, and in every corner damp or mould had taken hold, only to dry out and flake, leaving behind a musty odour.

But there was much to admire, not least the wide variety of Sir William's virtu – statues, vases, mosaics, coins – all extracted from the nearby ruins of Pompeii and Herculaneum. There were the stunning views that would suddenly manifest themselves through a window or embrasure; the Bay of Naples, an arc of off-white buildings backed by a smoking Vesuvius or, to the west, purple islands shimmering out to sea. There were ships, too, the few of his own victorious fleet that he had kept here for communications and repair. His own flagship, HMS *Vanguard*, bereft of masts, was hove down in the royal dockyard at Castellamare, next to Thomas Troubridge's ship, *Culloden*, in dry dock with a damaged bottom and stern from running aground at the Nile.

That turned Nelson's mind to the problems of his command, which were many, varied and worrying, not least because they fell squarely on his shoulders. Advice or approval on what action to take was, at best, two weeks away with Earl St Vincent at Cadiz. At worst, six weeks stood between him and his political masters in London, the people who had the final say of whether he had acted correctly or not.

The Nile victory had bottled up Bonaparte, and left him land-locked in Egypt with his army: hopefully the forces of the Sultan would bury him in the desert sands. But the legacy of his previous victories remained: Captain Ball was at this very moment off Malta, his task to ascertain if the island so recently captured and plundered by the French could be retaken. But Nelson would be expected to take responsibility for progress on land, as well – it was the lot of admirals on detached service to be accountable for things over which they had little actual control.

The northern Italian states, those that had succumbed to the French menace and those that still had cause to be fearful, must renew the struggle. Surely the Nile victory would give hope to the conquered and cheer the free, and encourage those who cared for their liberty to once more take up arms against the invader.

Yet in this, Nelson was only too aware of the limitations on his own ability to effect the outcome. British sea power had created the opening but it would be land armies that would decide the fate of Italy. News of his victory would not suffice – if he was to press home the advantage his fleet had provided, he must get powerful warships, of which he had too few, into the Italian ports to demonstrate to the populace that they had real support. He must overcome in the Italian mind the memory of defeat, occupation and expropriation and lift their eyes to what was possible.

The crux of that lay here in Naples, a country that was a byword for national lethargy. Nelson needed to persuade the Neapolitan court that the time was right to strike north towards Rome and the Papal States, and hopefully, in concert with the forces of Austria, to take on the French and throw them back over their own borders. Each freed tract of occupied land would add men and passion to France's enemies. There was enough latent power waiting to be unleashed – could he, from the sea and by persuasion, act as the catalyst to harness that strength.

'You are in a brown study, sir.'

It was Mary Cadogan, and Nelson's mind leaped immediately from professional to personal matters. Before him was an individual of some importance in the household. The dowdy dress and the heavy bunch of keys identified her as a housekeeper, and even her face, square, snub-nosed and common under a mob cap, marked her as a servant. Yet the expression in her dark brown eyes was far from submissive.

Mary Cadogan, as mother of the lady of the house, was clearly more than a servant. That Sir William esteemed her was obvious in that he unfailingly included her in any conversation at which she was present, and paid clear attention to her opinions. She gave the impression that she, and she alone, knew everything that was going on in the house. There were questions Nelson longed to ask her – the same questions that had troubled him as he lay in bed not an hour before.

It was never easy to separate rumour from fact, but he had heard that Emma's mother had been both a kept woman and a high-class trollop and that her daughter had followed in her footsteps. It had to be admitted that when it came to the daughter the gossip mill tended to completely race out of control. Messalina and Lucretia Borgia combined could not have committed half the sins with which Emma Hamilton was credited.

'I have much to ponder, madam.'

'I daresay you have, sir.'

What was in the flat tone of that voice? Irony perhaps, or an acknowledgement of the thought process she had interrupted – that he was the fulcrum on which events five hundred miles in radius would turn. Or was it closer to her home and attachments. His next comment was impulsive, and one he regretted immediately it emerged.

'I am informed that Sir William left the Palazzo Sessa after the ball.'

'He did that,' Mary Cadogan replied.' He often retires there, thinking as he does that waters are restorative.'

'You do not believe them so?'

'Depends what you're trying to mend.' There was enough light coming through the window to allow her to see the reddening of Nelson's cheeks, so she added hastily, 'He claims it is a help to old bones. I reckon a bit of good flannel next to the skin serves just as well.'

Mary Cadogan was thinking that this little admiral was a strange one. She had known hundreds of men in her life and was happy to have no further intimate connection with any of them – but none like Nelson, though there had been sailors aplenty. This fellow had probably never seen the inside of a house of pleasure. He was more the Norfolk squire: God-fearing, church-going, forthright on morality and drear company. There was a wife, she knew, and Mary Cadogan tried to picture what she might be like. Dry skinned and dry of passion was her supposition, the type to induce guilt, which made this fellow's coupling with her Emma doubly dangerous. This little blusher was likely to confess to Sir William and beg forgiveness, which would never do.

'Rest assured,' Mary Cadogan added, 'that Sir William mends easy. He never fails to return from his seaside villa in a better humour than when he left.'

Nelson couldn't resist fishing. 'Which supposes an ill temper when he departs.'

'I doubt you would ever see that side of him, sir,' Mary Cadogan replied, forcefully. 'I know of no man for whom he has more time and no other man to whom he would not gift all he had than your good self.'

Mary Cadogan was surprised by his reaction. Nelson seemed to grow before her eyes. She could not know that she had given him the reason for which he had been searching all morning to excuse what he must say to Emma Hamilton. That regardless of his feelings, what had happened last night must never be repeated. He would use the mutual regard in which he and Sir William held each other as a shield to deflect her disappointment.

'I must be about my duties, sir.'

'And I, Mrs Cadogan,' replied Nelson, in an almost jaunty tone, 'must be about mine.'

Francesca flitted about in her usual manner, moving much and achieving little, her soft singing for once grating on her mistress's ears. Emma knew that it would do no good to frown at her. She would only respond with a dazzling grin and the singing would continue.

Emma was wondering if she felt different, concentrating on each part of her body in turn to try to discern some fundamental change, without discovering much to either please or alarm her. There was a warm memory in her lower belly, that consciousness of having successfully made love, the recollection of that sated feeling that followed gratification. That induced a whole raft of memories. Mentally leafing through her previous lovers she ticked off first their attributes, then their failings.

The first, an overweight oaf called Jack Willet Payne, whom she could never recall without the epithet 'whale', was not recollected with any pleasure. Her deflowering had been painful and unpleasant. Harry Featherstonehaugh had been her first real lover. Uppark

Harry, with his overbearing mother, his stunning mansion, his broad Sussex acres and hearty rustic ways had been an elemental force in her life. Francesca stopped her singing as Emma chuckled, throwing her mistress an enquiring glance that Emma picked up in the mirror. Just fourteen at the time, she could recall the dreams she had toyed with looking across the deer park to the great mansion, dreams that one day she would be mistress of that place, chatelaine of one of the most beautiful houses in the land.

The glow had faded on Harry; he was selfish, vain, boastful, overbearing, violent and ultimately detached. To him Emma was just a chattel, of less account than one of his racehorses, to be parcelled out to any of his friends who wanted her and to be disposed of the minute she became a burden.

Charles Greville was one of those friends, but different. It was fitting that her thoughts should turn to him now, since that was the only previous time in her life that she had been knowingly and willingly unfaithful to the man who kept her. Of course Greville had known what she did not; that her dreams of a future of bliss with her keeper were nonsense; that at some point Harry would tire of her and he would be there to pick up the prize. Yet he too, having gained her trust and her love, had betrayed her.

There was a gentle knock on the door and Emma's heart missed a beat. She put up a hand, too late, to stop Francesca responding. It could be her husband and right at that moment she wasn't sure that she was ready to face him. She glanced over and saw Francesca take a note from Nelson's man, Tom Allen. The girl brought it over to her, and Emma recognised the untidy left-handed scrawl, familiar to her from all of Nelson's letters since he had lost his right arm.

'The Admiral's man is waiting for a reply?' she asked.

'Yes, Signora,' Francesca replied.

Nelson wanted to call on her immediately. Was that wise, Emma wondered, and was it generated by passion or remorse? Matters were at enough of a stand without Sir William coming home to find herself and Nelson closeted in her private apartments. Quickly Emma reread the note.

It is vital, my lady, that we speak without delay. Everything for the future of both our lives, our happiness and the fate of our nation's arms could depend on it! N.

It was too dramatic to be romantic, surely, but very much Nelson. Could she risk it?

'Tell Allen to convey to the Admiral that I will be happy to receive him in my drawing room in five minutes.'

Francesca rushed back to the door, then returned to the dressing table to brush her mistress's hair.

Nelson stood outside the gleaming double doors that led to Emma Hamilton's apartments thinking that he would rather be single-handedly boarding an enemy First Rate than here. Every word he had rehearsed had deserted him, leaving him without the faintest idea of what to say. His main argument, that the mutual regard between himself and her husband debarred further intimacy, so forceful just a half an hour before, now seemed feeble in the extreme.

All he knew for certain was that they had to call a halt now, that any future departure from the strictest self-control by either party might be disastrous. Sir William could not be expected to sit idly by while Nelson made love to his wife. And Nelson was not stupid enough to think that such an attachment could be kept secret: it looked as though Sir William knew already, and it was unlikely that Mary Cadogan had remained in ignorance.

If the servants had been too busy to notice because of the task of clearing up after last night's banquet, that would not last. And what had his own man, Tom Allen, made of the events of the morning? First a hastily scribbled note to Lady Hamilton, her reply, then Nelson's instructions for him to wait by the front entrance to the palazzo and hotfoot it upstairs should there be any sign of Sir William Hamilton. Tom might be slow-witted, but even he, Nelson suspected, could make four out of that.

On the other side of the door Emma was composing herself, trying to quell the thumping in her breast, worrying about how the folds of her dress lay, the angle of the light as it played on her profile, and most of all the calm face she must present to her expected visitor, an expression she knew would require all her skill to maintain. She realised now just how dangerous a liaison with Nelson might be, for to her he was not like other men: she had never felt for anyone the combination of tenderness and passion, hope and fear he evoked in her. If he was coming now to declare his undying love, she must send him away miserable.

She had ceased to worry about Sir William, her concern now was Nelson. Her reputation was tarnished, his was golden. He was about to be raised to the peerage, probably to a dukedom. Contact between them could only diminish him. Although, deep down, Emma did not believe this mattered, it was the part she was determined to play and it would be the performance of her life.

'Francesca, the door,' she said, when she heard the firm knock. 'Then you may leave Admiral Nelson and me alone.'

3

Francesca opened the door, but Horatio Nelson did not enter. He stood looking at the vision in the high-backed button chair before him, feeling the last vestiges of his resolve seep away. He knew, as he looked, that Emma had set out to entrance him: why else would she be sitting so that her loveliness was shown off to its best advantage? He took in the mass of russet hair, worn long and curled, the carefully powdered face that hid the rose-tinged glow of her cheeks. And even at this distance of several feet her eyes were huge and green.

Emma, her stomach churning, was fighting to stop herself smiling. Every feature of the man in the doorway was imprinted on her mind: the deep blue coat with one empty sleeve pinned across, the great star and ribbon of the Order of the Bath, the medal round his neck for St Vincent, held by black silk against his snow-white stock, the gilded epaulettes and frogging on his coat that marked him out as an admiral.

His entrancing good blue eye was on her in a steady gaze. She recalled the scar on his forehead, hidden by his bright silver hair, which she had kissed last night, still fresh enough to be red and angry. In intimate embrace it had been easy to see the scars Nelson bore from a hundred fights. She had kissed them all; cuts, dents and the stump of his lost arm, all the way to the puckered end that he had used to support his body as he made love to her.

'Lady Hamilton,' he said formally, with just the faintest trace of a tremor.

'Admiral Nelson,' she replied, in a voice so nervous and loud, it seemed to echo off the walls.

Formality insisted that Nelson kiss her hand, which he feared to do. He did not want to come any closer to her than this doorway. It was only the presence of her maid that forced him to step into the room. When she slipped out Nelson nearly followed her. It had never occurred to him that they would be left alone. He had no choice but to move forward, stiff-legged, and bend over the proffered hand. The contact did for them both.

'I am undone,' he said, his voice anguished, as he raised his head to look at her and saw tears gathering in her eyes. 'You're crying?' he said distractedly

Emma dabbed at her eyelids. 'It seems I am.'

'Why?'

'Do I flatter myself that I am about to disappoint you?' she asked.

'You would struggle to flatter yourself, Emma, and nothing you could ever do would disappoint me.'

The name came unbidden, but truly after the intimacy they had enjoyed it was only natural.

'Last night . . .'

Quickly he put a finger to her lips. He feared that she might say it had all been an aberration and he did not want to hear that: he wanted it to remain as he thought about it, the natural culmination of a shared passion. It might not be love, for Emma had made him wonder if he truly knew the meaning of the word, but it was something to be cherished.

'What I am about to say requires all my strength, more than I would ever need to fight a sea battle.' He was looking directly into her eyes, once more gripping her hand. 'Because of that I cannot say what I wish, cannot tell you the depth of the feelings I have, for to do so would make the rest impossible. Sir William is a man I consider a friend.'

Emma wanted to say, 'He is that to me, no more,' but desisted: she felt that he had reached the same conclusion as she, that any relationship between them was impossible. To tell Nelson that much as she esteemed her husband she did not love him would hardly aid matters.

'Apart from that, there is my duty . . .'

Tom Allen knocked, then opened the door and called, 'Sir William's carriage is coming up the hill.'

'Wait outside, Tom,' Nelson barked. The door shut with some force. 'I must not be found here, you know that, and if Sir William confronts me and refers to last night I must tell you I will not lie to him.'

'He won't, Nelson, be sure of that,' replied Emma, praying she was speaking the truth.

26

'And I wish to remain your friend.'

'For ever that,' Emma replied, a catch in her voice.

He kissed her then, a mistake he knew, but impulse overrode sense. When he tried to pull away her arms prevented him, and when he spoke his voice was hoarse and his head just inches from hers. 'You must let me go, Emma.'

She did so, feeling as her hands dropped a sensation of utter defeat. Emma had wanted many things in her life, to marry a prince when she was a young girl, to live in a grand house surrounded by children and doted on by an adoring husband. The memories she had reprised that morning flashed through her mind and Emma gave credence to the thought, for the very first time in her life, that she had failed. Nelson backed towards the door. He gave her a last longing look, then spun round and left.

Tom Allen was waiting outside, but he was not alone. At the end of the corridor stood Mary Cadogan. As Nelson passed her, she shook her head slowly and tutted, as if to say that even for a hero, he was living dangerously.

'Mister Tyson is waiting for you, your honour,' said Tom.

'Who?' Nelson said, before he collected himself. He had known Tyson since his first command and had taken him on recently as his new secretary. Tom seemed bewildered by his confusion. That made Nelson stop in his tracks.

'Tom. Not a word about this morning to anyone. Do you understand?'

As he nodded his servant tried to look innocent, and failed. A blind man could have seen that his master and the lady of the house were a mite more friendly than was proper. He waited for the Admiral to say more, but the sound of the carriage wheels, rattling over the cobbles at the front of the palazzo, had Nelson scurrying away. The last thing he wanted was to bump into Sir William.

Sir William Hamilton arrived home without ceremony and, having been informed by his major domo that his wife was about to leave for a meeting with the Queen at the Palazzo Reale, made his way to his own apartments. There he dealt with the morning correspondence, mainly composed of notes from various Neapolitan ministries that were empty of anything that could be considered meaningful. More interesting were reports from his own sources on the state of feeling in the kingdom to which he was accredited.

Naples was a city in which it was very necessary to possess two faces. Every nobleman, every person of rank, knew that he was sitting on more than one volcano. Vesuvius might smoke in the distance and erupt from time to time, but the more dangerous fault was political, not geological. Secret groupings abounded, in which the currency of entry was discussion of political change, and everything from peaceful overthrow to regicide was propounded as the best means of toppling the absolutism of the Bourbon monarchy.

Had foolish, childish King Ferdinand grasped, as he hunted and whored, dabbled in his Capodimonte pottery sheds, or received his most prominent subjects, that a good half of them belonged to societies dedicated to his removal? His queen, whose sister Marie Antoinette had perished on the guillotine, was certainly conscious of this. She lived in a state of perpetual terror that the same fate might befall her and her children.

Yet they would not fall victim to the peasantry. It was odd that here, in southern Italy, the only people on whom the monarchy could rely were the uneducated *lazzaroni*. They loved their king for the very same reasons that most nobles despised him: his lack of the attributes normally expected in a sovereign. Ferdinand's elder brother, who should have succeeded to the kingdom, had been harmlessly mad as a child and youth, and declared unfit to govern. It was suspected that the brain of Ferdinand himself might be delicate too, and should not be taxed too severely. Therefore the King had been raised with little education: no lessons in statecraft, finance or diplomacy, or even the rudiments of dignified behaviour. He was a boor with the manners of a rustic: he ate and drank to excess, preferred the company of peasants to nobles, took pleasure only in the chase and fornication. To men who desired Naples to be accorded respect he was an embarrassment; to those who hankered after constitutional change he was a tyrant. To the *lazzaroni*, unwashed, unambitious, and careless of the future, he was one of them, and nothing less than a hero.

When Sir William Hamilton thought of the components of the kingdom to which he had been the British representative for near thirty-five years, he almost succumbed to despair. Falsehood was more prevalent than honesty, laziness combined with bombast more apparent than activity and courage. Public revenues, with very few exceptions, were seen as fair game. Thus grand aims were never realised as the money set aside to pay for them disappeared into various deep pockets. Somehow he had to persuade this sclerotic structure to mobilise troops and warships, then attack a nation that had swept all before it in the last seven years.

'Admiral Nelson?' he asked his valet.

'Is in his chambers, Maestro,' the man replied, it being his job to know these things.

'A request that he join me,' said Sir William. 'We have important matters to discuss.'

John Tyson sat in the anteroom next to Nelson's bedroom, and noted how different he was from the young, gauche master and commander with whom he had first served on the sloop *Badger* in the Caribbean. It wasn't just the Admiral's uniform or the missing right arm: as always Nelson eschewed a wig, but his hair was silver grey now instead of straw blond, yet still untidy and tied at the nape of his neck in a queue. His face had lost its rosy colour but no lines betrayed the worries that must assail him. His one good eye was still pale blue and direct, the voice remained soft, friendly and encouraging, the smile still warm.

Knowing Nelson and others like him had often caused John Tyson to ruminate on the attributes required for leadership. Just as he knew he did not have such a gift, he had met many who claimed it and a very few who had that ability in varying degrees. But none had those attributes like this man.

'You know your predecessor ran off the deck at Aboukir?' said Nelson, without looking up from the mass of correspondence he was reading – letters and reports from every superior officer in his own fleet, as well as despatches from Earl St Vincent.

'There are those who vie to be an admiral's secretary, sir, and think that being shot at is not part of their brief.'

Nelson looked up and smiled. 'Not John Tyson, I hazard. I seem to recall you having to be restrained when an opportunity arose for a boarding from the deck of dear old *Badger*.'

'I'd be more content to stand still now, sir, since my bones have stiffened somewhat. But it's true I could not rest below with a fight going on above my head.'

Since those days as Nelson's first purser, Tyson had watched or heard of his rise in the service. The King's Navy was like an extended family in perpetual motion where news was eagerly sought regarding past compatriots. If Nelson had a ship, Tyson knew of it, and also if he had a success or a setback. His romantic adventures with the opposite sex were the cause of much mingled mirth and concern: Nelson was considered to be extremely unreliable in that department, forever in pursuit of the unattainable. Just as worrying was the passion with which he had imbued his suits in places as far flung as France, Canada and the Caribbean. The news that he had finally married a widow of good family, a seemingly steady woman with good sense, had been greeted with relief.

The disputes to which he was prone were common knowledge too: he had clashed with admirals and their wives, as with civilian and service officials. Then there had been the disastrous tour of the Caribbean Islands Nelson had undertaken with His Royal Highness Prince William Henry, the Duke of Clarence. It was generally held that Nelson had spent five years without employment before the present conflict because the King blamed him for allowing his son to make a fool of himself.

But that was all in the past. Now he was at his peak, and a peerage was certain. Tyson reckoned that if Nelson had been famous before, he had merely been one of a dozen others – Edward Pellew for his single ship actions, Jervis for the victory of St Vincent, Lord Howe for the Glorious First of June and Admiral Duncan for thrashing the Dutch at Camperdown. But after the victory at the Nile, Nelson would be elevated above all other mariners of whatever rank and he, lucky John Tyson, had landed the job of serving him as his secretary.

'I have here more correspondence, sir,' said Tyson, pointing to the pile of official papers, 'but I hazard of a nature more to your liking than that.'

As he handed them across the desk, Tyson reeled off the names of those who had sent these communications: the Sultan of the Ottoman Empire and various beys, deys, bagshaws and viziers of that dominion. There were letters from Vienna, from the Emperor of Austria and his leading ministers, from French exiles in Germany, the Prussian court, Italian grand dukes, deposed Venetian and Genoese doges; from occupied Rome, with the blessings of the Pope and his cardinals. And they were all, without exception, written in the formal diplomatic language, which was French.

'I fear I am good for no more than one word in three of this, Tyson.'

'I will have them drafted in English for you, sir, but if I may give you the gist, they are all fulsome in praise of the Nile victory.' Tyson picked up one. 'The Sultan, for instance . . .'

'Who sat squarely on the fence, Tyson,' Nelson interrupted. 'Had his navy been more active I would have found the French weeks before. Were they not his domains Bonaparte invaded, his Mameluke warriors he beat in battle by the Pyramids? The Sultan and his court did nothing, and left us to fight their cause for them.'

'The Sultan,' continued Tyson calmly, 'not only sends you written congratulations, but news that he is to confer on you the Order of the Crescent, as well as the most splendid special reward. An envoy is on his way from Istanbul with the decoration, a singular honour that is awarded only to those who have performed with the highest gallantry to the Ottoman State. It is a decoration known in Turkish as a *Chelenk*, and the correspondent describes it as an aigrette, a plume of triumph made from silver and diamonds, which is to be worn in the turban.'

'A turban for all love!' chortled Nelson. 'It would shake their lordships if I turned up at the Admiralty in a turban.'

Tyson grinned. 'I fancy the idea appeals to you, sir.'

'Oh, it does, Tyson. It so very much does.'

The door opened and Tom Allen announced, 'Captain Troubridge, your honour.'

'Tom,' said Nelson, rising.

'Sir,' Troubridge replied, punctiliously.

Nelson hated old shipmates to be so correct: it was just another example of the isolation his rank imposed on him. Right now this man was his second-in-command, yet he was still formal. It was never discussed because that was impossible, so Nelson could not explain how much he missed the easy camaraderie he had once enjoyed with men like Thomas Troubridge. They had served together as midshipmen, and it had been in Tom's company that he had witnessed his first flogging and fought in his first sea action. A series of movements up the ladder of promotion had meant leaving behind those who had once been brutally truthful with him and were now inclined to be deferential.

'How are you, Tom?'

'Spitting blood, sir, since I've just come from the dockyard.'

Both men knew that Nelson was not referring to that, and he looked into Troubridge's swarthy face for signs of the grief he must be suffering. They had sailed into Naples on the back of the Nile victory, only for Troubridge, who had run his ship aground and missed the battle, to find that he was a widower: news had arrived from England that his wife had died. Nelson, who had hardly had time to talk to him since, knew that anything other than the most perfunctory commiseration would be unwelcome.

Even as a youngster, Tom had been unsentimental and dedicated to the service, a magnificent organiser and executive officer, trusted if not loved by his crew. He had also been the only one with enough courage to mention his dislike of adultery after Nelson's dalliance with his Genoese opera singer.

The Good Lord help me, Nelson thought, if he ever finds out about last night.

They fell to discussing the shortcomings of the Neapolitan dock-yards – requests ignored, work avoided, planking, masts and spars nowhere to be found – like the money to pay for them. Was Troubridge, or John Tyson for that matter, aware that Nelson was keeping the conversation going to avoid that which he must undertake next?

He had a note on the table from Sir William Hamilton, inviting him to discuss the state of affairs in Naples, and how they must proceed if they were ever to stir King Ferdinand and his ministers into some kind of military action. Tom Allen forced the issue, with a polite reminder from Sir William's messenger that he was awaiting Admiral Nelson, only to receive from his master a look of venom.

'Admiral Nelson,' said Sir William, smiling as he came to greet his visitor, who, to his delight, looked somewhat nervous. That a man who had become the nemesis of every Jacobin the world over, who had laid the ghost of Bonaparte and the infallibility of the French Revolution, should dread to meet him was risible.

Nelson's throat felt as though it had a cord round it as he croaked his reply. 'Sir William.'

'I trust you are quite recovered from last night's exertions, Admiral,' Sir William paused just long enough to see Nelson blush, then added, 'at the ball.'

As he made the short journey from Posillipo, Sir William Hamilton had decided how he would respond to what had taken place. It was out of the question to make a scene; it would be both ungentlemanly and demeaning. Neither could he imply that he knew what had taken place between his wife and the Admiral.

He was determined to see the matter in the context of the city and the state in which he resided. In Naples, it was not just customary for a man of parts to have a mistress, it was considered essential. In fact, it was in order for men and women to have several lovers at the same time, and the shifting sexual alliances provided an otherwise dull royal court with entertaining conversation. Many observed their marriage vows with laxity – and even the prelates of the Catholic Church had their paramours.

The King couldn't be trusted with anything female, even his own wife, whom he had brought to bed with child eighteen times. Maria Carolina's only release was in his multiple affairs, either with the ladies of his court or with beautiful and willing girls from a less exalted background who knew that he would be generous when he tired of them. Sir William and Emma had been the exception to the rule in their mutual constancy, he an amused spectator as nearly every man that entered Emma's orbit tried to break that bond. Even the King had tried, only to find Emma very reluctant to entertain such a notion, and stopping him had taken all Sir William's diplomatic wiles.

Sir William did not wish to embarrass Nelson, who he suspected had little experience with women. He had known that as he grew older Emma might take a lover and could not deny there was some consolation to be had if it turned out to be someone he liked and admired. But Sir William still had a sense of mischief and, without Emma present, he could not resist having a little fun at Nelson's expense.

It was a delight to watch the confusion on his visitor's face as he continued. 'I do find balls so fatiguing, Admiral, and I attend a damn sight more of them than you do. Too much food, too much wine and a surfeit of tedious conversation make it hard for one to get a decent night's sleep. I myself went to Posillipo last night to recover.'

He gave Nelson a direct stare then, which from what he knew of the man, would normally have been returned in full measure. This time the Admiral had to look away, his face filled with the kind of despair that might precede a confession. Sir William decided he had teased him enough. Time to get down to business.

'I fear I must inform you, Nelson, that things have changed since your last visit to Naples. Those with whom you treated in '93 no longer have the power they had then.'

'Acton?' asked Nelson.

'His wings have been clipped,' Sir William replied.

Sir John Acton, an Englishman in the service of the Neapolitan court had proved himself a friend to the country of his birth. Nelson had arrived in Naples in November 1793, just after combined fleets of Britain and Spain had taken possession of the French naval port of Toulon. Nelson had been sent to request troops to help hold the place against the armies of the Revolution. Expecting lethargy he had been surprised when Acton announced that the troops were already being assembled. Six thousand men, with warships and supplies had reached Toulon in record time. That they had not performed very well mattered less than that Naples had provided them with such alacrity.

'He fell out with the Queen, I'm afraid,' added Sir William.

'They seemed so close, almost intimates,' Nelson mused, and regretted the allusion. It had been rumoured that Acton and the Queen were lovers, which was not a subject he wanted to raise.

33

'A rumour that Acton fostered, for by doing so he disguised his true inclinations.'

Nelson had heard that Sir John was a pederast. Indeed he had smoked a hint of that when they had met. Not that the notion bothered him. Nelson had met too many men of that stamp in the Navy, both officers and seamen, to care a fig for a man's sexual orientation. What mattered was how well they performed their duties, and in that respect Acton had been exemplary.

Sir William laughed. 'The irony is that he and the Queen fell out over an object of mutual affection, a young officer from Saxony, a tall blond blue-eyed Adonis. A foolish whim from the Queen of course.'

Nelson felt a flash of irritation. Sir William was gossiping, which in the circumstances seemed singularly inappropriate. He speculated that the British Ambassador was the not man he used to be – a fellow who had had razor sharp instincts for the essential. Perhaps age had withered his professional abilities just as it had atrophied his limbs.

'Forgive me for meandering off the point,' Sir William went on, making Nelson feel doubly a scrub. 'You will recall the Marquis de Gallo from your previous visit.'

'I do,' Nelson said gratefully, 'though I must admit the memory is not pleasant.'

'Well, it is our misfortune that he is the person with whom we will have to deal.'

4

Sitting across the table from the Marquis de Gallo, Nelson remembered why he didn't like the man: it was his insufferable air of superiority. Gallo had a bland face and a flat voice. He was constantly evasive and gave the appearance of deep boredom, playing idly with a jewelled snuff box whenever anyone else was speaking.

Nelson wanted evidence that Naples was prepared to take advantage of what he and his fleet had delivered to them. More than anything he wanted a firm declaration of war on France, which would encourage the other Italian states either to take up arms or rebel against the invaders. De Gallo had the ear of the Queen, who was the true ruler of Naples, plus the trust of the King, which implied political dexterity of the highest order. What it clearly did not imply was any predilection to zeal.

Looking at the Marquis, as he accompanied his passion-free words with tiny negative gestures, Nelson was reminded of something that had happened to him as a youngster. A fellow midshipman on his first ship, Tom Foley, who had later become a firm friend, had invited him to partake in a pissing competition, he who achieved the greatest distance to be declared the winner of a silver sixpence. Nelson went first, only realising when soaked how he had been guyed into pissing into the wind. He felt a little like that now as he reiterated once more the reasons why Naples should act swiftly.

'What if the news of Aboukir Bay reaches Paris before I can inform my ambassador there?' Gallo protested.

Sir William translated, then told Nelson of his intended reply: that even the rogues who ran France would respect diplomatic credentials. Then he reminded the Marquis that on his northern border the French had fewer than nine thousand troops of indifferent quality.

That was followed by a rapid incomprehensible exchange before Sir William told him what had transpired.

'The Queen's brother, the Emperor, who shows no sign of movement himself, is sending an experienced general from Vienna to take command of the Neapolitan forces.'

Evidently Nelson failed to respond with the enthusiasm de Gallo had expected for the Marquis frowned. The Admiral had had much experience of Austrian generals in past campaigns centred on the northern Italian states and nothing he had seen inspired him to expect from them either courage or military skill. All they had ever offered him was prevarication, obfuscation, or a terse note to say they were retreating or suing for peace.

'Baron Karl Mack von Leiberich,' Sir William added, 'is already on his way.'

'When will he arrive?' Nelson demanded. The response from the Neapolitan Chief Minister was a shrug, so he added, 'And the Navy?'

What followed was a long explanation, blaming the British for the delay. How could the Neapolitan fleet be fully fitted out when the dockyards were occupied with Nelson's battle-damaged ships? It was a far cry from the time when Sir John Acton had been in charge.

Emma was playing Blind Man's Buff with Prince Alberto, the youngest of the royal children, aware that the Queen was only intermittently watching them as she paced between her work-table and a window overlooking the bay. That was rare for a woman who had such a deep affection for her numerous offspring. Maria Carolina was troubled – indeed her life since coming here as a young girl from Vienna had seemed one whole sea of such. Her husband was suspicious, cunning at the same time as stupid, wont to leave the running of the state to her only to interfere at the most inappropriate time to ruin whatever consistency of policy existed.

Compared to the ordered world of the Austrian Court Naples was chaos. The Queen had never felt comfortable here, and even now was surrounded with a forty-strong cohort of German speaking servants. If Ferdinand was unaware that many of his aristocratic subjects were disloyal to him, his wife was not. She had seen her own sister brought to the guillotine in Paris, and was shrewd enough to know that although the rabble made the noise, it was disaffected noblemen that made revolutions, and weak servants of the state who failed to stop them.

The Queen's nephew, the Emperor of Austria, heading one of the mightiest states in Europe, had been forced into an ignominious peace. If her homeland, which was huge and capable of putting large armies in the field, could not resist, what chance had Naples? Maria Carolina had to take a decision that she longed to avoid: what advice should she give regarding relations with France?

A few years before, the decision would have been exclusively hers, a time when she had leant on the support of Sir John Acton, but no longer. Acton had not stolen money, but he had turned out in his own way to be just as corrupt and disloyal as the others. His successor, the Marquis de Gallo, was too slippery to control, having succeeded in getting Ferdinand interested in the management of his kingdom – mainly by engendering suspicion in him about the true motives and the fidelity of his wife.

That brought an ironic smile to the Queen's lips. Ferdinand could not comprehend that she was not, like him, a slave to physical passion. Maria Carolina had desires, but of the variety of courtly love, that medieval construct by which a lover committed his soul to his paramour, yet suppressed any carnal thoughts. That was the kind of man she liked, and any intimation that matters should go further was instantly rebuffed. She got enough of that kind of attention from the slavering beast to whom she was married.

A high squeal made her turn. She saw Emma mock-wrestling with Prince Alberto, who was six, and third in line to the throne. He still wore the blindfold, yet protested his invisibility, although Emma held him in a firm embrace. If only, the Queen thought, she could emulate that childish ability to believe that if you cannot see, you cannot be seen. Then she could avoid the coming meeting which her husband had insisted she attend because the Marquis de Gallo had convinced him that it was the best way to stop her plotting.

To Maria Carolina Lady Hamilton was a true blessing, and she regretted that protocol had kept them apart for the first years of Emma's stay. As the mistress of a diplomat, Emma had had no standing in Naples, but meeting her had been unavoidable. She had surprised the Queen by speaking German, which endeared her to Maria Carolina. A bond had been struck and Emma had quickly become an intimate.

But it remained unofficial; protocol insisted that only those who had been received by their own sovereign could be received at a foreign court, and King George III flatly refused to entertain the notion of meeting Emma, even after she had married his childhood friend. But such a ruling could not stand in the face of the needs of a lonely queen or a fearful nation. Good relations with Great Britain had to be maintained and part of that meant that Sir William must be kept content.

Emma was now a *confidante* in the sense that Maria Carolina spoke in her presence about matters of state, her relations with her husband and what to do with her children. But the Queen was never subjected to a question, never ever probed for motive, because that was forbidden. It was possible for Emma to advance ideas that had advantage for her husband's mission as British Ambassador. But absolute intimacy was impossible: a ruler could never entirely trust anyone.

'Enough, children,' Maria Carolina said, waving away a barrage of protests. The various German women who had care of the children came forward to collect their reluctant charges, who would now be taken off to their lessons. The Queen persevered with studious application to their education, not least because she did not want them turning out like her husband. Before departure, each was required to kiss their mother, and none went without a peck from Emma. Maria Carolina felt a pang of jealousy that she received dutiful embraces, while Emma's were given out of affection.

'So, Emma, what onslaught must we to face today from your little admiral?'

Emma started at 'your', then realised that the word had been used in innocence. 'He will not attack you, madam, but he will try to persuade you to attack the French.'

Maria Carolina laughed. 'Believe me, Emma, if I were a man, I would need no persuasion. My sword would be stained already with the blood of those swinedogs.'

'Why change sex, madam? Perhaps what we need is a regiment of women.'

'Look no further than Naples for that, Emma,' the Queen replied, bitterly. 'A true man in this forsaken place is not easy to find.'

There were things about which the two women disagreed, and Naples was one of them. Emma loved it for dozens of reasons, which seemed to be the same ones for which Maria Carolina despised it. The climate was benign in winter and bearable in summer, as long as they went out of the city. Society was frivolous, the peasantry idle but good-humoured, the scenery beautiful, even rumbling Vesuvius. There was the warm sea to bathe in, an idea that made the Queen shudder, and abundant highly scented flowers, which made her sneeze.

The only thing of which they seemed at one was the Neapolitan love of superstition. Maria Carolina was a firm believer in the Evil

One, who could damn you to perdition with a look: thus she was covered in charms to ward off the actions of the devil and his acolytes. She had persuaded Emma to wear them too, because their friendship would render her person vulnerable if Emma was not protected. It was hard to argue with a queen, and Emma didn't try.

In fact, she was careful in what she said, though not from weakness. Emma knew that she could speak to the Queen in a manner that would see others put firmly in their place. She didn't try to understand why this should be so, but knew that Maria Carolina disliked falsehood or disguised feelings. Therefore, ever since they had first become close, she had behaved naturally.

'You would oblige me, Emma, by telling your admiral that my inclinations are to oppose France, but I may not be able to say so in his presence.'

'He will believe that without any words of mine, madam. He knows and esteems you from what I have told him of you in my letters.'

'Do you always write well of me, Emma?'

Intended as a joke, it was taken the wrong way, with Emma insisting, 'I keep fair copies, madam, that you are at liberty to read.'

'No, no, Emma, my dear,' Maria Carolina said. 'You have often read to me Admiral Nelson's replies and that will suffice. I am often left to wonder if the person he talks of as Queen of Naples is me or someone imagined, so virtuous does he make me sound. Now, take my arm, and escort me to the door of that nest of vipers my husband calls his council.'

That Nelson emerged frustrated from de Gallo's room came as no surprise to him. He had never expected to be greeted with news that the strategic and tactical moves he had recommended had been implemented. But he had expected political action. However, the man on whom he relied to pressure their putative allies had seemed reluctant to press his case. As he had perceived that morning, Sir William had lost some of his fire.

The best interpretation that Nelson could essay was that the Ambassador realised the limitations of what he could do and was determined not to raise Nelson's hopes. But Sir William had been too soft on the Marquis. He had let him control the conversation instead of reminding a man who was a silk-clad scoundrel what he owed to Great Britain; to tell him that, years ago, without the shield of the British fleet, Naples would have been under French control.

That thought was reinforced as they entered the council chamber to face the several men and one woman who ran the kingdom.

Ferdinand was there, of course, looking bored, although the proceedings had not even begun. Nelson observed the huge nose and heavy, dark features, the prominent brow made more so by thick eyebrows. The King had near-black eyes that never seemed to settle on any object for more than a second, and a hand that seemed to be continually scratching at his groin.

Ferdinand didn't twitch; he was after all not actually mad, just very strange. A tall, broad-shouldered man who should have looked splendid and majestic in court dress, he was the most unkempt person in the room, with traces of food on his coat front. His wig was poorly dressed and very slightly misplaced which gave him the air of some character from a comedy of manners.

As usual a high cleric was in attendance, a hawk-faced individual that Sir William informed him was Cardinal Fabrizo Ruffo, apparently one of those divines who, rich before his elevation, spent most of his time increasing his wealth rather than tending to the needs of his flock.

The Queen was seated beside Ferdinand and Nelson saw her as no more regal than her husband. She was squat at the hips and narrow at the shoulders, with unhealthy skin, a heavy, gloomy mouth and a long face that ended in a double chin. Only the eyes betrayed animation and intelligence. What was it that made Emma friends with this woman? In every letter he had ever received from her Emma had never failed to praise the Queen. And it was an attachment that had paid handsome dividends. Without Maria Carolina – and possibly Acton acting in his capacity as Minister of Marine, Nelson would have had to abandon the chase after Bonaparte. Then he recalled that it had been Emma, using every ounce of influence she had on behalf of her country, who had persuaded the Queen to break the rules of neutrality. For that she deserved a medal, and he resolved there and then to move heaven and earth to get her one.

A delegation from Malta was shown in, to tell the King and Queen that their islands, captured by Bonaparte, were willing to submit to the suzerainty of Naples if they could be recaptured. The home of the Knights of St John since the time of the crusades, Malta had been just the kind of prize craved by revolutionary France; rich, undisturbed for centuries, and with an abundance of treasure to steal. That treasure had been sent to the bottom of Aboukir Bay with the French flagship *L'Orient*.

Through whispered translation, Sir William kept Nelson abreast of the submissions of the Maltese delegation and the King's response; that his forces would kick the French out. To Nelson's mind the

Maltese could invite away and give credence to Ferdinand's promises if they wished. Valetta was the only place that mattered and Malta would be a hard nut to crack with the French holed up in the main fortress. They were not like the Knights of St John, grown soft and corrupt through decades of luxury, an easy target to a determined invader.

De Gallo had arrived while the Maltese were making their case. After their departure he began to talk as though he was barely part of the proceedings, reiterating what he had told Nelson and Sir William already regarding the arrival of Baron Mack. Equally bored Horatio Nelson looked around the overly elaborate decor of the chamber; painted ceiling panels showing the various stages of some celestial contest; feats of a more modern nature graced the wall panels, with knights slaying everything from dragons to Saracens. He was unable to resist the ironic contrast between Neapolitan art and reality.

He needed soldiers and would have given his one good arm for British regiments that would march to his commands. As de Gallo droned on Nelson let his imagination run to lines of red-coats advancing under his instructions, taking Rome and the states beyond and rolling the enemy back beyond Nice.

Sir John Acton was called upon to speak. Nelson ceased his meandering and concentrated on what his fellow countryman had to say. Acton had always had an agreeable countenance but age had sharpened his features considerably. Though dressed plainly in a dark silk coat and buff breeches, he was immaculate in a way that others present were not. Everything about his person spoke of a fastidious attention to his toilet, from his short well-powdered wig, to his gold-buckled and highly polished pumps. Nelson could see that his fingernails were even, manicured and clean.

Nelson had always liked him because he was a positive force in this gimcrack court, too professional to be dismissed. He might not have the power he once enjoyed, but he was still a potent minister. His information, which was far more encouraging than de Gallo's, revealed that troops were available and more could be recruited. The royal regiments were up to strength and all the noblemen of the mainland and Sicily had been called upon to serve with horse and carbine.

Acton called upon Commodore Caracciolo to speak about naval preparations. An old adversary of Nelson's, Caracciolo, despite his squat and muscular frame, had the same courtier-like arrogance as de Gallo. He declined to be specific – in fact, he did little more than invite Nelson to dine on board one of the Neapolitan capital ships as a guest of the King. Nelson could see what that meant without explanation from Sir William. Ferdinand was telling him that Naples was still neutral. To dine a British admiral on shore would breach the obligations of neutrality, giving the French envoy every right to object. Naples was sitting on the fence.

Which was where Nelson wanted to be on the way back to the Palazzo Sessa, preferably a fence miles away from Naples. The meeting he dreaded, at which he, Emma and Sir William would be present, was about to take place. He contemplated an immediate return to his ship, but dismissed that out of hand. Even if *Vanguard* had been ready for sea, which she was not, his flight would strengthen rather than allay suspicion.

There would be a brief respite while each party returned to their own apartments, or so Nelson thought until he opened the door to his and found his stepson, Josiah Nesbit, waiting for him. The sight of the young man brought forcibly to mind an image of his wife, which induced feelings of deep guilt. This he tried to disguise by giving the young man a hearty greeting.

'I have come to proffer an apology, sir,' Josh said, as Tom Allen took Nelson's hat and removed his cloak.

Stiff, non-familial, typical of the grown up Josh. 'An apology?'

His stepson was looking at a point above his head. 'For my behaviour last night, sir.'

Nelson looked perplexed. 'I was not aware that your behaviour gave any cause for an apology.'

'Captain Troubridge does, sir, and also, it seems, Captain Hardy. I am here at their express wish.'

There was still no eye contact. 'Josh, you can come and go here as you like. We are, if not blood relations, family nevertheless.'

'Sir.'

Nelson wondered what had become of the boy he had once known, whose company he had so enjoyed. In a life in the Navy Nelson had seen hundreds grow from nervous boys to confident men, watched them lose that sense of frolic on taking up an officer's responsibilities. But Josh had surpassed them all. His golden hair had turned dull brown, his happy countenance had soured.

That he drank more than was good for him was obvious from the puffy face, bloodshot eyes, and the protruding belly in an otherwise spare frame. On his desk, Nelson had a letter of complaint from the commander-in-chief that alluded to transgressions without being specific. This was odd, because when they had met at the beginning

42

of the year, prior to the Nile campaign, St Vincent had been full of praise for the same person his letter damned.

'For what offence do Hardy and Troubridge say you must apologise?'

'I made some remarks regarding you and Lady Hamilton, which they deemed inappropriate.'

Nelson turned away, with a sharp look at Tom Allen, which commanded him to leave the room. 'Tell me, Josh, did you drink much last night?'

'Several of your officers told me I was drunk, yes.'

Nelson turned back, smiling. 'Was it not an occasion to over-indulge? We were celebrating a great victory.'

'You will recall, sir, that I was not present at Aboukir Bay.'

Nelson was angry now, but he sought hard not to let it show in his voice. 'For God's sake, Josh, stop being so damned formal. I am your stepfather, and while I acknowledge that such an estate is not perfect I hope and pray you believe that I regard you as my own son. I have done everything in my power to advance you in the service and will continue to do so. Now, let us put aside the events of last night for a moment. Tell me what you did to upset St Vincent.'

'I became engaged in various disputes with my fellow officers on the Cadiz blockade, sir.'

'I can hardly fault you for that,' replied Nelson, with a laugh. 'I have, as you know, spent half my service life arguing with some of them.'

His attempt to lighten the atmosphere fell flat. Nelson had already replied to St Vincent, requesting a more detailed explanation, while at the same time requesting that Josh be given a frigate and the right to serve under his stepfather's command. Better to wait for a response from the Earl than to tax his stepson about his misdemeanours. However, although he didn't want to ask what happened at the ball last night, he knew he had to.

'Tell me what was it you said that so upset Troubridge and Hardy?'

'I complained, sir, that the attentions you were paying to Lady Hamilton were those you should have properly been paying to my mother, and I said so loudly enough for a great number of people to hear.'

'She was our hostess, Josh. And I do recall that when you came here with me in '93, she was the soul of kindness to you.'

Josiah Nesbit positively spat his next words. 'Just as *I* recall, sir, telling you that she was a whore who had tricked Sir William Hamilton into marriage. And I also remember how severely you chastised me for that statement.'

'I thought you wrong then, Josh,' said Nelson, softly, 'and further acquaintance with the lady means that now I know it.'

'She's ensnared you too.'

The realisation that his stepson was jealous came as a flash of insight, though Nelson had little time to examine it. For five days in 1793, Emma had doted on the youth, flattered him, made him feel special, and broken through his shyness. How had she treated him on his return? As just another naval officer, perhaps, well connected but of less account than the abundant Nile heroes?

'Lady Hamilton has ensnared no one, Josh. I will not lie to you when I say I find her a most pleasant person to be with.'

'I doubt you are alone in that, sir,' said Josh. 'I should think that half the cocks in Naples share that notion.'

'How dare you, sir!' Nelson shouted, regretting it immediately. Too stout a defence of Emma could only confirm the young man's suspicions. 'How dare you bring your vulgar filth into my presence? Do I have to remind of my rank, as well as my status as your legal parent?'

'No, sir,' said Josiah stiffly.

'I have it on very good authority,' Nelson went on, 'that the lady in question gives no cause for scandal. Have I not written to your own mother these last five years to tell her so, and point out that whatever demeaning gossip she might have heard about Lady Hamilton cannot be true? Do you not know that Lady Hamilton, out of the kindness of her heart, also wrote to your mother to praise you, and to tell her that, having taken you under her protective wing, she felt that you would grow to be a man of whom she could be proud?'

'I am aware of that, sir.'

'Then by your behaviour you are denying the truth of that assertion. Captains Troubridge and Hardy are right, you do owe me an apology. But more than that you owe a greater one to someone else who has shown you nothing but kindness. Lady Hamilton, herself.'

5

As he made his way towards the main reception rooms of the Palazzo Sessa Nelson was seething, yet he sensed that the ground was shifting beneath his feet. Who else had noticed his behaviour with Emma? Troubridge for certain, and his flag captain Thomas Hardy. Did they think the same as Josh? Had they, in fact, sent his stepson to apologise as a way of alerting him to the obvious nature of his behaviour? His own weakness, which he experienced that very morning, would work against him. Proximity to Emma shattered his resolve so he must never be alone with her, nor show her too much attention when they were in company.

The doors opened before him to a room full of people engaged in polite applause. As he bowed he saw Emma glance at him proudly. The look on Sir William Hamilton's face was a combination of admiration and perplexity.

It was easier to avoid being alone with either Sir William or Emma than Nelson had supposed. Few occasions arose in the endless round of balls and receptions when they were not in the company of others. The Palazzo Sessa had always played host to a stream of visitors; expatriate or travelling fellow countrymen, locals and foreigners interested in art, antiquities, music, literature and gossip. Sir William Hamilton's reception rooms were home to wit and malice in equal measure and, over the years of his tenure, they had become one of the focal points of Neapolitan society. With Nelson in residence the number of callers increased and The Palazzo always seemed full. When either the crowd, the contemplation of Emma's beauty, or a stab of jealousy at the attentions paid to her by another man became too much for him, Nelson had his own apartments to retire to, where Tyson waited with sheaves of correspondence requiring his attention.

Most days and every night they went elsewhere to be entertained. In the main, Nelson travelled to these events in a separate carriage with his officers because whenever he appeared a crowd gathered to cheer him. Walking in the streets was impossible – he was mobbed whenever he tried.

The nights were the worst: alone in the dark he half feared, half hoped that Emma would visit him. A man with a lively imagination, he could easily conjure up the pleasure of her presence, just as easily as he could let his mind rip on the consequences. Often he feared to close his eyes, lest the images that assailed him came once more to mind.

He saw more of Sir William on matters pertaining to duty since the Ambassador was his conduit to the Neapolitan government. Slowly and haphazardly his ship was being refitted, the army was being mobilised and trained, supplies and armaments were being stockpiled. And Baron Mack von Leiberich was on his way. The frustration lay in the time it all took, and the way the whole of Naples society seemed more intent on dancing, gossiping, drinking and eating than war. As he wrote to St Vincent, they were no more than 'a bunch of fiddlers and rascals'.

Ferdinand and Maria Carolina made good their promise to receive him aboard one of their capital ships, the 74-gun *Tancredi*. His own barge crew, under the watchful gaze of his coxswain, Giddings, rowed him there. A stocky Londoner with a battered face, who had served with Nelson for years, Giddings never looked quite right in the neat blue jacket, white straw hat and gaily striped trews of his office. He looked like what he was: a bit of a brawler, a man who would never shy from a fight be it against a fellow sailor or the whole French fleet.

On coming aboard, Nelson's professional eye was employed in comparing the Italian vessel with one of his own. The ship was dry and weatherly, the rope work neat, and the decks were pristine, all of which testified to time spent at anchor, not the quality of build. The ships of his own fleet were worn, having been at sea for months, in blazing sun, howling gales, rain, sleet, heaving seas and battle. Hardly a rope was not spliced or a sail lacking a patch, the decks gouged at the edges where the guns had been run in and out and in other places where shot had ripped out splinters. Even an amateur eye would spot repaired bulwarks and masts fished with spars and gammoned with ropes to strengthen them where cannonballs had struck or a hard blow had loosed them from their seatings.

'What do you make of it, Mr Pasco?' Nelson asked the young midshipman at his side as the ceremony of piping aboard was completed.

Wherever Nelson went he took with him one of the midshipmen, youngsters who alternated between fear of making a gaff and the even greater dread that should food materialise they might not get enough. It was a means of introducing his young charges to polite society, but it afforded him a chance to get to know them better, and to ensure that their life in the midshipmen's berth was bearable – it could be hellish if it was not carefully supervised. He also felt that contact with these youths kept him young.

He enjoyed their company too. There were exceptions, morose individuals or those too nervous to relax, but in the main, once they had realised that Nelson was not going to devour them, the midshipmen were talkative and informative. He had formed the habit when he took his first command, and malicious tongues had wagged. He had pretended not to care, but before his marriage he had worried that there might some truth in the accusations covertly made against him.

'Tidy, sir, very tidy,' Pasco replied.

He was a white-faced youth, whose clear skin seemed impervious to either the ravages of his age or the Mediterranean sun. He was slim, with black hair and lively, dark brown eyes, keen as mustard to do well, bright, intelligent, with the right mix of mischief and capability. Pasco was just the kind of young man Nelson liked; one whom, should he survive, would rise to become a credit to the service.

'And?'

'The men, sir,' said Pasco doubtfully. 'They seem timid. They fail to meet the eye.'

It was true. Smart though they were they lacked the spark that animated a British crew. Britannia's sailors had a way of looking at their officers which let them know that while they would be afforded all due respect, they were dealing with souls who knew how to go about their business. Not insolent – that would only bring down punishment – but assured.

'Well observed, young Pasco,' Nelson said, as they were escorted across the maindeck, 'd'you know, I quite missed that.'

It was good to sense Pasco swell a little beside him. No doubt he would regale the midshipmen's mess with the tale, embellished a trifle, of how he had put his admiral right. As they came up on to the sunlit maindeck, the midshipman fell a step behind so that his commanding officer could raise his hat to the Commodore of the

Neapolitan fleet and the flag of the kingdom that streamed from the masthead.

The commodore was Caracciolo, and by waiting on the quarter-deck, the Count had inflicted a minor insult on Ferdinand's guest: given Nelson's rank and what he had just achieved, Caracciolo should have greeted him at the entry-port on the maindeck. He looked at Nelson keenly to see if the slur had been noted, and his disappointment, when he was greeted by a bland British admiral, was almost palpable.

Nelson and Count Caracciolo had met before, when the ships and troops of Naples had been despatched to Toulon in '93. After that unfortunate town was abandoned to revolutionary reprisals Caracciolo, in one line-of-battle ship, had stayed with the British fleet as part of the squadron under Admiral Hotham. Able to speak clear if heavily accented English, he had served in the British Navy as a youngster attached to Admiral George Rodney, a man he admired greatly. At a dinner aboard Hotham's ship, Nelson had questioned Rodney's reputation. There was little doubt that the late, successful admiral had been corrupt. Everyone knew that in every command he had held, he had stretched the rules to near breaking point to line his own pockets and promote his followers, however dubious their abilities.

He soon discovered that Caracciolo would not hear a bad word said about Rodney – nor it would seem, a true one. To the Italian the man was a paragon and any attempt to dent his reputation exposed the critic to contemptuous questions about their own capabilities and honesty. Everyone soon learned, including Nelson, that in Caracciolo's company, Rodney was a subject best left alone.

'The Commodore and I, Mr Pasco,' said Nelson loudly, 'were at the battle off Genoa in March '95, he on this very 74-gun and I in command of *Agamemnon*.'

'Your favourite ship, sir, I am told.'

'By whom?' asked Nelson, ignoring Caracciolo who seemed offended that the guest of honour was more interested in talking to one of his midshipmen than to his host.

'All the old Agamemnons aboard *Vanguard* say it is so.'

Three things pleased Nelson about that remark: first, that it was true, second, that his old shipmates were not shy of telling anyone, and third, his recollection of the large number who still served in whichever ship he sailed. It was comforting to have around him faces he knew.

'Then while we are waiting for the King and Queen I shall tell you

48

all about that day. I'm sure the Commodore will oblige you with a description as well. Having stayed close to the flagship he was so much better placed than I to observe the whole action.'

Nelson knew by the man's pursed lips that he had paid Caracciolo back for the slight, and he took the opportunity to move away from him to tell Pasco of what had occurred that day. It was another Nelson habit to regale his midshipmen with tales of battles, sometimes those he had fought himself, more often those he felt would inspire them.

To call what happened in March 1795 a battle was to elevate it somewhat, Nelson rating it as no more than a skirmish. The French, sighting the British fleet had run for their home base of Toulon, with Admiral William Hotham in pursuit. Yet he had proved timid when a chance came to trounce the enemy, seemingly more afraid of damaging his own ships than those of the enemy. It was a day of high hopes that ended as dust. In the initial excitement he had dashed off a note to Fanny.

My character and good name are in my own keeping. Life with disgrace is dreadful. A glorious death is to be envied.

He could have written a hundred pages as they sailed all through the afternoon and into the night. As the dawn mist cleared, the enemy lay ahead, still running, and Hotham ordered the fleet to give chase on a parallel course in line-of-battle. As one of the fastest sailers in the fleet, *Agamemnon* was soon well ahead, with half-a-dozen other ships who had also out-sailed the main body forming a block between him and Hotham, and a clutch of frigates out ahead almost in touch with the enemy.

One of the rearmost French ships, an 80-gun two-decker, had run foul of one of her consorts, carrying away her fore and main topmasts. The frigate *Inconstant*, with a mere twenty-eight cannon immediately closed with what was identified as the *Ça Ira*, a bold step given the respective firepower of the vessels.

Pasco was enthralled as he listened to Nelson, watching his hands as they traced the various ships' positions on the hammock nettings.

The frigate had received heavy fire and was force to haul off to avoid destruction, but had achieved the aim of slowing the enemy, towards which *Agamemnon* was now standing. The *Ça Ira*, under tow, was vulnerable, unable to manoeuvre, and unable to gain enough speed to get clear. Coming up in the wake, Nelson overhauled the Frenchman under a raking fire from his stern chasers. Nelson had had his own worries – *Agamemnon* was short of men through death, disease and the manning of prizes. He had too few hands aboard to sail the ship and fight the guns, so he resolved that the crew would have to do both.

'Once in range, Mr Pasco, I called the men from their guns to man the braces and let fly the sheets. At the same time the quartermaster spun the wheel to bring *Agamemnon*'s head round. In the minute it took to come broadside on to the *Ça Ira*'s stern we had taken several knocks to our hull and observed a couple of balls nearly nick the mainmast. But those gun crews were soon back at their pieces, in time to pour a devastating fire into the Frenchman. That was repeated several times with our ship being cut up quite badly on the approach. Sailing straight in *Ça Ira*'s wake, we were unable to return fire.'

'Hot work, sir,' said Pasco.

'Two hours that went on, and though we took a bit of punishment we inflicted a damn sight more. *Ça Ira* was a perfect wreck. The pity is that we could have overhauled her, for she was a sitter, and by passing her to windward taken on the next ship in the French fleet.'

'The *Sans Culotte*, sir.'

'You know about this?' Nelson asked.

'Yes, sir,' replied Pasco proudly. 'We mids know of every battle you've been in. We re-fight them on our mess table.'

Nelson nodded and smiled, for he had done the same thing himself as a youngster, and every time he and his messmates re-fought a battle they always did better than the original admiral; taking more ships, inflicting more casualties, and employing superior tactics.

'I fear to continue this, Pasco, lest you inform me of where I went wrong.'

'The opinion is, sir,' said Pasco, guilelessly, 'that it was Admiral Hotham who went wrong.'

'I am forgiven on your mess table for not getting amongst the French laggards for the lack of any ships to support me?'

Pasco replied in the same natural way. 'Oh no, sir. You are reckoned brave but never foolish.'

Nelson laughed out loud. 'Not an opinion you will find unanimously shared in certain high places.'

Had he been foolish? Tired of the punishment, the captain of the *Ça Ira* ordered his towing frigate to bring his head round and aim a broadside on his tormentor. The Frenchman had every right to expect his enemy to shear off, but Nelson did nothing of the sort – he sailed on boldly as most of the French shot screamed harmlessly over his head. What had Admiral Hotham seen? One of his smallest line-of-battle ships, isolated and outgunned, racing into battle as if nothing mattered but contact, a sitting duck that lost would weaken the fleet and rebound badly on Hotham's reputation. That was when the Admiral raised his flags and ordered the recall, forcing Nelson to break off the action.

'It would never do, Pasco, to say that Admiral Hotham was wrong that day. I had tested my luck, but it is not a good idea to push that particular lady too far.'

The following morning the *Ça Ira* had been taken, along with *Censuer*, a 74-gunner then towing her, another engagement in which his Agamemnons had distinguished themselves. Yet Hotham, instead of continuing the pursuit and trying to bring the French to battle, had declined to agree with Nelson and his own second in command, Admiral Goodall. He, supported by the third admiral, Hyde Parker, had claimed 'that they had done very well.'

As a captain Nelson had strongly disagreed and said so. Now he was himself an admiral he knew that his opinion would have been the same.

His tale was interrupted when a lookout shouted and all eyes turned to the shore, where the royal barge was pushing off. It was so like the day, five years before, when he had entertained the King on the deck of *Agamemnon* – the sun had shone then too. The royal couple and their court had come aboard to be fed and wined by splendid comestibles at the expense of Sir William Hamilton, who had been there too, with him his wife.

And on that deck, close to a woman who excited him like no other, Nelson had very nearly committed the mortal sin of telling her so publicly. Just in time the news had come that a French warship was in the offing, which had given him the excuse to turf the royal party off the ship, Hamiltons included, and sail away from temptation.

Now a whole flotilla filled the sparkling blue waters of the bay, timing their arrival aboard so that the royal party would arrive last. Of course, the Hamiltons were there, Emma in layers of white and cream muslin, a shawl of heavy lace preventing the sea breeze ruffling her hair. As he was not the host, Nelson was not obliged to welcome her as she came aboard, for which he was grateful.

As they approached, the King and Queen were greeted by a twenty-one-gun salute, stamping marines and whistling pipes. The Queen and her entourage made straight for the cabin where they would remain until dinner. Maria Carolina was not a lover of the sea, and preferred to be surrounded by wooden walls and eager servants than stand on a windswept deck.

Ferdinand arrived alone on the quarterdeck dressed in the uniform of an admiral, splendid for once in dark blue silk coat edged and buttoned with gold, sparkling white waistcoat and breeches, with a fine hat, trimmed with ostrich feathers, on his head. Graciously he tipped it to Nelson, a signal honour from a sovereign to a commoner, before insisting that his guest accompany him on the ritual inspection of the ship.

'I do not believe, young sir, that we have been introduced.'

William Pasco turned from watching the broad back of the King, to be faced by a vision. Emma was smiling at him, and his heart raced. He knew who she was and snatched his hat off his head. 'Midshipman William Pasco, Lady Hamilton, at your service.'

'I find myself without an escort, young man. You will observe that my husband, Sir William, is engaged with Count Caracciolo.'

'If I can be of service, my lady?' replied Pasco hoarsely.

'You may take my arm, young sir, and tell me about yourself.'

Pasco had found that he could talk to Horatio Nelson with ease, but the notion of conversing with this woman rendered him tongue-tied. Like every blade aboard ship, he had heard tales of her past and her beauty, and had speculated with his shipmates by candlelight about the sybaritic practices of which she was capable. He had lain alone in the dark, as well, thinking about that very same thing.

'You are, I would guess, serving on *Vanguard*?' Pasco nodded. 'And you were at the Nile?'

That brought out the pride that he, like every other man in Nelson's fleet, felt at having shared in that battle. 'I was.'

'Good. I wish to hear as much of that engagement as I can. Admiral Nelson has told me about it, of course, as have several of his officers, both Vanguards and others. But I confess to you Mr Pasco, that I cannot hear enough.'

Pasco could talk of the Nile with ease, even to a famous beauty, for not even the potency of his fantasies about her could dent his self-satisfaction. Like all of his shipmates he had thought about it, discussed it, embellished and honed it in preparation for a lifetime of recounting. They all knew they were heroes, and they could not wait to get back to their homeland to bask in the glory their story would bring them.

And Pasco had an imaginative and colourful turn of phrase: he could describe the dying light as they approached Aboukir Bay, the way the sky turned first gold then orange. Even though he had spent most of the battle on the gundeck below, he knew enough to give a good description of the events of the night: of the coloured lights above every British vessel that identified them to each other, of the shot, shell and fire, the screaming of men in the water, the blasted stumps of masts trailing over the side and blood running out of the scuppers to stain the sea, of the boy Casabianca refusing to leave his father, the captain of *L'Orient*, then the final great cataclysm as the French flagship exploded taking father, son and six hundred crew to perdition.

'Why, Mr Pasco,' said Emma, clutching his arm a little tighter, 'you tell your tale so well as to render me fearful.'

'I will not lie to you, my lady,' the boy said, his shyness now quite gone, 'when I say that my heart beat as fast as it ever did that day, and there were occasions, seconds only I grant you, when I was frozen with fear. But my need to do my duty saw me through.'

As he gazed into those amazing green eyes, Pasco felt pleased with himself. In perfecting his version of the tale he had reckoned that undiluted heroics would never do: humility and an admission of fear would be more believable.

'You are lucky to have such a commander, Mr Pasco, are you not?'

Pasco replied with genuine feeling. 'The greatest sailor and the best man that ever lived, my lady, and there is not man in the whole fleet who will say otherwise.'

Emma had heard often enough from the lips of Nelson's officers how highly he was regarded, but she felt a warm glow as she encouraged this young fellow to tell her again. An admiral he might be, but Nelson could joke with the lowest swabber on the ship, and talk knowledgeably to every warrant officer about his duties and methods. The gunner reckoned the Admiral knew more about cannon, powder and shot, as well as range and trajectory, than any man alive. The master, whose job it was to plot navigation and see to the sail plan would never fail to listen if Nelson cast an opinion, and only once in a blue moon advised against whatever course or change of sail he suggested.

Nelson swapped tales with the carpenter about some of the rotten ships they had both served in and discussed changes to the ship's design that would facilitate some fighting task. He even treated the purser as a human being. No man could go further than that, since pursers, in any sailor's opinion, were robbing bastards.

Pasco talked on and on as they circled the quarterdeck and Emma was content to listen. Edward Berry had been flag captain at the Nile, but he had been sent home with despatches and replaced by Thomas Hardy, another of Nelson's protégés. Hardy was nicknamed the Ghost for his way of appearing silently in any number of places on the ship, as well as his disinclination to engage in trivial conversation. His elevation, it seemed, had brought the cat out of the bag for Hardy, unlike Berry, was a strict disciplinarian.

Emma could see the royal head emerging from below, then Nelson's head appeared, and she felt a deep surge of emotion.

'My dear,' said Sir William.

As she turned to her husband the admiration was still in her face and it took all of Sir William's self-control not to acknowledge it. The most telling pang came from the knowledge that, while he and Emma had been happy together, she did not love him. The look on her face was one he had never seen. It made him jealous.

'Allow me to name Mr Pasco of the *Vanguard*,' said Emma. 'He is Admiral Nelson's escort today, and I must say he has entertained me handsomely.'

'Thank you, my lady,' said Pasco, beaming. He would be top dog in the mess tonight just for having spoken with her. That she had enjoyed his company was a bonus he would admit to with care.

'You will find, young man,' Sir William said, 'should you get to know my wife, that no one can turn her head like a sailor.' He regretted saying it before the whole sentence was out of his mouth. To have spoken with such obvious pique was a breach of his own standards and those of his occupation. And he saw by the way Emma turned her head that his barb had hit home. He could not tell her that he had appalled himself, nor could he apologise, for that would require him to allude openly to what had happened between her and Nelson, which he could never do. He said instead, 'I think, my dear that we are about to dine. I wonder, would Mr Pasco escort you to the great cabin?'

'Delighted, sir,' crowed Pasco.

'It would please me too, Mr Pasco,' Emma replied, offering him her arm as she threw a forced but sweet smile at Sir William.

6

The bells pealed all over London and within days the news brought by Captain Edward Berry had spread throughout the nation. Strangers stopped each other in the street to ask if they had heard the stupendous news of the battle of the Nile, and it was the sole topic of conversation in coffee-house, home or place of employment. Disbelief was rampant, because the success of the British fleet, and the Admiral who commanded it, had been so absolute.

Every theatre owner in the land was lashing together a patriotic show to tell the tale, creating an overwhelming demand for the artefacts of Egypt; pyramids, sphinxes, obelisks and crocodiles. The risk that a whole building might burn down in a massive conflagration was ignored in the interests of re-enacting the climax of the battle: the explosion of the French flagship *L'Orient*. Any one-armed ex-sailor prepared to tread the boards could command his own price to play Admiral Sir Horatio Nelson, the hero of the hour.

Lord Spencer was cock-a-hoop, too overwhelmed with gratitude to notice that the men who had damned him for a fool before Berry's arrival were now praising his sagacity. Even Farmer George openly lauded Nelson: being King no one would dare to remind him of his previous long-held animosity.

In the City of London, meetings were held to decide how such a success should be rewarded, and an already amazed public was stunned by the announcement of an award of ten thousand pounds to the victor of the Nile. Alexander Davidson, Nelson's long-standing friend and appointed prize agent, employed extra clerks for what was sure to be an increased workload, and ordered gold medals struck for the officers of Nelson's fleet, to be paid for out of his own pocket.

The government moved more slowly, which allowed euphoria to be tempered by time: those forced to disguise their distrust of Nelson after the news had broken began to reassert their malignant opinions. At the same time the King was asking himself why such a victory had not been granted to an officer he liked.

To a nation waiting with bated breath for the announcement of Nelson's elevation to the rank of duke, the award of a barony came as a bitter disappointment. The populace decided that the official excuse, that Nelson was only an admiral in command of a detached squadron, not a commander-in-chief, had been prompted by small-mindedness.

Fanny Nelson had only one wish: that her husband would come home. Who could achieve more than he, who was now styled Baron Nelson? Now that he was the hero he had always wanted to be, surely he would cease to put himself in life-threatening situations and come home for a well-earned rest. If not, she was resolved to join him in the Mediterranean, and she wrote to tell him so.

Even such a spacious cabin as that of the *Tancredi* struggled to accommodate the numbers who sat down to dine, and around Nelson conversations flowed in French, German and Italian, with little English. As guest of honour, he was seated next to the King, a privilege he had been granted previously, and one that, given the man's boorishness, he would gladly have surrendered.

Ferdinand was not a fellow to talk to his neighbours if he could hold a shouted discussion with someone at the furthest end of the table. This he interspersed with stuffing his mouth with food and wine so that his deep blue nautical garments were soon as food-stained as those he habitually wore. Occasionally he would turn and beam at Nelson then raise his wineglass in a way that forced his guest to follow suit and consume the entire contents. The King's glass was immediately refilled, and so was that of the man he had toasted.

Horatio Nelson knew he had a limited capacity for alcohol and that over indulgence in the past had got him into trouble. But caution evaporates as quantity increases, and even if he had been determined to fight the effects, whatever resolve he had was weakening. He tried to concentrate on others at the table, like young Pasco, who was in an animated conversation with one of Maria Carolina's younger ladies-in-waiting.

When that failed he turned his attention to Count Caracciolo, distrust surfacing. Yet fair-mindedness forced Nelson to consider that just as he was a patriot to his own nation so must be Caracciolo. Perhaps the Neapolitan nobleman experienced the same feelings that surged in Nelson when he thought of his country. His devotion to those things for which Britannia stood made him want to do well for her.

He recalled the vision he had had on his way back from Calcutta as a youth. He had been in the grip of malaria and fever had generated in him a conviction that he was destined for great things: that his love of God and his country would shield him as much as it would raise him. Did Caracciolo hanker for a shrine in the cathedral of San Gennaro, as Nelson dreamed of a statue in Westminster Abbey?

Nelson knew that Britain was far from perfect. Thanks to a survey he had undertaken during his five years on the beach he was well aware of the depths of rural poverty, the despair and fecklessness it engendered, and the lack of alleviation that stood in stark contrast to the statements of concern that issued from the hypocritical mouths of those who claimed to care.

The politics of his country could appear just as venal as those of Naples, and in some cases just as corrupt. Was the Marquis de Gallo any worse than Lord Holland, who in the 1770s had used money entrusted to him as Paymaster to the Forces for private gain, and remained embroiled in dispute till the day he died? Nelson's superiors at the Admiralty were not always given to acting in the best interests of the officers and men of the service. Politics was a constant bugbear: people of little merit were advanced to senior positions in the administration merely through the power of their sponsors. The common seaman was paid sporadically, often by warrants that, for want of cash to feed their families, the men of the fleet had to sell at a discount to the crimps who thrived in every naval port.

Conditions aboard some ships of His Majesty's' fleet were downright shameful: rotten food, hard-horse captains too fond of the lash, commanders and pursers who misused their office for private profit, while dockyard workers stole anything that was not nailed down. Abuses abounded, and though he had a care as to whom he voiced his opinions, it was well known in the service that Horatio Nelson had some sympathy for the men who had mutinied at Spithead and the Nore in the previous year. And yet for all that was wrong, the system worked. There were enough good men to see that the fleet remained effective.

Under the influence of the wine, Nelson, every so often, had to look at Emma, and it was not easy to be discreet given that she was seated to his left: any attempt at eye contact required that he sit forward to look past the boisterous King. If he wished, Sir William, seated next to Princess Esterhazy, could observe him. Nelson found that he no longer cared. And Emma met his eye, although she was engaged in conversation with the neighbour to her right.

Things were easier during the ritual speeches: all the toasts – to Naples, Britannia, Ferdinand, King George, the Austrian Emperor, the British fleet, its sailors and, most of all, Nelson himself – required him to gaze around the company. During the toasts news was delivered to Ferdinand that his Austrian general had reached Caserta. Clearly fuelled by the amount of wine in his belly, the King felt the power of his office: in a display of personal braggadocio that made the slippery Marquis de Gallo blench, he raised his glass, said, 'Damnation to the French,' and drank, breaking in that simple phrase the neutrality of his kingdom. Nelson could not help but be delighted, although he knew that the matter about which he cared so passionately had been resolved by drink, rather than wisdom.

'Admiral Nelson.'

He hesitated to turn round. He had been standing on the windward side of the deck, gazing out at the sea, deep-blue under the late afternoon sun, hoping that the breeze would remove the brassy taste of stale wine from his mouth. Like everyone on board he was waiting for royalty to depart – or, more specifically, Maria Carolina and her suite of German servants. Ferdinand had gone an hour before in the *Tancredi*'s cutter, but the Queen had insisted on waiting till the sun dipped and the temperature fell, which would ease the breeze and the choppiness of the water.

'Lady Hamilton,' he replied as he turned.

'I require a private word with you.' Nelson glanced around the deck for Sir William as Emma added, 'It is on behalf of the Queen. I am, as you know, at Her Majesty's disposal.' Emma walked towards a less occupied part of the deck, obliging him to follow her. 'If I may refer to something you said when you arrived in Naples.'

'Why so formal, Emma?' Nelson whispered.

'You said,' she continued, as if he hadn't spoken, 'that you would remain here for no more than two weeks, that once your ships were repaired you would sail to Cadiz.'

'I have a commander-in-chief to whom I must report, Emma, and St Vincent is off Cadiz. I must look into Malta on the way – that is a pressing concern.'

'You also said that you would base the fleet on Syracuse.'

'It is the best place to hamper French movements, Emma. You, of all people, know that. From there I cover both the Straits of Messina and the waters between Taranto and the Barbary shore.'

She wouldn't look at him. 'So that is still your intention?'

Now Nelson adopted a formal tone, because he felt wounded by hers. 'I intend to meet with Baron Mack to find out what plans he has to attack the French in the Papal States. Once I have done that I will make whatever dispositions are necessary to support him.'

'So Cadiz is not a necessity?'

'I have the trust of St Vincent, who allows me to make my own dispensations. I will do whatever I see to be in the interests of our country.'

Still she wouldn't look at him. 'And Naples?'

'Thanks to the King's wine-fuelled bravado, the two are now the same, although I will be convinced only when I see the French Ambassador sent packing. I don't trust de Gallo not to change the King's mind when he returns to a state of sobriety.'

'Would it help you to know that the Queen feels the die is cast, that Naples cannot live at peace with France, and that she and her husband cannot ever feel secure until the cancer of Revolution is excised from their patrimony?'

'Those sound like her words, Emma.'

At last she smiled. 'They are.'

'I would be happier if you used your own.'

'You must be aware that Maria Carolina fears her own subjects as much as she fears the French. Perhaps the army will march now that Mack is here, but you know as well as I how hard it is to beat the French.'

'On land,' he said, smiling, which earned him a squeeze of his good arm.

'The Queen feels she will not be secure without you anchored in the bay.'

'Me?'

'If you are here, the fleet is here.'

And the means of escape, thought Nelson, for a royal family who could not be sure in a crisis if their own naval officers would be reliable.

'I cannot decide on any action until I have met with Mack.'

'Can I tell her, then, that you will not desert us? It would ease her mind.'

Nelson was required, he knew, to say no: he could not hobble himself and his duty to his own sovereign by making such a commitment to another. But neither could he look into those green eyes and say the word. 'Yes, you may tell her that.'

The royal party, led by the ladies-in-waiting, began to assemble on the deck. Emma breathed, 'Thank you,' and went to join them, no doubt to tell the Queen what Nelson had said. That she did so was obvious, since Maria Carolina looked straight at him and inclined her head. Nelson wondered at her perspicacity: had she asked him herself he would have been obliged, however diplomatically, to refuse. How had she known that if she used Emma Hamilton as an emissary he would say yes? He was under even more scrutiny, by many more people, than he had assumed.

He felt very much under Emma's scrutiny at dinner than night – a private affair for him, his senior officers and several close friends of the Hamiltons – from the numerous paintings that lined the walls of this private dining room. Three, he knew, were by Romney, Emma as herself, young and stunningly beautiful, in a classical pose as a *bacchante*, others by Gavin Hamilton and Angelica Kauffman, and the one he liked best, by Madame Vigée Le Brun, of Emma in white, hands clasped in supplication as St Cecilia.

In every picture her eyes seemed to be on him and he almost squirmed to think that Sir William had bought them all. A man who had so many portraits of his wife was likely to be enamoured of her. She was sat halfway down the board with an eager midshipman to one side and a stiffly formal, and hopefully chastened, Captain Josiah Nesbit on the other.

There was much talk of the war, as well as of London and country society: friends, acquaintances or public figures to commend or damn. Others, once assurance had been given that no person at the table was a cousin or comrade, were condemned outright. Whatever scandals had reached Naples from London were dissected, and compared with the more disreputable local ones.

Nelson was seated at one end of the table next to Emma's friend Cornelia Knight, whose mother, the widow of Admiral Sir John Knight, was on his other side. He liked them both, the older lady for her sagacity, the daughter for her verve, though he found Cornelia's voice a trifle blaring. They had been shunted down to Naples from their residence in Rome by the French invasions of '96, forced to settle in Naples when the armies of the anti-revolutionary coalition made peace with Bonaparte.

Lady Knight was an invalid, yet she swore that, but for her daughter, she would have stayed in Rome and 'not given a damn for the consequences'. Nelson believed her: you only had to look at her to see that she had a truly steely determination. More importantly, on her last visit to England Lady Knight had become a friend of his wife:

she had met Fanny with the Reverend Nelson when his father made one of his frequent visits to Bath.

Cornelia was a writer of books, which to a man who hated to pen a letter was astounding. He could not comprehend how anyone could sit down voluntarily with a quill. As a writer Miss Knight was agog to hear his own experience of the battle of the Nile, and Nelson told her his tale in great detail, concluding, 'I believe Miss Knight, that my hand was guided by divine providence.'

'God must hate a Frenchman, sir,' Lady Knight interjected, 'for they are demons and apostates,' and Nelson realised how like his mother she was. The words she had used might have come from Catherine Nelson's lips, for she had hated the French with a passion, and often told her little Horatio that when he grew up it was his duty to confound that damnable race.

'You flatter me, sir,' Lady Knight responded, when he said as much to her. 'I know your mother to have been a Suckling, and I had the good fortune when my husband was alive to meet your late uncle on many occasions. He was an upright man, and modest about his own achievements.'

'Apart from my dear mother, Lady Knight, I can think of no person who has inspired me more.'

Captain Maurice Suckling had taken his nephew as a youngster into his ship and made sure he learned his trade. He had chaired the board that examined him for lieutenant and used his influence to get him promoted to the rank of post captain. It was no exaggeration to say that, as a fighting sailor, Nelson owed him everything.

'Inspired?' Lady Knight exclaimed. 'You surpass him, sir. His actions were splendid, but they cannot compare with yours. Imagine his pride, Admiral Nelson, if from some celestial realm he observed your recent victory. His heart must swell at the sight.'

'The Nile, sir,' added her daughter, loudly, 'must have been the happiest day of your life.'

This coincided with a lull in the conversation and Cornelia's voice acted like a clarion. Every eye at the table was now on him, including those of Sir William Hamilton and his wife. Lady Knight corresponded with Fanny on a regular basis, and if Josiah, sitting looking morose, had noticed his behaviour with Emma then others could do so.

'No, Miss Knight,' Nelson replied. 'I have to tell you that the happiest day of my life was the one on which I married Lady Nelson.'

'Bravo, Admiral,' cried Cornelia's mother.

That pleased him, although Emma's eyes bored into him with an amused accusation that he lied, while others, embarrassed by such a fatuous and maladroit statement, coughed and looked at their plates. Josiah glared at him.

'Such a sentiment does you great honour, sir,' said Sir William.

Nelson had no idea if he had spoken the truth or indulged in deep irony, and had no way to find out – the mood of the gathering picked up and the conversation was flowing again.

Nelson made the journey to meet with Mack, now resident at the royal country palace of Caserta, in the company of the Hamiltons. They were travelling on an oft-used royal highway in a well-sprung carriage, free of attendants or guests, the only bar to conversation being the hum of the ironbound wheels on the smooth *pave*, in an atmosphere that was somewhat strained.

Sir William applied himself to keeping up a flow of witty anecdotes about the stream of English visitors who came to the Palazzo Sessa. He had a great store of such stories, being a man who could highlight a fault or a weakness, recall an attraction or a peccadillo in even the most puissant of his guests, and then recount them with humour. Yet even he faltered at times, obliged by the circumstances to leave out any reference to seduction or adultery, the normal mainstay of his tales.

Nelson's fear of making some revealing remark led him into a rather didactic repetition of the problems he had in his command and in dealing with their Neapolitan allies. Emma took refuge in defence of the Queen, maintaining that if Maria Carolina had her way, none of Nelson's problems would exist.

What was most telling to Sir William was Nelson's inability to meet his eye, for the Admiral was famed for his direct gaze. Emma too, normally a light-hearted companion, was behaving in an odd, stiff way. The question for her husband was obvious; did such manifest guilt spring from mere embarrassment, or did it disguise some deeper feeling that neither party dared express?

Nelson was thinking that with *Vanguard* finally ready for sea, he must get away from Naples, and remove himself from the hothouse of his emotions. In his present circumstances he couldn't think and guessed from the way Emma was behaving that she was similarly distracted. He could not know that she was wriggling with frustration at the restrictions imposed on her. She wanted to speak out, to break the shackles with which she and Nelson had bound each other.

The sight of the guards of the Royal Regiment at the gates to the palace brought an almost audible sigh of relief from all three occupants.

Baron Karl Mack von Leiberich was a pleasant surprise, a Bavarian not an Austrian, a scarred survivor of many battles against the forces of the Ottoman Empire, both as a junior officer and as a commander. Nelson found him refreshing. He was a man who been raised to his noble rank not born to it, which also pleased Nelson. He had met too many officers of the Austrian army who appeared to have achieved their elevated status without dirtying their manicured hands in a fight. The French army might be composed of riff-raff, but at least its men were fighters, who would battle to take what they wanted and hold on to what they had.

The introduction was made by the King and Queen in person, and Maria Carolina begged Baron Mack 'to be on land what Nelson was to Naples at sea', before they repaired to dinner. Given that the royal palace of Caserta was a huge, sprawling edifice built to rival Versailles, the setting of the meal was intimate, taking place in one of the smaller salons rather than the great echoing state rooms. Baron Mack had no English, and Nelson no German, so the conversation was conducted in French, with Sir William and Emma translating.

Baron Mack insisted that the French would grow stronger if Naples delayed, and Nelson agreed. In fact a despatch had already come in to Sir William from the consul at Leghorn hinting at rumours of French reinforcements, but the decision had been taken to keep this information to themselves. It was not confirmed, but the very thought of greater French strength would only give Naples an excuse to delay.

Having assessed the force at his disposal Mack wished to march north within ten days, his aim to drive the French back from the Papal States and take Rome. Then he would attempt to form a junction with the Austrian forces, who would surely break the treaties forced on them by Bonaparte and push down the valley of Adige.

'Please tell the Baron that I will undertake whatever tasks he sees fit to designate to me, but . . .' Nelson paused '. . . I hardly think such a pleasant dinner is the place to discuss our future strategy.'

There was stupidity around this table, Nelson was sure, men whose gossip would alert the French. There might even be true disloyalty: people present who would write to the French commander at Rome with an outline of the planned movements of troops and ships.

'And please tell the Baron that while he makes his preparations I

63

will use the time to visit Captain Ball off Valetta to assess the situation of Malta.'

His openness about his intentions was deliberate: Malta was no more than a day's sailing on a fair wind. If the French knew he was coming they would expect action, which might unnerve them. Bonaparte's reputation had helped the French to capture the island; perhaps Nelson's would assist in taking it back.

The Queen enquired anxiously. 'You will return, my dear Admiral?'

'Of course, Your Majesty. Did I not give you my word.'

Ferdinand's head jerked up when that was translated, his large nose twitching and the black eyes suddenly suspicious, making it very obvious to everyone in the room just how much he mistrusted his wife.

The rest of the day was spent in consulting maps, and Ferdinand boasted about the advances he would make and the Frenchmen he would kill, although he had yet to actually declare war on France. Away from him and the ears of his courtiers, Nelson and Mack, with Sir William translating, discussed various scenarios in which the Royal Navy could assist. Emma was with the Queen, bolstering her resolve and allaying her fears.

On the journey back to Naples, she said, 'The Queen wishes me to assure you that de Gallo will not be made Minister of War. That position will be given to Sir John Acton.'

'Even though she mistrusts him?' asked Nelson.

'She distrusts de Gallo more when it comes to a conflict with France,' said Sir William. 'And she knows how highly you regard him. The appointment will be made to ensure that you keep your word to return.'

Nelson looked at Emma then. 'It disturbs me that she can doubt it.'

'Which only goes to prove, my dear Admiral,' Sir William responded, with irony, 'how strange to you are the ways of Italy.'

7

Nelson felt clean merely being at sea again, leaving behind his own evasions and Neapolitan chicanery in exchange for his naval command. He had entertained Ferdinand and his second son, Prince Leopold, at breakfast before raising anchor, in part to show them gratitude for the fact that the dockyards had finished the works on *Vanguard*, but also to seek their help in speeding up work on Troubridge's ship, *Culloden*, still waiting for the metal pintles that would hold the rudder in place, without which she was useless.

From Prince Leopold he learned that orders had gone out to the governors of the Sicilian cities of Messina and Syracuse. They were required to send troops to Malta, with whatever stands of arms they could spare, ammunition, and victuals to feed the Maltese insurgents. Sir William Hamilton had attended that breakfast, and Nelson was grateful that Emma had not. An awkward public farewell had thus been avoided.

Their parting had taken place in the vestibule of the Palazzo Sessa, with coachmen and servants scuttling around them. Their words had borne little relation to what their eyes seemed to say. There was a tinge of doubt in hers that, even though he had promised to return, he might sail away for another half-decade. He had tried silently to reassure her that her fears were groundless.

The routine of the naval day soon imposed itself, although the crew seemed a little slack after a fortnight in the dockyard. Every man on board knew that there was prize money on the way for the captures at the Nile, ship money, gun money for the cannon and head money for the prisoners. Sure that it would be paid without any of the usual fuss, Captain Hardy had advanced his men a portion to make pleasant their Neapolitan stay.

The problem for the crew was that every whore and cheapjack trader in Naples knew they had money, so it was doubtful if many of them left Naples with a single penny piece. The 'tween decks of *Vanguard* this past two weeks had been like Paddy's Market; singers, jugglers and dancers performing while traders sold everything from sweetmeats, silks and cloths, to charms and false gold trinkets. Naturally, the local whores had come aboard in droves.

There would be endless sore heads from sour wine, pox aplenty, as well as the odd tar who, in a drunken stupor, had somehow got himself married. The 'bride' would emerge at sea, often disguised in male attire, sometimes to remain undiscovered and meld into part of the crew. If he cared to look closely, Hardy might also notice an increase in the number of ship's boys. There were numerous home-less urchins in Naples who would happily swap a damp culvert for regular meals aboard a British man o' war. If that involved sharing a hammock to get themselves on the muster roll, so be it: such things happened in every port at which a warship called. In time they, too, would become part of the crew, indistinguishable from the rest, good sailors who could hand and reef with the best.

Like the females their real identity might be known, but unless it was made too obvious their superiors would turn a blind eye. Every ship, unless a captain made a special effort to clear them out, had its portion of such pairings. In the main they kept themselves to themselves, and as long as they showed a proper degree of discretion they would be left in peace. The smooth running of the ship came before unenforceable Admiralty statutes: better to accept and man-age the situation, than be forever in front of courts martial.

Tom Allen was happy to be back aboard ship too. At sea he could look after his master with his eyes shut; the pre-dawn awakening, the early morning shave, assistance to dress, and a quick tidy of the cabin as the Admiral took a walk on the windward side of the quarterdeck.

Tom hadn't liked the Palazzo Sessa. There were too many servants, as well as that Cadogan woman who was forever turning up unex-pectedly like a wraith, able to make him feel guilty without reason. And things had been going on there between the lady of the house and his master of which he wanted no part. Better to be aboard, where Tom Allen was a somebody instead of a pawn, accosted frequently by his shipmates asking to know how the Admiral was feeling.

The men of HMS *Vanguard*, especially those who had sailed with Nelson on previous ships, had an almost superstitious attitude to the well-being of their admiral. They knew he was prone to bouts of fever, the victim of any ailment that was going the rounds, and was even prey to black moods brought on by doubt. But they also knew he was a fighter; that any disorder fell away at the prospect of action. And the men who sailed with Nelson relished a scrap as much as he did.

Tom could tell them happily that 'He's at his very best, his old self so to speak. Wouldn't surprise me to see them guns run out, mate, as soon as we sight the Maltese shore.'

Most of Nelson's time was spent in writing letters. He dictated the official missives to Tyson, who could turn a neat phrase, but he scrawled more intimate notes, with his left hand, to family and his wife. When he came to mention Emma Hamilton in a letter to Fanny, Nelson paused. He had referred to Emma many times since his first visit to Naples, and to omit her now would generate curiosity. He had told Fanny that malicious stories about Emma's past could be safely ignored, that she was kind, clever and patriotic, that she and her husband had been, individually, for the last five years his regular correspondents.

Emma had written to Fanny too, to tell her that in Josiah she had a fine son who would one day make her proud. Nelson was tempted to say in his own letter that the young man was a snake in the grass, who had bitten the hand that had been kind to him, but he contented himself with observing that, with his moodiness, Josiah was in danger of ruining his career.

He wrote of Emma uneasily, praising her as he had always done, asking Fanny to let all know that without Lady Hamilton's intervention in securing supplies for the fleet the Nile battle might never have happened. Longing and guilt fought each other as he tried hard to strike the right tone, and he could not be sure he had. The way he thought about Emma had changed so dramatically that his judgement was suspect. He felt a pang of loneliness that there was no one to whom he could turn for advice.

The following day at first light they raised Malta. As well as the masts of his own warships and those of Naples he could see a clutch of Portuguese men o' war, a squadron whose arrival he had been anticipating for weeks. That they had made a rendezvous with Ball was to be commended, but he wondered if Malta was the right place for such a force.

'A message to Captain Ball, if you please, Hardy,' he said softly, as they approached the main island, 'that he repair aboard.'

Hardy smiled, which did little to light up his face, and Nelson reckoned that Thomas Hardy hadn't changed from the rather grave midshipman he had taken into his ship. He had always had a heavy countenance, sad eyes, well-rounded cheeks and down-turned lips over a heavy jaw, which made him appear dull and a touch slow-witted. But he was painfully honest, without guile, as brave as a lion and a very competent sailor. Nelson loved and trusted him for that.

'I think you will find, sir,' Hardy said, handing him his telescope, 'that his barge is already in the water. Mr Pasco, oblige me by seeing to the arrangements for the reception.'

Nelson fixed the glass on the entry port of HMS *Alexander* in time to see Ball, in a boat cloak to keep the spray off his uniform, step nimbly into the waiting boat. The boatswain was ready to pipe Captain Ball aboard at the entry port. That was where Nelson would greet him: by taking *Vanguard* under tow in the most danger-ous of circumstances, Ball had once saved him from going down in this very ship. He had been one of his Nile captains, and was therefore one of his 'Band of Brothers'. The captains had commem-orated the victory by the formation of the Egyptian Club. They called each other 'crocodiles', had subscribed to a portrait of their admiral and patron, and had presented him with a sword. The Canadian, Captain Ben Hallowell, had had his carpenter make a coffin from *L'Orient's* mainmast, and had given it to Nelson so that his admiral could carry it with him wherever he went.

Nelson gazed through the telescope at Malta's splendid natural harbours, backed by the island's barren hard-baked earth. The town of Valetta stood to one side of the choke point that formed the entrance to a secure anchorage, with Fort Ricasoli on the other. The whole was dominated by the citadel and the gun-bristling bastions that stood at the horns, the most potent being the four tiers of can-non, from water level to topsail height in Malta's Fort St Elmo.

Now he recalled the promises Ferdinand had made to the Maltese delegation. The King had assured them that once supplied with guns, ammunition and troops, the islanders, in concert with the forces of Naples and Sicily, would take it back from the French in a week. With a better eye and a damn sight more experience, Nelson reckoned it too formidable to assault without several regiments of British troops, and Ball agreed. He pointed out that a land attack was fraught with difficulties and major forces would have to be deployed. Nelson could see for himself that no ship could get within range of the main fortress without facing fire from those formidable bastions – and even if the bastions were knocked out the entrance to the harbour would still be under heavy fire from the forts. As only one ship at a time could make the passage, it would be reduced to a hulk before it could even begin to bring fire to bear on the citadel. Bonaparte, with a force big enough to invade Egypt, had bluffed the previous owners out of the castle. The British Navy must either do the same or blockade the place and starve them out.

'Boat approaching, your honour,' said Tom Allen, 'from the Portuguese flagship.'

'The Marquis de Niza,' said Ball, his dark and handsome face creasing in a frown. 'He will expect a salute, sir.'

'Of what kind?'

'The same as that due to you, sir.'

'Will he, by damn?'

Nelson was fussy about flags and salutes – who was entitled to fly or receive them and who was not – which had got him into disputes throughout his naval career. On one occasion his objections had led to censure from the Admiralty, creating among certain members of the body that ran the navy the impression he was something of a pest.

'The Marquis,' Ball continued, 'rates himself as equal to an English admiral in detached command of a squadron. He has tried to issue orders to me. Naturally I have declined to oblige him.'

'I should hope so,' said Nelson emphatically, 'and so shall I in the matter of a salute. Tell me, do you perceive his presence as an asset?'

'No, sir. His ships are poorly manned, with under nourished and ill trained crews. Heaven knows, a Portuguese sailor is as good as any, but their officers are more interested in their rank than their duties. We cannot assault the main island from the sea without heavy losses, as we have already concluded. If I am not prepared to risk my ships, then there is even less point in risking those of an ill-equipped ally.'

The Marquis de Niza turned out to be a pompous oaf – who, as Nelson informed St Vincent by letter later that day, 'is a complete nincompoop in matters pertaining to the sea'. He had to resist the desire to chuck him overboard, either just to the left or right of his barge. It was Nelson's task, as commander in the Mediterranean, to hold together a coalition that included allies who were often more of a burden than an asset. De Niza had ships, which Nelson was short of, so the idiot must be humoured before being sent to Naples.

Nelson's Neapolitan allies were no more helpful. The supplies and troops demanded by de Gallo were nowhere to be seen; no guns, no food, no ammunition and not a single soldier. Nelson was obliged to supply the Maltese insurgents from his own stores. He also called on the French commandant at Valetta to surrender or face destruction, but the man knew he was bluffing and answered accordingly.

Useless here, Nelson resolved to return to Naples, but first he used the force at his disposal to frighten into surrender the French garrison on the second Maltese island of Gozo. The defenders, without the fortress protection of their compatriots on the mainland, sailed for France with their arms and flags, leaving Ball a safe anchorage from the coming winter storms and good supplies of wood, water and food on the fertile island, while denying those commodities to the enemy on Malta. It ensured that if all else failed, and no reinforcements got through with supplies, the fortresses could be starved out.

Correspondence between Nelson and Naples was constant, as was the reverse, and Sir William and Emma knew of every step taken at Malta – while Nelson was well aware of what little progress had been made in Naples. Baron Mack talked more than he acted and planned more than he executed.

Emma threw herself into the task of keeping up Maria Carolina's morale. This proved increasingly difficult as it became more and more obvious just how many Neapolitan nobles were in touch with the French. Some were genuine republicans, but others hoped to save their wealth and possessions by appearing to support the Revolution.

What was evident was that the Queen had little support in Naples among the nobility or the peasantry. Through various ministers, she had used spies and informers to root out the more vocal of their enemies. Torture, confessions, several executions or banishment followed. Called a 'White Terror' by Jacobins it was a pale copy of the same regimen that had racked France, but whatever odium resulted fell squarely on the shoulders of the Austrian-born Queen. Ferdinand, as usual, was held to have been manipulated rather than responsible.

Even the peasants who loved him had no time for Maria Carolina. The sobriquet *lazzaroni*, originally applied to the numerous beggars of the city, was a corruption of the name Lazarus. Feckless they might be, but the beggars and paupers were also organised, with strict bounds to territory and a court of their own which handed down harsh punishments for transgression. Since Ferdinand loved them and protected them it was little wonder that they reciprocated. Neither was it a wonder than when some statute was issued limiting their activities he was never held to be at fault.

Blame centred on the Queen. Good King Ferdinand they would save from his own nobles, his wife they would happily burn at the stake.

The task of reassuring the Queen was made easier by Nelson's return and the fact that Baron Mack finally declared himself ready for battle. He invited Nelson and the Hamitons to inspect his forces before their move to the north. Nelson stood on a podium with Mack as the contingents marched by, drums beating, trumpets blaring and flags waving. Bursting with martial pride Mack declared them 'la plus belle armeé de l'Europe'.

'And splendid they look,' Nelson replied in halting French, while thinking in plain English, 'all that glisters is not gold'.

His own task was to transport a force of soldiers and artillery to Leghorn, land them behind the French and secure that port. Thankfully *Culloden* was now ready for sea and her captain Thomas Troubridge bursting for action. However Mack and Nelson, alert to the likelihood of treachery, did not even tell the Neapolitan in command of that army their destination. General Naselli was told he was bound for Malta. His demeanour made it plain that the only place he wanted to be was back in front of his own hearth. He was scared stiff and the appalling weather as they sailed north rendered him less than useless, since he was convinced they were about to drown.

He was no better when they arrived. After accepting the surrender of the city, he was more interested in appeasing the local Jacobins than corralling them, and horrified by the suggestion that he might undertake offensive operations. The same applied to the numerous French privateers that filled the harbour: Naselli wished to let them depart, ships and all. Nelson knew he could leave Troubridge to see to that dilemma, so he parted with *Culloden* and sailed south, happy to hear by despatch that the corsairs had left without their ships.

The return from Leghorn was made on the same storm-tossed sea under a low grey sky as the outward journey, yet Nelson ran into a messenger sent by Emma Hamilton, bearing despatches from England. One informed him of his elevation to a barony, an occasion for toasts in his cabin. In her private correspondence Emma wrote that she feared for his well-being at sea: she was worried about the stormy conditions. Unaware that he was on the way back she also begged him not to go ashore at Leghorn, which was home to many a republican sympathiser who might take his life on the blade of a stiletto. The better news was that no one in Naples knew where he had been or when he would return.

Another *felucca* found them off Stromboli, bearing tidings that had Nelson ordering Allen to break open the wine for a second time. 'Gentlemen, I have received news that King Ferdinand is in Rome.'

It was dour Thomas Hardy who asked, 'But is it true, sir?'

That earned him a wry smile. 'Lady Hamilton writes to tell me it is, that the French have abandoned the city and retreated north.'

On this occasion Nelson could not fault Hardy for being wary. He viewed Neapolitans as grubby, thieving rascals, and the notion that they could beat the French was one of the few things that made the Ghost laugh.

The waters of the bay reflected the grey colour of the sky, even Vesuvius losing its double-domed majesty as its plume of gaseous smoke merged with low clouds, and the mood of the locals was no more cheerful. When Nelson landed he was greeted with none of the usual huzzahs, and the glances he was thrown ranged from anxious to hostile. It wasn't long before he found out why. The 'most beautiful army in Europe', sent to eject the French from Italy, had disgraced itself: Neapolitan troops had plundered their own baggage train long before they made contact with the enemy so that their fellows went without rations. The King and his entourage suffered too, spending two whole days without food, their baggage scattered throughout the army. The guns were in the wrong place, the cavalry nowhere to be found and information had come in that a French force of thirteen thousand men was holding a strong position at a place north of Rome called Castellana.

That meant their main force had abandoned the Papal capital as indefensible. The latest information put Ferdinand in Rome, where he was accepting the fealty of the Roman nobility and dreaming of an expanded kingdom. But he was far from master of the city, since the French had left a contingent of some five hundred men to hold the Castel St Angelo, a vital hilltop fortress overlooking the Tiber. Everything depended on Baron Mack beating the French force to the north.

'Your opinion, Admiral?' asked Sir William, looking tired and older than his years.

Like all civilians behind the lines, he had heard rumours of the most depressing kind – that Baron Mack had been captured; that the army of Naples was in full retreat; that half of the Neapolitan commanders had deserted to a republican enemy with whom they were in sympathy. More worrying was information that was not in doubt: the Austrians had declined to move to support Naples. Mack must defeat the French on his own.

'Mack has superior numbers, Sir William, but not the quality of troops, so the issue must be in doubt.'

'And if he loses?'

'The road to Naples is open. The French have nothing to fear from their rear, and the Baron does not command a force that will stop running once it is in motion. Their officers are fond of display and boasting but they don't like fighting – and I said that before they marched north.'

The next few days were anxious indeed. Nelson saw Emma often but fleetingly, as she hurried between the Palazzo Sessa and the Queen's apartments in the Palazzo Reale. The weather, overcast and dull, seemed to match the mood of the city. Everyone went about armed, fearful of a secret knife, and that applied to those who supported the Bourbons as well as those who opposed them. Sedition was now discussed openly.

Nelson could do nothing but write fulsome reports to his commander-in-chief. He received word from Troubridge at Leghorn, corresponded with Ball off Malta, smoothed the feathers of the Marquis de Niza and made sure his ships were ready for an evacuation. At the same time he was brusque with the admiral of a Russian squadron that had arrived, ostensibly to assist, but seemed too interested in Malta for his liking.

The news from the north was constantly depressing, the only hope that French sympathisers were spreading false tales. Baron Mack had asked permission to sabre half the army for cowardice; the King had fled south ahead of a retreating army; half of what remained of that army had gone over to an enemy who were on the march, coming south to take and sack a now undefended Naples.

And all the while three people bobbed around each other, Sir William observant but determined to be detached; Emma concentrating on boosting the Queen and keeping her promise to herself about Nelson; and Nelson, who felt increasingly secure that his one transgression weeks before would be the last. Sometimes it was agony to be in the same room as her, but he took comfort from the pain. He longed to ask Emma how she felt but could not, knowing that to do so would open the floodgates of his emotions.

'The rumours are true, Nelson,' said Sir William. In his dressing gown and slippers, without the wig that usually hid his wispy grey hair, he looked worn and tired, while his voice reflected the despair he felt. 'King Ferdinand returned to the Palazzo Reale in the garb of a common soldier. The *lazzaroni* heard he was back and demanded he appear. The man has no shame. He came out on to the balcony, and when he did so his peasants cheered him.'

'God knows, he had little honour when he marched, but he has forfeited that now.'

'The concept of honour is alien to Ferdinand,' Sir William replied sadly.

Sir William had always rather liked the King for his simple ways, and for being a committed fellow hunter. They had shared many a chase together and many a drunken meal after the sun had gone down. Now, though, he was forced to see him in a new light; not as the fun-loving sovereign at one with his land and his people, but as a coward who, to get here so far ahead of his own men, must have fled at the first whiff of enemy grapeshot.

'The army?' Nelson asked.

'In full retreat. The French beat them at Castellana.'

'Tom,' Nelson said softly to his servant, who was hovering in the shadows, 'raise me Mr Tyson, would you, please?'

'Beat them, did I say?' Sir William continued. 'I rather think they beat themselves. They ran away and their officers were ahead of them. How can a man stomach such disgrace?'

Looking at him, Nelson felt a wave of pity – here was a man seeing his life's work disappear before him – but he had much to do, and his head was filled with the orders he must give to get all his ships ready for sea.

Tyson came in, looking as dishevelled as the Ambassador. 'You must, I hazard, have matters to attend to Sir William,' Nelson said.

The washed-out eyes regarded him vaguely for a moment, then Sir William answered, 'Yes.'

'I will require an audience at the palace as soon as possible. Perhaps it would be wise to tell their Majesties beforehand that I have three transports available for them and their retinue. Naturally, should it become necessary to abandon Naples, I will take them and the royal family into my own ship.'

'Such a thing must be carefully planned. The flight to Varennes looms large in the royal imagination.'

Varennes, half way between Paris and the Rhine, was where Louis of France and Marie Antoinette had been apprehended trying to flee with their family to the frontier.

'This is not France,' said Nelson, forcibly, 'and we have the sea and

British sailors behind us. But you are right, Sir William. There are so many traitors in this place that an attempt will certainly be made to stop them leaving.'

'Perhaps at your audience . . .'

'No!'

Brusquely interrupted, Sir William was seeing Nelson as he had so often heard him praised: commanding, decisive, the master of his own surroundings. Perhaps this was the man his wife saw?

'No,' Nelson repeated. 'We must plan it, and they must do what we say. Whatever we decide must be arranged here and not a word of it breathed in the Palazzo Reale.'

'You can do nothing without the consent and co-operation of the Queen, and in that, Admiral, you would do well to take advice from my wife.'

'Sir William, I fully intend to include Lady Hamilton in whatever plan we devise.'

The two men exchanged a look, one which underlined the subtext of what had been said, but it was equally plain, from the sudden breaking of eye contact, that neither party wanted to pursue it.

8

~

Nelson admired Emma for her beauty, and over the next week, as they planned the evacuation, he had more reason to appreciate her application and courage. Only she had the total trust of the Queen – Ferdinand, having seen his martial hopes dashed, had taken refuge behind his stupidity and was now no more than a cipher, doing as he was told, only throwing occasional tantrums to establish that he still had some rights as the king.

Sir William was anxious about his possessions. He had no intention of leaving a lifetime collection to be plundered by looters, who would surely raid the empty palazzos as soon as order broke down. There was a great deal of virtu, even though most of his collection had gone already in HMS *Colossus*, a 74-gun ship so in need of repair that Nelson had ordered it home. Left were the things he valued most, a personal possessions with a sentimental or an aesthetic value. It mattered little – when it came to planning a daring escape the skills he had honed as a diplomat were of scant use.

With no force of soldiers to hand, protection must be provided for the King and Queen, their children and the king's ministers – the royal regiments had gone north with Mack and were still fighting. It was suspected the gunners who manned the forts were republicans, while the crews of Caracciolo's flagship and the frigate *Archimedes* were discontented and unreliable. British marines from Nelson's ships would create suspicion – and cause no end of complications when it came to getting them back aboard.

Ferdinand's peasant supporters provided the solution. The leader of the *lazzaroni*, a barrel-chested, moustachioed peasant called Edigio Bagio had acted on his own initiative, sending men to the north of the city to disarm the deserters from Mack's army who were fleeing south. He was busy forming bands to protect his beloved king, with guards outside the Palazzo Reale and armed bands close to the royal person. Ragged they might be, but it worked; if there was one thing a traitorous Neapolitan nobleman feared more than the monarchical state, it was the cut-throats of the streets.

Numbers were another problem, for it was obvious that even with the ships at Nelson's disposal more people would want to embark than he could readily accommodate. Nelson had sent messages off to Troubridge at Leghorn to come back with all haste. He had also requested from Alexander Ball, who was lying off Malta, that he send one of his 74's to Naples. But on no account was he to allow any Neapolitan ships to leave the blockade. Even if the ships requested did come in time, Nelson feared overcrowding.

Priority must go to the royals, their retainers and ministers, in short the government. But Nelson had to get his fellow-countrymen away as well and there were too many for the available transports. His solution was to allot them the Portuguese ships commanded by that nincompoop the Marquis de Niza. To disguise the fact that he would be taking the Bourbons aboard *Vanguard* he told him he intended to remain in the bay and bombard the city as the French tried to take it, which he could not do with a ship full of passengers.

Emma undertook to get a list of attendants and supporters from the Queen, but equally pressing were the royal possessions; clothes, state papers, money and jewels that would go with them. No one could say how long their exile would last, just as no one could say for certain where they would finally find refuge. Sicily would be their first destination, since the occupants of that island hated anything to do with Naples, and could confidently be expected to do the precise opposite of their mainland cousins and support a King and Queen that the capital city had repudiated.

But would the French leave them there in peace? They might invade Sicily, leading to a further evacuation and an exile at a foreign court. Thus everything must be taken to form a government in exile and that could not be left till the last moment; getting such a quantity of possessions aboard on the night of the evacuation would take too long. Emma again showed her worth. She had all their chattels brought secretly and in small quantities to the Palazzo Sessa. Sir William's virtu, when packed, was loaded into *Vanguard*. No one observing packing cases leaving the ambassadorial residence knew that a good number of them belonged to the royal family.

There was much more: when to evacuate – something that could not be decided until the French threat had been properly evaluated: Mack was still fighting a rearguard action. How to get them from the Palazzo Reale to a safe part of the shore – that solved by the information that there was a secret passage for that very purpose. Every move Nelson made was the subject of intense interest, and that applied equally to his ships. When he transferred them to an anchorage less exposed to gunfire from the forts it caused near panic, the assumption being that he was about to weigh anchor and leave Naples and everyone in it to stew.

And on one day, Emma and Nelson, wrapped in cloaks to keep out the winter chill, walked the shore, he to pick the spot of embarkation, the protection it would need and the number of boats; and she must work out the time required to get the royal party to the chosen spot. And if by walking arm in arm without attendants they gave rise to gossip, so be it. That was enough to keep idle tongues wagging, in the hope that their equally idle minds would not suspect what was being planned.

Proximity to each other was a dangerous thing. Yet they had the excuse of conspiracy to mask what was actually the desire to be together, to talk in an intimate way, without any chance of showing a physical expression of their feelings. The fact that Sir William, preoccupied with his own cares about the forthcoming evacuation, seemed to give them a nod of approval imbued what they were about with false innocence.

Nelson knew very little about Emma Hamilton that was neither impersonal, the stuff of correspondence, or rumour. And she made it hard to extract information about her past, regularly turning the conversation so that Nelson was obliged to describe some exploit or embarrassment of his own.

Thus she learned of his family and his birthplace: of the domestic despotism enforced by his widower father, of a cheerless house in which there never seemed to be enough food for a growing boy or his half dozen siblings. They had eaten under the eye of a parent determined that they should sit upright, while he told them repeatedly of their noble antecedents.

Edmund Nelson was not a bad man, just a dour one who lacked faith in his own abilities both as an ecclesiastic and as a father. That he had loved his deceased wife could never be in doubt. He had inscribed on her grave, set into the floor before the altar of his church, 'Let these alone, let no man touch these bones'.

'You were always destined for the navy?' Emma asked.

'I have no idea,' Nelson replied, making a mental note of the suitability of the southern mole as an evacuation point, being as it was, protected from fortress gunfire and close enough to the arsenal to make any gunner cautious.

He had been a rebellious child, a scrapper who started many a brotherly fight and a sore trial to his father. He had been a prude to the elder brother, William, with whom he went to school. Not that William had used the word prude. 'Pious little turd' had been his expression. Did William now, as an ordained minister of the church himself, remember that and blush?

'I think it was decided upon when my Uncle William came to visit.'

'He was a hero too.'

Nelson tried a shrug of modesty, but it felt uncomfortable. He was aware that he liked to be called a hero, just as he was aware that the sin of hubris was one he must avoid. There was the other pleasure too, in hearing this woman refer to him thus, that brought an even warmer glow to his being.

'I sailed past the site of his battle at Cap Francis Viego, in the Caribbean.' Nelson smiled. 'There was nothing to see, of course. That is why we sailors talk of sea battles so much. There are no fortresses to see, no hills or valleys, forests or rivers to point to bold attack or stout defence. The sea closes over our exploits, so they must be retold time and again so that all remember.'

'You loved your uncle?'

There was a slight hesitation, because Nelson was forced to admit to himself that he hardly knew William Suckling. A lifelong bachelor, his uncle had been a rare visitor to Norfolk, a larger than life presence when he was there, a distant memory soon after he left. But he was a somebody, a man who had friends and influence enough to keep command of a King's ship in peacetime when many another officer languished on the beach.

'He was an easy man to admire.'

'Then it must be in the blood,' said Emma. 'And what would he think of you now, your Captain Suckling, to see his nephew termed Baron Nelson of the Nile and Burnham Thorpe?'

Emma said that with pride, but her reaction to the news of his elevation had been less than effervescent. In fact she had been incensed. She had railed against her own government, reeling off the titles she would have granted him; Duke Nelson, Marquess Nile, Earl Aboukir, Viscount Pyramid, Baron Crocodile, and for good measure Prince Victory. And she had damned the official reason for such parsimony, that Nelson was not actually a commander-in-chief but a subordinate officer, as sheer jealousy.

'Where does that secret passage begin?'

The Palazzo Reale occupied a frontage of over half a mile on the Naples shore. No point in picking a potential embarkation point that was too far from the point at which the royal party would emerge. There were numerous postern gates leading to the working parts of the palace; kitchens, storerooms, butteries, bakeries and wineries, but only one led to the private royal apartments.

'It is so secret, that I have not been told,' Emma replied.

'Not been told?' Nelson demanded, only to look into her face and observed he was being joshed.

Emma laughed. 'I think we have passed it, though I felt it prudent not to point it out.'

'Very wise,' said Nelson, taking the paper, glancing at it, then spinning round. Those who were following the couple, a dozen middling Neapolitans of an idle disposition, stopped. He surmised one or two would be spies eager to know what he was about. Emma had been quite right to remain discreet under such observation. Nelson pulled out his watch, and said, 'Let us retrace our steps to this gate, and count the minutes.'

This is how Nelson must feel as he goes into battle, thought Emma, as she watched him receive from the Turkish envoy the Order of the Crescent and the Plume of Triumph aigrette that had been brought to him from Constantinople. Her heart was beating faster than it should, but her head was clear and she felt that her eyesight was more acute than she had ever known it to be. Standing to one side she saw the diamond and silver plume twinkling in the light that filled the salon in which the reception was being held.

Nelson lifted it from the case in which it lay, to hold it up so that those gathered could admire it. Kemal Effendi, the sultan's envoy, had no idea that this presentation had been chosen as the cover for the evacuation of the royal family of Naples. Neither did the cream of Neapolitan society, gathered to watch the Victor of Nile honoured. It had been Nelson's inspired choice to use this glittering occasion to cover the planned escape, aware that a number of the men prepared to betray Ferdinand would be bound to attend the function.

The French were moving south slowly, subduing the Campanian countryside as they went, and were not expected to try to invade Naples for at least a week. Everyone knew the crisis was approaching

– some in this very room would be planning what bloody fate to visit upon Ferdinand and Maria Carolina. They would be looking at Sir John Acton and the Marquis de Gallo, and savouring the thought of seeing, in only a few short days, their heads on the block of the guillotine.

Perhaps too they would be relishing the sight of this British admiral taking his leave. Certainly they would applaud politely at the presentation of the aigrette: Nelson was undoubtedly a hero, but he was an enemy to the formation of a republic in Naples, so the sight of him sailing out of the bay was another event to look forward to. There was no doubt he was going and the distrust he felt for the Neapolitans was obvious, he having moved his ships from under the guns of the forts to an obscure part of the harbour.

The Hamiltons would go with him of course, and that to many was a pity. Sir William was well liked, had been here a long time and had many friends, even amongst the seditious. And his lovely wife? In many a male breast there was regret that such a bastion as her virtue had proved unconquerable. And her gaiety would be missed as much as her husband's urbanity. But perhaps there was time for one last visit to the Ambassador's residence, once last chance to enjoy his famous hospitality.

Had anyone bothered to enquire, they would have been told that there was indeed time to visit. The Hamilton carriage was waiting to take them back to the Palazzo Sessa, where, at this very moment the table was being laid for dinner.

Captain Josiah Nesbit had arrived at the reception just after the Hamiltons. In what had become his habitual stiff manner he stood to one side in the dress uniform of a post captain. When the ceremonies were over he would escort Kemal Effendi and his entourage to the ship which his stepfather had prised out of Earl St Vincent. HMS *Thalia*, a 28-gun frigate, was tasked to take the Turkish envoy home. There the stepson could present to the Sultan the personal thanks of Lord Nelson for these gifts. That it would also remove his morose gaze from the actions of his stepfather was a bonus.

At that very moment small parties of British seamen were fanning out through the city, quietly rousing out their fellow countrymen, telling them to make their way to the northern mole, where the boats of the Portuguese Squadron were waiting to embark them and their possessions.

Emma found it hard to be patient while speeches were made, thanks professed, drink consumed in between toasts to every enemy France had, but mostly to Nelson, King George's Navy, and insincere thanks for the protective shield at sea of Britannia. Her calculation was that from the time of leaving this reception, she had at most fifteen minutes to take up her station. In her imagination she could see the boats being lowered from HMS *Vanguard*, each with its component of armed sailors. Nelson's marines would already have secured the mole at the southern end of the harbour, the point of embarkation. She must make her way to the secret passage that ran from the Palazzo Reale to the shore. Admitted to the royal apartments Emma was the one who would have to tell her charges that it was time for them to leave.

As Nelson, Sir William and Emma emerged, the empty carriage left, to return to the Palazzo Sessa and take on board Emma's mother, the servants of the family and the final load of possessions. The trio, escorted by a party of armed *lazzaroni* provided by Edigio Bagio, hurried down the steep hills towards the harbour, parting with a whispered farewell as Sir William and Nelson continued towards the mole and the waiting marines.

Emma, with her part of the escort made her way to the secret gate. She was aware that the wind was strong, and that the sky above her head, seen between the high buildings, was full of scudding clouds flitting across the moon. It seemed appropriate, as if the gods had arranged for a stormy backdrop to a dramatic episode. One of the Queen's German servants was waiting at the gate, opening it to her as she gave the password in his native tongue. Soon she was following a lantern along whitewashed and musty damp passages, climbing worn stairs to face the door she knew led to the private royal apartments.

Nelson, not for the first time in his life, was cursing the conditions. On a night when he needed calm water the Bay of Naples was choppy, and if his instincts were anything to go by it was going to get worse. The scudding clouds presaged foul weather coming in from the open sea, which would make the task of getting the evacuees aboard that much harder. He could hear the hiss of the waves on the shoreline and smell the tangy odour of sea-spray. Ahead, at the point where the mole joined the shore, the phosphorescence from breaking waves showed a line of shadowy figures, one of whom, by his height and the way his pale skin reflected the moon, looked very familiar.

'Is that you Mr Pasco?'

'Sir,' the midshipman replied, rushing forward.

'Take Sir William to my barge,' said Nelson, gently urging the

Ambassador forward, 'then find me Mr Giddings. He has my sword and pistols.'

'I'm here your honour,' Giddings called, moving forward and unshading a lantern. As usual, he ignored the injunction that no sailor should speak to an officer unless asked to do so. He always had, since the day he had discovered over twenty years earlier that here was one officer who didn't mind.

'This be a rum do an' no error, your honour.'

'What is, Giddings?'

'This 'ere rescuing lark,' his coxswain replied, speaking as usual out of the corner of his mouth. By that one physical trait Giddings had the ability to make everything he said appear to be a closely guarded secret. The irony was that this time it was just that.

'Comes to a sorry pass when Kings and the like can't trust their own. Worse'n than the bloody frogs, I say.'

Nelson was tempted to ask how he knew, since it had been a well kept secret just what the crew of HMS *Vanguard* were being employed to do. But he decided not to bother; he had learned from experience that the crew of a man o' war always seemed to know what was going on. He took the proffered weapons then, accosting one of Hardy's lieutenants, requested confirmation from him that all was in place. The man could only reply regarding what he knew: that the mole was secure, the boats manned and ready and since there had been no sound of gunfire, the armed parties that had fanned out through the city were going about their business quietly.

'Then,' he said, hauling his boat cloak around him to ward off the night chill, 'we wait.'

Emma emerged into a brightly-lit chamber to find the entire royal party assembled and dressed for the outdoors. Having curtsied to the indifference of the King, who was determined not to look her in the eye, she did the same to Maria Carolina, seated on a chair, who beckoned her forward. She smiled at the silent children, and mentally ticked off that the numbers in the room, including retainers, tallied with what had been agreed.

'Emma,' Maria Carolina said, and proffered her hand, which Emma took as she executed a low curtsy. A folded piece of parchment was pressed into her hand, that followed a whisper low enough to evade the hearing of the Ferdinand. 'We have had this note from Commodore Caracciolo.'

Emma hesitated to unfold it. Time was short and the danger that their proposed flight would be discovered very real. But at an insistent nod from the Queen she moved over to an oil lamp and began to read, slowly, since her ability to read Italian was not as good as her speech. Not that the message was difficult. In it Commodore Caracciolo, as commander of the Neapolitan navy, stated that the situation was grave; that the royal family could not be sure of being safe in the city, and that he felt their security could be better guaranteed if they were to take refuge aboard his ship.

Her thoughts would be the same as those of Maria Carolina. Was this a genuine offer or did he know of the plan to go aboard Nelson's flagship? If so, was there a trap waiting to be sprung if the King and Queen failed to respond to his invitation? The *lazzaroni* were not the only armed men in Naples. Every disloyal nobleman had retainers to use against them and Caracciolo had half the officer-class of the navy at his disposal, all aristocrats, but how many loyal to the crown? Fortunately, he had few men – the sailors, fearing for their homes and loved ones, had deserted their ships and come ashore to swell the ranks of fearful mobs that had begun to rule the streets.

Emma suddenly felt very isolated. There was no one to ask, no one to consult, and she could feel, by the silent atmosphere in the room, that this letter has been the cause of some friction.

'Your Majesty,' she said, addressing the broad back of the King, sensing that to appeal to his more sensible wife would not aid matters. 'Do you have complete faith in Commodore Caracciolo?'

'I have never had any reason to suspect him of being disloyal,' Ferdinand boomed.

Emma wondered if he suspected a single member of his court. If anyone was capable of occupying cloud cuckoo land it was Ferdinand. Emma saw the Queen's head drop, and knew that she had her support, but she also knew that such support would count for nothing if she could not persuade the King. This was typical Ferdinand; to let matters reach such a stage then to throw in some objection. But he held the ultimate power: everyone else in the room, Francis, the Hereditary Prince, his pregnant wife, the Princes Leopold and Alberto and the three royal princesses, did not matter.

'I agree with you.' Emma said, emphatically. That made Ferdinand turn round, and he aimed a glare at his wife, now reduced to looking at her own twisting and anxious hands. 'His ship will, of course be in the company of the rest of the other ships of the Neapolitan fleet at present in Naples?'

Ferdinand frowned as though the question was a difficult one.

'Which means that he will also be in the company of all the officers of that fleet.' Maria Carolina looked up, her eyes showing that she knew the route Emma was about to take. The fact that Ferdinand turned away again demonstrated that he was not completely stupid either. 'If you can assure Admiral Lord Nelson that you have complete faith in all your naval officers then I feel he would be forced to recommend that you accept Commodore Caracciolo's offer. If not?'

The question was left hanging, but truly it was one that answered itself. Ferdinand was no more certain of the loyalty of Caracciolo than he was of anybody else. Even he must know that the most profound protestations of fealty were often the ones that masked the deepest treachery: the notion that there were no Republican sympathisers amongst his naval officers was patently absurd. Royalty reasserted itself as Ferdinand, with that inability to admit an error, which was a hallmark of his character, said. 'Naturally, that is the conclusion I myself have reached.'

There was a moment then when no one moved, the enormity of what they were about to do taking hold, at least in the adult minds. Once out of the palace, the royal family was beyond the pale. They were deserting the city and their state, so that even men who had been supporters would curse them for abandonment, the indifferent would hate them, and their enemies would bay for their blood, claiming that only the spilling of that could cleanse their new dominion.

It was the Queen who moved first, she was a woman who expected no clemency anyway. Maria Carolina stood by the door to the secret passage and willed her husband to enter first. Looking at him, the slow way he turned, the look in his eye and the deliberate way he responded, Emma sensed that this was what he wanted. To be able to say at any future date, should his motives be called into question, that he had been reluctant to depart but that his Queen, lacking the same love of patrimony that filled his breast, had forced him.

Maria Carolina held her tears well, not so Francis, the Hereditary Prince, though he was outdone by the wailing of his pregnant wife, which was soon added to by the cries of her first born, still a baby in swaddling cloths. Young Prince Alberto, six years old and Emma's favourite was not crying, but he was pale and shaking as though in the grip of a fever, so much so that Emma requested that one of the servants carry him. She brought up the rear, the last person to leave that well-appointed apartment, the private drawing room of the royal couple, the palace of three hundred rooms were she had spent so many happy times. If she felt saddened, Emma could understand the depth of feeling that must affect her charges. The closing of the door was like a clanking death knell for a whole way of life.

9

Ferdinand, who knew the exit well, had stopped before the last turning in the passageway, forcing Emma to pass and be the first to risk herself at the postern gate. As she went, she had to impose silence on the party, no easy matter with a princess in the throes of panic, and a baby given to wailing.

The King's self-elected *lazzaroni* guards, who had escorted Emma to this place, still manned the gate, a quartet of swarthy, ragged individuals bearing muskets as tall as themselves. When Ferdinand emerged they knelt to kiss his hand, and were patted on the head like pet dogs. It was noticeable as the party moved off that they did not follow. They had an open gate to the palace: loyal to their king they might be, but with him gone his chattels were there for the looting.

Emma's nerves were jumping as they made their way along the shoreline. It had been her idea that Nelson's men should not venture from the mole: then if the royal party was accosted they could say that they were shifting to a Neapolitan ship, not fleeing into British custody. Now she wished that she had around her a party of Nelson's tars, whom she knew she could trust. .

They were on the mole at the point where it met the shore, with Nelson ordering all lamps shaded and his men to make themselves as obscure as possible, most staying in the boats, the rest pressing themselves against any dark object to hide their profile. As always, Giddings, his coxswain, was right behind the Admiral.

'Bit like press-ganging, your honour,' Giddings whispered.

Indeed it was, Nelson thought: the dark, wild night, men hiding in wait for an unsuspecting individual to meander into the maw of the naval net. He had always hated that duty, and counted himself lucky that he had only rarely undertaken it. Ships were manned easily in peacetime, and when war threatened his name and reputation provided him with a crew.

'Trade,' Giddings added, employing the phrase he had used as a press-ganger.

'*Aeneid*,' said Nelson, stepping forward to give the agreed pass-word, appropriate, since it was the title of Homer's tale, which was partly about the flight of royal survivors from the sack of Troy. He unshaded a lantern as he said it and immediately saw Emma's pale but beautiful face. As their eyes met Nelson reckoned that, for a moment, they both forgot their purpose, but it was fleeting for Emma stepped aside to let the royal party through.

'Your Majesty,' Nelson said, raising his hat to Ferdinand with Emma translating. 'I have arranged for the ladies to be placed in the cutter, which is the steadiest boat we have. May I suggest that they go aboard first?'

Even by faint lantern light Nelson could see that Ferdinand had to weigh this against his royal prerogative. He looked as if he was about to demur, when Nelson added, 'I know you to be a fine sailor, sir, and the waters of the bay, which will indispose the ladies in their present disturbed state, will not affect you.'

That mixture of truth and flattery made the King step to one side and Nelson said to Emma, 'Lady Hamilton, pray go with the Queen, the smaller children and her ladies. My own quarters have been set aside for their accommodation.'

It was dark enough to take her hand and squeeze it, but in the lantern light he gazed in to her deep green eyes, framed by the fur-trimmed cowl of her cloak. In that instant both Emma and Nelson felt everything else fade to insignificance: the presence of their charges, the hissing of the wind as it bent the branches of nearby trees, the crash of a wave against the brickwork of the mole.

'The men are waiting to assist, sir,' said Midshipman Pasco, breaking the spell.

Nelson watched as Emma got aboard nimbly and took up station in the prow. What followed was a pantomime of cries, squeals, protests and entreaties as the rest of the ladies embarked. There was no steady gangplank as there would have been for the royal barge – the boat was bobbing unevenly through several feet of air, with just a sailor's hand to steady them.

Eventually the Vanguards got them aboard, with several marines to provide protection, and shoved off into waters that were much more agitated than those around the mole. That brought forth renewed wailing which turned to near panic as a flash of lightning illuminated the western sky, followed by a deep roll of thunder.

Getting the royal servants into the boats was just as bad – they screeched like banshees, almost outdoing the ladies – but Ferdinand, to his credit, boarded Nelson's barge easily, while Prince Leopold, like the sailor he had always wanted to be, assisted others to take their place. Then he leaped back on to the mole and bent to kiss the soil of his homeland, before boarding again to watch the receding shore as the crew bent to their oars.

The waters were vicious: a cross sea that added to the local currents set up waves that headed the barge, and others that slammed into the quarter to create a corkscrew effect. All the while, to the west, Nelson could see the approach of a storm. *Vanguard* showed just how bad the sea-state was, rolling and pitching at single anchor. If such a swell was prevalent in this relatively sheltered part of the anchorage, Nelson knew that out of the lee of the land it would be much worse. His plan had been to weigh for Palermo as soon as the passengers were aboard and accommodated, but that would have to change. There would be few good sailors amongst the royal party, and seasickness was inevitable.

Could he stay in the bay and ride out the worst of the weather? The royals' escape would not remain secret after daylight, neither would it take much to deduce where they were. How disloyal were the officers of the Neapolitan fleet? Would they, knowing that their king and queen were aboard the British flagship, attempt to force a change of circumstance?

The scene at the entry port of *Vanguard* was one of utter confusion. Those Britons in Naples who had been alerted by Nelson's shore parties had hired boats and, even if instructed to head for Portuguese ships, were determined to clamber aboard his. In the cries, shouted curses and commands that followed, he could hear the voices of many nationalities, including a whole host of French. There were hundreds of *émigrés* in Naples, who had fled the Terror in France. They needed to get away too, sure that any revolutionary army would guillotine them without hesitation.

In the chaos it took an hour longer than Nelson had anticipated to get the King aboard. By then he and every other passenger in the barge was soaked to the skin and chilled to the marrow. Yet still Ferdinand took the salute as he came aboard. Dripping seawater by the bucket-load and shivering, he was still an anointed sovereign.

If it had been chaos in the boats it was even worse on board: there were too many people and not enough room to accommodate them. The wardroom had been allotted to the King, his ministers and the British Ambassador. With *Vanguard* riding at single anchor in a heavy swell it was hard for someone without good sea legs to make any progress from one part of the ship to the other. Most of the passengers had succumbed quickly to seasickness, which rapidly turned the ship into a near cesspool. This mixed with rainwater and spray that forced its way through every gap in the straining planking.

The royal servants, with only one exception, were useless and the lot of tending to the stricken passengers fell to Emma and her mother, both of whom seemed impervious to the tossing of the ship. There were bruises and broken bones, and cries of fear mixed continually with the sound of retching.

Emma took charge of the Admiral's quarters and the ladies, while Mrs Cadogan saw to the men. In this she earned the admiration of Ferdinand, who as a good sailor did not suffer but whose dignity would not allow him to offer help to any of his less fortunate companions.

Nelson's great cabin was a mess, with anything not fixed to the deck sliding back and forth as the ship pitched and rolled. The smell was worse between decks, but not much worse. Emma was comforted by the steadiness of her own stomach and asked Tom Allen to provide warm water to bathe the shivering baby. Meanwhile she comforted the Queen and the Hereditary Princess, and cradled the suffering Prince Alberto, singing to him and telling him stories, while she reflected that those born to rule seemed to lack any resource when the careful pattern of their lives was disrupted.

Nelson appeared at the doorway, one hand on the lintel, swaying easily on well-attuned sea legs, water streaming off the oilskins he had donned on coming aboard. He had come to tell his royal passengers of his decision to wait for the weather to moderate before he set sail, but it was obvious, from their prostrate condition, that they couldn't have cared less.

Emma was thinking that with her clothes streaked with grime and other people's vomit, her cheeks unpowdered and red from seawater, she must look a frightful mess. However, to Nelson, she looked magnificent.

Dawn brought some respite, though as Nelson emerged from the chart room, where he had snatched a much needed nap, the horizon looked just as grey and unwelcoming as it had the day before. The weather had eased slightly, and the low cloud was lifting so that the shore had ceased to be an indistinct line, and had become again a series of identifiable locations. The harbour area was still full of boats, some surrounding the British transports and Portuguese warships as the fearful of Naples sought refuge. Most surrounded *Vanguard*, endless petitioners seeking an audience with their sovereign to persuade him to return to his palace, either to oversee the defence of Naples or to stop the disorder and looting that had already broken out.

This kept the King and his ministers busy, and Nelson, who had concerns of his own, grew impatient. Time and again he sent Tom Allen to the wardroom, with a request that the Marquis de Gallo, Sir John Acton and Sir William Hamilton join him in the fore section of Captain Hardy's cabin, but half the day had gone before that request was satisfied.

'Gentlemen,' Nelson said, 'I have requested you join me so that we can decide what to do about the Neapolitan ships remaining in the harbour.'

Acton, who saw himself, quite rightly, as the Admiral of the Neapolitan fleet, looked as though he understood what Nelson meant. Not so de Gallo, who, once it had been translated, looked perplexed. Sir William sensed what might be coming and prepared himself to deploy a degree of diplomatic emollience.

The capital ships of Naples were off Malta with Captain Ball, who had been requested to keep them there, but two heavy 40-gun frigates, commanded by Caracciolo, were anchored close inshore under the guns of the Neapolitan forts. 'They cannot be left to fall into the hands of the French,' Nelson said.

'Then they must be persuaded to sail with us,' said de Gallo.

'Without crews?' asked Nelson. Attempts to bribe the crewmen – who had gone ashore to protect their own homes – to return to their ships had failed, obliging Nelson to send over some of his own seamen to help man them. But Caracciolo showed no sign of wanting to weigh. 'I suggest that if we cannot get them away they must be burned.'

'Impossible,' erupted de Gallo. 'Huge sums of money have been poured into creating the fleet, and those are two of the newest vessels.'

'It will be nonsense, Marquis, if crewed by Frenchmen I have to engage them in battle.'

'Can you not crew them, Admiral?' asked Acton. As the man who had initiated the construction of these very ships he was clearly on the horns of a dilemma, with pragmatism fighting sentiment.

'No,' Nelson replied.

His tone was a trifle brusque for Sir William, who winced. But Nelson was not prepared to tell even these men how short handed *Vanguard* was. He had shifted men into Troubridge's ship off Leghorn, which meant the men he had sent to the Neapolitan ships, twenty-five in number, were all he could spare. Nor was he going to say openly that if his request that *Culloden* return to Naples was fulfilled in time this conversation would be redundant. With Troubridge here he would either take Caracciolo's ships or sink them.

'The King will never agree to this,' said de Gallo, 'and I doubt even the Queen could be brought to consider it.'

'Considered it must be,' Nelson replied, 'and I would ask that you put the matter before the King.'

It was a forlorn hope that Ferdinand would agree, and never had the Queen's indisposition been more unfortunate. Nelson reckoned, as he watched the three courtiers file out, that she would have put aside any considerations of money and ordered them to be taken or sunk – if for no other reason than to tell the traitors in Naples what they could expect of a future restoration of royal power.

He was still ruminating as the cabin door opened to admit Midshipman Pasco, as alert as ever although he had probably been up all night. 'Boat approaching, sir,' he said, 'and Captain Hardy reckons Baron Mack is in the thwarts.'

The man Nelson greeted at the entry port bore little resemblance to the glittering white-uniformed general that Nelson had last seen reviewing his beautiful army. That force was now shattered, and so was their leader. Mack's hair was awry, his uniform stained and tattered. He looked as broken as the force he had led to defeat.

Nelson felt sorry for him, although he suspected him to be an incompetent soldier who had led a very inept army. Reports of the deployments Mack had made, and the way he had used his inexperienced troops, had made many question his sanity. But now he was being asked to shoulder all the blame. It was telling that King Ferdinand, his titular commander-in-chief, who had shown no signs of seasickness hitherto, had declined to receive him, claiming illness as his excuse. The Queen, who would certainly have received him was genuinely sick, a fact endorsed by Emma Hamilton, who Nelson had been forced to send for.

'I must entertain him in some way,' Nelson said quietly, 'and try to restore his spirits. But I cannot commiserate without an interpreter.'

Emma used the back of one hand to sweep her wayward auburn hair from her eyes. 'Sir William?'

'Is with the King.'

Emma fell in with Nelson as he led Mack towards Hardy's cabin for a quiet conversation – there were officers sleeping in the ante-rooms on each side. Refreshments were served by Hardy's steward; wine for him and Emma, a stiff brandy for Mack. The Baron listed the events that had led to this moment, naming Neapolitan officers, nobles to a man, who when they were not behaving like cowards showed an alarming degree of military stupidity. As he detailed the orders he had issued he was unaware that the Admiral was mentally praising some of those subordinates for showing sound common sense.

But Nelson's mind was only half on Mack. It was delicious to watch Emma in profile as she listened to the poor man, who spoke slowly and deliberately, head bent over, with none of the ardour he had shown before the campaign. Then she would turn to translate, looking at him directly, and he could gaze in to her eyes.

Emma was mentally comparing the two men, knowing she would never see Horatio Nelson like this. If her hero suffered defeat, the only thing anyone would have to look at would be his corpse. As they exchanged glances that excluded Mack, Emma felt no danger, or any sense that she was risking her future. The words she trans-lated tripped off her tongue without effort as she held Nelson's good eye.

Nelson was aware that he had a stark choice – the kind of choice he had to make in battle. And he realised that he had known it since he first met Emma Hamilton. Looking at her now, not carefully combed and dressed, a real woman in a real situation, he knew that he must either live with her or entirely without her. There could be no middle way. He knew she was tired and so, too, was he, after a night of almost constant exertion, but that added clarity to his thoughts rather than diminishing them and he sensed that Emma was thinking the same way. He was tempted to say, 'I love you,' but did not, because he knew it to be superfluous.

As Emma told Nelson what Mack had said, that the last line of defence outside Naples was near to being breached, she could not help but try to impart in her words that she was not talking about the city but herself. She understood suddenly that the constraints she had placed on herself with regard to this man had everything to do with her previous settled existence, her life of entertainment, friends and routine. The truth that this life had been shattered forever was evident in the disconsolate pose of Baron Mack, who had come to ask the King's permission to surrender so that lives might be saved. Ferdinand being too much of a coward to oblige him, Mack looked like a man who had lost his faith as well as a campaign.

Emma felt as though she was gaining faith: faith in her own judgement, free from the attitudes of her mother and the pain she would cause her husband. There was only Nelson, and a further surge of electricity coursed through her as she saw in his look what was also in her mind.

'The crisis is clearly reaching a conclusion,' said Nelson, looking right at her.

'It has already done that,' Emma replied, as Mack drained his glass and pulled himself to his feet.

Mack spoke sharply then, with some of his old fire, as though the brandy as well as the needs of his command had restored him. Emma informed Nelson that Mack would return to the shore, and take upon himself the task of surrender. Ferdinand had deserted him and he had the right to do the same, but he would do his duty, and Nelson could only admire him for that. He called for the marine sentry to fetch an officer to escort Baron Mack to his boat.

'I should have gone myself,' whispered Nelson, as the door closed.

'He deserves the courtesy,' Emma replied.

They were standing a little apart, swaying easily on the swell of the sea, eyes locked, yet there was one final barrier they had still to cross. Nelson knew in his own heart that he had already made the leap. He had never been in love before – he knew that now. All his previous romantic attachments seemed foolish, especially his initial regard for his wife. He was incapable of imagining a future without Emma, and nothing – neither career, fame nor glory – would serve to fill the void of her absence.

Emma had been in love, and knew, too, the heartbreak of rejection. She wanted Nelson to make the commitment that her previous love, Charles Greville, had not. She wanted him to say the words that would break down that final barrier.

'Emma,' Nelson said, holding out his hand. His mouth was dry. 'I cannot live without you.'

'I must see to the Queen,' Emma replied.

Nelson smiled, for he had seen what was in Emma's eyes and felt her affirmative squeeze. 'Does that make you happy?'

'Yes.'

There was no need for more, even though his heart was pounding.

He kissed the back of her hand – not the kiss of a courtier, but that of a lover.

Emma had to compose herself as she made her way back down to Nelson's cabin and the Queen, passing officers and men, all of whom tipped a hat or touched their forehead in respect. These were Nelson's men, who were said to love him. So did she. Could they love her too? She felt calm, was not plagued by second thoughts. She was certain that what had just been pledged was right and that the consequences of that decision did not matter. She felt different, too, as she walked into the cabin, as though it was somehow her own.

The sharp tang of watered vinegar tingled in her nostrils. The cabin had been cleaned in her absence, with the furniture in its proper place. The first to greet her was young Prince Alberto, dressed in fresh, clean clothes and it gladdened her heart to see some colour in his cheeks. Alberto, coming aboard shivering in the grip of a fever, had been more violently sick than either his siblings or his mother. Yet now he looked as he always had, black eyes shining and ready for mischief as he rushed over to kiss Emma.

Tom Allen was there, too, standing over the large round table that Nelson used as a desk, a tub of beeswax and a cloth in his hand. 'Had a right good breakfast, His Highness did, milady, oats and goat's milk laced with a tadge of the Admiral's brandy.'

Emma realised that she was hungry, not having eaten since Kelim Effendi's reception.

'Been helping me put things to rights, has young Prince Alberto,' added Tom. 'He be a dab hand as a swabber, ain't you, young sir?'

Alberto had enough English to understand that and he looked proud that Tom rated his ability to ply a mop.

'Your mama?' Emma asked, nodding towards the sleeping cabin.

Alberto made a face and moaned, then asked eagerly, 'Will I be allowed to go on deck, Lady Emma?'

It was Tom Allen who replied. 'Why that comes later, Master Prince.' He pushed a cloth in Alberto's direction and aimed a finger at Nelson's mahogany, brass edged wine cooler. 'You ain't yet complete here.'

Emma exited the cabin to the sounds of Tom Allen's quiet instructions, that, 'too much applied was just making work, an' it be best to keep it off the brass if you can.'

When Emma went into the sleeping-cabin it was dark, drapes having been put over the casements to keep out the daylight. Maria Carolina lay in Nelson's cot, swaying with the motion of the ship. Her eyes looked hollowed and her skin waxen. She held one hand out to Emma, a damp handkerchief rolled in the fist, her voice weak as she muttered, 'Oh Emma, what is to become of us?'

Emma wasn't thinking of Maria Carolina, Naples or the approaching French when she replied, 'Everything will work out for the best, Your Majesty.'

10

On deck the weather had moderated, though it was far from calm. Nelson watched as Mack's boat dipped and swayed back to the shore, then lifted his telescope to look at the grey arc of the bay as it ran from the island of Procida to the southern arm at Capri, glowering Vesuvius in the centre. There was nothing more he could do here, Mack had made that plain, and the safety of the royal family meant that he should leave.

A glance at the lowering clouds above his head told him little more than the grey water of the bay. Many years at sea had given Nelson an acute sense of the weather, which allowed him to interpret what might come from what he saw and what he sniffed. The feel of a breeze, steady or gusting, the run of the clouds or the way they masked the sun, or the disturbed state of the water between him and the horizon. Experience also told him that his forecasting was inexact. He had been right more times than he had been wrong but he knew that he had not conquered the art.

However, given that the weather these last weeks had been foul it seemed that any observations should have little bearing on any decision he made. Those of his passengers likely to succumb were sick already, and the sooner he got them to dry land the better. Told by the officer of the watch that the Admiral was on deck, Thomas Hardy appeared silently, awaiting orders. Nelson, as was his habit, asked Hardy's opinion, which was much the same as his own.

'A signal to the transports, Captain Hardy, and to the Portuguese. We may prepare to weigh for Palermo.'

An hour after they had cleared the bay, his little convoy of ships was in a violent gale that was worsening by the minute, the screaming of the wind in the rigging increasing in pitch. The bowsprit dug deeper into troughs of waves that grew more and more unpredictable, the stern of *Vanguard* lifting clear of the water then slamming down again. In the wardroom all the men were hanging on to something, pale-faced and fearful – none more so than Ferdinand himself, who was convinced, and prepared to tell everyone else, that his house and his person were cursed.

Above, the Admiral's cabin was in chaos again, and Prince Alberto lay prostrate on a bed Emma had made up for him on the lockers that ran under the stern windows. Strapped in by ropes, with the boy's head on her lap, Emma was talking to him to keep up his spirits, using Tom Allen as a messenger to the Queen, laid too low to nurse her own child, to tell her of her son's progress.

Alberto's black, thick hair was soaking, and his skin translucent, as though the flame of life was struggling to maintain itself. Emma prayed, feeding Alberto sips of the brandy that Tom Allen had fetched at her request, trying to raise him by recalling the games they had played in the royal palaces.

'I's done my best, milady,' said Tom, nodding towards the other cabins. Just as in harbour, none of the palace servants, bar one retainer who seemed able to withstand the motion, had been an ounce of use. Yet Emma could forgive them now – the way the ship was heaving even Tom Allen could only make his way around the cabin by clasping on to the ropes he had rigged.

'They're all afeart we're going to drown,' Tom continued. 'I telt them that as long as the sticks stand – that be the masts like – then there's now't to worry about.'

On deck, Thomas Hardy and the Admiral, wrapped in oilskins, were watching those sticks with increasing alarm, as daylight gave way to dusk. Both knew that *Vanguard* had always been a roller, apt to show the copper that lined her bottom, a ship that sat higher in the water than was good for her: a heavy sea made the hull sway alarmingly from side to side. She had rolled out her masts twice before in this very sea, once off Corsica, where only the bravery and application of Alexander Ball had saved her, and again on the way back from the Nile.

'You have a party standing by, I trust?' yelled Nelson. Hardy's response was carried away on the howling wind, but he aimed one mittened hand towards the nearest companionway, to tell Nelson that men were ready with axes to cut away any mast that went over the side.

In truth Nelson shouldn't have been there: this was Hardy's deck, not his. But he could not abide inactivity and, with the wind battering them from west-south-west, they had a dangerous, rocky coastline to leeward that would turn the ship to matchwood if she was driven ashore. He justified his presence on the grounds that he had known Hardy since he was a slip of a lad, had educated him in his duties as an officer and a sailor. Anyway, he knew this ship better than Hardy did.

He did not know that Hardy was glad of his presence. He had had command of a brig and a frigate, but a 74-gun ship-of-the-line was altogether different and his responsibility for the safety of the hero of the Nile was an added burden. Ships foundered, it was part of the risk of life at sea, and the storm was violent enough to send *Vanguard* to the bottom. At least with Nelson here, he had someone to share the responsibility of whatever action he took.

Hardy did not hear the topsails shred, for the wind carried away the sound, and neither did Nelson – he had stepped into the chart room to check the ship's position with the master – but the crack of torn canvas alerted everyone close to the quarterdeck. By the time the driver and the foremast staysail went, bringing down with them a mass of rigging, chains and blocks that clattered on to the rolling deck, Nelson was back. He could hear Hardy ordering extra hands to the wheel, a party of seamen forward to cut away the debris, and yet more to get aloft to bend on new canvas. Nelson was half intending to go forward with the axe party when Giddings yelled in his ear.

'Best stay put, your honour. With only one pin you can't do owt and keep a safe grip an' all.'

The advice was sensible, but it angered Nelson. He never complained about the loss of his arm and how it constrained him, but he missed it, and such situations brought it home to him. He had always been an active rather than a magisterial captain – some rooted themselves to their quarterdeck station throughout a crisis, but he wasn't like that: in a storm or a battle he wanted always to be at the forefront. Fellow-officers condemned him for seeking popularity, but Nelson was merely responding to the way his blood raced. Giddings knew that, which was why he made sure he was always close to Nelson to stamp on temptation that might see him harmed.

The ship was in peril, though not mortally so. But below decks the sound of falling debris and running feet echoed through the planking, and sounded truly alarming. Mary Cadogan saw Ferdinand go white, and all around the wardroom men who had relished power and thought themselves immortal were silently praying to gods both Christian and pagan.

Emma held tightly to Prince Alberto, whose fever had worsened, his small body now racked by convulsions. Emma knew the storm was strengthening, just as she knew that in her arms her charge was sinking. Yet there was no way to bring relief – the sea controlled the motion of the ship, moderated only by the skill of those on deck to anticipate the flukes of the gale and the run of the waves. In the cabin, the howling wind found every crack in the casements beside which she sat, sending in freezing air and water. The floor of the cabin was awash, full of debris, running under the cabin door as the bow dipped, then surging back to splash around the hem of her dress. Every few minutes Tom Allen was there, hanging on to one of his ropes, gazing anxiously at the youngster's face, or exchanging a glance with Emma. His face offered encouragement, but his eyes reflected despair.

From the side cabin the wailing of the other royal passengers was a background din to the cacophony of the storm and a ship that, with groaning planking, sounded as if it might tear itself apart. Above her head, on deck, barefoot seamen, cursing, wielded axes and knives to break wood and ropes or slash canvas, freeing debris which, trailing over the side of the ship, would further endanger them. Men slipped on the water-lashed deck, only saved from perdition by the quick thinking of their mates. Others in even more exposed positions were trying to replace what had been blown out.

Occasionally, through the pouring rain, Nelson caught sight of the topsail yards swinging in the wind. He had served up there as a youngster in weather as foul as this, so he could imagine what he could not see: the bare feet struggling to keep a grip on the drenched foot ropes slung beneath wooden poles, the yardarms that carried the sails as the ship arced forwards, back and sideways through the air. Men with the top half of their bodies hanging over that spar were fighting with freezing fingers, he knew, to bend on a replacement sail so that the way of the ship could be restored and *Vanguard* could haul off the jagged shore that was not far to the east.

Horatio Nelson envied those men aloft: he missed the comradeship that went with being a topman, the elite of the sailing tribe. It was where he had served as a common sailor on his first voyage to the West Indies, and on his first long-service naval commission. He had formed friendships in the rigging that he would have liked to keep, only to watch them fade as he attained higher rank. Those who had taught him his trade would be ashore now, if they were not dead, sitting snug, he hoped, in some warm taproom. They would be telling avid listeners of the places and sights they had seen, with just enough exaggeration to keep the free ale flowing. They could well describe a storm: men overboard in seas from which they could not be rescued, dropped blocks or spikes that scarred the deck or mutilated some unfortunate soul, the exhaustion in the face of toil that could not be avoided, for to rest was to risk damnation. But would they describe the bond that grew between men who served in such a station? Nelson doubted it, because it bred a closeness that could neither be breached nor comprehended by outsiders, with its private language, the cryptic looks, particular jokes and human intimacies that would seem strange to the ears of a landsman.

As these thoughts ran through his mind, Nelson also admired the quality of Thomas Hardy's calm seamanship. He was in a storm, surrounded by over twenty ships of their evacuation convoy, without much knowledge of where his consorts lay, but he did not appear anxious, nor had he sought advice. Hardy had issued his orders, had ensured that the men on the wheel kept the head into the run of the sea, and waited without impatience for matters to be put right. Hardy trusted his men, and Nelson knew he was right to do so.

Mary Cadogan did not see what Sir William had fetched from the screened-off cabin he shared with Prince Esterhazy, but she noticed alarm in the Hungarian's face, Sir William's furtive air as he staggered out of the wardroom, and the bulge of substantial objects under his coat.

Tottering along the lower deck, Sir William crammed his body between a lashed cask and one of the uprights that held the deck-beams above his head. Using the top of the cask as a table he laid out two pistols, his powder horn and lead balls. It wasn't easy to load them as the ship pitched: he spilt much of the gunpowder and lost several balls. But he was an experienced hunter, and handy with a gun, so the task was eventually completed. Raising the pistols, long barrelled and gleaming, he opened his coat and jammed them into his waistcoat pockets, then set out with a more determined tread, handing himself off from the obstacles he met on his way, finally descending to the orlop deck.

Emma was approaching despair. She had seen little of death in her life. Samuel Linley, her first love, whose death had wrenched her heart. A neighbour or two in Hawarden as a child, the odd cadaver in the streets of London when she had been a homeless waif with no bed but a pile of rubbish in a stinking alley. She knew Prince Alberto was slipping away – his waxen skin told her that – and several times she had thumped at his heart fearing it might stop. Alberto's breath came in great wracking gasps and saliva dribbled from his mouth on to her hand.

She felt lonely and helpless. Tom Allen's attempts to fetch a physician had produced no one. The ship's surgeon was busy tending the cuts and broken limbs of both crew and passengers, and could not spare time to deal with a child's fever. The court doctor, who had come aboard in the wake of Ferdinand and Maria Carolina, was in a cot groaning, convinced he was not long for this world.

Emma asked Tom Allen to fetch Nelson. She felt that he alone might be able to light in Alberto's breast the spark of life. But when he came, Emma knew that the crisis was upon her. The convulsions were more acute, as was the lack of breath in the few periods of respite. She took strength from Nelson kneeling beside her, as he whispered encouragement into Alberto's ear.

Nelson had seen a lot of death; from sickness and from war, and just as much from the perils of the sea; he had sat beside many a fevered fellow sailor and reckoned to know who was a survivor and who would expire. As he spoke he tried to compose in his head those words he would need to comfort Emma.

The death throes saw the small body stretched to its limit, three massive convulsions that caused deep and terrifying pain that contorted the beautiful young face. The cry that emerged was a scream of agony that grew till it filled both the cabin and the ears of those attending. Tom Allen was openly weeping, Nelson still trying with words to stave off the inevitable, while Emma called Alberto's name. The last paroxysm forced his mouth to expand in a silent rictus. Alberto's eyes were wide open and full of fear as the last breath of his life escaped from his tiny frame in a horrible hiss. Then he went limp, and the light left his eyes.

Emma, through her moans, heard Nelson praying. He was using words he knew too well, learned from his father, who had stood over so many bodies in his time. As he prayed he took Emma's hand and put it to his forehead. Tom Allen had dropped to his knees by the casement lockers and was deep in prayer as well. But Emma, for all the despair she felt at the loss, had a task that only she could perform.

Gently she pulled her hand free, unlashed the rope that held her to the seat and stood up. Nelson stood, too, trying to steady her, but it was he with only one arm who failed to keep his balance and had to clutch at a rope.

'I must tell the Queen,' she said.

Nelson heard the keening cry of a bereft mother seconds after Emma closed the door. Maria Carolina had suffered much: eighteen confinements had resulted in the death of more than a dozen of her children, some at birth, some within weeks. Nelson knew this would be the hardest to bear: Prince Alberto had been a favourite with everyone.

It seemed like an eternity before Emma emerged. She left behind her a woman racked with guilt that her own afflictions had taken precedence over that of her child, that another had comforted him through his illness.

'Tom, I leave it to you to tend to the body,' said Nelson.

'Your honour,' Tom replied, sobbing.

Nelson patted him on the back, and went to Emma, who was still leaning against the door to the sleeping cabin. He took her hand and let the motion of the ship press him against her. 'I have no words, Emma, to tell you how sorry I am, nor to tell you how much I admire you.'

Her response was to lay her head on his shoulder. Then she began to sob, but even through her tears she could not forget her responsibilities. When she collected herself, she said, 'Someone must tell the King.'

'I will do that.'

The shake of the head was violent. 'No. I will.'

'Now?'

'Yes.'

'Very well,' Nelson replied. He turned to see Tom Allen glance surreptitiously at him and Emma, with a knowing expression that held a good measure of concern. 'I shall go back on deck.'

The first face Emma saw on entering the wardroom was her mother's. It bore the faraway expression of someone under the influence of drink. She sat in a chair set tight against the wardroom table, clasping a goblet, and gave Emma a lopsided smile. That disappeared when Emma told her of Prince Alberto's death, to be replaced by a shocked expression. By the time she had spoken to the King, and seen him drop his head in his hands, Mary Cadogan was crying. The boy had been an imp, but a charming one, a visitor to the Palazzo Sessa as often as his mother would allow. Ferdinand did not lift his head, and did not seem to mind when Emma took his hand in hers to comfort him: for once the king was completely immobile, stunned by his loss.

'Sir William,' Emma asked her mother.

'Gone,' Mary Cadogan slurred. 'Went out an age ago, never saying where to. Had something with him under his greatcoat.'

'What?'

'Couldn't see.' Mary Cadogan nodded to the screened off cabin. 'Happen Prince Hazy will know.'

Emma called softly, then pulled back the canvas screen. Prince Esterhazy, normally the most fastidious creature, was dishevelled. He had jammed himself into a corner, and was sitting fiddling with a sparkling object. Emma was close enough to see it was a jewel-encrusted snuff box. Esterhazy held it up to show her the miniature painting on the top, a nude study of his beautiful Neapolitan mistress, the Princess Pigniatelli.

'Do you think if I offer this to the Gods of the sea it will appease them?'

'My husband?' Emma asked.

'He took his pistols from his chest and went out.'

'You didn't think to stop him?' Emma said, trying to hide her alarm.

'No gentleman can require an explanation from someone unwilling to volunteer it.'

Before he finished the sentence Emma was gone, cursing him for a courtly fool. A look at her mother produced no more than a shrug, so she went out on to the lower deck to look for Sir William. In a crowded ship, no one could move anywhere unseen, so Emma found him quickly enough. He was in another screened-off cubicle on the orlop deck, sitting on a tiny cask, his coat wrapped round him for warmth, the two pistols held ready for use.

'The motion is more tolerable below sea level,' he said, with a slight scowl to show that he was displeased at being disturbed.

'Those?' asked Emma, gesturing towards the highly polished and decorated pistols.

'For me, my dear,' he replied. 'I have no intention of dying with the guggle-guggle of seawater in my throat. It is something I have always feared. Should we founder I will blow my brains out to avoid it.'

'Would I be allowed to observe, husband, that you are being very foolish?'

'Am I, Emma? Perhaps I will just take this route to perdition anyway.'

Emma had never seen Sir William behave like a chastised child before, but now that was what he looked like. His lips were pursed together with the kind of determined look a stubborn youngster might adopt. She felt that if Sir William had looked in a mirror now he would be shocked at his aged appearance. But what she was seeing was the face that greeted him every morning before his toilet; the wispy grey hair, the lined and thin face that needed to be dabbed with powder to be made presentable.

It had rarely occurred to Emma that her husband suffered black moods, perhaps because he was so careful of his demeanour, always the diplomat, able to cover a gaff with a witticism, an insult with professional deafness and a didactic statement with just the right measure of levity. He would hide his moods from her, of course, that was his nature, but she guessed he had been in one since the night he had spent at Posillipo after the Nile ball.

'Admiral Nelson assured me that we have no cause for real concern.'

'Our dear friend obviously feels he can vouchsafe to you things he will tell no one else.'

That remark was uncharacteristic of him, but instead of regret Sir William was suffused with a feeling of contentment that his pique was out in the open: he might not like to feel jealous – he might do everything he could to disguise it – but he did and it was uncomfortable. Nelson could say what he liked, and try to reassure his nervous passengers. But Sir William knew that the ship was *in extremis*, and so the chance of drowning was high. To dissemble in such circumstances was absurd.

'I would not hurt you for anything,' Emma said softly, stretching out a hand to push back her husband's wayward hair.

'For Nelson?' Sir William croaked.

It was as if the words had stuck in his gullet, so reluctant was he to use them: to pose the question was to invite an answer he dreaded to hear. Had Emma shown any signs of dalliance in the past, perhaps the present situation would be easier to bear, but it was her own fidelity that made what had happened so momentous. It was Nelson's singularity that made his attentions a threat.

'You admire him as much as I do.'

Sir William could hardly deny that. The day he had introduced Nelson to his wife, five years before, he had told her that Nelson was a remarkable fellow who would go far. Quite why he had been so enthusiastic seemed odd now, although he had been proved right. Until then he had always had a jaundiced view of sailors, never ever offering visiting captains hospitality under his roof. But he had accommodated Nelson in rooms set aside as royal apartments. The man had impressed him from that first day, and still did. Old enough to be the Admiral's father, Sir William wondered if he saw in him the son he had never had.

'Yes, I admire him, but not quite as much as you do, my dear.'

11

Emma knelt in front of her husband and removed the pistols from his hands, releasing the hammers to render them safe. She laid them on the floor and took her husband's cold hands in hers.

How to say to him that the pleasures they had shared were now so diminished as to have almost ceased; no man wants to hear such a thing, that the companion of his bedchamber is rarely present, and then only through a sense of duty not anticipation. How to tell him that she didn't admire Nelson, she was in love with him; madly, passionately, uncontrollably, totally. That would be even more unwelcome to a man who had craved that very emotion, only to never have it granted.

'Tell me the truth, Emma.'

They locked eyes, she wondering if somehow she had communicated her confusion through touch, the fact that whatever she said would cause him pain and that in turn would make her feel dreadful. Sir William, looking into those green, confused eyes, was reminded of the first day he had clapped eyes on her. There, in Greville's Edgeware Road hideaway, he had seen the beauty his nephew had acquired, a veritable Venus, so alluring that, as a fifty-five-year-old, Sir William was forced to recall his age, which was enough on its own to dampen any fantasies he might harbour about the girl.

Emma was older now, the face a little more full than that of the stunning beauty he had so admired. Yet that recollection produced another memory, of a young woman who had lacked guile; who was so natural and open in her behaviour it was often mistaken by other men for that of a practised coquette. If Emma had lacked one thing it was certainty, being a person who had always seemed to need guidance. Perhaps that was what she needed now.

'Do not fear that what you say will shock me,' Sir William added. 'Remember, I have been your intimate companion for a dozen years.'

Emma stroked his lined, unshaven cheek. 'I never thought I could shock you.'

Nor had he. When they had become lovers Sir William had revealed himself to be a proper disciple of the two-faced god Janus: urbane, witty and formal outside the bedchamber, but a true vulgarian behind closed doors. He was an avid reader of lewd French books, a lover of ribald conversation, a man who relished a robust fart just as much as he enjoyed the private performances Emma kept for his eyes only.

'You have made me happy.' He squeezed her hands reassuringly and continued. 'Do you believe, Emma, that your happiness is of paramount importance to me?'

She nodded.

'You know, then, that you have made me jealous?'

'Yes.' She indicated the pistols. 'But I thought not enough for you to see those as a solution.'

'I confess, my dear, that I contemplated such an exit when I had them in my hand, and not because of the fear of seawater. But I have always held that those who take their own life for something as paltry as being cuckolded are at best fools and at worst cowards.'

'You are neither.'

'I am a coward when faced with drowning,' Sir William insisted, before adding, 'There is some similarity, I suspect, between drowning and jealousy, the one a physical manifestation, the other a submerging of the spirit. I speak as someone new to the emotion. The night I saw you enter Nelson's bedchamber . . .'

'You saw me?' Emma interrupted.

Sir William laughed. 'I came to ensure our guest was comfortable. I knew him to be fatigued, and still suffering from his head wound. I arrived at his door just as you entered, and I thought to wait till you came out.'

He cocked his head then, as if unsure. 'Or did I? Was I anticipating what might occur, hoping to beat you to his apartments and so deflect you? I watched you at the banquet, saw how often you laughed and touched our hero. I suspected, even then, a greater attachment to him than to all those other suitors who have pursued you over the years.'

'You are making yourself unhappy, husband.'

'No, Emma. It does me good to question myself, for I must tell you that jealousy is not a feeling I ever imagined I would experience, and having done so I can also tell you that for a man like me it is damned uncomfortable. I spend all my time watching you and Nelson for signs of your mutual regard, which is foolish, since any I see wound me, and I am convinced and made uncomfortable by the thought that I may have missed more. Have I missed anything, Emma?'

The import of that question was plain: had she and Nelson made love more than once? 'No.'

'But I sense a craving not wholly satisfied.'

'Would it hurt you more,' Emma whispered, 'if I was to tell you that I cannot help myself.'

'The pain, my dear, is acute enough to be beyond augmentation. But tell me, how does he feel?'

'I know he loves me, for he has said so.' Sir William's arched eyebrow made her add quickly. 'It is not just words. It is in his eyes, his whole being. Yet I think he fears it. He is, as you know, more God-fearing than either you or I.'

Sir William, excluding paganism, hated all things religious, and responded sharply. 'I should think, then, he anticipates eternal damnation.'

'I think he fears more to lose me,' replied Emma, with equal force.

'*Touché*,' said Sir William.

'Yet I think he would rather offend his God than you.' Sir William's humourless laugh made Emma continue. 'It is true husband! I doubt any other man could have caused him a second's doubt.'

'The morning after your assignation, while bathing at Posillipo, I was forced to review my life.' Emma made to speak but Sir William pressed a finger to her lips. 'I have always been concerned about what would happen to you after I am gone. You are so much younger than I, and I have accustomed you to a degree of extravagance that what I will leave behind me cannot sustain.'

Having promised his estates and the income from them to his nephew, there would be no comfortable inheritance for Emma. Having used up the best years of her life he had taken her to a point where she might struggle to find another benefactor, and she would have only a small annuity plus the money left after the settlement of her husband's debts. The style in which she was now wont to live, with three homes, carriages, servants, dressmakers, milliners and never a thought for the cost, would cease on Sir William's death.

'I must confess,' Sir William continued, 'that in idle moments I had thought on this before, the possibility that another man should come into your life, who would be able to maintain you after . . .'

'You have many years left, husband.'

'Have I, Emma? I am nearing seventy, the allotted biblical span. My bones ache even on the warmest morning. My ardour, which I hold sustains a man against all manner of ailments, has cooled to the point of . . . Well I need hardly tell you that. In conclusion, faithful as you have been to me all these years, I was contemplating the notion of advising you that such behaviour was no longer wise.'

Emma smiled. 'Yet you did not.'

'The diplomat in me, my dear', Sir William responded wryly. '"Nothing precipitous" has always been my motto. And I must own how different the intellectual pursuit of an idea is from the reality. Is it because Nelson is a hero? Is that why?'

The suddenness of those questions jolted Emma, so that her reply was unconsidered. 'No.'

'When?'

'The first day I met him.'

There was a flash of pain in his eyes, quickly masked. 'And you carried your torch for five years.'

'I never thought to see him again. We exchanged letters, as did you and he, but nothing in his correspondence or mine touched on anything other than mutual regard.'

'And then the Nile.'

Emma raised herself up, crouching over Sir William's head, using his shoulders to steady herself against the motion of the ship. 'I must go back to the Queen. She is distraught.' The look her husband gave her then made Emma realise that she had not told him of Prince Alberto's death. She told him now, ending in a whisper, 'I think the King would benefit from your company in the wardroom.'

The torn topsails had been replaced with fresh canvas, and although the storm wasn't over, it had eased enough for everyone on deck to feel more sanguine about the ability of ship and crew to ride it out. Their actual position was unknown, but the island of Sicily was too big to miss, and Nelson knew that as soon as they sighted land they would be able to steer for Palermo.

As the night wore on the weather eased steadily, allowing those unused to the sea to sleep. The motion was still greater than they would have wished, but it was no longer violent enough to toss them from hammock or bed, or send them tumbling down a companionway as they made their passage from one part of the ship to the other. Nelson went once more into the chart room and dozed off, half-aware of what was happening on the quarterdeck. His eye would flicker as the bells of the watches tolled, and as he sensed each change of course.

The comatose interludes were punctuated by snatches of vivid dreams; of old faces and strange ones, real battles and imagined encounters, until he heard, 'It be coming up dawn, your honour'. Tom Allen was shaking Nelson's shoulder. 'Time for your shave.'

Nelson smiled before he opened his eyes. Routine made the Royal Navy what it was. No matter that the ship was still tossing about on a troubled sea, that his cabin was all ahoo and occupied by others. Tom Allen shaved him at the same time every naval day, and this morning was not going to be any different.

'And may I be the first, your honour,' Tom added, 'to wish you good cheer on Christmas Day.'

'It is that, Tom,' Nelson replied, and closed his eyes again. 'I had quite let it slip my mind.'

What would they be doing in England? Would the family have gathered at Burnham Thorpe for a special Christmas service and a celebration meal? Would his eldest brother, Maurice, with his indifferent health, have been dragged from London and the Navy Office to see in a New Year in Norfolk? His father would be there and Susanna, his favourite sister, now Mrs Bolton, with her seven children, and brother William, now the Reverend, the closest companion of his youth.

There were deaths to mourn, his sister Anne and brothers Edmund and George, but the baby of the brood, Catherine, had married George Matcham and the couple were steadily producing children. His other brother Suckling he had never cared for, and he checked himself for that unchristian thought. But the face that drew his inner gaze was the one he wanted least to imagine – that of his wife, Fanny.

She would play consort to his father and gently scold Susanna's litter as though she was the matriarch of the household, a position she assumed, much to the annoyance of Nelson's eldest sister. Her face filled his mind now, gentle, refined, and smiling as he had first seen it on Nevis, pinched and frozen with chapped lips as she had been in Norfolk, during those five years he had spent without employment.

He fought to keep the comparison from surfacing, Emma's gaiety and abandon with Fanny's reserve and physical coldness. She was his wife before God, and deserved his devotion. But he could not force out the lovelier, livelier face or the memory of the freely offered passion that contrasted so sharply with Fanny's restrained emotions.

His eyes snapped open. It was the best way to blot out dreams. 'A Happy Christmas to you too, Tom.'

'Wonder what they're up to in Burnham?' Tom said, smiling. He was from Burnham Thorpe as well, baptised by the Reverend Nelson at the font of All Saints.

'A shave, yes,' Nelson insisted.

Tom had set up the chair, water bowl and strop in Hardy's cabin, and had also conjured up a welcome cup of coffee. The cook had got his coppers relit so that there was something hot for all. By the time the razor was under Nelson's chin, the officer of the watch had sighted land and HMS *Vanguard* had put up her helm on a true course for Palermo.

Dressed and ready for breakfast, John Tyson appeared. He had spent the time since the flight from Naples well out of the way, mewed up hugger-mugger with the ship's purser. But official business could be delayed no longer and that it was Christmas made no odds. Rarely a day went by when an admiral did not have to deal with a mass of correspondence, and Tyson wanted that which was outstanding cleared before the day's work came in. There might be despatches – there would most definitely be lists – of ship's conditions, masts, spars and sails, which would be dire after such a blow. Each would report the state of their water and biscuit, how many men they had left in Naples or lost on the way to Palermo, the mass of detail that was the bane of a commanding officer's existence. And that was before Admiral Lord Nelson must write both to the Admiralty and Earl St Vincent to apprise them of his actions.

Then, and only then, could he attend to personal matters.

Hardy was sensible enough of the occasion to arrange that his officers should gather to raise a glass to Their Sicilian Majesties on the anniversary of the birth of Christ. Yet it was a stilted affair, everyone conscious of the losses that those being toasted had endured: their kingdom and their youngest son. Outside, snow fell in a part of the world usually immune to such a phenomenon, while in the cabin small gifts were offered and graciously accepted, the very lack of intrinsic value seeming to make them more potent than jewelled or golden objects. Ferdinand, for once showing the courtly manner that went with his rank, thanked the ship's officers on his family's behalf. Thomas Hardy then made a brave little speech in which he apologised that more cheer was not possible, but he felt sure, he said, that the protective arm of King George's Navy was there to see them safe, now and in the future.

As he finished the lookout yelled to alert the quarterdeck that the harbour of Palermo was in sight.

Sir William was on deck as HMS *Vanguard* manoeuvred to clear the mole, half of his mind on the way the snow obscured the view, the other on the conversation he had had with his wife. Matters were out in the open now and thus had to be dealt with. The question was how? With another man little would have had to be said, but Nelson was so naïve in matters of the heart that Sir William contemplated that he might need to invite him directly to proceed with Emma.

He balked at the idea. Suddenly, the gruff voice of Mary Cadogan addressing a sailor made him turn. She was so wrapped up against the chill that not much more than her snub nose, reddened by the cold, was visible from inside her closely tied bonnet. But it was enough to remind him that, years before, it was she who had smoothed the way to her daughter's acceptance of him as her protector.

She had challenged him and his intentions in a manner that had made him feel as if she was the master and he the servant. Her attitude had been based on years of experience in dealing with men, and the fact that she suspected he was engaged in a conspiracy with his nephew.

Mary Cadogan had smoked out all the details of how he and Charles Greville had intrigued to transfer Emma from the nephew's arms to the uncle's. And she had known that what had looked simple to the schemers on paper would founder on her daughter's good nature and fidelity. Sir William had anticipated her anger, only to find her eminently practical. Mary Cadogan had deduced one obvious truth: that the chance of Emma's return to Greville's affections was remote. What mattered to her was comfort and security, and once she had established that the best chance of that lay in Naples, she had set out to alter her daughter's mind.

Looking at her now, it occurred to Sir William that she was the solution to his problem. If anyone knew how to alert Nelson to the fact that he might proceed, without embarrassing anyone, it was Mary Cadogan.

Despite the chill December sleet it seemed that half the population of Sicily was on the shore waiting to greet their king and queen, a silent mass of citizens who believed that royal residence in Naples was foolishness. Sicily was loyal where the mainland was suspect, true to the Bourbons and with a visceral hatred of revolution. There were no Jacobin clubs here, no seditious nobles, only true subjects.

In the calm of Palermo harbour, inching in to tie up at the mole under the great hanging rock and the forts, the ship was now in a ferment of preparation. Ferdinand was berating his valets for the state of his clothes, which had been spoiled by seawater. In Nelson's quarters the Queen was patient, distant almost, as her ladies-in-waiting prepared her to meet her subjects, everyone trying to ignore the plain wooden coffin that had been made by the ship's carpenter to hold Prince Alberto's body.

Emma had found space in one of the side cabins to repair the damage of the last forty-eight hours. Gazing at herself in a looking glass she saw lines on her face, the result of extreme fatigue. Sir William had already gone ashore with the King's chamberlain and some of the more astute courtiers to secure the best available accommodation at the Colli Palace.

A bed for Sir William in the royal residence could only be temporary: as the British Ambassador he would be required to rent suitable accommodation from which to represent his country, and prices, once the locals realised just how many fleeing royalists had arrived, would shoot through the roof. As an early bird, he might save some money.

The death of the prince was enough to still any cheers from the populace, which would have been inappropriate in any case. As the King and Queen, the Hereditary Prince and his wife, their baby and the royal princesses made their way through the streets, they were accompanied by the quiet murmur of prayers, and the onlookers made the sign of the cross as the cortege bearing Prince Alberto passed.

Nelson, with Hardy and his officers, watched the procession begin from the poop, vaguely aware that the ship was being put to rights around him. The transports and the Portuguese men o' war began to unload too, which turned the mole into a mass of gesticulation, as those landing sought accommodation and avaricious monks from numerous monasteries bargained with them.

Some of the faces he knew from balls and receptions he had attended, but he couldn't recall many of the names. He spotted Commodore Caracciolo and wondered how he had got there since no Neapolitan warship had left Naples. He half considered offering him accommodation aboard *Vanguard*, but the Commodore was not much given to either grace or gratitude, so he might be an unpleasant dining companion. Added to that, he was probably still smarting because his king and queen had chosen a British ship in which to flee Naples, rather than one he commanded.

When he returned with Tyson, Tom Allen had seen to his cabin. The furniture was in place and polished, and when he sat at his worktable it seemed to Nelson as though he could put the clock back to a point where there had been no Nile battle, no Naples welcome, no Emma Hamilton. Then he concluded that the lady had been a presence in his life for a very long time.

'Mr Tyson,' he said, 'we are required to inform Earl St Vincent, Captains Ball and Troubridge of our situation.'

There was almost pleasure in immersing himself in work.

Sir William felt unwell, sitting up in bed wrapped in blankets and his dressing gown. He had caught a chill on the journey from Naples, which had moved from his chest to his stomach. His discomfort was made worse by the cramped quarters he and his wife had been allotted by the chamberlain. The room was dark, with cracked marble flooring and peeling paint on the walls, and barely big enough to hold his possessions – and that was without the packing cases still snug in the hold of HMS *Vanguard*. The luxury of separate suites that he and Emma had enjoyed in Naples had been replaced by cohabitation, with a couple of his servants forced to sleep on the floor outside the door. It was all very well for the court officials to insist that the Colli Palace was packed to the rafters with courtiers and ministers but he was, after all, the British Ambassador.

His only consolation was the thought that this setting was likely to be temporary. He was sure his early arrival ashore was about to bear fruit, and a promising villa had been proposed to him, albeit at a staggering rent, in which he could assume once more his usual comforts and the duties of his office. The door opened to reveal Mary Cadogan with a steaming bowl of liquid.

'Not another of your damned possets,' he moaned.

'Got to get you well, Sir William,' she replied, giving him a hard stare as she approached the bed. 'An' if it don't taste like nectar that's all to the good I say, 'cause what seems foul is often best to restore a man's humour.'

'The only humour to be gained from that,' Sir William sniffed, 'is gifted to the person watching the victim consume it.'

'Then you won't mind, sir,' said Mary Cadogan, positioning herself on a cramped chair, 'if I partake of the pleasure.'

The temptation to damn her to hell and tell her to get out was overborne by the realisation that he had a chance to engage in a conversation he had been delaying since coming ashore. His high fever and low spirits had been the excuse, but he was aware that procrastination had brought no joy. Emma was absent, Mary Cadogan was here, and it was too good a chance to miss.

'You have a ghoulish turn to your nature, Mrs Cadogan.'

Emma's mother discerned the amusement behind that remark, even if it was delivered with a grimace. 'You arrange a good hanging and quartering, Sir William, and I'll happily go to that and leave you in peace.'

For all his diplomatic skill, Sir William found the next step difficult. 'I had a mind to talk with you anyway, but intended to wait till this ague had passed.'

'Would it be about matters domestic?'

'No!'

The emphatic response was met with the merest lift of her eyebrows, and since Sir William had no desire to state the details of the matter, a silence ensued. Eventually after what seemed an eternity of a mutual stare, Mary Cadogan spoke. 'Would it be about my Emma?'

'I have often had occasion,' replied Sir William, 'to remark, Mrs Cadogan, upon your sagacity.'

There was little doubt in Mary Cadogan's mind as to what he wished to discuss. She had been watching the parties involved with a tight eye since the night Emma had gone to Nelson's room and, sensitive to atmosphere, had noticed the tensions.

'God gave me eyes to see,' she said finally, if elliptically.

'And the good grace to be discreet,' replied Sir William, nailing the subject.

'Would it ease your mind if I said it were bound to occur one day?'

'No, Mrs Cadogan, it would not.'

'If I may speak plain, Sir William.'

'I have always found that you do so when matters require it,' Sir William observed, in a mordant tone.

'Fidelity has always been one of my Emma's better traits.' The Ambassador nodded. 'She can be lacking in sense, but even with your nephew, who didn't deserve half the consideration due to your good self, she was true.'

The last part of that sentence betrayed a bitterness that Mary Cadogan had never sought to hide and that had remained constant throughout the twelve years since she and her daughter had come to Naples. She held Charles Greville to be a scrub, and made little attempt to disguise this from his uncle.

'I know it,' said Sir William.

'It is without a boast,' Mary Cadogan snorted, 'that I can claim to have not only smoked your game, but made my Emma party for it.' It was no time for Sir William to interrupt, since he might open himself to censure, so he stayed silent. 'And now you'll be asking me to tell

Emma, in a way that you cannot, that this here nonsense with Lord Nelson has got stop.'

There was some comfort there for Sir William in that, with all her natural acuity, Mary Cadogan had not seen just how much her Emma was smitten, had not made the obvious connection between her daughter's natural fidelity and the depth of feeling that would be necessary to break it. For once he knew more of what was happening in Emma's head and heart than her mother.

'Quite the reverse, Mrs Cadogan. I admit to needing your assistance, but it is not to badger my wife into breaking off her friendship.'

There was no need to say more. The surprise on Mary Cadogan's face said it all.

12

There was an uncomfortable sensation in Nelson's breast as he wondered why Sir William Hamilton had come aboard *Vanguard* to see him. The ambassador was fully recovered now and they had met many times ashore in the last week at the daily levee the royal family insisted on holding even though they were in mourning for Alberto. Any discussions of a military or diplomatic nature had taken place then, usually in the company of Sir John Acton or the Marquis de Gallo.

Not that there had been much to discuss. The French had occupied Naples, but had found that although the nobles welcomed them the peasants were another matter. Rumour had it that no Frenchman dare walk the streets alone for fear of being murdered. The Neapolitan naval officers who had remained had surrendered their ships to the enemy, which caused Nelson to curse the fact that he had failed to destroy them.

At least one officer, Commodore Mitchell, ex-Royal Navy and British in the Portuguese service, had taken it upon himself to attack the Neapolitan ships, forcing them in under the guns of the Naples forts. Meanwhile Nelson was busy making dispositions that would not only keep them there, but cause as much trouble to the French occupiers as he could with what were strictly limited resources.

An uprising was underway in the countryside. Cardinal Fabrizo Ruffo, religious advisor to the King, had sailed to Sicily with the royal evacuation, only to return immediately to the mainland. He had sent word that he was traversing the hinterlands of Calabria, where he had huge holdings, raising a force, the Army of the Holy Faith, under the banner of the cross, to fight the heathen invader. Religion was the mainspring of this enterprise, though no one in Palermo had much faith in what it could do. If a trained army could not beat the French, what chance would a rabble of barefoot peasants have, however much they loved their king and their God.

'The villa I spoke of, Lord Nelson.'

'Yes,' Nelson replied warily. He recalled a discussion he had had with Sir William several days before, when the Ambassador had declared himself eager to move out of the crowded royal palace into a residence he could call his own.

'The Villa Bastioni,' Sir William added.

'You mentioned it, I recall,' replied Nelson.

What Sir William recalled at that moment was the discussion he had had with Mary Cadogan who, once she had discerned the direction of Sir William's intentions, had reverted to practicality. He had admitted that his admiration for Nelson as a man and for what he had achieved was unbounded. He also admitted to his jealousy at Emma's regard for the admiral and his cares for her future.

Emma's mother had shown swiftly where her sentiments lay. She assured Sir William that he had a good few years left, but had enough sense to know what the future would be like without him and the protection of his income. She was willing to damn her daughter for fanciful notions and for her outrageous extravagance in the article of clothes, hats, pets, jewellery and the like, which, in her humble opinion, 'Sir William should have clapped a stopper on some time past.'

Mary Cadogan offered an astute opinion of Nelson's nature and his character. He might be God-fearing but he was also impulsive: he was man who could go from social shyness to dominating a gathering in a few seconds. As to his knowledge of her sex, however, 'why I doubt he has an ounce of it'. But he had passion nonetheless, and was at this moment a man with 'ants in his pants', lashed tight by his country-squire upbringing, nothing but a mass of ardour bursting to get out.

Sir William had listened until Mary Cadogan had reached the crux of her concern. It was all very well for Sir William to be saying that the time had come for him to surrender exclusive rights to his wife's bedchamber. That was as maybe and up to him. But was this sailor just toying with Emma's affections? There was a wife back home, a shrew she had heard, 'who is not the type to take kindly to liaisons.'

It had been odd for Sir William to hear himself insist that should Nelson succumb to his natural desires, he was not the type to leave the lady in the lurch. That given the Nile victory and the fame and wealth that was bound to bring him, he would be able to support

Emma – and her mother – in the manner to which they had become accustomed.

'Then it be simple, Sir William,' Mary Cadogan had said, with an emphatic toss of the head. 'You're planning to take a place away from the palace, a villa of your own. Lord Nelson resided with you in Naples and he can do so here. If you put the two of them close enough to let their blood boil, nature will do the rest. Then we will see if you are right about your little Jack Tar, or not.'

The feeling that a problem had not necessarily been solved, but at least had been acted upon, was shattered by her last words: 'And let's face it, Sir William, it would be no harm havin' another to share in the expense, what with these Papist heathen charging sinful prices for a place a decent person can lay his head. You needs to preserve what you has when you gets of an age.'

Sir William realised that Nelson was staring at him, that he had been lost in recollection, which made the barbed remark about old age all the more pertinent. 'I have secured the use of the Villa Bastioni for six months. Naturally my wife and I would be only too happy that you should see it as your home while you are based on the island.'

Nelson did not react, so Sir William carried on, his voice deliberately enthusiastic. 'I grant it will not be as commodious as the Palazzo Sessa, my friend, but I daresay we will manage.'

'I had thought to stay aboard ship,' said Nelson cautiously. 'It is not uncomfortable in such a well protected harbour.'

Sir William smiled in a way that showed he though the notion absurd. There was no need to add that at this time of year, and with the foul turn of the weather, the whole ship, even Nelson's well appointed quarters, felt damp. There was a draught coming down the companionway that led from the cabin to the quarterdeck, even though it was secured by a hatch. The stoves in each of the partitioned cabins belched away, yet failed to warm the place. Nor did he say that Nelson would succumb to a chill if he insisted on remaining aboard a berthed vessel.

'I think you must admit that you would be more at ease on dry land.'

Nelson bit off the temptation to insist that he would not. He had seen Emma every time he had been ashore, but with the protective shield of numerous company only their eyes had met. Hers were often red, from the time she spent weeping with the Queen, who could not reconcile herself to her son's death. But those shared looks had been troubling.

'And I must add, my dear Lord Nelson, that my wife will insist. Lady Hamilton is of the opinion, and so I must say am I, that the Palazzo Sessa was never so complete as when you were in residence. It felt, somehow, more of a home.'

Sir William, staring intently at the rock-still Admiral, was convinced he could say no more. If the man could not read between those lines there could be no others to replace them. An open invitation was out of the question; whatever happened between Nelson and Emma, Sir William had his dignity to maintain. Yet he could not help but feel that Nelson, with his lack of social skills, had somehow missed a point as obvious as the proverbial barn door. He was forced, after all, to go further. 'It has often seemed to me, Lord Nelson, that our fates are inextricably linked, that we are bound together not just by mutual regard, but by circumstances.'

In his mind Sir William was screaming for Nelson to respond, aware as he added the next observation, that he had comprehensively breached the limits of what he been prepared to say when he came aboard. 'We are, as I pointed out to Lady Hamilton, like the inscription of the knightly order of the Bath we both wear, a *tria juncta in uno.*'

When Nelson still failed to respond, Sir William stood up and said, rather testily, 'I will have my servants prepare your apartments.'

Nelson did speak then, to say maladroitly, 'You are too kind.'

The Villa Bastioni was a marble summer mansion that stood on a wide statue-covered promenade that ran between its noble facade and a clear view of the sea. It had an air of exterior magnificence, yet inside it seemed a desolate place after the Palazzo Sessa. The vast under-furnished rooms, stone-floored without chimneys or fireplaces, were prey to every draught. With the unusual weather – snow, sleet and a biting cold *tramontana*, a cold north wind that came straight off the ice-covered Alps – the place was freezing. Sir William had placed braziers in some, one being Nelson's bedroom, but his guest considered himself just as much at threat from chills here as he was aboard ship.

That was until Emma came, wrapped in a heavy velvet cloak, the hood framing her shining hair. Nelson was suddenly reminded of a day in London, at Charing Cross, of the sight of a beauty he had seen heading through a teeming crowd of travellers for a coach, an enchantress he had seen the night before. He had visited a charlatan doctor who had dosed him with electricity to cure a painful arm. Only the discomfort of the treatment had taken his eyes of a scantily clad vision of a nymph standing in a raised alcove. When he had first met Emma, there had been the faintest feeling of recognition, and he had it again now.

A liveried servant opened the door for her, and she threw Nelson a look of deep longing. That was followed by a glance at Tom Allen, who was unpacking his master's sea chest. Tom was slow to react, but eventually the meaning of that look penetrated his skull. He slammed the lid of the chest, edged towards the door, tugged at his forelock and left.

An eternity seemed to pass as they stared at each other. Then Emma moved forward, her eyes alight, her hands coming from inside the cloak to take his. The knowledge that contact between them would be his undoing did not stop Nelson's arm from responding, and as he had known it would, his resistance crumbled.

The need to say something foundered when Emma kissed him full on the lips, then took his hand and slipped it inside her cloak. The feeling of naked flesh was electrifying, as potent as the knowledge that Emma had come to this room with only one purpose. He rested on her hip for only second, moving up first to cup the ample flesh of her breast, which brought a slight moaning gasp. Her hands, expertly working at his breeches produced a corresponding moan from him.

He felt the edge of his sea chest touch the back of his knees, which forced him to sit down heavily, the vision of Emma's rounded belly before his face. Nelson buried his head in that, his hand pulling to increase the pressure. Emma had straddled the chest and him, moaning incomprehensible endearments behind his head.

The greatest number of charcoal-filled braziers had been placed in a salon without windows, with a semicircle of screens to create a feeling of intimacy. The same people who had been constant visitors to the Hamilton palazzo in Naples were gathered round the table; the Knights, mother and daughter, the painter Angelica Kaufmann, the Prince and Princess Esterhazy. Sir William sat at the head. Cunningly he had placed Emma closer to himself than to Nelson, but with the pair on opposite sides of the table. Thus the Admiral had looked at him every time his wife addressed him, and Sir William could watch his friend's face unobtrusively as Emma dominated a very light hearted conversation.

Sir William supposed that she and her mother had spoken. He knew his Emma well, that patience was not one of her virtues. On arriving back from the King's shooting party he had sensed an odd atmosphere in the villa: the way the servants would not meet his eye, and his valet, not by nature convivial, had seemed more taciturn than usual. As this was an unfamiliar household, he might have read something into innocent acts that did not exist. But he had lived with servants all his life and he knew them to be an infallible barometer of domestic life. Nothing happened in a household that the servants didn't know about, and it imperilled any master or mistress who forgot that. He had attended law courts aplenty to watch and laugh as everyone from skivvies to head footmen gave evidence of their employers' shenanigans, which provided grounds for an injured party to win that near impossible prize: a legal divorce.

Seeing Emma in her present mood, he realised how constrained she had been these last four weeks with the proximity of war and the prevalence of death. Now she was quite her old self, in a newly made dress of burgundy silk over white lace, laughing, making risqué sallies, forcing by her sheer brio everyone at the table to share in her good mood. Everyone except a preoccupied Nelson, who could barely smile.

Nelson felt as though he was at sea, with some sixth sense warning him of a threat over the horizon. Emma's beauty was heightened by the soft light of the candles in a way that he had not seen since the night of his victory banquet. The memory of the afternoon produced remorse and a feeling of radiance in equal measure.

Those emotions had to be suppressed. He knew that, much as his host tried to disguise it, he was under scrutiny. A man raised in the tight confines of a naval wardroom was always conscious of the feelings and surreptitious glances of others. Sir William might suppose himself discreet, but to the sensitive Nelson he was as obvious as a ship's bell.

For a great deal of the time, Nelson castigated himself for his weakness. Why had he not merely insisted to Sir William that by staying aboard ship he was best placed to get to sea quickly should any opportunity present itself to take on the enemy? Any number of reasons had occurred to him to turn down residence here and avoid what had happened. Yet he was here, allocated draughty but spacious apartments, Tom Allen with him, and his sea chest, the thought of which made him blush.

Emma felt wonderful. Gone was the hankering for Naples, the social round, the three houses and half dozen carriages she had had at her disposal. Even the weather, clear sunny and sharply cold, had conspired to add to her feeling of wellbeing. She felt that ten dozen cares had been lifted from her shoulders. That morning, as the Queen had wept once more for her dead son, Emma had stayed dry-eyed, not from any lack of grief but from the knowledge that what she had never dared hope for had been gifted her. When she returned to her new home, the man she loved would be there. She knew that her husband, ever the gentleman, had accepted the inevitability of a liaison between her and Nelson. The rules were those she knew well, having seen others observe them over several years. In public, all the proprieties must stand. Sir William was to be deferred to in the manner to which he was accustomed, treated as both her husband and the companion of her heart, praised, flattered even, and always the first person with claim on her time. The world, even if the truth were no secret, would see a happy and devoted couple.

In private it would be different. Night and day, as he had of old, Sir William would use his own apartments. However, he would no longer call upon her in her own rooms without first sending a servant to ensure that a visit would be welcome. Should he be absent from the residence, notification would always be sent ahead of his imminent return. Under no circumstances must he be embarrassed. What he knew and what he saw must remain separate.

It was odd to be sitting here, leading the conversation, guying the man she loved, even when it was obvious that he was uncomfortable. Nelson had not believed her when she had told him of the change in circumstances, and Emma wondered at the innocence of a man who could not see what should have been obvious. He was free to be gallant, indeed to be forward, because the idea that they should be lovers and keep it hidden was impossible. Everyone would know, merely observing the etiquette of never saying openly and publicly that it was so. Everyone was well versed in the rules of such a game – except Nelson.

'Are you too hot, Lord Nelson?' asked Sir William. He had noticed the blush, and something prompted by years of experience had told him it was the time for a pointed sally.

Nelson obliged him with a deeper blush.

'Have a care you are not falling prey to a fever, sir, for if you are, I would advise that you take at once to your bed.'

It was impossible for Nelson to redden any more, but he squirmed. Then Sir William caught Emma's eye: her expression told him plainly that guying her lover was not to be borne.

'Whist!' he exclaimed, after a deep and rumbling cough.

The ritual of saying goodnight, of being escorted by candle-bearing servants to each set of chambers, was the same as it had been on any other night under Sir William's roof, but the way Emma came to

Nelson's apartments, without a hint of subterfuge, gave the lie to that. She had changed from her burgundy dinner dress into a loose dressing-gown over a linen nightdress, worn with a lace cap. She bore in her hand a five-branch candlestick, guttering in the draughts, that must have looked like an alarm beacon in the dimly lit corridors.

She found him in boat cloak and nightgown writing personal letters at a desk, one a short missive to his wife. When Nelson protested she laughed, a loud pealing sound that he loved in daylight but considered inappropriate in an establishment at repose. He knew he should be angry with Emma, but that was a feeling he found hard to apply, especially where she was concerned. And she made going to bed together seem natural, as if they had been doing it all their lives. The proximity of her body and the freedom of her hands and his wiped away his mortification. They made love with less breathless passion than they had earlier that day, and soon, by the light of the only candle Emma had not extinguished, they lay in each other's arms, talking quietly

'I cannot imagine myself ever looking Sir William in the eye again.'

'From what my mother tells me you have not done so for weeks.'

Nelson raised his head enough to look at her. 'Your mother?'

'That is what my husband told her.'

'Then he did know.'

'He saw me enter your apartments on the night of the banquet. He was outside the door when I locked it.'

'He told your mother this too?'

'Yes,' she murmured into Nelson's breast. It was a lie. but Emma had no desire to impart to him that her husband had told her himself.

'God in heaven.' Nelson groaned. 'How could he bear it? Had I been him I would have called me out.'

That made Emma laugh, and when gently chastised she was forced to explain that she was amused by the notion of a one-armed man duelling with himself.

In the explanations that followed Emma's mother assumed a greater role than she had held in reality. Forced to the truth, Emma would admit that most of what she knew of that night had come to her, so to speak, from the horse's mouth. But she was reluctant to tell of that difficult conversation she had had in the lower decks of HMS *Vanguard*, and the sight of her husband, whom she considered an upright, brave man, in despair with a brace of pistols in his hand.

The feelings she had for Sir William Hamilton were deep, based on delight in his company and appreciation of his manifest kindnesses. He had made her a lady in spirit as well as in name and it was not only convention that obliged her to protect his character and reputation. It was a deep regard for the man who, while he had been her lover, had also been in many respects the father she had never had.

'I cannot fathom your fears, Nelson. It is, if not commonplace, then so frequent as to deny comment. You have had it pointed out to you by me, if not by other people, Count so-and-so is the lover of X, and the Duke of Blah is deeply attached to Madame whoever.'

Looking into Emma's face as she leaned over him, he could not bring himself to say that what might pass for mundane in Naples would not in many other places he had been; that the society of the Neapolitans was lax in a way that few others were.

'And do not play the hypocrite, my dear. Do not tell me, Nelson, that you have no knowledge of dalliance.'

'You have lost me.'

'Genoa? A certain opera singer.'

'You know about that?'

'Would it surprise you to discover that your officers are no more discreet than any other men?'

Nelson had a vision of that awkward interview with his stepson. 'Was it Josiah who told you?'

'No,' Emma insisted, then added in a slightly wounded tone. 'Your stepson has barely said a word to me since he came back to Naples. I cannot think what I have done to offend him.'

'Then who did?'

The information had been given to her, in all innocence though tinged with drink, by Alexander Ball before he left to take station off Malta. He insisted that his commanding officer needed to relax, that he was wound too tight for his own good.

'Surely you would not wish me to tell you,' Emma said. 'Be satisfied that it was told to me out of affection not malice, and by a fellow officer who reckoned that a bit more of the same would do you good.'

Emma had one thigh over his groin, and the gentle motion of her flesh was having a profound effect. It was with a husky voice that Nelson agreed his indiscreet officer had been right.

When he awoke, Emma was gone, habit ensuring that he was the first guest in the Villa Bastioni to be up and about. Tom Allen found him, as Emma had, in candlelight at his desk, writing. He had opened and reread the letter to Fanny, first having read her missive from home in which she related, among news of family and friends, that he was the most famous man in England and that his name was on everyone's lips. She had been showered with visits and invitations from the great and the good, all eager to touch his glory by association, and had even been to court where the King had been very kind.

It was the last part of her letter that alarmed him: Fanny had stated her intention of exercising the right of an admiral's wife to be at her husband's side on foreign service. The misery of being apart was too much to bear, the thought that he might do something that would take him into the arms of a loving God without her being able to gaze once more on his countenance. She was making plans to travel to the Mediterranean to join him, and had added a request that he might procure, for them, suitable accommodation.

The reply he had written before Emma came to his room had warned Fanny off such a move. He had reminded her that he was a serving officer at the mercy of a commander and government that might send him in all directions, that she might arrive only to find him ordered home. He did not want Fanny out here, fussing and worrying.

But he rewrote his letter with more insistence, instructing her – damn near ordering her – to stay put, and to look for a house in England suitable to their rank and station. Whatever doubts he had harboured about their union over many years were laid to rest: he had found what he knew to be true love.

Fanny was his wife, and as such she had to be accorded all respect. She would have his name, his title, and a reflection of his glory. When he was back in England he would live with her as her husband in whatever accommodation she found. But his heart was elsewhere, and far from feeling unhappy about this, Nelson realised he was entirely at ease with it.

Tom Allen approached the task of shaving his master with some trepidation, since he knew what had happened the day before and last night. But as he looked down into the smiling face, he relaxed, and began to burble away in his customary manner about matters inconsequential.

13

It was a less sanguine admiral who prepared to meet the eyes of the rest of the household over breakfast. Emma had been so indiscreet in her nocturnal meanderings that Nelson was sure that only a blind, deaf fool could have been unaware of what had happened. As if the fates were against him the first person he encountered was Emma's mother, in her usual housekeeper's garb, a huge new bunch of keys at her waist to replace those she had left in Naples. The thought of what she knew, which was everything, made him feel queasy.

'Good morning to you Lord Nelson,' Mary Cadogan said, with unusual gusto. 'I trust you had a good night?' Nelson saw the twinkle in her eye. 'I can assure you that Sir William slept the sleep of the just,' she added.

When he smiled, so did she, although he was unaware that Mary Cadogan's motives were more calculating than his. It was in Nelson's nature to be friendly with people. Emma's mother, in the light of recent events, reckoned she should be a mite more pleasant to Lord Nelson. She was still concerned about his suitability and Emma's security.

'I'm glad to hear my host enjoyed a peaceful night,' Nelson responded, thinking that with those words he had entered fully into the intrigue.

Mary Cadogan chuckled, salaciously, which bounced off the walls of the long passageway that led to the main reception rooms. 'When a man reaches his advanced years, for all he's a sprightly cove, a good night's rest is something to savour.'

Nelson managed an embarrassed laugh, then took refuge in the safest of topics. 'At least the weather has eased.'

'Thank Christ,' Mary Cadogan replied, blissfully unaware of the blasphemy. 'That wind had my chaps red raw. Never did I think I'd need to put goose fat on my lotties in these climes.' She shook her ample breasts, leaving Nelson in no doubt as to what she meant. He laughed inwardly: a sense of vulgarity must run in the family. Emma sometimes shocked him with her open way of referring to her body and his. But he loved it too.

Sir William stood up from the breakfast table to greet him with a wide smile, and the knot of anxiety in Nelson's breast loosened. 'The weather has turned, my dear fellow,' he cried, linking an arm and leading Nelson to an open window. 'And my bones no longer ache.'

Together they stood by the window, gazing out on a calm sea, which, if it wasn't the blue of a summer's day was very different from the dull grey, choppy mass of the previous weeks.

'That damned *tramontana* cast me low, Nelson. I feared to raise my head of a morning only to hear more bad news from the King's ministers. But the southerly wind is with us, and the heat of the North African plains will warm our blood. Perhaps it will stir something in these supine Neapolitan breasts as well, so that we can begin to put right all that has passed to mortify us this last month.'

It was easy to see that Sir William was being deliberately hearty, since such behaviour was not a normal component of his urbane and cultured nature. Was he trying to tell Nelson, in his own way, of his acceptance of the situation? If he was, then Nelson was prepared to take it at face value. Within a minute they were sitting at the table, talking like the two friends they had always been.

'Oh! The news is mixed,' said Sir William, when Nelson enquired of the latest despatches from the mainland. 'Cardinal Ruffo and his band of ruffians have enjoyed some success, and that will lift the mood of the court. But Commodore Caracciolo's behaviour will erase that.'

To Nelson's lifted eyebrow, Sir William continued, 'He asked permission of the King to return to Naples to protect his estates from the French. He landed, met Cardinal Ruffo, declined an invitation to join his army and went north. We have had word, as yet unconfirmed, that he has gone over to the Republican cause.'

Nelson recalled the morose countenance of the Commodore both on arrival in Sicily and on the various occasions he had seen him at the Colli Palace: squat, square of face, swarthy with piercing eyes. As he gazed upon his king and queen there had been no love in his face. Now, to Nelson's way of thinking, Caracciolo had seemed a man who felt himself betrayed, and was conjuring up reasons to justify an act that others would see as treason.

'It is to be hoped that the rumour is untrue,' added Sir William, 'for if Caracciolo has defected it bodes ill for the reconquest of the King's dominions. It is on men like him that the royal couple must rely.'

'I would not place too much weight on the likes of Commodore Caracciolo, Sir William,' Nelson replied, with some asperity. 'You are in danger, if you do, of sharing the high opinion he has of himself.'

Others joined them for breakfast, Sir William repeating to each new arrival what the change of weather had done for him. He was looking forward to another day's hunting, and pronounced himself certain that court mourning should be suspended for the deleterious effect it was having on morale. He abjured everyone to be a philosopher and accept whatever fate threw their way, oblivious to the fact that the admonishment flew in the face of his own recent behaviour.

Perhaps it was the change in the weather, but Nelson, too, felt different, and as he boarded his flagship his step was lighter. However, there was the usual mass of correspondence to deal with, and money matters to sort out with John Tyson. A fleet could not run on air and Nelson needed money, a great deal of it, to keep his command supplied, and it was Tyson's job to ensure a steady flow. In a war-torn world where armies and fleets competed with governments for coin, it was in short supply. Nelson lamented that with the treasures of Malta and the money Bonaparte needed to pay his army on board, there had been enough on the sunken *L'Orient* to keep him supplied for a year.

'Ships carrying money and the like should fly a special flag, Tyson saying, "do not sink me",' Nelson moaned, as he studied the state of the accounts.

Tyson shook his head at a man who seemed unaware of the greed of many of his fellow officers. Nelson could not fathom that there were captains who would let a whole fleet go to secure a Spanish plate ship. He merely informed Nelson of his efforts to raise coin from sources close by and from England, it being his job, also, to ensure that every penny pledged was properly accounted for: his personal credit was at stake and he operated for his profit on a small margin. A minor error in the accounts might be picked up by an Admiralty clerk, which would cost him dear. A major miscalculation would see him ruined.

Nelson had to account for every pound spent, too, and there was always a difference between what the Admiralty considered proper expenditure and that which any admiral on station needed to spend.

With the well-being of his sailors his paramount concern, Nelson used money with a prodigality that prompted a steady flow of censorious correspondence. Sums expended months, even years before, in storms, battles or even on a calm day in port, had to be explained to an official who sat close by a fire at work and had his home to go to at night. That sailors at sea might want for some comfort was none of this fellow's concern.

'Lady Hamilton is preparing to come aboard, sir. Captain Hardy has undertaken to greet her on the quarterdeck.'

Immersed in his letters, the name shocked Nelson. He looked up at the midshipman who had brought the message, dying to ask him if Sir William was in attendance – but, of course, he could not be, or his name would have been announced. No one else had been announced either, which implied that Emma had come alone. Why had Hardy sent for him so swiftly? He looked at Tyson, who seemed intent on keeping his head down, like a man who knew something and feared eye contact. Nelson grabbed his hat and left. Tyson exchanged a glance with Tom Allen, which confirmed for him the truth of a rumour that had been flying around the fleet since before they left Naples.

That every man aboard was privy to that rumour was obvious as Lady Hamilton made her way up the companionway to the quarterdeck. As always aboard a square-rigger tied up to a mole, a mass of work was being carried out. Blocks and pulleys were being greased, ropes spliced or replaced, sails hung out to air, men below with vinegar soused the 'tween decks, with hatches open to let in some air. Under the supervision of the gunner, the cannon and the gun carriages were being serviced, while other men worked on the breechings that held them to the side of the ship. The carpenter and his mates were hacking out damaged wood and replacing it with new timber. Men were over the side with paint, the smell of which mixed with the tar used to caulk new planking, crane parties were hauling aboard supplies while water barrels were being scrubbed clean for refilling. The pace of that work slowed perceptibly, since everyone had one eye cast towards the quarterdeck to see Captain Hardy and the officer of the watch raise their hats to the visitor. When Nelson came on deck, his haste to greet the lady was plain to see. His sailors were too shrewd to murmur approval when he, hat off, kissed her proffered hand, but there were many satisfied sighs and nods – mixed with the odd snort from those who saw a broken commandment.

'Lady Hamilton,' said Nelson, 'you have come alone?'

Emma spoke in a clear voice, easy to hear over what was now a silent ship. 'I need neither companion nor chaperone to visit such a close friend.'

Suddenly the air was full of shouting as the officers, petty, warrant and commissioned, realised that HMS *Vanguard* was quieter than a church hosting a funeral. Now each worker sought to assure those in authority that if all the other fellows had been curious, he had not, which created a great babble of noise that made Nelson laugh.

Hardy was blushing, while the officer of the watch made himself as frantically busy as everyone else close by: they all wished to pretend they had not seen confirmed what they had all suspected. Nelson might not be a good reader of social signs ashore but he knew his sailors too well to be fooled. What he had thought secret had been, if not common knowledge, certainly a shared suspicion.

Emma leaned a fraction closer. 'Have I missed something, Nelson?'

'No, my dear,' he replied in a soft voice. 'I fear you have just confirmed something.'

'I should be angry with you, Emma. You were flitting about last night in the most obvious way and you must have considered the consequences of coming aboard my ship without a companion.'

She was lying along the cushions on the footlockers, her head in his lap, looking up, green eyes squinting as the sun sparkled on the panes of the casement windows. 'Why consider what I do not fear to be known?' she asked.

'Discretion?' he asked.

'Is for mere mortals, not the Hero of the Nile – the Hero of the Nation is nearer the truth.'

'Please!'

She sat up, her face close and level with his. 'You are that, Nelson, though it does you credit that you seem to be the only man unaware of it.'

Nelson wanted to admonish Emma and tell her that what might pass in the confines of a villa would not pass in the street or on a naval deck. But what he had sensed on his own deck not ten minutes before prevented that. Though he could never be brought to admit it, Nelson had a preternatural knowledge of mood, a most essential attribute in a commander. He could sense discontent merely by walking the deck: it was in the cast of a shoulder or the avoidance of an eye, in the bearing of a midshipman or ship's boy. A happy ship was a fighting ship and, while he would not step too far outside the rules of his profession, he was prepared to push them to whatever limit was required to look after his officers and crew. There was a warm glow in his breast at the thought that his men were pleased for him. There would be those not happy, men who hated the sin, but he had felt a wave of affection at the moment he had kissed Emma's hand.

'It is not uncommon,' Emma asked, 'for officers to have their wives aboard, is it?'

'Unusual, my dear, but not uncommon. Thomas Freemantle rarely sails anywhere without his beloved Betsy.'

'A lady who is young and lively?'

'Very! A beauty and a favourite of every officer who knows her husband.'

Her face was very close to his now. 'I was just wondering . . . Where do they . . . Captain Freemantle and his Betsy . . . you know . . .?'

'Emma, you are shameless.'

She giggled. 'I do hope so.'

An hour later, dressed and with all repaired, Nelson and Emma strode the decks as he explained the function of each article needed in the construction of a fighting ship. As he talked, or introduced her to some sailor or petty officer, Nelson watched their faces, pleased that there was no hint of a blush anywhere. He was used to the way the midshipmen dogged his footsteps, but the open admiration for Emma in the faces of these boys cheered him.

A woman who had never lost sight of her original station in life, Emma was not the type to play the *grande dame*. In fact she had the same ease in common company as Nelson, and beauty enough to win over anyone whose heart might waver at the thought of her being their hero's paramour. Thus their progress was one of pleasant asides, smiles, much doffing of sailors' caps and officers' hats.

The fellow stapled to the foredeck by locked leg irons had such sad eyes that he touched Emma's heart and she pleaded for him to be released. Nelson pointed out quietly that he had no rights in the matter, that discipline aboard his flagship was the province of Captain Hardy and his officers. Also, he had no idea what the miscreant had done. It was some minor offence for sure, like getting drunk or losing his hammock: Thomas Hardy was somewhat stricter in matters of discipline than Nelson, and did not shy from rigging the grating for a flogging as often as he considered it necessary.

'Then I shall ask Captain Hardy for clemency,' Emma insisted. 'I cannot abide that on a day when I am so happy anyone should be in discomfort.'

Nelson stopped and said, with some force though he was still smiling, 'My dear, you must have a care not to let the kindness of your heart take you into such an area. By your beauty and nature you will place a burden of reaction on Thomas Hardy that will lead only to resentment. Not from Hardy, I think, for he is so very fond of you, but other minds will not be so well disposed.'

Looking at Nelson Emma understood that he was talking less about Hardy than himself, saying that in matters naval she must not interfere.

'You have seen a man flogged?' Emma asked, as he took her arm to lead her away from the unfortunate sailor.

'More than once I have ordered it, my dear, but only as a final sanction. It is a device of discipline that I dislike. It tends, I believe, to make a good man bad and a bad man worse. There are many officers who share my view yet more who do not. You know Tom Troubridge as a gentle soul.'

'A touch humourless,' Emma interjected, though she added hastily that she was fond of him.

Nelson grinned. 'He is a serious sailor, and that makes him somewhat dour ashore. And there is also his recent loss, for he was devoted to his wife. But Tom is also a ferocious captain who will not tolerate dissent on his decks. When the cancer of mutiny spread from England to the fleet he was at the vanguard of the hangings that saw it squashed.'

'You have never hanged a man?'

Nelson stopped and looked at her. 'With God's good grace, Emma, I have never had the need.' That was a subject too melancholy to dwell on, so Nelson set himself the task of restoring the previous mood, helped by the attitude of the crew.

The carpenter, repairing damage from the storm that brought them to Palermo, was eager to let Emma ply a saw. The gunner, normally a most capricious and temperamental cove, welcomed Emma into his screened-off lair, lit only a by a lantern shining through a glass panel in the bulkhead that ensured the flame could never reach the powder. Few were admitted to this den, though Nelson was always welcome. Emma was shown the various grades of gunpowder, invited to smell them crushed to pick up the odour of saltpetre. Given a charge to make, the gunner pronounced that she had a natural eye for measure. Sailmakers stitched for her, ropes were specially spliced and knots created, and Nelson bemoaned in good humour the loss of an arm that made it impossible to compete. Men who had known him with two arms attested to their admiral's old skill.

Emma, observing the attention of the men when it shifted from her to him, was sure she had never seen anyone so elevated converse so easily with the commonalty. Sir William was urbane, gentle and kind, and very good with his people, but there was never a hint in his aristocratic behaviour that the relationship was anything other than that between master and servant. But Nelson was different. In his case it was not *noblesse oblige*: he was one of them. Take away the blue coat, the gleaming orders and the hat, and there would have been nothing to tell you that he too was not a common sailor. Though they had a care to be polite, Emma got no sense from his men that they felt they were talking to anyone other than a professional equal. They even joshed him gently, or shared a well-worn joke. Loving him, she had never doubted his qualities as a leader; observing this she felt he could never fail, for these men would never let him down.

Nelson could not recall ever having been so happy. It was as if he had changed places with some other man, so different were his feelings about everything: his duties, the problems of the Mediterranean command, his relations with his commander-in-chief, the Admiralty and government at home.

Ashore it was the same, with everyone accepting quickly the status of the pair. It was just taken for granted that they were lovers and that Sir William knew it. Throughout January, Nelson was struck not by the change in people but by the lack of it. The Queen was just as effusive in his presence, insisting that he was the only one who could restore her to her rightful station. The King noticed little that did not relate to his own concerns.

As a full member of Sir William's household, Nelson learned to relax. He entertained in the company of the Hamiltons as though he was as much the host as they, and watched as Emma played cards well into the night, at which she won and lost prodigious sums that he had either to lend or hold for her.

While still eager to defeat the enemy he knew that he had done, for the moment, all that he could do: without soldiers he could not recapture either Naples or Malta. His cruisers, British, Portuguese and a few loyal Neapolitans, were at sea, ensuring that the shipping lanes were covered to strangle French trade, and that any French warship that ventured out would therefore meet a force large enough to destroy it.

At night, he and Emma retired to bed where, to his delight, her passion increased. He could not and would not explain to her how her ardour pleased him. As a shy man, to have the burden of initiation removed was bliss. He had always been easily rebuffed, especially by Fanny. That was never the case with Emma.

For Emma, marriage to Sir William had entailed duties, pleasant enough but rooted in a degree of practicality, but with Nelson she could recall the excitements of her youth. She could not get enough of him: his company, his gentle wit, his forgiving nature – for she knew that she sometimes overstepped the bounds of good taste – his naked presence.

Like any lovers, a great deal of their conversation was inconsequential, yet physical. Familiarity brought with it an intimacy of mind, the beginnings of a private language, an awareness of desires unfulfilled, not least Nelson's to be a father. Emma did not make an issue of her craving to oblige that, but after six weeks of close company, Nelson knew that she had abandoned all attempts to avoid a pregnancy.

Emma was thrilled that when she talked he listened to her. Nelson, the most powerful man in the Mediterranean, lionised by his fellow countrymen and foreigners alike, from the lowest to the highest, discussed his most pressing concerns with her. The Queen – who had lost most of her power to her husband and ministers who seemed to blame her for the loss of Naples – had come to depend on Emma more than ever. Now she acted as a conduit between Nelson and Maria Carolina to ensure that Nelson knew of every stratagem hatched by Ferdinand and de Gallo.

Gifts and praise poured in from foreign courts. Disappointed that his request to London regarding recognition of Emma's services had been ignored, Nelson was delighted when the Tsar of Russia bestowed on her the Order of St Catherine. This came with a jewelled cross that Maria Carolina pronounced a sad affair: to prove her own attachment to Emma, she had it reset with precious gems, and Emma wore it at her neck with pride.

On her advice, Nelson, despite initial unease, had taken to wearing his *Chelenk* in his hat. The plume of triumph glittered mightily in the Sicilian sun, and gave him an exotic air to go with his surroundings.

Emma was Cleopatra to everyone in the fleet, most happy, others less so. Some were furious, even if they were well disposed to her, convinced that the association would tarnish Nelson's reputation. Yet another group cared nothing for that reputation, or for Emma, and letters winged their way back to England, to become part of a tale that would not rebound to the credit of the man who had thumped the French.

For Emma and Sir William trouble emerged with the sudden arrival of a Mr Charles Lock and his wife, Cecilia, daughter of the well-connected Duchess of Leinster. Without much wealth, Charles Lock was a man in a hurry who made no secret that he had designs on Sir William's position as ambassador, a natural step up from his present appointment as Consul General to the Court of Naples. But natural only if Sir William retired, on which he was rumoured to be keen. Emma knew how her husband wavered, depending on his increasingly volatile moods. One minute he would proclaim his intention to stay in harness till the Grim Reaper took him, the next that if Naples ever again became a place of peace he would live out his life there in retirement. At other times he would damn Italy and all its works, then declare that he would go home to England within the month.

Good manners forced Sir William to accommodate Lock, along with his wife, two children and dog. As a guest in the house Lock picked up on his host's indecision, and interrogated the servants for their views. The vagaries of this left him in an agony of frustration, which manifested itself in attempts at irony so inept that Emma found him tiresome. Less diplomatic than her husband, she made it very plain that she did not like him.

The wife was sweet-natured enough, but rather feeble and prone to faint at the sight of blood. An envoy arrived from the Sultan and, on seeing Nelson's *Chelenk*, immediately prostrated himself, as was the custom at the court to which he belonged. A gross, ugly fellow he was subsequently persuaded by a flirtatious Emma that rum was not barred by his religion. In his cups he claimed to have cut off the heads of twenty Frenchmen with one blow, a feat so impossible as to be humorous. Encouraged by a laughing Emma, the weapon was produced, stained with dried blood, and Cecilia fainted when Emma, to the delight of the Turk, kissed it.

What to Emma had been a jest became, in the letters penned by Charles Lock that night, a sybaritic rite, one in which the evil Emma Hamilton, not content with an outrageous attempt to seduce the Mussulman, had communed with powers no decent Christian could abide. He also added that Lord Nelson seemed under the spell of this depraved creature, and that Sir William was an old, doddering fool, well past the labours required of his office.

Surveying his handiwork, Lock could take comfort in a good hour's work. No harm could be done to his prospects by tarnishing, at home, reputations that shone in the Mediterranean. And he could rely on his correspondents to share with all they met what they read from a good and trusted friend.

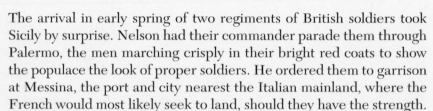

14

The arrival in early spring of two regiments of British soldiers took Sicily by surprise. Nelson had their commander parade them through Palermo, the men marching crisply in their bright red coats to show the populace the look of proper soldiers. He ordered them to garrison at Messina, the port and city nearest the Italian mainland, where the French would most likely seek to land, should they have the strength.

That looked increasingly unlikely. For all that Nelson thought Cardinal Ruffo 'a swelled up priest', the prelate was proving effective, commanding an army that now numbered some seventeen thousand. Ragged and disorganised they might be, but such a host struck terror into the hearts of the Republican sympathisers who had taken over the towns and cities of Ferdinand's domains. It was also an army that the French, much weaker in numbers, declined to meet in open combat, so it became a war of thrust and parry.

The whole of southern Italy was blood-soaked – little quarter was given by either side. The Army of the Holy Faith would take a Republican stronghold and exact horrendous revenge on those suspected of Jacobinism. Mass rape was common, as were hangings, quarterings, crucifixions, beheadings and burning, all the terrors of ancient sack. If they took those towns back, the French army then inflicted even worse punishment on those loyal to the King, leaving behind a desert devoid of human life. Needless to say, any Frenchman caught by the insurgents suffered a fate that rendered death a welcome release.

Elsewhere, the effects of Nelson's Nile victory were beginning to be felt. The Russians and the Turks had taken Corfu and were now masters of the Adriatic. In northern Italy Austria had moved, and the armies of the Emperor were inflicting defeats where Bonaparte had routed them three years previously. The Russians crossed from Corfu to Italy to support Ruffo, which made his army even more formidable, squeezing the beleaguered enemy back into a shrinking pocket of possession.

Troubridge sailed for Naples to take command there, immediately sending back news that all the islands off Naples had surrendered to the King. He also informed Nelson that he had several dozen prisoners who, it was claimed, were traitors, and added a request for Neapolitan judges to try them. Nelson obliged him, but later regretted it, given the nature of the justice meted out.

Trials were held at which the accused were neither represented nor present, where 'witnesses' could speak against the supposed traitors without the truth of their statements being checked. Troubridge was ordered to arrange hangings that he declined to undertake, suspecting that a great number of old scores were being settled under the guise of royal retribution. It had ended with Troubridge turfing the 'judges' off his ship, and refusing to be party to such a sham affair.

'Doubtless there is much to be desired in the way these matters are handled,' Sir William commented, on reading Troubridge's latest despatch, 'but I do think we must look to our primary aim.' That, he and Nelson had long agreed, was to get the King and Queen back to Naples. 'Not just to Naples,' Sir William insisted, 'but to a place in which they will be secure and the body politic stable enough to support the interests of Britain's policy.'

Sir William, Nelson noted, was in a positive mood, forceful in his opinions and clear as to his ambassadorial objectives. The evening before, at dinner, he had been distracted and feeble. 'You do not hold then with Cardinal Ruffo's suggestion of an amnesty?' Nelson asked.

Ruffo had written to the King to insist that the simplest way to retake Naples was to offer those who had espoused the Republican cause a pardon for their sins. His aim was to avoid a bloodbath. Edigio Bagio, the leader of the *lazzaroni*, claimed to have enough followers to cleanse the city. What Ruffo saw in this was a variation of the Terror that had gripped France: peasants would kill anyone of gentle birth, regardless of their allegiances, just as they had in the interregnum between Ferdinand's flight and the arrival of the French in Naples.

'Only a committed Papist believes in redemption through forgiveness,' said Sir William. 'I have rarely known a single blackguard change his ways through absolution.'

'Ruffo is a Catholic,' observed Nelson.

'He is also a cardinal, Nelson, not a simple priest, and should know better. Can we really hope that those who plotted against their King will settle for a restoration? They will not. They will plot and plan for their damned republic as they did in the past, treating again with our enemies, undermining the state, merely waiting for another opportunity to rebel – this time with more success in the article of regicide. We cannot always have a fleet in Naples Bay. Therefore we must root out the need.'

'And Troubridge's reservations about justice?' asked Nelson.

'Let the Neapolitans worry about the justness of what they do.'

Less formal discussions with Emma produced much the same response. She had passed through Paris in '89 and seen how the mobs controlled the streets, how they had been manipulated by clever men, who finally got the heads of their anointed sovereigns. For Emma the loyalty was personal as much as political: she was a partisan of the Queen, a friend to her children.

Nelson disliked treachery, and the society which Ferdinand and Maria Carolina had ruled was rampant with it. Many of the rebels had fawned upon their king and queen, had taken everything that royal generosity could bestow, only to turn on their benefactors for personal advantage. Officers of the army and the marine had sworn a personal oath to their sovereign only to break it. It was easy for him to understand the prevailing mood of the court, which was anticipation of a bloody revenge.

Ferdinand would not hear of an amnesty, waving an imaginary blade to lop off endless traitorous heads. If the judges he had sent Troubridge were hanging renegades, the only question arising for the King was this: were they doing it fast enough? Yet when it was mooted to him that he should return soon to Naples to oversee the recapture of the city, he fell silent.

Then news came from Troubridge that the French had abandoned Naples, leaving only a garrison at the most potent fortress, St Elmo. Almost simultaneously Nelson learned that a French fleet of nineteen sail-of-the-line had broken out from Brest, their supposed destination the Mediterranean, and the period of repose came to an abrupt end. The time had come to get back to sea.

What frigates Nelson had were sent to range far and wide, to look for the approach of the enemy. Despatches were sent to Cadiz to tell Earl St Vincent that he felt confident if the French did come he could defeat them. Meanwhile, shifting his flag to HMS *Foudroyant*, he would take station off Naples. Would the King take command?

It was left to the Marquis de Gallo to inform Sir William and Lord

Nelson that the King's Council felt it imprudent to risk Ferdinand's person, on which so many hopes were based, aboard a ship that might well see action. The reptilian de Gallo was as much a realist as Sir William Hamilton. He knew that it was in Britannia's interests to retake the city, which would be risky, even given Cardinal Ruffo's successes. The forts covering the bay were held by committed Republicans. Let Nelson succeed and Ferdinand would reap the reward. If he failed, the King would be absolved of blame.

'Of course His Majesty is conscious of what you do, Lord Nelson, and wishes you to know that he has complete faith in your abilities. Therefore he wishes to appoint you his personal representative.'

Nelson sailed with full powers to make peace or war, and to hang whomsoever he chose.

HMS *Foudroyant*, a dry, weatherly vessel, in much better condition than the battered *Vanguard*, led the fleet into the Bay of Naples. Nelson had aboard Hardy as his flag captain, Tyson, several officers and midshipmen, as well as Sir William and Lady Hamilton as interpreters. In the first week of June, the scene sparkled. Emma could believe, as she stood on the poop looking at the city, that it was as she had always known it. But the huge tricolour flying above Fort St Elmo disabused her of that idea; that and the gimcrack flag of what the rebels called the Parthenopean Republic flapping everywhere else.

The bay was full of boats, but only one took the eye, a splendid barge canopied in red, bearing a great white flag with a golden cross. There could be no doubt of whom it carried, and soon Nelson made out the arrogant figure of Cardinal Ruffo, sitting on what looked remarkably like a throne.

'I think we had best give our swelled-up priest a C-in-C's salute, Hardy. Thirteen guns, if you please.'

Sir William, standing next to Nelson, nodded sagely, knowing that it was wise to flatter Ruffo. The guns banged out, and Nelson imagined he could see Ruffo tallying them off on his fingers. The cardinal was piped aboard with all due ceremony, with smiles and greetings being exchanged. That mood was shattered by Ruffo's declaration that he had arranged a truce with the rebels.

'Then you must repudiate it,' said Nelson. 'You do not have the authority.'

'I cannot,' Ruffo replied sententiously. 'I have given my word.'

'Your cabin,' said Sir William, quietly, the maindeck of a ship being no place for such a discussion.

In fact, it was a full-blown argument, made worse when Ruffo outlined the generous terms he had granted the insurgents. These rebels were to be allowed two alternatives: they could return to their homes, as if nothing had happened, unmolested, and the King would ensure they remained so; in return they would swear once more to uphold the monarchy and abide by the laws of an autocratic state. Or they could take ship into exile, carrying with them all their portable property.

Nelson argued for several hours through Sir William, but he let the Ambassador point out the flaws in Ruffo's proposals: that Ferdinand would never agree to it, that Nelson, his representative could not approve it, and that the only reason the rebels were surrendering was because they lacked the force, without a French garrison, to do anything else. When Sir William tired, Emma took over, but there was no shifting the priest: his honour and word were pledged, and his principles of forgiveness invoked.

The way Ruffo talked it seemed as if the rebels were merely errant children instead of treacherous opportunists. He could not grasp that if they had taken the King and Queen they would probably have executed them, along with their grown-up children. Nelson preferred not to think about the infant child of the Hereditary Prince. No sensible sovereign, let alone a half-mad one, could live with such a threat hanging over his head.

'Tell the cardinal,' said an exasperated Nelson for the tenth time, 'that a few lopped-off heads will solve the business much quicker than all the overtures he makes.'

But Ruffo argued on, forcing Nelson to accept that the matter should be passed back to the King and his council to decide, and obliging him to accept that the truce was valid.

'I know his game,' Nelson opined, as the cardinal was seen into his barge. 'He hopes for a *fait accompli*.'

'Who is to say, Nelson,' said a restored Sir William, 'that he does not know his sovereign better than you or I?'

As expected Ruffo's amnesty was repudiated by the King, which put those who had accepted it in an impossible bind. The forts were no longer fully manned, for a goodly number of the defenders had sneaked out to their own homes. Faced with Ruffo's army and Nelson's fleet, those left had no option but to surrender. What followed was the full bloody revenge of the counter-revolution that Ferdinand had prophesied. Men who thought they had surrendered with the honours of war were imprisoned in disease-filled hulks or in the dank, rat infested dungeons of the fortresses they had so recently controlled.

The news arrived that Earl St Vincent had gone home through ill health, to be replaced by Lord Keith. The first despatch from his new commanding officer indicated to Nelson that the trust he had enjoyed until now, and the right to make his own dispositions, might be under review. Nelson could not be sure if strategic concerns or a desire to put in place an over-mighty subordinate prompted his new superior's views. All he knew was that they were wrong.

With the French in the toe of Italy, albeit tenuously, and Bonaparte still in Egypt, Nelson was sure the fulcrum of Mediterranean control still lay around the Straits of Messina and the seas between the African coast and the toe of Italy. Keith disagreed, and insisted it was necessary to subdue Malta. Nelson met that with a request for troops to carry out the task, it could not be done otherwise. Then Keith worried that the two ships that had escaped the Nile battle, *Le Généraux* and *Guillaume Tell*, which Nelson dearly longed to take, posed a threat out of all proportion to their strength, therefore Toulon must be blockaded. The notion that they might combine with the fleets of Spain and the French fleet supposedly making its way from Brest terrified Keith. Nelson was more sanguine, for he had met them and beaten them. Let them put to sea, was his opinion, because it was only there that they could be destroyed. He had arranged his fleet in Naples Bay to do two things: first to form a defence that no attacking fleet could breach, and second to lock in the still rebellious subjects of King Ferdinand. He declined to change that plan.

Ruffo's Army of the Holy Faith controlled the country around Naples, as well as the city, and a steady stream of captured rebels were brought aboard *Foudroyant* by the cardinal's ruffians. One prisoner, handled none too gently, was Commodore Caracciolo, no longer proud and disdainful but ragged, unshaven, dispirited and in handcuffs. Hardy, seeing a fellow sea officer in distress, and unaware that the Commodore had been dragged from a hiding place in a well, immediately ordered the handcuffs to be removed and put a cabin at his disposal with a sentry. Caracciolo needed protection from his own countrymen, who appeared to have administered a sound beating before handing him over.

Arraigned before the officers Ferdinand had sent along for the purpose, the Commodore swore that his sole intention in leaving

Sicily had been to see to his estates; that he had been forced to take command of the rebel marine, and that even when he had fired on his own one-time flagship *Minerve*, he had had no choice. The majority of his six judges did not believe him, and Caracciolo was swiftly condemned to be hanged.

The execution was Nelson's to approve or commute, he being the King's representative. It was his own dislike of the man that made him hesitate, the memory of his arrogance. Caracciolo had resented the flight of the royal family from Naples in a foreign ship, was that the cause of his disaffection? Nelson turned to the two people aboard whom he trusted to advise him.

Emma was troubled. She was no partisan of the Commodore, but she had a mental list of those who had rebelled, many of them personal friends and former guests at the Palazzo Sessa. She had no idea if they were still in Naples, or if they had fled. But it was certain that if they were taken, they would suffer a similar fate. Sir William seemed unconcerned: his own mind was fixed on what he called 'the necessities': a stable kingdom that could take due part in the war against the French. For that, rebellion must be punished with full rigour. Clemency would only be construed as weakness.

Nelson had never hanged a man, though he had seen it happen after the mutinies of '97 at Spithead and the Nore. Some of that discontent had spread to infect St Vincent's fleet, and the old Admiral, Sir John Jervis before his peerage, had reacted with a swift harshness that many of his captains admired, stringing up several malcontents after a short trial. But that fleet had been in sight of the enemy: they were just over the horizon, armed and in well-found ships. He could have faced battle at any minute, and that had taken precedence over everything else. Nelson knew that most of his officers would not hesitate: Hardy and Troubridge would have signed without asking a soul.

In the end, what moved his pen was the knowledge that, though he might be the King's representative, he was not empowered to interfere in an internal matter. Caracciolo's Neapolitan peers had condemned him. All a British admiral could do was confirm the sentence, state that it should take place at five o'clock in the evening – and attend it.

It was a dishevelled, shambling figure that came on to the deck of *Minerve*, hands and feet secured by chains, a priest beside him murmuring a steady incantation for his soul. Every Neapolitan officer, including the men who had judged and sentenced him, were also on that deck, some to whom he had once been a commander. Alerted to what was about to happen, *Minerve* was surrounded by boats full of silent spectators. Aboard HMS *Foudroyant* the sides and rigging were lined with Hardy's crew. The chains were struck off, and Caracciolo's hands were bound behind his back, as his eyes raked over both his accusers and the man who had signed his death warrant.

Gently the Neapolitan sailors led him to the scaffold, for it was no part of their nature to be unkind to a condemned man. Too many of them feared death to do other than sympathise with their old commander. Placed on a platform that projected over the side of the ship, Caracciolo was afforded another chance to discomfit Nelson, who, not wishing to look at the man, took refuge in examining the Italian officers. He saw in their eyes an almost malignant glow of satisfaction. They had fled with their king, abandoning homes and possessions; this man was to pay the price for their discomfort and they were happy.

Caracciolo was offered a cap to place over his head, which he declined. All watching could see in his black eyes that he was determined to die looking at men he despised. A gun was fired as the noose was placed round his neck, pulled enough to grip without being tight. The men who would hang him stood ready, in their hands the end of the rope that ran up to a well-greased block on the yard high above. Then the second gun banged out.

The sailors steadied themselves, then ran barefoot along the deck, rope over their shoulders, hauling the jerking body into the warm summer air. Nelson saw Caracciolo's feet kick out at the nothingness beneath them, and the face suddenly suffused with blood. The tongue shot out of his pain-filled mouth as the noose cut off both air and the ability to scream. The man's feet performed a frantic dance for more than a minute before the final spasms racked him. Then he was still, no more than a lifeless bundle twisting on the rope, moved by the breeze.

Nelson ordered the body to be cut down at sunset, less than two hours hence, so that at least the man would be given a decent burial. Ashore, he knew summary trials and executions were taking place, as the full force of the counter-revolution exacted its revenge.

The arrangements aboard *Foudroyant* were more circumscribed than they had been ashore. Sharing a bed with Emma was impossible in a ship of war ready for action. Certainly Nelson had ample space, but he also had a flag captain, Sir William Hamilton and a steady stream of Neapolitans begging temporary accommodation. Time alone with Emma was limited, although, as in all history, the lovers found the means to be together.

This required much use of the blind eye not only by Sir William but also by Tom Allen, John Tyson, Thomas Hardy and every officer on the ship. And the matter was no secret to the common seamen who remained aboard. In the main they were not as accustomed to Nelson and his ways as the old Agamemnons or the men who had served on *Vanguard*, so a certain amount of ribaldry was to be expected whenever Emma appeared. Those who had served with the Admiral before saw it their duty to put in their place these new-come upstarts, and if that took a clip round the ear, so be it.

Giddings was the handiest in that department. He might be getting on a bit but he was still a proper hard-case, as many of the *Foudroyant*'s crew found to their cost. But what made Giddings's view prevail was not fisticuffs but the nature of Nelson and Emma. They were so obviously happy in each other's company, their relationship lifted the spirits of everyone aboard ship. Nothing could seem more natural in a beautiful sunlit bay, with matters proceeding well ashore, than Lady Emma Hamilton playing her harp on the dappled quarterdeck, while the Admiral paced, listened and occasionally stopped to admire.

It was hard to admire a monarch like King Ferdinand who, when he finally came to Naples, took up residence in Nelson's flagship and refused to set foot ashore, where British sailors and marines, aided by the Russians and Edigio Bagio's *lazzaroni* had laid siege to Fort St Elmo. Instead, he held his royal gatherings on *Foudroyant*'s quarterdeck. Those who visited him looked exactly like the courtiers who had fawned on him before he fled, and Sir William pointed out to Nelson several of the nobility whom he suspected to be less than wholehearted monarchists.

The meetings took place to the background boom of siege cannon playing on the walls of St Elmo. Less frequent was the crack of signal cannon as hangings were carried out on the Neapolitan ships. But the routine of a British man o' war went on. Hammocks were piped up each morning; decks were wetted, sanded, holystoned and flogged dry. Boats plied between ship and shore carrying ammunition and men. And Nelson was still to be found each morning pacing his quarterdeck, head bowed, gnawing on professional and private concerns. Was he right about the Brest fleet? What would they think in London of his actions, and his questioning of Lord Keith's orders? What was he to do about his wife?

'Sir.' Nelson looked up to see Pasco, looking bewildered. 'There's a fisherman come alongside, and from what one of the local marine officers tells me he is ranting about Commodore Caracciolo having risen from the sea bottom to come in on the tide and get his revenge.'

'Nonsense.' growled Nelson, then seeing Pasco's face fall, he added, 'forgive me.' The lad was only conveying what he had been told to impart.

'The King has been informed, sir.'

'Not by you, I hope?' asked Nelson, grinning. The thought of Pasco barking out such news to Ferdinand amused him.

'No, sir, by his own fellow. The one who translated the fisherman for me went to tell him.'

By the time they made the main deck Ferdinand was there, questioning the near prostrate fisherman. Clearly what the man had seen had alarmed him because every sentence was accompanied by the sign of the cross, and a wild-eyed look at those who stood round him. Ferdinand was as superstitious as his subjects and was furiously fingering a green agate charm. The upshot was that Hardy, less than pleased, was obliged to raise anchor and stand out to sea so that the royal fears could be laid to rest.

The body bobbing in the water was unmistakably that of Caracciolo, and it looked as if his hands were still tied. The square head and firm jaw were recognisable, and the fixed stare seemed more threatening, the sea birds having pecked out his eyes. The noose that had killed him was still tight round his neck.

Ferdinand was mumbling prayers under his breath when Sir William came to the rescue: he pointed out that Caracciolo had only risen from the deep to beg his king's forgiveness for his treachery – that his soul would never rest in peace without it. Ferdinand swallowed the explanation whole and shouted a hasty royal pardon at the bobbing corpse, which seemed, by the touch of a wave, to bow in acknowledgement.

'Mr Pasco,' whispered Nelson, 'oblige me by getting that body out of the water as soon as we port our helm.'

'Sir.'

Nelson was angry with himself. He should have ensured that what he had assumed had been carried out. But he was even angrier with the Neapolitan officers who had committed what he considered an outrage. How could Christian men who had sailed with Caracciolo and dined at his table behave like that?

Pasco didn't relish the idea of touching the corpse, that was obvious by his look of distaste, so Nelson said, 'Tow the body ashore and find a priest. Then ensure the Commodore has a decent burial according to the rites of his faith.'

15

Fort St Elmo surrendered on August 1st, the anniversary of the Battle of the Nile, and so became the occasion of a huge illuminated fête to celebrate both the victory and the man who had brought it about. Twenty-one gun salutes were fired to honour both sovereign and British admiral, all the Neapolitan ships were illuminated and a specially constructed Roman galley was rowed round the bay carrying a portrait of Nelson at the stern. Both Nelson and Hardy anticipated that King Ferdinand would now go ashore to reclaim his kingdom. Instead, he informed them of his intention to return to Sicily.

A second despatch arrived from Lord Keith, to tell his junior admiral that he had been out of touch with the French Brest fleet for more than three weeks, and had no idea of its whereabouts. Every available ship was to proceed to Minorca, which he believed to be under threat. To Nelson this smacked of tactical nonsense, and he declined to oblige his superior. He suspected that the ships Keith was worried about were unlikely even to be in the Mediterranean, and that if they were, the only place they could be of any use to the French cause was where he was already, in the Bay of Naples.

Minorca, to his mind, was not as important as a whole kingdom, though he felt it prudent to write to Lord Spencer, as he had to Keith, stating that he was so sure of the rightness of his decisions, that he was prepared to take whatever opprobrium came his way.

They sailed back to Palermo, the King to his hunting, Sir William to the shocking news that his treasures, valued at ten thousand pounds, which he had sent home for sale, had gone down with HMS *Colossus* off the Scilly Isles, leaving him with only what he had rescued when they fled Naples. Nelson went back to Emma and to their communal existence in another rented villa, and to the permanent presence of Cornelia Knight who had lost her mother. The main task for all three was to console Emma's husband for the loss of his statuary and classical urns. Nelson also found out from Emma that Ferdinand, who had already presented him with a jewel-encrusted sword, intended to grant to him the Duchy of Brontë, an estate in the south of Sicily with an annual income of some three thousand pounds.

He was mightily pleased, and wrote home at once to tell Fanny that she was a duchess. From then on, his letters and despatches, the first of which was a description of the huge ball thrown in his honour, were signed, Nelson & Brontë.

On the morning after the ball Emma came aboard *Foudroyant*, this time in the company of Cornelia Knight, claiming that the heat of the town was too great, and only on a ship berthed in the outer roads could a body find a cooling breeze. No one batted an eyelid when she requested that a harp she had left on board be brought on deck for her to play, and men worked contentedly as she plucked a gentle air.

'Emma, my dear,' said Cornelia Knight softly, and pointed to a bruised looking midshipman who was hopping from foot to foot, clearly eager to talk to her.

'Mr Pasco.'

'I am flattered, my lady, that you remember me.'

Emma smiled, noting the lad's voice was rather thick, due to a swollen upper lip. 'How can I forget such a fine storyteller? Cornelia, you must get Mr Pasco to recount his version of the battle of the Nile.'

'If I could beg your indulgence, Lady Hamilton, I have a service to ask.'

'Mr Pasco, if I can do it, you may have it.' Pasco looked at Cornelia Knight, and Emma said, 'You may speak openly, for Miss Knight is my best friend.'

'The ball, last night, my lady.'

Emma suspected she knew what was coming, but thought to delay it a little so that Pasco might relax. 'A magnificent affair, was it not? The fireworks were outstanding. I particularly enjoyed the moment that Prince Leopold thanked Lord Nelson.'

Pasco had found that rather mawkish, the nine-year-old Prince placing a laurel wreath on an effigy of Nelson before naming him guardian angel to his family.

'Are you aware that there was some misfortune to do with the local gallants?'

'Who could not be, Mr Pasco? The noise was tremendous. I believe it drowned the orchestra.'

'It was not we mids who started it, my lady.' Pasco wasn't sure if that was the truth. He, and his companions, had been as drunk as lords before they ever left the ship. There was a Sicilian coster-monger who might still be looking for his horse and cart since they had commandeered it as soon as they got ashore. Their behaviour at the ball had been far from perfect, but no olive-skinned rascal, to Pasco's way of thinking, had the right to insult the women of his country, which is what they had done.

That a fight had broken out between the hot-headed young Sicilian noblemen and Nelson's midshipmen was not in itself surprising. Both groups were of an age to be bravadoes. But the locals had been armed, which obliged Pasco and his fellows to reach for their ceremonial dirks. Twenty mids against a greater number of blades had gone the British way, because they were all fighters by nature. The problem was that a local youth had been stabbed, this com-pounded by a musket-ball wound to one of the mids when the Royal Guardsmen intervened. They could hardly be blamed for firing, seeing as how the drunken mids had, with their knives still in their hands, charged them with a whooping war cry.

'I fear I am the culprit who wielded the knife too well, my lady, and I fear also that the fellow I stuck was badly hurt.'

Emma looked up at Pasco, at the fat lip and a yellowing eye. 'We enquired of the fellow this morning, Mr Pasco, and he is well on the mend.'

'Thank Christ,' Pasco exclaimed, then added quickly, 'saving your presence, ladies.'

'Is that what you wanted?' asked Emma. 'To enquire after the fellow's well-being?'

'Well . . .' Pasco hesitated.

'You will find, Mr Pasco, that if you want something, it is best to come right out with it.'

'I fear I have been brought up before Captain Hardy, who intends to lay the matter before Lord Nelson.'

Emma laughed again, which turned quite a few heads. 'I suspect, Cornelia, that I am about to be asked to intervene.'

Cornelia Knight pursed her lips. It was well known to her and every other British national in Palermo that Nelson had admonished Emma many times not to intercede in matters of discipline, just as she knew that Emma was forever doing just that. Everyone from a common seaman to a fellow like Pasco felt he could approach her to use her good offices, and it was also well known that Lord Nelson was like melted butter when Lady Hamilton asked for clemency.

'Lord Nelson has stopped leave for six months for all us mids, my lady,' added Pasco hopefully.

'How barbaric, young man. What will social life ashore be without your presence?' Emma was being sarcastic, and Pasco knew it. Midshipmen ashore in numbers were a menace: loud, brash and no respecters of local custom. But seeing the effect of her words she added, 'Leave it with me, Mr Pasco, and I will see what I can do.'

'I have asked you time and again, Emma, not to interfere in these matters. Hardy resents it.'

The truth that he did too was left unsaid.

'Oh, the Ghost, must I ask him? He will glower at me with those great fish-like eyes of his.'

'No,' Nelson said, knowing that Hardy would, for his sake, deny her nothing. If the ship's company ever found out that Hardy was susceptible to Emma's wiles there would be no discipline at all.

'So you will reject me?'

'I fear I must.'

Emma went easily into dramatic mode and she did so now, her voice changed to that of a supplicant waif. It was wonderful the way she could use her scarf and straw bonnet to create an effect of downtrodden poverty. 'Oh, sir, do with me what you will but do not 'arm them poor lads who don't know no better than to slash at a local who insults their womenfolk.'

'Emma!' said Nelson emphatically.

'You can tie me to a gratin' if you wish,' Emma continued. 'I care not if you rips the garments off my back, and goes to it with a whip.' She was behind him now, her hands over his shoulders. 'You has got a whip, your honour, I suspect, and I'm sure it be a terror to any young lass exposed to its ways.'

As her hands slipped down inside his waistcoat and her head rested against his, Nelson could smell her body. Much as he hated the idea that came into his head then, it was unavoidable. Cleopatra had struck again. Pasco would be forgiven, there was little doubt of that, and so, probably, would the other riotous mids. But would he ever forgive himself for being so weak where she was concerned?

Still, surrender was so pleasant.

His correspondence with Lord Keith was not going well. Though careful to be diplomatic, the despatches between the two admirals became increasingly terse as Keith sought to impose his authority and Nelson fought to maintain his independence of action. Nelson wrote often to the First Lord in London, well aware that his commander was doing the same, no doubt insisting to Lord Spencer that Nelson be either brought to heel or replaced.

The inferior officers, the captains of the men o' war, divided too, and for the first time Nelson sensed a hint of fragmentation in their loyalty. Knowing broadly what orders were coming from Keith at Cadiz and how Nelson was responding, they were conscious of the impact on their own careers. Some thought that his refusal to obey Keith had more to do with his relationship with Emma, and a number of captains, much as they liked her, saw her presence as pernicious. Set against them were officers who observed only the benign effect she had on their over-burdened commander.

Nelson alternately worried about it and dismissed it as none of their concern. Yet his stepson Josiah nagged at his conscience. Even though he was mostly at sea, his stepfather always knew where he was and that what had been disapproval in Naples was turning to something worse. It was a forlorn hope that Josh had not alerted his mother to the state of affairs in Palermo. The most painful moment came when Thomas Troubridge, fresh from the capture of Rome, felt that he had to tell his friend the error of his ways.

The interview started badly and what followed made it worse. By his own standards Troubridge was being circumspect, but he was such a direct fellow that what he saw as subtle could be, when spoken, damned rude. He had questioned Nelson's response to Keith's latest orders, pointing out that as a subordinate admiral he had little choice but to obey.

'Even if I disagree?' asked Nelson. He spoke without rancour, still with that well known half-smile, for it was one of the tenets of his method of command that no subordinate should fear to tell a superior what he thought. Nelson reckoned any number of battles that should have been victories had been lost by the silence of inferiors.

He was fond of telling his midshipmen the tale of the wondrous Admiral Sir Cloudesly Shovell, who had hanged a flagship master who had dared to tell him that the course he was steering was wrong and, worse, that he was not in the chart position he thought. The man was still swinging from the yardarm when Shovell ran his whole fleet into the Scilly Isles, losing dozens of ships, thousands of men, and drowning in his own intransigence.

'Perhaps, sir, it is a case you could put to him in person. Go and see Lord Keith.'

'I would waste my time by sailing for the Straits, and I would also leave matters here in a state of flux. A party around the King is urging him to sue for peace with France. The only thing that keeps him true to his alliance with Britain is our presence and protection. Take that away and . . .' Nelson left the rest hanging in the air. 'Believe me, Tom, I have it on the very best authority. My information comes from the Queen herself.'

'Brought to you by Lady Hamilton?'

'Yes.'

There was an awkward silence. Nelson knew that, much as he liked her personally, Troubridge did not approve of his liaison with Emma. Tom had always been upright to the point of obsession and, having just lost a wife of whom he had been deeply fond, was scandalised by what Nelson and Emma were engaged in.

'Are you sure, sir, that you are not being manipulated?'

'How so?'

'Are you being fed what the Queen wants you to hear, being advised of conspiracies that do not in truth exist?'

'To keep me here?'

'Yes,' snapped Troubridge, who had allowed the idea to raise the level of his ire. 'It gives me no pleasure, sir, to tell you that among a goodly number of your officers you are perceived to be unduly influenced.'

'The word "unduly" sits ill, Tom.'

Nelson's face had stiffened. But Troubridge had crossed a point where telling what he perceived to be the truth outweighed his sensibility to his commander's feelings. Old friend or not – hero or not – Nelson had to be told.

'You are seen, sir, to care more for our comfort than your duty to your King, more for the charms of Lady Hamilton than the defeat of the enemy. Do you not know that Lord Keith complains about you constantly to London? You are rightly admired, but I fear that you are dissipating that in the arms of a wholly unsuitable woman.'

'You will have a care, Tom,' said Nelson sharply. 'Do not assume that the liberties I allow you as an old friend apply to Lady Hamilton.'

'What of her reputation?'

'I will not deny she has one. But I would remind you that I was born the son of a far from wealthy parson. Nothing in my background gives me the right to sit here. I am in this place because of my own efforts to raise myself, that and the outstanding abilities of my officers and sailors.'

Nelson softened his voice. 'We all have a past, Tom, even you. Do you not lie awake at night sometimes, remembering an action of yours that brings a feeling of shame? Yet often what you recall was done in ignorance, caused by circumstance not malice. For that reason you can ask God for forgiveness. We do not, any of us, choose the course of our life. All we can pray for is that on Judgement Day the scales will tip away from damnation towards salvation.'

Troubridge was torn between trotting out a truth that would wound his old friend deeply, that Nelson was becoming a laughing stock, and staying silent. He would have avoided such an entanglement like the plague. Emma Hamilton had an engaging sense of fun, a lively intelligence and a fading beauty. He had even written to her to warn her that she had enemies. But she had manifest flaws, to Troubridge's mind, that totally outweighed her assets, the greatest that she lacked any notion of what constituted a sense of virtue.

Nelson could not see this because he was blinded to it, but she flirted with every one of his officers. Some would call it innocent: Troubridge saw it as an insidious attempt to command them as she commanded her lover. She drank too much and then what little self-control she had evaporated. The card games at the Hamilton villa had become notorious: Emma flinging money, usually Nelson's, around with abandon, losing regularly and laughing as she dragged her exhausted paramour, who had been yawning for hours, off to their shared bedchamber. Troubridge also felt that what happened behind closed doors between her and Nelson did little to aid clear thinking in the man he loved and esteemed.

And then there was her husband, smiling, telling jokes and anecdotes, ever the superb host, unconcerned that another man was rogering his wife. He could say all of this or nothing. He felt that what he did say was feeble in the extreme. 'Will you consider what I have said?'

'Yes, Tom, I will,' Nelson replied.

Both knew he would not.

Sir William had settled into a limbo, curious about the way he had taken to observing the two lovers, almost as if he was not involved. That Emma showed him respect in public was gratifying, but he worried that this did not extend too far into the evening. Too much wine made her tease people: it was uncomfortable to realise that he occasionally became the butt of her jokes.

Sir William's ambassadorial cares had multiplied since the arrival of Charles Lock, who sought to undermine his authority and gave what he called advice that sounded more like commands. The man's ineptitude was astounding. Presenting his papers as British Consul, Charles Lock had seen fit to lecture Ferdinand and Maria Carolina on the gratitude and duty they owed to England. That it was true did not make it a proper thing to say to reigning monarchs, who, discovering that he was connected by marriage to the rebellious Irishman, Lord Edward Fitzgerald, thought of him as a dyed-in-the-wool Jacobin before he ever spoke a word.

Pique at his reception by the royal pair redoubled the venom of his letters home, in which all the supposed failures of policy were attributed to Sir William's fading powers. And he did not fail to mention Emma and her affair with Nelson, asking how an openly cuckolded near-septuagenarian could possibly represent his country. Nor was he content to leave Nelson free of scandal, accusing him in writing of financial peculations that played well with the Victualling Board in London, always in dispute with far-flung admirals. In Palermo, when these insinuations came to light, Lock was forced to withdraw with a grovelling apology, but at home his letters added to the growing disquiet about Nelson's actions and activities.

To this were added the stories that appeared in the French press, fed by those in Palermo who disliked both Nelson and the English alliance. Reports circulated that the Admiral and Ambassadress haunted low-life taverns in the disguise of common seamen, with hints that they sought young male company to share.

To those who cared about Nelson, and who knew of these things, it was troubling that, as the year slipped to a close and a new century blossomed, their hero seemed unaware of any trouble he might be storing up for himself.

That Nelson had been proved correct about the French – that the fleet had returned to Brest, that no combination had been possible, that Minorca was safe – cut little ice with Keith. The position into which he had been thrust in taking over from the successful St Vincent and with the nation's darling as an inferior, exacerbated his irritation. The moment had come for him to look this trouble square in the face, and the opportunity presented itself when he was ordered by the Admiralty to proceed into the Mediterranean. But his dignity demanded that Mohammed come to him – after all, he was the mountain – so he ordered Nelson to join him at Genoa. The rich trading city was held once more by the French and the whole of north Italy stood in peril. Bonaparte had abandoned his army in Egypt and returned to lead the armies of the Revolution on the plains of Lombardy.

Keith knew he had to be careful: like every other senior officer he had his own troubles with the Admiralty, and he had good cause to be worried about his own standing while he had only limited knowledge of Nelson's. His greeting, in the great cabin of his flagship *Queen Charlotte*, though stiff, was polite, and his enquiry as to why his orders had been ignored posed as a query rather than as a demand for an explanation.

'You will be aware, sir,' said Nelson, 'of my view of the independence of inferior officers.'

Keith had to take a deep breath to stop himself choking on his own bile. He was a man who ruled his inferior officers with a rod of iron. No ship in his fleet was permitted to be an inch off station on his flagship, no officer allowed any autonomy in the matter of dress, orders, or of how his ship should be handled. The Beechey portrait that hung in his cabin, which Keith thought excellent, told all who treated with him of his acerbity: a frowning forehead over heavy brows, full cheeks and a ponderous nose over unsmiling lips, the tall, broad shouldered body leaning forward as if to impose.

He was trying, with a weighty look, to do that to Nelson now, and was aware that it was having little effect. The man before him was half his size, thin, tired looking and pale. He had a light voice, in contrast to Keith's booming gravel, and was festooned in the most vainglorious way with stars, medals and that Turkish thing in his hat. But just as he knew that Nelson should be intimidated, he was aware that he was not, which smacked of arrogance.

'Our task as fleet commanders is such an onerous one,' Nelson continued, 'because we cannot know all that we need. Like you, sir, I have had chimeras rear their head, fleets that turn out to be no threat, an evasive enemy that reports tell me is in three places at once or is not to be found at all. I cannot tell you how often I have heard that *Guillaume Tell* and *Le Généraux* are over the horizon, only to find they are snug in harbour. We operate, too often, in a fog.'

'Quite,' was all Keith could say.

'It has ever been my way, even when, as a captain, sending a lieutenant away in a prize, to ensure that they know they are free to act as they see fit. My instructions are general, in that I would like to see them safe in harbour, but not at the risk of passing up any opportunity that presents itself.'

That, too, was at odds with Keith's method: he gave tightly written orders that he expected to be obeyed to the letter.

'Before the Nile . . .' Nelson paused, to let Keith acknowledge that the battle had been special, which he did with a nod. '. . . in all my conferences I stressed that any captain sighting the enemy was not to wait for my signal. By covering I hoped, in discussion, all the alternatives, I felt I could trust them to do as I would in the circumstances.'

'You must be lucky in your captains,' said Keith, with what he thought was unmistakable irony.

Nelson missed it. 'That sir, has been my greatest asset. Captain Foley sailed inshore of the French at the Nile without any request to me for permission to do so. I point to the success of that as vindication of my way. Therefore you will readily understand that on receipt of your orders I applied the same principle, adding my judgement to yours.'

To damned well ignore them, thought Keith.

'I knew you would agree with my dispositions once you had a chance to examine them.'

The man's confidence was staggering and, to Keith, impertinent. He was tempted to tear a strip off Nelson, but good sense made him hesitate. He had already told everyone at the Admiralty that Nelson was a menace. He had seen the depth of Nelson's insolence now. In future he would word his orders to make sure that they must be obeyed, so that this pipsqueak could never wriggle out of doing as he was told.

Nelson was still enthusing about his officers: Troubridge who had taken Rome, helped by a division of Russians. Alexander Ball, who had been made governor of Malta, even although Valetta was still in enemy hands, Hardy, Foley and the others, so that Keith reckoned they must fawn on the man. Then it was the turn of the Hamiltons, whom Nelson could not praise enough, Sir William for his long knowledge of Italian politics, Lady Hamilton for her connections to the court, which meant that he, as an admiral, was always abreast of the thinking of Ferdinand's ministers.

Keith had heard rumours of the Lady Hamilton business, indeed he had even discussed them with St Vincent before the old rogue went home. Some said she ruled the fleet, that Nelson was putty in her hands. Worse, that the Hamilton woman was so enamoured of the Sicilian Queen that ships that should have been doing what Keith ordered were kept in waters that suited the Neapolitan cause. That he would stop.

'It is my intention to accompany you back to Palermo, Lord Nelson, so that I can form a personal impression of how matters stand there.'

Nelson's face stiffened. He had come all the way from Palermo to Genoa only to be told that they were going right back there, which to his mind was coming it pretty high. He was tempted to make some remark to the effect that St Vincent had been better in his manners. But the look on Keith's face stopped him: it was as if the fellow was hoping he would say something untoward. And Nelson had come to smooth troubled waters, not rough them up.

Nelson had not liked the sound of Keith from his despatches, and exposure to the reality had only served to confirm that. Even with his well-known habit of looking for the best in everyone, he could find little in this Scotsman's manner to enthuse him.

He would have been even angrier if he had been aware of Keith's thoughts which were, 'There you are, my laddie. For all your baubles and your dukedom, your self-importance and your Jacobin notions of how to handle a fleet, it is I who rule here.'

What Keith said was, 'My wife is with me aboard *Queen Charlotte*. She would be mortified if you failed to dine with us tonight.'

16

Nelson returned to the news that Sir William Hamilton had been recalled, that a new ambassador had been appointed and was on his way by frigate from England. This despatch cast gloom over the shared villa, intensified by the February weather and the dour presence of Lord Keith and his equally staid wife.

Sir William felt he had been swindled, never having asked to be retired. He had requested some leave, and failing that the Foreign Office could dispose of his post, but that was not the same thing at all. In his view it was a design to secure a plum post for Sir Arthur Paget, heir to the Earl of Uxbridge.

'Yet the notion has its attractions, Nelson,' said Sir William, when his friend had ceased commiserating. 'It will be of some comfort to treat and deal with people who have only one face instead of several. I have to say these Neapolitans have worn me down with their manoeuvres.'

'I don't want to go home,' said Emma, when she and Nelson were alone. 'I have become accustomed to life here.'

Home frightened Emma. It was no place of mists and mellow fruitfulness to her but a cold locale that spoke of standards more duplicitous than she had ever encountered in Naples or Palermo.

Nelson had told her many times that one day he, too, would be recalled, indeed he had asked for that on several occasions when the burden of the tasks that faced him grew too wearisome. He was at the disposal of the Admiralty, and no commanding officer was left in place for ever. In London there would be any number of rear admirals pursuing his post and they could not all be denied indefinitely. But when he wondered aloud what was to become of them, Emma had made him concentrate on the delights of the present. And Nelson had not the heart to insist they discuss the matter since it made her so miserable. Now she talked of being in England just long enough for Sir William to see to his affairs, his Welsh estates, collect the money owed to him by the Government, sell his remaining virtu, before they could return.

Sir William was no more insistent than Nelson that Emma look at the realities, but it would be impossible for his successor to feel secure if he was still in the Kingdom: Paget would see him as an alternative source of influence, and what he would make of Emma's friendship with the Queen did not bear thinking about. He would also struggle, without Government support, to maintain the style in which they had lived. Certainly they would be comfortable, but to a woman who had become accustomed to grand living and to being at the centre of affairs, that might appear as a comedown.

Maria Carolina refused to accept that her, 'dear Sir William,' should go home, and sent a messenger to London to request that he be reinstated. When Nelson sailed with Keith to look at the situation in Malta, matters were still at a stand.

The two admirals arrived off Malta to be greeted by the intelligence that the garrison of Valetta, close to capitulation, could only hope for succour from a convoy of supply ships that had already left Toulon. The sole capital ship escorting it was *Le Généraux*, one of the two line-of-battle ships that had escaped from the Nile. *Guillaume Tell* was locked up in Valetta harbour, snug under the guns of Fort Ricasoli, but rotting at its moorings and a prime target for a cutting-out expedition to every captain who could see her.

If there were two ships that Nelson longed to see with a British ensign above their colours, they were *Guillaume Tell* and *Le Généraux*, because they had fled Aboukir Bay. Objectively, Nelson knew that their captains had chosen wisely in leaving a scene of defeat, saving their ships for the future, but he wanted them badly because then the Nile victory would be total.

If Nelson had any doubts as to how he stood with Lord Keith he was soon disabused of them. Used to independence, it was galling to have to obey orders that he felt to be inappropriate. The landfall for the supply fleet was Valetta: they had nowhere else to go. By standing close to that harbour there was no doubt about the notion of interception, the only caveat being weather so foul that they could sneak in unobserved.

Keith sent Nelson off on a chase to intercept them in open sea, beating into the wind in foul weather. His blood was boiling with the certain knowledge that Keith was about the same sort of business to leeward, leaving the approaches to Valetta harbour unguarded. If the enemy convoy made its landfall, a whole year of siege would go to waste. The French garrison would be supplied with enough to keep them there for two more years.

As usual, when things were not going as he wished, Nelson spent every waking hour on deck. To the disgust of Tom Allen these were many, for disquiet ensured that Nelson could not sleep. He was jumpy, irritable and frustrated. He developed his usual raft of ailments over the three days and nights as he and the four line-of-battle ships he commanded beat into oblivion. He was close to a human wreck when the distant sound of gunfire came to *Foudroyant* through the fog.

'Gunfire, Mr Pasco.'

'I reckon it so, sir.'

Pasco had developed even in the short time Nelson had known him. His reply, which would have been tremulous a year ago, had been confident. Pasco had heard cannon fire, and he knew of what he spoke.

'Pray for the *Le Généraux*, Mr Pasco.'

'There's not a Nile veteran that doesn't every day, sir. We vie with each other to gift you that prize.'

Nelson was touched, and as he stared into the mist, he hoped that the wetness around his eyes was from vapour in the air. He was weary, of course, but he also loved the men with whom he served in a way that he suspected not even perspicacious Emma understood.

'Do you, Pasco, do you so?'

'Masthead, what do you see?'

That cry came from Sir Edward Berry, who had replaced Thomas Hardy as flag captain. Keith had put Hardy into another ship, a slack vessel that required his ability in the article of discipline. Berry had been with Nelson at both the battle of St Vincent and the Nile, his knighthood having come from the latter. He was a true fighter, and if there was to be an encounter, and Nelson prayed that there would be, the presence of Berry boded well.

'Line-of-battle ship, sir, going large on the starboard tack. She has a tricolour aloft. There's a hint of other ships in the offing but no clear way of saying what they are.'

'I would like to close with that ship, Sir Edward. I believe I may ask for the signal, general chase.'

'A signal to Lord Keith, sir?'

Nelson's mind worked on the relative positions of the two groups of ships, the weather, the wind, a fast piece of triangulation that produced only one answer. The signal could only be got to *Queen Charlotte* by a repeating frigate: she was too far off to see it in this foul weather.

'A waste, Sir Edward, we would put him to a chase for no purpose. Keith cannot come up on the enemy before we do.'

Berry didn't look at Nelson. He did not have to, having seen him many times change from weakling to ardent warrior in the wink of an eye. What he did know from the masthead observations was that the enemy had gone hard about and had put herself before the wind.

'A chance to show your mettle, so make *Foudroyant* fly.' As the mist lifted Nelson made two observations: one that the chase was very likely *Le Généraux*, the second that HMS *Northumberland* was in a fair way to head reaching the flagship. 'We will require to do better, Captain Berry. That ship must strike only to my flag.'

Berry was ruthless. Within minutes he had the fire engine playing to wet the sails, so that they would draw better on the gusting wind. Hammocks were removed from the leeward side and shot put in their place to right the ship. Wedges were knocked from the masts to give them play and finally Berry had the drinking water started over the side to lighten her. And slowly, almost imperceptibly, *Foudroyant* began to pull ahead of *Northumberland*.

Now that he could see her Nelson knew it was *Le Généraux*, and his blood raced. He was pacing up and down, his short stump working furiously, aware that the Frenchman had a fair chance of escape. Then the masthead called that a strange sail had appeared ahead of the chase.

'Demand her number!'

The flags flew aloft and were answered. 'HMS *Success*, milord.'

'Signal her to engage.'

'Tall odds,' said Edward Berry. 'Thirty two guns to face eighty.'

'They will do it, Sir Edward, mark my word.'

The truth of that was clear in ten minutes. The tiny frigate put herself across *Le Généraux*'s hawse and let fly with a broadside that, aimed high, took out all the canvas above the topsails. But the enemy was not to be tickled, and had let her head fall off just enough to return a compliment in double measure, and with guns of twice the calibre. Hardly an in-drawn breath was expended on *Foudroyant*'s deck as they saw the French guns belch forth, to envelop *Success* in a cloud of smoke and spray. When the smoke cleared there was the frigate, battered, but doing all in its power to continue the pursuit.

The task allotted to *Success* had been carried out: the chase had been forced to slow, and the damage the Frenchman had sustained aloft meant she could not immediately regain her speed. 'Success to come under our stern, Sir Edward, she has done well for her size, and the range tells me it would be worthwhile to try our lower-deck cannon.'

They were waiting below, guns loaded and run out, wedges rammed under metal to raise the elevation, the fingers of the gun captains twitching to pull on the lanyard that would fire the lock and send a thirty-two-pounder ball flying towards wood and flesh. Nelson felt the thunder of shot and recoil through his feet as they let fly, then watched as the great black balls flew over the enemy to raise great spouts before her dipping bowsprit, evidence that the range was excellent.

That applied to the Frenchman, too, who opened up on *Foudroyant*, sending a ball through her mizzen staysail that brought a light to Nelson's good eye. He called to Pasco to ask him how he rated the music as his ship and *Northumberland* closed on *Le Généraux*, who had no alternative now but to fight. Soon both British vessels were raking her with massive broadsides. Berry had gone for masts and yards, his consort for the deck, and both were accurate. The tricolour flag was half way down from the masthead before they could fire again, and Giddings was in a ship's boat, with Berry, heading for the defeated enemy deck to find a French admiral too wounded to hand over his sword.

'The convoy is scattered, sir, no more to be, which leaves Valetta in a sorry pass. I reckon we will have Malta complete in a month or two. Added to that, we have a fine large store ship full of everything from meat to brandy, which I suggest be spread through the squadron.'

Keith should have responded to that with appreciation, but he sat there, as he had throughout Nelson's report, stony-faced and silent. It was that lack of a signal, of course, which would only ever have been a courtesy. There was no way *Queen Charlotte* could have taken *Le Généraux*, but he was probably miffed that, out of sight of the capture, the officers and men of his flagship were out of the running for the prize money too. Keith would get his eighth of course, but that signified little in a situation where he felt that it was not a subordinate's job to assume anything. Nelson had left him out of the only action that was likely to be seen in these waters for quite some time, and pinned another laurel to his already overblown reputation.

'I said, after the Nile, sir, that should I take *Le Généraux* and *Guillaume Tell* I would be content to strike my flag.'

Keith continued to stare at Nelson with what appeared close to loathing. He had enjoyed a good career, if not a spectacularly successful one, yet now he was faced with a man who could toss off a line like that. And why did Nelson have to keep mentioning that infernal Nile battle, as if he was determined to emphasise his superiority?

'You cannot strike just yet, Nelson,' Keith said finally. 'I need you off Valetta. Perhaps with you there the French will give in a little quicker.'

'Captain Ball, sir . . .'

Nelson never got a chance to say that Ball deserved whatever honour came from a captured Malta, for Keith interrupted him. 'I will draw up your orders in writing. And I suggest that there are anchorages better suited to the task at hand than Palermo.'

Any lingering respect for Keith died in Nelson: it was no part of the man's task as a commander to tell him how to live his private life and his suggested alternatives as anchorages were merely a smokescreen for the intention to keep him apart from Emma. But he stayed silent, leaving Keith to assume that he would be obeyed. In the past he would have spoken up, and damned the consequences.

Troubridge protested furiously when, after only a few days beating to and fro off Valetta, Nelson told him that he intended to sail for Palermo. Keith's orders had been specific, but he had gone back to Genoa, to take station off a city now under siege.

More worrying to Nelson was the letter from an old naval friend at home, which he read in Palermo. Admiral Goodall sought to tell him that enough people knew of his relationship with Emma for it to be the subject of gossip. He advised Nelson to be content with what he had enjoyed, and draw away from his enchantress. To Nelson, she was that and much more, though less than happy at preparing to surrender her position to another at court. He sent Berry back to Valetta and hoisted his own flag in a transport, which Nelson declared to be about right, given the trust he enjoyed in higher quarters.

It was a sad day when Sir William Hamilton came to hand in his letters of recall. Thirty-seven years of diplomacy concluded in a scene where Maria Carolina shed a tear for her 'brave Chevalier'. This while the King looked vague, as if he could not comprehend a court without the Hamilton presence; hardly surprising since Sir William had been there before he had attained his majority and properly ascended the throne.

Nelson had *Foudroyant* back, plus the news that, in a hot action, Berry had taken the last French Nile ship, the proof of which was apparent. Part of *Guillaume Tell*'s figurehead now decorated his great cabin. Nelson knew for certain that his task was complete and that he would now be going home, but to ease matters for Emma and the unemployed Sir William he arranged a cruise that would take in Syracuse and Malta. Sir William loved a ruin, and the old Greek City of Syracuse was filled with traces of three thousand years of classical history. He went off with Cornelia Knight and several other members of the party, leaving Nelson and Emma alone. With the whole of the great cabin to themselves and a lookout who would give them ample warning of the party's return, it was possible to spend a day in each other's arms.

Off Valetta, their next port of call, *Foudroyant* got into a scrape when she dragged her anchor in a storm and found herself under the guns of the French defenders. The crew were treated to the spectacle of their admiral alternately angry and pleading with Lady Hamilton to leave the deck, with her refusing point-blank as his flagship and the enemy traded fire.

Emma did not budge as the cannon boomed and waterspouts soaked the deck. Her hair and face pitted with the burnt grains of powder blown back from the guns, Emma stood rocklike on the quarterdeck, proudly wearing her latest decoration from the Tsar of Russia, a ladylike diamond-studded cross, daring the French to do their worst.

Nelson knew that the island would fall soon and both Troubridge and Ball begged him to stay. He could not, for Ball had been there at the inception, and Nelson knew that if he stayed the capitulation would be credited to him. Let the man who had done the work have the glory, a man who was a friend to both him and Emma. Troubridge would garner some glory, too, and that was only right. But let the name of Alexander Ball forever be associated with the fall of an island that had proved impregnable to most invaders over centuries. Let him rank with Bonaparte.

To wish to go home and achieve it was no easy matter: the Admiralty had to approve, which took weeks. Sir William, likewise, could not just depart: he had an endless series of balls and banquets to attend in which he said farewell to all those whose position demanded it: the King and Queen, of course, but also de Gallo whom he hated, and Acton whom he liked. The latter had just married for the first time, by proxy to a niece not yet fourteen. No doubt the union had been prompted by the need to protect an inheritance than by any carnal passion, but Emma and Nelson spent a happy evening trying to imagine the consummation of such a misalliance.

Maria Carolina was going home too, to Austria, knowing that with her power so diminished in Naples, her presence there would not be missed. It was time, she told Emma, to introduce her younger children to a proper court. Besides, her girls needed husbands and if they stayed here they might end up in the marital bed of some Neapolitan nincompoop. Better to be in Vienna, at a court that knew how to arrange such things. That was not as easy as it looked, given that Bonaparte, now First Consul of the French Republic, was fighting to reverse the gains the Austrians and Russians had made the year before.

Only passage in a British man o' war offered security to a nervous Queen, although Keith had taken Genoa from the French. As her suite ran into hundreds, Nelson was obliged to send for another warship to transport them all, making swift passage to Leghorn before he went to join his commander-in-chief.

The farewells were attended by many gifts, the most valuable a diamond necklace for Emma. Nelson was unsure whether to be pleased or amused by a miniature of King Ferdinand, the surround for which the Queen had made herself. The parting was postponed after the news of the battle of Marengo, in which Bonaparte had routed the Austrians, forcing them to surrender the whole of northern Italy. The Queen, convinced that the people of Leghorn would take her hostage wanted to return to Palermo. Nelson and Emma persuaded her that they were anti-Jacobins, which was hard, but not as hard as having to disperse a mob that had gathered to defend Maria Carolina and monarchical rule.

Still she insisted on going home, but Keith, who must have had a fair idea of what was going on, sent orders from off Genoa that no British warship was to be employed to transport her. This annoyed Nelson, but sent Emma into a fury that someone who had been so loyal to Britain's cause could be so treated. Then Keith arrived in person to hold with Nelson another of those cold interviews that was the hallmark of their relationship.

'I have in my charge the best of what represents Naples, sir, and I feel it is certainly my duty, if not that of the nation we both serve, to secure the safety of those royal persons.'

'At the expense of our nation?'

'We stand in no peril at sea.'

'Do we not, Lord Nelson?' barked Keith, for once stung out of his habitual stony reserve. 'I would remind you that the enemy still has a powerful fleet.'

Nelson was equally sharp. 'In Brest, blockaded, several weeks away even if they could break out.'

'It will not be your reputation that suffers if they do, but I take your point.'

Nelson rehearsed every argument he had as to why Maria Carolina and her suite deserved British help and Keith refuted each one. Then Keith commanded Nelson to proceed to Spezia, an order which was declined, Nelson asking instead that he be allowed to strike his flag at once, a request which was granted without even the slightest show of reluctance.

When Nelson left, Lord Keith sat for several minutes, wondering if what he had done had been wise or foolish. Then he slammed his fist down on his desk and declared in a voice that could be heard in the tops, 'Lady Hamilton has had command of the fleet long enough.'

Nelson knew that Emma was nervous about going home, but her reluctance to travel by sea mystified him as much as it did her husband. Keith had offered him a frigate, and had accepted that it was only right and proper that a returning ambassador and his wife should share it. Now Emma was refusing point blank to travel by warship and insisted that they go overland, which from someone who was a good sailor was madness.

Nelson argued, Sir William cajoled, Cornelia Knight begged – the two latter had made that journey and knew how uncomfortable it was in peacetime, let alone in war. They would be obliged to travel through Austria and Germany all the way to the Baltic and take ship there. Only Mary Cadogan stayed silent, with a look on her face that implied to all who examined it that she was privy to information they were not.

Finally Emma was saved from the need to explain by the news that Maria Carolina and her daughters were to travel to Austria through Tuscany to the Adriatic, thence by ship to Trieste and on to Vienna. Her request for Lord Nelson and his party to accompany her was one that he could not refuse.

Emma thought she was pregnant. Although she had planned for it, she was shy of telling Nelson, uncertain of how he would react. What had seemed simple in its inception took on a new aspect in reality, and brought home to her once more that they were both married to others. Now, with this journey imminent, he had to be told.

'I wish you to be seated,' said Emma, when she had found a spot where they could speak, away from chattering princesses, Cornelia Knight and Sir William.

Nelson obliged, but a shaft of apprehension shot through him. She seemed nervous, twisting her fingers.

'You have said to me many times Nelson, that you long to be a father. I must ask if you still do?'

Nelson felt the need to be careful in the face of what must either be reluctance or the inability to conceive; he must reassure Emma, without in any way being false. 'I will not deny to you my desire to be the father of a child, because I would not lie to you. But be assured, my love, I would not press you to any inclination that did not make you happy.'

'Do you think of the problem of a child?'

Nelson smiled. 'What problem, Emma? It could only be by you that such a thing could come to pass, and if that happened it must be God's will. If it was a boy, what joy to take him to sea. If a girl, it must be another Emma. What rapture that would be!'

'Those are men's words.'

He looked at her quizzically then, seeking the thought behind the assertion, which could only be reluctance.

Seeing his crestfallen face, she had to respond. 'I am . . . I am near certain, with child.'

He was on his feet, touching her, before walking away to turn and look at her with amazement. He grabbed her and made her sit down, then knelt at her feet and pronounced himself the happiest man alive.

'You cannot stay here, you cannot go home, you must go back to Palermo,' he said.

'You would cast me aside.'

'Trust me, Emma, I will never do that. I think only of you, and now of the child within you.'

'Tell me again that you are happy, Nelson.'

'Look at me, Emma, and tell me how you cannot know that I am the happiest man alive.'

But behind the joy in his eyes lay a hint of anxiety. She had a pregnancy that would need to be disguised, and a birth that would have to take place with the maximum discretion, and it was something she knew as well as he.

'I fear I cannot advise you, my love.'

'I have a notion of what to do,' said Emma. As usual her mother had come up with the solution. Patiently she explained it to her lover, who nodded with a confidence he did not feel. 'And that, Nelson, is why we must travel overland.'

'Put both your hands in mine, Emma,' he said. 'Whatever happens, that is my child. For the sake of the unborn and you, all discretion must be shown. But should that fail, never fear that I will abandon you, Emma, for I will not.'

Sir William was angry with Nelson, because he had still hoped to persuade Emma to travel by sea. Now the man he relied on as his ally was waxing lyrical about the benefits of travelling overland: the way they would be greeted at the Austrian court, his desire to visit the states of north Germany, how his health, which had been appalling, would benefit from the numerous spa towns along the way.

So Sir William found himself buying, albeit with Nelson's money, a large travelling coach for them, with a lesser conveyance for their attendants, and arranging for possessions they would not need on the journey to be shipped home. Given the size of her party it was necessary for Maria Carolina to travel a good forty-eight hours ahead, otherwise Nelson and the Hamiltons would have shifted to find anywhere decent to lay their heads.

The Queen had gone and was not a witness to the moment when the most successful admiral Britannia had ever sent into the Mediterranean struck his blue rear-admiral's flag, to the sound of banging guns and bosun's whistles, and the very obvious absence of Lord Keith.

Nelson had a despatch from Lord Spencer in his hand – a reprimand for his decision to quit Malta three months before in flagrant disregard of Keith's orders. Spencer asserted that he had been 'inactive at a foreign court,' and that it would be better if he struck his flag and came home rather than let such a situation continue.

Giddings had his own dunnage in the barge as he ordered it rowed ashore for the last time, with the shrouds and yards of *Foudroyant* and all the other British warships in the harbour manned to cheer Nelson on his way. Every officer and midshipman raised his hat, some openly in tears at the departure of one who had brought many of them such glory. Nelson had to struggle for control, but his resolve held until Giddings, ashore and having waved the barge crew back to the ship, handed him a note.

My Lord,
 It is with extreme grief that we find you are about to leave us.
We have been along with you, tho' not in the same ship, in every

*engagement your Lordship has been in, both by land and sea, and
most humbly beg of your Lordship to let us proceed with you to
England as your boat crew in any ship or vessel, or in any way
that may seem pleasing to your Lordship.*

*My Lord, pardon the rude style of seamen who are but little
used to writing and believe us to be my Lord,*

Your most humble and obedient servants,

Barge crew of the Foudroyant, late of Vanguard.

'Damn the First Lord,' said a damp-eyed Nelson.

'Amen to that, your honour,' said Giddings.

17

~

The sight of the thin strip of land lit by the low eastern sun produced mixed feelings in Nelson's breast. It was the coast of Norfolk, and wherever he had gone in the world it was a place for which he hankered: nothing had ever stood comparison to his home county. The people were honest, the women fair and faithful, the men bred to the sea, slow to anger, but terriers in a battle. The landscape, be it the flat, dyke-cut marshland or the low hills to the north, entranced him and, like the local food and ales, had a flavour the mere sense of which opened a whole treasure chest of memories. But most of all it was the light, that translucent glow from the setting sun that created mile long shadows across open fields, the light with which he had grown up.

That he was arriving here in the *King George* mail packet still rankled. The Admiralty, despite repeated requests, had failed to despatch a frigate to Hamburg to fetch him and the party of the returning Ambassador. It was a slight both to Sir William Hamilton and himself.

Four months was a long time to be unavailable for service, but he had told his superiors that he needed to restore his health, and he had done something beneficial as well in the political sphere. The diplomatic effect of the victor of the Nile turning up in person at the central European courts while Bonaparte was rampant had been of immeasurable importance, but this seemed not to have registered with the Admiralty.

From the Grand Duke of Tuscany, the Emperor of Austria, the aristocracy of Bohemia, to a raft of German dukes, margraves and electors, he had set out to charm his hosts and encourage them to see that France was not invincible. His visits had been well received, and he looked forward to stressing this to his political masters when he met them. Sir William and Emma, both accomplished in the diplomatic *milieu*, had aided that cause admirably. And at no time had it seemed to Nelson that their hosts suspected he and Emma were lovers.

Sir William, with a sharper eye and more experience knew differently. The attentions paid by Nelson to Emma were more evident than the Admiral supposed, not least the open admiration in his look whenever Emma spoke, sang or moved around the room at some distance from him. She would sit with him at the Faro table, playing cards with his money, gifting him her winnings or burdening him with her losses, all the time in such close physical proximity that a blind man would have suspected an association.

Yet even Sir William had to admit that Emma had handled her pregnancy, which she had never admitted to him, with discretion. She was visiting places where she was known only by reputation as a beauty and a performer of classical attitudes, and in the earlier stages of their travels the bloom of her condition had added to that. In northern Italy and Vienna she had scored no end of triumphs: the elderly genius Joseph Haydn, who had insisted she sing for him, had made it plain that he was prepared to be more than just a distant admirer.

The only one who seemed oblivious to the true nature of affairs was Cornelia Knight. Emma's close companion seemed unaware of the affair and its burgeoning consequences. Perhaps it was enough for her to bask in the fame of the man with whom she was travelling: perhaps it was a desire to see nothing but good or simply that Cornelia Knight was unworldy. No great beauty, she was not particularly attractive to the opposite sex and her tendency to gabble and her very strident voice were off-putting too. Sir William had often seen male companions frown when she brayed some remark. When she laughed, which she did frequently, Cornelia could be heard across a crowded room.

But she clearly loved Emma and admired Nelson, forever penning songs and odes to the hero that she recited at every opportunity, her favourite being the new words she had put to the tune of Rule Britannia. On the road, in the discomfort of a swaying carriage, her enthusiasm for any sight, sound or event that took her eye lifted rather than diminished the spirit. As a travelling companion, Emma claimed she was without peer, given the ease with which she could make her laugh.

As the journey progressed Emma began to put on weight, but that mattered little; she was amongst strangers or people who had not seen her for years. Nelson watched her closely for any sign of ill health, Sir William with the jaundiced eye of a man who had at one time contemplated fatherhood by the same woman. Emma had the excuse that the endless feasts and balls were ruining her figure, and by constant alteration to her wardrobe she was able to disguise each increase in her waistline.

From every point of the journey, letters flew back to Naples and on to London, impressions of Nelson and of Sir William and his wife. Most, even couched diplomatically, could not avoid reference to the way the Hero of the Nile fawned over Emma Hamilton. Hosts heard from their servants of nocturnal traversing and morning retching in Emma's apartments, and while never precise, hints were dropped that the recipients would fully understand.

Approaching England, Emma was beginning to show the full bloom of her pregnancy. In private it was the start of a bulge that Nelson loved to caress, taut skin to which he put his ear hoping for a heartbeat or a kick. In public it would be hidden under a newly extended set of garments. Nelson hoped that the Hamiltons, while people would be aware of them, would not excite as much attention as he himself would, and thus Emma would escape scrutiny.

He knew that he was in bad odour in certain quarters, and not only for the extended mode of his travel. There were his relations with Lord Keith to account for, the fact that he had ignored his instructions. The more he thought about it, the more he had concluded that Keith's orders had been designed for one purpose only: to get him under his personal, close command and curb his independence. In short, Keith had been motivated by jealousy, not sound tactical thinking. So he was not minded to turn up in London and apologise, though that did not prevent him worrying.

The Board of Admiralty must have concurred with Lord Spencer before he had sent the admonitory despatch. There were members of that body, and yet more who had the ear of one, who were less than fond of him, officers and officials whom he had offended long before his own exploits had made him a substantial person in the public eye. While proud of his natural inclination to speak the truth, he knew it tended to create enemies. The envy of service superiors, who felt he had been over-indulged and given commands above his rightful station, would be added to that, which left Nelson to conclude that despite his successes, nothing in his future was certain.

If the Board of Admiralty backed Lord Keith to the hilt it could be very difficult. Suddenly that strip of coastline conjured up a sense of impending danger rather than welcome.

It was known to all sailors that news, both good and bad, travels faster than the ship carrying it, and the town of Yarmouth had been alerted to the arrival of the nation's hero well before his merchantman cleared the harbour entrance. The bells of every church rang out, while every window that faced the sea contained a waving flag. The quay and the harbour wall were lined with people, obliging Nelson to move on to the poop to accept the accolade. Sir William, who had joined him on deck, stayed in the waist, alternately grinning at him and at the cheering crowd. The sun, well above the horizon now, seemed especially ordered to illuminate the hero, sparkling off his jewelled orders and the diamonds of the *Chelenk* that adorned his hat.

Below decks, preparing to land, Emma's heart swelled at the sound. Fêted in the Mediterranean, courted throughout the whole of his European journey, Nelson feared that what fame he had achieved might have faded. With what sounded like the whole of Yarmouth yelling his name, how could he feel that now?

Sent ashore in a boat while the ship edged in, Tom Allen had hired a carriage to supplement the travelling coach, now lashed to the deck, and had booked rooms at a modest inn called the Wrestler's Arms. By the time the party landed the hired horses had been removed from the shafts and replaced by a dozen sturdy fellows. The leading burghers of the town, the Mayor and Aldermen, formed a double line from the quay edge to the carriage door, behind which there rose the one-word clamour for 'Nelson'. It was difficult to hear the voice of the Mayor, who informed Nelson that a meal had been prepared in his honour at the leading hotel in the town, that he was the honoured guest of Yarmouth, and that a resolution to grant him the freedom of the town had already been passed. The younger men, as a signal mark of honour, had volunteered to pull his coach through the streets.

Hats were doffed to Lady Hamilton and her mother, and Sir William received hearty slaps of congratulation, blows that were too powerful for his sparse frame. But there was no complaint, just wonder at a reception the like of which he had never seen. Looking into the eyes of those cheering his friend he could see tears of joy and open rejoicing. Not even the *lazzaroni* of Naples acted with such fervour.

Though the Royal George was close by it took nearly an hour for the coach to get to it, so thick was the throng. The same dignitaries who had lined the quay, had used the back streets, so were there to greet the Nelson party and to show them to the upstairs room. A table was set, lit by chandeliers and candelabra, sparkling with glasses, crockery and cutlery. A pair of double windows opened on to a balcony, so that Nelson could step out to overlook the main square, full of people, with yet more crowded in to the roads that led to it.

His name greeted him in various forms: ropes spliced and nailed to a garlanded board; flowers encircling a huge N, banners proclaiming both him and the Nile victory, one arranged like an army battle honour, listing in a scroll his greatest battles: St Vincent, Tenerife, Calvi and Bastia, Toulon and the action off Genoa, all dwarfed by the four huge letters spelling Nile. When he lifted his hat to the crowd they lifted their voices to a deafening pitch, banners and victory talismans bobbing in accolade.

'My dear,' he said, holding out a hand to Emma. One look from a local worthy caused Nelson to extend the invitation to Sir William, this while he informed the gathering, 'Gentlemen, rest assured that whatever fame I have garnered for the cause for our nation's arms, it could not have been achieved without the aid of these, my two closest companions.'

'Hear him, hear him.' Sir William felt his back slapped again with excessive force, and as men vied to hand his wife on to the balcony, he whispered to Nelson, 'If this is to be the state of things, my friend, I fear I must buy a cuirass. My back aches from the pummelling.'

'They love you, Nelson,' said Emma, her face radiant, 'they truly love you.'

He leant close, though over the clamour no one could have heard him. 'They will come to love you in the same manner, Emma. Love you as I do. I swear it.'

The word 'Never' she mouthed, but it was accompanied by a smile.

Giddings was adept in such situations: to be coxswain to a commander like Nelson he had to be. Ignoring the celebrations, he oversaw the unloading of the luggage, chiding a slow-moving Tom Allen to, 'shift his arse and help him load the handcart.' Even using back roads that took them in a wide arc, the roars of acclamation carried, as they struggled to pass a stream of people rushing in to the town.

'What a to do,' said Tom Allen.

'You'll see plenty more of where this came from Tom, boy. Close to, you have forgotten just how famed your master be.'

Tom replied in a cross tone, his breathing heavy. Lugging chests and the like was a job he was accustomed to delegate to others and he was short of breath. 'How could I, Giddings, when her ladyship never leaves off reminding him. Hero this, hero that. He has vanity enough of his own, Christ knows, but she is forever stoking it.'

'With what he's got in his trumpet, mate, it don't do no harm to blow.'

'He's blown hard from more than one shaft, I can tell you.'

Nothing was secret to Giddings, who had a sharp eye and a close mouth. If the man he had served for so many years wished for silence about his relationship with Lady Hamilton, it was up to those loyal to him to do the same. And that applied in spades to Tom Allen, who was the closest of the lot. He had known Allen a long time, but Giddings could not say he knew him well: their worlds, though they meshed, did not actually mix. Giddings saw to the Admiral's barge, kept the boat crew smart, and was always by Nelson's side in a fight. But he messed, like all sailors, before the mast. He was required to be efficient rather than polite and took some pride, in his smart jacket and flat sennit hat, in being a bit of a ruffian.

Tom had been a sailor too, but had never excelled. After years of being a servant he seemed polished, a weak man when it came to fighting. He had grown soft with his pantry and a cubicle to sleep in, officer's food to eat and as much wine to sip as he liked. The sailor servant kept himself to himself, rarely mixing with the lower deck hands. There was wisdom in that: almost a part of the great-cabin furniture, Tom Allen overheard most of Nelson's conversations. He served the officers at every conference they held to discuss tactics, heard Hardy, Nelson and the ship's master plot the course to what-ever destination had been decided on. It was his duty to keep what he heard to himself.

Not that secrets could be kept aboard a ship. Mewed up together, six hundred and fifty souls hugger-mugger in their wooden walls, not even a determined admiral could keep from the crew much of what was going on. There hadn't been a man jack aboard either *Vanguard* or *Foudroyant* who was not aware of the nature of Nelson and Lady Hamilton's friendship. They discussed it openly, made lewd jokes and wavered between pity and respect for Sir William. But it was kept to the confines of the ship. What everyone knew and what they were prepared to say to outsiders were two different things.

'You wouldn't be sounding off to others like you have to me, Tom, would you?'

Tom Allen was in a bad mood. Aware of his own deficiencies, he hated to be ashore at the best of times, since the few certainties he harboured seemed to evaporate. Out of the ship he was no longer master of his own domain, and that had been true in Naples, Palermo and on the route home. England would likely be the same. Being in an irascible frame of mind he spoke more forcefully than was wise. 'It won't be needed, mate. I overhears enough to know what is knowledge and what ain't, and this here coach is not taking us to calm waters, I reckon.'

'What are you saying?'

'I'm saying that enough folks in Palermo and Naples were not as happy as the fleet about our Nellie and his Cleopatra. That there were those who mightily condemned them.'

'Like who?' demanded Giddings, with a look that implied he would silence the lot of them.

'A few captains had high words, Troubridge not least, and there were ten times more civilian tongues that were wont to wag. That Lock cove was forever trying to dig out dirt.'

'Let them wag, I say.'

'It's not the wagging, mate, but the writing that will do for him. There must have been any number of letters home.' Tom made a gesture at his belly. 'And you can't say my master hid away what they were up to, nor can we maintain we don't see the result.'

'I reckon, then, it be best not to talk of it, even with shipmates.' Tom Allen looked at Giddings then, well aware that a threat had just been issued, telling him to button his lip. 'You got to reckon Tom, that if you can pick up on idle chat so can other folks.'

'Have a care,' said Tom suddenly. 'The dragon's ahead.'

Giddings looked to where Tom nodded to see Mary Cadogan waiting for them. She had come to sort out the domestic arrangements at the Wrestler's Arms, well aware that left to his own devices, Tom Allen would make a poor fist of it.

'They reckon she was a beauty once,' said Giddings quietly, 'and she ain't so bad yet that I wouldn't have her over now.'

'You'd get more pleasure out of a piece of knotted wood, mate,' Tom replied, head turned away from eyes that he knew could read his mind. 'Take my word for it.'

Much as he hated the idea, Nelson had to make a speech to the assembled Yarmouth worthies. For a man who could address with confidence the entire manpower of a ship-of-the-line he made a poor fist of talking to his awe-struck fellow countrymen. Halfway through, moving the praise from himself to his friends the Hamiltons and the officers and men of the Nile fleet, he realised what hampered him.

Sailors looked at him differently from these worshippers, whose uncritical adoration unnerved him.

Thankfully, the peroration in which he thanked Yarmouth for its welcome was easy, its message that, much as he esteemed their town and those who inhabited it, he must make plans for his onward journey.

'For there are people waiting to see me, my friends.' He had trapped himself and he knew it: he had meant his superiors at the Admiralty and the ministers of the government, but there was one person he could hardly leave out – in fact she must come first. It was with some effort that he imbued the words with sufficient force. 'My wife, Lady Nelson.'

The cheers for her were nearly as great as those for him, which made Nelson blush. He looked at Emma to reassure her.

'Gentlemen,' he said to his hosts, when he was back in the room. 'I fear I will need your strong arms once more to get myself and my companions to our accommodation.'

It was true. Just getting out of the Royal George was hard enough, with people jostling for position on the stairs and in the hallway claiming precedence for some real or imagined standing in the community. The owner was not going to let the victor of the Nile leave without a written testimonial to his visit that he could display on his wall for posterity, so pen and ink had to be fetched. Nelson longed for a party of sailors to clear the doorway since the leading citizens of Yarmouth were too feeble. All the while he tried to interpose himself between the mob and Emma, for fear that she might be crushed.

Emma could not avoid being jostled, but she tried to hide from Nelson that she was somewhat downcast. At first, the cheers and adulation had lifted her spirits, but as she had listened to the speeches of the Yarmouth elite, to toast after toast to the King, the nation and Nelson, to the endless damnation of the French, her good cheer had evaporated. Emma had seen cheering mobs before, but never had she witnessed anything like this. As she stood beside Nelson on the balcony and looked into that sea of faces, it had come home to her just how famous he was. Triumphant Roman generals must have been accorded this honour in ancient days, or an Egyptian pharaoh – but a British admiral?

She loved him and was sure that he loved her. But how could she hope to hold on to someone so beloved by his fellow countrymen, whose every move would be accompanied by a besotted crowd of admirers? It was one thing for the common people to cheer so, but even the most potent citizens of this town had been close to grovelling in his presence. Emma knew it was deserved, but the depth of feeling had shocked her.

And then he had mentioned his wife

With a crowd constantly present outside the Wrestler's Arms it was far from peaceful, but at least the stream of visitors had dried up so that Nelson could write some letters, the first to the Admiralty to say he was home and once more fit for active service. After a light supper, Emma retired to bed, Sir William and Cornelia likewise, propriety demanding that each guest had a chamber of their own. Nor, in a strange establishment, could Nelson contemplate a visit to Emma. He stayed in the parlour, wrote a second letter and addressed it to his wife at Roundwood, near Ipswich, Suffolk.

This was a small country establishment Fanny had taken on his instruction, as much for his father as for herself. It was not very grand accommodation for a couple like the Hamiltons, but it would give him a chance to return some of the hospitality he had received in both Naples and Palermo.

Nov 6th 1800

My dear Fanny,

Nelson contemplated what to say. Should he hint that things could not be as they had been before? Although he had thought about it endlessly since leaving Naples, the enormity of the difficulties he faced now bore down on him. Within forty-eight hours he would introduce Emma to Fanny. What had his wife heard? She could not be in ignorance of his behaviour in the Mediterranean. The way in which he had ignored this seemed to haunt him now, the way he almost invited observers to question his actions, which could hardly have been left out of letters sent home to England. He knew the power of gossip, just as he knew that not everyone he had dealt with had been happy with his arrangements. Apart from the well disposed who had felt uneasy, there were people who disliked or envied him and would do all in their power to damage his reputation. He had given them plenty of ammunition.

He wanted his wife to take to Emma as so many others had. She must be brought to realise that happiness was as necessary to her husband's wellbeing as fame or appearances. Fanny had the title and she would enjoy all that flowed from his success. He would attend upon her socially as a husband should but she must share him privately, and accept what was, after all, a not uncommon relationship in the circles in which they would now move. He had a high regard for her, but it was not love, given the lack of physical passion that had existed between them for years. That was something he had wanted throughout their married life – that and children. Fanny had poise, grace and exquisite manners, and when Nelson thought of her it was with an abiding fondness. She would grace his name and rank splendidly, but he would seek his comforts elsewhere. He knew that in writing this note he should start as he intended to continue. The quill moved again, but the words he should have used would not come.

The note stated that he and a party would be arriving at some time on Saturday, setting off from Yarmouth on Friday, following a service of Thanksgiving to which he had been invited.

We are this moment arrived and the post only allows me to say that we shall set off tomorrow noon, and be with you on Saturday, to dinner. I have only had time to open one of your letters, my visits are so numerous. May God bless you, and believe me ever your affectionate,
 Brontë Nelson of the Nile

It dawned on him as he reread it that he had failed to mention his father, also that he could hardly turn up with two elevated guests without letting her know. He added,

Sir William and Lady Hamilton beg their best regards, and will accept the offer of a bed. Mrs Cadogan and Miss Knight and all the servants will proceed to Colchester.
 I beg my dear Father to be assured of my duty and ever tender feelings of a son.

That would do. It would tell Fanny all she needed to know, if indeed she had been on the receiving end of any gossip. If not, it was an innocent communication. He sanded and folded it, in the knowledge that Tom Allen was waiting to talk to him.

18

'There's a naval gent to see you, your honour.'

Nelson looked up, his expression grim. He might have sent a civilian away, but how could he shun a fellow officer. It was with a forlorn last hope that he asked, 'In uniform?'

'Aye, your honour, but it be of a fair old cut.'

'Who is he?'

Tom Allen replied with a negative shrug, adding, 'He claims your acquaintance.'

'Yet he does not give his name?'

The man who entered a few moments later was tall and spare, somewhat stooped with age, but with a lined face that had once been fleshy and was now loose-jowled. He had a pair of jug ears, which were obvious when he removed his hat. They pricked at Nelson's memory, and had him searching for a name that was just out of reach.

'Admiral Lord Nelson.'

His visitor said those three words as if he had been rehearsing them for an age, his voice carrying the tremor of his years. Nelson took pride in his service memory, his ability to identify by name the many hundreds of men with whom he had served, but this fellow, who was looking at him in an almost avuncular fashion, eluded him.

'It is many years ago now, sir,' his visitor continued, 'but I recall a miserable youth who made my acquaintance at the gates to Chatham Dockyard.'

'Frears,' said Nelson suddenly, taking in with a swift glance the information provided by the coat. 'Lieutenant Frears?'

'The very same, sir.'

The memory was clear to Nelson now: of the trials and tribulations he had encountered on joining his first ship at Chatham. It had been a cold, friendless introduction to naval life, a wet, freezing day; indifferent locals induced increasing misery in the thirteen-year-old midshipman. Frears had taken him in hand, insisting that he join him for a warming meal by a hot fireside, then he had delivered him and his sea chest to HMS *Raisonable*, the ship his uncle commanded.

'My dear Lieutenant Frears,' cried Nelson, standing up and holding out his hand, 'pray take a seat at once. Tom, some wine, at the double. Have you eaten Mr Frears?'

Frears was grinning now, and nodding, happy to seat himself at Nelson's table, 'Obliged, sir, obliged.'

That whole period of his life ran through Nelson's mind. Of the feuds and fights he had had aboard that ship, the way he had driven his Uncle William Suckling to distraction. And he also remembered the cause of those fights, the gross attempt by a very knowing senior midshipman to take advantage of his youth and sexual inexperience. His face must have closed up at the memory, for Frears looked alarmed. Nelson smiled warmly at the man he recalled with nothing but affection, banished the bad memories, and sat as Tom Allen poured some wine.

'It is near thirty years, Mr Frears,' said Nelson. 'You have weathered well.'

'Tolerable well, Lord Nelson, tolerable well.'

'I see our service did not grant you the rank you deserve.'

Frears looked sad as he fingered the old fashioned coat. 'Luck eluded me, sir, and I lacked the influence to change it. My posting aboard *Victory* was sustained until she was finally commissioned, but nothing like it followed.'

Had he been a good officer? Nelson did not know, never having served with him. That he was a kind man was not in doubt. The rank at which he had remained might point to inefficiency in the way he carried out his duties, but Nelson knew the Navy too well to assume that. Many a good officer had been stuck in a lieutenancy and spent his life watching others less competent or deserving get their step to a post captain's rank, even rising as he had to an admiral's flag.

'You had three sons, I recall?'

'Aye,' Frears replied, taking a deep swig of wine, 'and seeing to their needs forced me to take merchant service.'

'Then they have prospered, I hope?' said Nelson, now aware of why Frears had remained a lieutenant. By taking a merchant ship he had removed himself from the active list. To think that Fanny, fed up with freezing Norfolk and little income, had once wanted him to do the same. If he had given in to her, would he be like Frears now: a touch sad, certainly disappointed, wandering about in an out of date uniform coat?

'I got one a berth, sir, but he succumbed to the Yellow Jack on West Indian service while still a mid. Poor lad never saw his fifteenth birthday.'

That occasioned another understanding nod. Nelson had almost lost his own life, as well as the best part of an entire crew of two hundred men to that dread malarial disease while fighting up the San Juan river at Lake Nicaragua. The graveyards of the West Indies were full of crosses bearing the names of soldiers and sailors who had succumbed.

'Another prospers reasonably in the law,' Frears continued, 'while the youngest, I'm afraid to say, is of a rakish nature and lost to me and his family.'

'Then let us drink to him, sir,' said Nelson, raising his glass, 'for he has a bloodline that is good and noble, and I am sure one day he will play the prodigal and come home to you.'

Frears obliged, though there was a hint of a tear in his eye. Nelson surmised that of all his brood, the scrapejack was the one the old fellow loved most. It made him think of his own father. How much had the Reverend Edmund Nelson agonised over his son's behaviour? What would he say about it now, for he was by nature unworldly? Nelson put the thought firmly to the back of his mind.

They talked for an hour, with Frears eager to hear from Nelson's own lips the story of his exploits. The old man showed signs of resurgent pride as the tale unfolded, and as much interest in stories of the stripling Lieutenant Nelson taking Caribbean blockade-runners as in the great fleet actions. The hour grew late, and Frears realised that he had outstayed his welcome. Nelson felt nothing of the sort: he owed so much to this man that Frears could have stayed all night. And why, now that he was making to leave, was he looking so bashful?

'I hesitate to place before you a request.' Nelson smiled for him to continue, which Frears did, albeit stuttering now. 'I have . . . a grandson . . . of twelve years of age . . . near thirteen.'

Nelson held up his hand. 'Lieutenant Frears, leave me his name and where I can contact him. Be assured that as soon as I have a command I will request my flag captain to take him in.'

'You are too kind, sir.'

'No Mr Frears. My kindness, if you call it that, pales beside that which you showed to me.'

✻

Emma woke in the night to the sound of rolling, distant thunder and lay, rubbing her swollen belly, surprised yet again that she was indeed pregnant, still unsure if she should rejoice or despair. What would this child be like? She hoped for a boy because her lover so wanted a son.

In the next bed Cornelia snored, an unladylike trait that Emma had never felt able to tell her about. Her companion slept like the proverbial log and could bring the roof down if she wished. She had thus provided, without knowing it, a shield of respectability throughout the travelling months that had allowed Emma to go to Nelson at night, to enjoy gentle sex and quiet conversation. She had been happy to let him talk, and knew all about his family, how they stood in his affections, their good points and bad. On the subject of his wife he was guarded. If he noticed that Emma was evasive about her distant past, Nelson never commented on it or pushed for revelation. Emma could talk happily and openly about her childhood and her time in Naples, but the period between was to her thin ice, to be skated over with delicacy. Complete openness might diminish his love for her.

When she thought of it, the impending birth did not frighten her. She had gone through it many years before with Little Emma, producing her with such ease that the child's first cry had surprised her. She worried at the thought of bringing up a child alone. Little Emma had grown up under the care of her great-grandmother, and after a brief few weeks in a Southport boarding house with her mother, the child had, at Charles Greville's insistence, been sent to a good family to be brought up. The memory brought a pang that Emma had not felt for years, part affection, part guilt, when she recalled how her child had been reared by others.

It was easy in that atmosphere, a dark room, the thunder outside, to feel self-pity, to recall the despair that had animated her then. And it was easy with another child in her womb to sway to the negative and contemplate a repetition of that rejection, to wonder if Nelson, dear, sweet, soft-hearted Nelson, might reject her.

If he did would Sir William continue to support her? Her husband had never mentioned her pregnancy, though he could hardly be unaware of it. Did it make him angry or sad? He had withdrawn from her intimate life with surpassing grace, but he could not keep off his face the occasional flicker of pain, jealousy, or longing. Had she so wounded him that he would cold-shoulder her too?

'It will not be!' Emma said aloud.

Cornelia stopped snoring, but she did not wake, she merely moved to get more comfortable. Emma lay, eyes open, as various dramas were acted out in her mind. The one in which she lost Nelson was banished each time it surfaced, replaced with the one in which she had her hero to herself and to hell with the wife.

She had corresponded with Fanny Nelson, exchanging with her news and pleasantries over hundreds of miles of sea. But she had never met her and knew of her only what Nelson had divulged. A picture had emerged of a quiet woman, a bit of a mouse, pious, far from colourful, no friend to the physical and fearful of the taint of scandal.

That they were rivals had been disguised by distance. That would cease soon: they would be face to face, the companion of Nelson's heart versus the woman who held him in the bonds of matrimony. Emma had a rosy vision then of she and Fanny as friends, confidantes, frequent visitors to each other's parlours. They would take tea, and Emma, out of sensitivity would keep the child out of sight and never mention it in conversation.

Fanny would accept the inevitable, as Sir William had done, and would become reconciled to the liaison. Like Sir William, she would lend a shield to the two lovers so that all the proprieties would be observed. With this idyllic dream in her mind, Emma went back to sleep.

Having read late into the night, Sir William was trying to avoid gnawing on his indebtedness. He wanted to sleep, but knew that age had sapped his capacity to do so, and every time he put aside the book and lay in the semi-darkness he contemplated a less than untroubled future. The loss of HMS *Colossus* had been a disaster: ten thousand pounds of his finest possessions now lay at the bottom of the sea off the Scilly Isles.

Those vases, statues and ancient coins had been headed for the auction rooms of London and the proceeds would have allowed him to set up house in the style to which he was accustomed. When they had been despatched that had included Emma too, but now he was no longer sure that she was his responsibility. He allowed himself a flash of irritation as he contemplated the fact that she was with child, and just as clearly she felt it was none of his concern. She had not seen fit to confide in him or ask for his opinion.

Did Emma think she could hide such a thing from someone as worldly as he? And what a complication should the truth emerge, for there was not a soul in London society who would assume that after so many years together, and at his advanced age, that he was the father. The thunder rolled outside his window and seemed an appropriate sign to Sir William that trouble was brewing. But thinking of Emma and Nelson only brought him back to the knowledge that he was now dependent on Emma's lover, which was a damned uncomfortable position to be in.

All Sir William's money was gone, his income from his estates pledged to creditors for some time ahead. It had been spent on his ambassadorial office, on renting villas, throwing balls, entertaining royalty, buying them gifts and feasting his numerous guests. In his valise was a bill to the government requesting that he be reimbursed for monies expended on his office as well as his domestic losses from the looting of the Palazzo Sessa, plus his application for a pension as a retiring ambassador. Both, given the sterling service he had performed in Naples, should be certain, but Sir William knew too much about the ways of Treasury clerks to feel secure. He doubted that they would withhold the money altogether, but haste was anathema to such people.

On the journey from Italy he had had to leave Nelson to pick up those bills not met by whoever was their host, and that looked set to continue in London. The prospect of retirement, which had seemed so alluring in the south of Italy, looked less so now that he was at home. Would malicious tongues say that he had sold his wife to the Hero of the Nile to keep a roof over his head?

Troubled by those and other thoughts, Sir William tossed and turned in his bed. He did get to sleep as dawn broke, only to be awoken by what sounded like an invading army.

The clatter of hoofs woke Nelson from another turmoil-filled dream that promised happiness one minute and disaster the next. The wine he had shared with Frears tasted stale in his mouth and the excessive bed coverings had made him sweat profusely. He opened the curtain to see the first hint of dawn. The sky was overcast, but there was light enough to see the serried ranks of cavalrymen dismounted and attending to the horses' harness.

Within minutes the door opened and Tom Allen entered, bearing a pitcher of hot water to wash and shave him and to inform him that the men outside were the local Yeomanry. They had, it seemed, been up half the night polishing their brasses because they were determined to escort him wherever he went this day, right to the edge of Norfolk county.

'Then please ask the owner of the Wrestler's to provide them with breakfast on my account, and hay for their mounts.'

'Ain't the Wrestler's no more, your honour.' Tom was so full of pride he was nearly bursting. He pulled Nelson's nightgown over his head and proceeded to flannel him briskly. 'Ain't just the local horse soldiers who've been busy, either, so has the local limner. I was consulted about the image he painted, and I can swear to a true likeness. The sign outside this establishment now has a fair study of your own face and the Wrestler's Arms is now to be known as the Nelson.'

'Reckon there'll be one from now on wherever we go,' Tom added.

The cavalry provided an escort to the church, packed to the rafters for the Thanksgiving service. Nelson stood in full dress uniform and glittering stars with Emma and Sir William to one side and Cornelia Knight to the other, singing hymns of praise to his country and his king. He listened as the vicar lauded him from the pulpit, not forgetting to add that all victories were the work of God, and that the Hero of the Nile should be humble before Him. But he was also Englishman enough to add that the Supreme Being, with his all-seeing eye, was well aware of the just cause of Britannia, which was why he had cast the heretical French into the deep waters of Aboukir Bay.

By the time they emerged the carriages were waiting – Mary Cadogan had supervised the packing and bill paying so that they could leave Yarmouth immediately. Cavalry to each side, they left the town, to the renewed cheers of the populace, under a lowering sky with a gusting wind that threatened foul weather but could do nothing to dampen the enthusiasm of those who lined the route.

Every stop to change horses was a repeat in miniature of Yarmouth, the crowd, the cheers, folk desperate to touch him as if to transfer to themselves a sliver of his glory. They skirted Lowestoffe to avoid another civic reception and spent the night in a small country inn, free of their cavalry escort, well away from any crowd. The next day the party was off at dawn, the heavy-built coach rolling at a steady pace along the well-laid turnpike roads. These were travelled free, since no toll-keeper, aware of the identity of the main passenger in the pair of coaches, could bring himself to levy the fee.

There were still crowds, because the news had gone ahead of them that the Hero of the Nile was home and making for London, so just as on the day before, every change of horses occasioned a small amount of ceremony. There were toasts, food, open-faced men, women and children who would swear years later that this was the high point of their life. They were greeted by beaming innkeepers eager to tell Lord Nelson that his name would now grace their establishment, as well as the odd notable person who had come from their large house and insisted that their station gave them the right to a private conversation. That they all had a young relative eager to go to sea was only to be expected and by the time the two coaches parted company Nelson's pockets were stuffed with requests for a place.

It had remained heavily overcast all day, and several times it had teemed with the kind of rain which reminded Sir William of why he had so loved Naples. By the time they turned off to make for Roundwood House, the sky was streaked with lightning, and the coach now bucked along rutted, muddy tracks.

'At least we will be spared another set of speeches,' said Nelson, a remark that was greeted by a grateful murmur. Even Cornelia Knight seemed tired and subdued, no doubt eager for a decent room, hot water and food. 'I don't know the layout of the house, but I doubt it is spacious, though I trust my wife will manage to make us comfortable.'

Nelson felt as jittery as he had before they found the French fleet at the Nile, jumping at each crack of thunder, each bright flash of lightning, for the storm was now right over their heads. The sudden right-hand turn on to crunching gravel told him he was home, before he realised he could not call it that. It was just a rented place he had never seen. He tried very hard to convince himself that with his father in residence no crisis could occur. If Fanny was concerned about his behaviour she would say nothing before the Reverend Edmund Nelson for fear of upsetting him. It did no good to Nelson's state of mind to remember that his father might be privy to certain matters, and he shuddered at the thought of facing his stern parent in a mood of disapproval.

There was no welcoming party at the porch, no light in the doorway or from the small paned windows. Indeed, with the red brick of the house soaked dark with rain, the place looked forlorn. Tom Allen had jumped down, water streaming off his oilskins, to pull at the bell, but it was minutes before anyone appeared. Seconds later Tom was at the open door of the coach.

'Lady Nelson ain't here, your honour, and hasn't been for weeks past. There's now't but a housekeeper.'

'Fetch her,' snapped Nelson. For once he was angry enough to put out someone instead of himself.

With a shawl as a cowl over her head the housekeeper, a middle-aged kind-looking soul appeared at the coach door. As soon as he saw her shiver he relented, and insisted she shelter inside so he could question her.

'Lady Nelson never took to the place in my way of thinking, milord, forever saying it reminded her too much of the Reverend Edmund's Norfolk home. The old man, your father, seemed happy enough, even after her ladyship departed, but he got a mite sick of no company and went off to join her in London. Post still comes here for both, of course, and I have been sending it on to Portman Square.'

Nelson spat, 'Portman Square?' The housekeeper recoiled.

'That be where Lady Nelson has taken a house.'

Nelson had to bite his tongue, although he wanted to curse Fanny. He could not say in the presence of Emma and Sir William that he had expressly asked her, when renting a London house, to avoid the Portman Square area, since that was where Charles Greville had engaged in some speculative building. The last thing he wanted was to find himself renting a house built by Emma's ex-lover. But to say so would let Emma know that he was in possession of such information, and he had been careful in talking with her to avoid alluding to knowledge of her past. Added to that it would wound Sir William, who was still fond of his nephew, despite the manner in which he had behaved.

'I could make up beds if you so require, milord, though I have not the food for a meal in the larder.'

'No. Bring me the address and we will be on our way, but I would take it as a kindness if you could direct the coachman to a decent inn.'

'You would oblige me by taking what post has come, milord, for the address has been appended to that already.'

'Of course.' Nelson fished for a coin and slipped it to the house-keeper. 'And I thank you for your care of the place.'

The package was delivered to him, letters that included his own sent from Yarmouth, re-addressed to 64 Upper Seymour Street, Portman Square, London. Nelson wondered if by disobeying him on two counts, to wait for him at Roundwood, and by taking a house in Portman Square, his wife was in some way sending him a coded message.

'We shall send a messenger ahead from Colchester, to London,' he said suddenly. 'To find us all a hotel.'

He looked away from Emma and her husband, leaving them to speculate. It was understandable that they should stay in a hotel, but for him, with a wife and a rented house in which to take residence, it looked very like he intended nailing his colours to the mast.

19

Fanny Nelson was apprised of her husband's arrival in England by a polite note from Mrs Nepean, wife to the secretary of the First Lord. This lady was a firm friend, who probably knew more about what was going on in the naval world than anyone, since all correspondence, both outgoing and incoming, was seen by her husband. But she was the soul of discretion.

In the four months that her husband had been travelling from Naples Fanny had received any number of disturbing letters, some from the points on his journey, given that the party seemed to be in no hurry to get home, others from Naples. To add to these she heard from other correspondents, passing on snippets of gossip and heavy hints that matters were not as they should be, all well wrapped up in disclaimers of any true knowledge of the state of affairs.

In the privacy of her own boudoir Fanny fetched them, dating from before the battle of the Nile and read them again. The change wrought by the aftermath of that event was plain to see. When she compared letters preceding her husband's return to Naples with those that followed she perceived two things. The first was his change in tone, which lacked the fulsome affectionate touches of his earlier correspondence. The second was his praise for Lady Hamilton. That had been in his letters before, and Fanny had known that her husband admired the woman. But the way he lauded her in the later epistles grated mightily: she was the queen of sagacity as well as beauty, as much a hero of his victory as Nelson himself. He even praised Lady Hamilton for the way she had knocked the rough edges off Fanny's own son, Josiah, making her so angry she had under-scored several passages and put many an exclamation mark in the margin. The cruellest letter of all had been the one in which he had abruptly informed her to stay at home: that her presence in the Mediterranean would not aid him in the execution of his duties.

Had his infatuation with Lady Hamilton gone beyond admiration to something else? That was the one thing to which those numerous well-disposed people had hesitated to allude directly. There was much hinting at intimacy without any proof and Fanny was not going to condemn her husband on hearsay. There was little doubt that Emma Hamilton was a loose creature, capable of seducing an innocent, but had it come to that? If it had what was the cause? The actions of a temptress eager to add the name of Nelson to her conquests, or the infatuation her husband had failed to disguise in his most recent letters?

Fanny Nelson was prey to moods, one night unable to bear the thoughts that assailed her so that she went to sleep sobbing, on others so incensed that murder was not out of the question. Over the months of living with this quandary she had plotted a course by which she thought she could proceed. She had no intention of giving up her husband, but if she must win him back, she knew that to do so would require her to remind him of why they had married in the first place.

Horatio Nelson was a God-fearing man who cared much for the state of his soul. Fanny must remind him that damnation waited for an unrepentant sinner who dared break the commandments. This Lady Hamilton might be a beauty, and celebrated socially. Hot, teeming Naples and a voluptuous woman might have turned his head, but did she have good manners and the kind of grace that Fanny knew she herself possessed? Her plan was not to chastise him: all men were weak creatures when it came to matters of the flesh. Fanny would prevail by example, by the certain knowledge that in the places where Nelson would want to be received his 'veritable Diana' would not be welcome. He would, away from the bright sunlight of southern Italy, realise in the more sobering climate of his native land, where his true interests lay.

The Nelson party arrived in London in the middle of a tempest. The streets of the City were strewn with roof tiles, and in parts of Westminster roads were closed because of the danger of falling masonry. Emma was grateful for the weather conditions as Nelson could enter the capital without fuss: most sensible people were content to huddle indoors and read about rather than witness his return. They were finally decanted at a hotel in St James's with only a small, chilled crowd outside to greet him.

Emma was the only one who stopped between coach and entrance, to look around at what were familiar buildings. Arlington Street was not so very far away, and there were a dozen places round this area where she had spent time in the company of various suitors. They had passed through Whitechapel on the way, where one lover had abandoned her, and from which Greville had rescued her. Covent Garden lay to one side as they passed along the Strand. Emma had been one of a thousand waifs and strays scratching a living there once, selling flowers occasionally for the price of some food, ever alert to the possibilities of falling even further in to wretchedness.

To Nelson, London was a strange place, a great metropolis full of preoccupied strangers who had no sympathy for their fellow men. Emma never spoke it: to do so would bring an admission that it was as much home to her as Naples: familiar, with sights that invoked both pleasant and unhappy memories. But then so much of what she had experienced was alien to her lover. She suspected he knew more of her past than he let on, but was grateful to him for his silence.

'Lady Hamilton!' His voice brought her sharply back to the present. The look on his face was troubled, making her wonder if he had read her thoughts. Then he smiled. 'I fear we have a busy day ahead.'

He was correct, of course, the first duty being to ensure that while those he wanted to see were shown up to his rooms, others were politely turned away. The Marquis of Queensberry, a relative of Sir William Hamilton, called, and was introduced at his own insistence to Nelson, a courtesy that was not extended to the next Hamilton caller, Charles Greville.

Nelson's first naval visitor was Thomas Troubridge, on his way to take up an appointment as captain of the Channel Fleet, now commanded by Earl St Vincent. He would be the senior executive officer to Nelson's old chief, probably his last appointment as a captain before he, too, earned his admiral's flag. That gave the pair plenty to talk about that did not include Emma, not least the notion that Nelson himself might serve under St Vincent again, notwithstanding the fact that their lawyers were locked in a dispute about the distribution of Mediterranean prize money.

Troubridge loved Nelson, but despaired that his old friend would ever see how other matters impacted on his service prospects. St Vincent wasn't sure that he wanted him, given that the Channel Fleet was confined to blockade. The chances for independent action of the kind Nelson always craved were near non-existent. He would go mad beating back and forth before Brest, occasionally retiring to Spithead when the weather turned too foul to remain at sea. Worse, if the way he had behaved in the Mediterranean was anything to go by, Nelson would crave time ashore with Lady Hamilton, no doubt to the detriment of his responsibilities.

The correspondence between the commander-in-chief of the Channel Fleet and his new executive officer had not left out discussion of their old friend and comrade, and little of what they had said to each other had been flattering. Nelson's ability was not in question, but his judgement was. Also Troubridge, as a highly regarded officer without a blemish to his character, was popular enough at the Admiralty to know that Nelson was not.

He had done nothing less than run insubordinate rings round Lord Keith, who was no mean sailor himself and had deserved more respect. The despatches Keith had sent detailing Nelson's conduct, though couched in the language of officialdom, had done much to tarnish the glory of the Nile victory. Between the lines of Keith's reports it was obvious that he felt Nelson put proximity to the body of his mistress before the needs of his country, a view that had subsequently been disseminated in high places.

His relationship with Emma Hamilton had given his naval detractors a stick with which to beat him. Lord Spencer might love the man for his victory, and Lady Spencer might be ever grateful for the way it had aided her husband politically, but there was a steady drip of venom from old adversaries and folk eager to be scandalised. Although Nelson had been instrumental in defeating one enemy fleet and had destroyed another, there were admirals senior to him who could say without a blush that he was too bold, too much of a chancer, to be entrusted with another command.

'Davidson,' said Nelson, grasping the hand of his prize agent and friend. 'It is so good to see you after so long.'

Alexander Davidson hadn't changed. He still had the same high colour under ginger hair, though that was showing the first hints of grey, the same piping voice and soft Northumbrian accent. He was a true friend, one of the few people not naval that Nelson could utterly rely on and he loved him like a brother. He envied him, as well, because of the speed with which he and his pretty wife quickly produced the children to whom Nelson stood as godfather. He enquired after them, bursting but unable to tell even Davidson that he too would soon be a father.

What Davidson saw was a man not much different from their first meeting in Quebec: older, yes, wiser, no. Then Nelson had been, just as he was now, a victim of his enthusiasms. The only person to whom

Nelson had confided the breakdown of his relationship with Fanny, Alexander Davidson was less surprised than most about his affair with Lady Hamilton.

'How could you let Fanny take a house near Portman Square?' Nelson asked suddenly. 'It was my express wish that she should avoid that area.'

If Nelson hadn't changed, his wife had. The rather mouse-like creature Davidson had met and got to know over the first years of her marriage to Nelson had turned lately into something of a shrew. Fanny Nelson was no longer content meekly to obey her absent husband's instructions. She had taken to questioning some and disobeying others, which could only be ascribed to her disquiet at information she was receiving regarding her husband's behaviour. Fanny had never said anything to Davidson, but her demeanour told those with eyes to see that she knew about Emma Hamilton and her husband. Nelson was in for a turbulent homecoming – of that Davidson was certain.

'Nelson, I am your agent, not your executor. I can dispose of your prizes and instruct your lawyers to sue that greedy old goat, St Vincent, but I can only advise Lady Nelson and if she chooses to ignore me I'm not sure what I can do.'

'Are you saying she chose deliberately to disregard me?'

Davidson shook his head, although he suspected that the answer was yes. It was not a subject on which he wanted to dwell, so he moved swiftly to business matters, reassuring Nelson that his finances were reasonably sound. While he was not rich he was comfortably situated, though Davidson thought he should be less free with his disbursements to his family – and once he had perused the accounts of the journey from Italy, more circumspect with support to his friends.

'I would never deny Sir William Hamilton anything.'

'So it would seem,' Davidson replied. 'But he is already in debt to you for some two thousand pounds and that is not, I'm sure, a situation with which he is comfortable.'

Nelson wasn't good with money, mainly because he cared so little for it. Even as a half-pay post captain stuck in Norfolk he had been a soft touch for a beggar. With a steady stream of income from prize money and gifts, he could afford to be generous now, but only up to a point. Davidson had seen too many naval officers come ashore wealthy only to soon find themselves strapped by their own profligate spending. And some of the monies Davidson had counted in were sums owed rather than paid.

Disputes were ongoing with the Admiralty, St Vincent and Lord Keith about prize money distribution, all designed to keep the lawyers busy, and Davidson had to report that his attempts to settle these without litigation had failed. It was the same after every commission, ten times worse after a battle, with every officer in the fleet convinced that he had been cheated of his just deserts. Added to that, the Navy Office, the Victualling Board, the Sick and Hurt Board, and His Majesty's First Lord of the Treasury would never agree to the amounts expended on keeping a fleet at sea. It was part of Davidson's job to take issue with them as well so that any monies Nelson had paid out of his own pocket could be recouped in full.

Nelson sighed as the state of his accounts was finally disclosed. 'I swear Davidson, if I had not a headache before, I have one now,'

'To more pleasant tasks, then,' said Davidson, pushing forward a letter with a heavy seal. 'It is the Lord Mayor's banquet tomorrow. The City of London has asked me to pass on to you a request that you consent to be the guest of honour.'

It was a signal accolade, and Nelson couldn't keep the pleasure from his countenance. He would occupy a seat often reserved for royalty at a dinner that was near the top of the social calendar and attended by the most elevated persons in the land. It must have been planned for months, with a guest of honour in place well before now: someone had either stood down or been displaced by his return. He longed to ask who, but did not dare.

'Can I ask if you will be remaining here?' Davidson asked, bringing him back to earth. The inference was plain: would he be moving in with his wife?

'For the time being, but I would ask that you find me a house of my own.' Nelson turned away as he added. 'It should be spacious as I anticipate the need to accommodate guests. Also, I will need a full complement of servants since a degree of entertaining will be unavoidable.'

In the rear of the hotel hallway, with Davidson gone, Nelson was finally alone. Fanny, alerted by messenger to his arrival in London, and invited to come to the hotel, had replied that she would meet him at three. She must have wondered why he had taken residence here, and not come straight to Seymour Street, but the note she sent back only stated that she looked forward eagerly to their reunion.

All the worry was gone now. Nelson felt the same calm descend on him as he experienced before an action. Odd to think in those terms of meeting his wife, but he did. He heard the hackney pull up on the cobbles outside and stopped pacing, standing, feet apart, facing the doorway, for all the world as if he was on the quarterdeck of a ship gliding into battle.

Fanny did not rush to greet him. Ever the lady, she allowed her cloak and hat to be removed, waited while her father-in-law was likewise cared for, before she looked to where her husband stood. When she advanced it was only far enough to get away from draughts and street noise. Nelson was already moving towards her, his eyes searching her face, unsure of what he was looking for – hurt, anger, determination. What he saw was calm certainty.

'Fanny,' he said, with a slight croak, and he kissed her gently on each dry cheek, his nose taking in the lemon verbena with which she habitually scented herself.

He looked past her. Edmund Nelson stood as erect as ever, though his son looked with concern at the near white hair and the increased lines on that stern dark face, now almost cadaverous.

'Father.'

The Reverend Edmund Nelson stepped forward to put his arms round his boy. Taller by several inches he hugged him with the kind of warmth that should have been exchanged between Nelson and Fanny, and in doing so he unwittingly underscored the distance between them.

'It is good to see you home, Horace,' he said, gruffly, 'and I think you know how proud you have made us.'

Then he stood back, his hands on his son's shoulders, wondering that a child of his should have achieved so much. He had loved his Horace as much as he had despaired of him, had been proud of his son for just being a post captain in the King's Navy. The battle won off Cape St Vincent had astounded Edmund Nelson as much as the reverse at Tenerife had depressed him, but the Nile victory had made him wonder at the possibility of an Immaculate Conception. Had there been so much fire in the bloodline of his late wife, Catherine, to make such a hero? He was certain that there was none in his.

'They have set aside the parlour so that we can talk,' Nelson said, taking his father's arm to lead him forward.

Seated out of public view in the small salon, Fanny perched alone on a chaise-longue while the two men occupied chairs. Conversation was stilted, but Edmund Nelson brought his son up to date on the doings of his siblings. Nelson said little, but Fanny sat in near silence, only responding when her father-in-law sought confirmation regarding a sister, a brother or a grandchild. Eventually, after some twenty minutes, realising that a married couple who had not seen each other for two and a half years needed time alone, Nelson's father took his leave.

When he had gone, Nelson said, 'You look well, Fanny.'

'Then it only proves, husband, how appearances can deceive.'

It had been a feeble opening, and Nelson knew he deserved that sharp response. But it had also been necessary: he had no idea of what his wife knew. All he had was his own determination.

'You are unwell?'

Fanny was nervous. She had expected some shyness in Nelson, some evidence of guilt, but it was absent. He was behaving as though nothing was amiss. Perhaps that was the truth. Could it be that all that gossip was wrong?

'I am troubled – not least, husband, to find you staying here in a public hotel instead of at the house I have taken for us both.'

'Hard by Portman Square,' Nelson replied, without rancour, 'a location I expressly requested you to avoid.'

'I cannot see that makes a jot of difference, and nor will it till you vouchsafe to me the nature of your objections.'

'I admit I did not issue a direct command . . .'

'Command?' Fanny interrupted.' Are you still at sea?'

'A word ill chosen,' Nelson said hastily.

Fanny fought hard to control her emotions. She must be patient, must play upon his sentimental feelings for her. If he had indeed strayed she wanted him to come back to her of his own free will. 'You know I hate the winter, husband.'

Nelson smiled. 'Even in London.'

'I grant you it is not Norfolk,' said Fanny, feeling on safe ground, 'though Roundwood ran it close. Even your own father admitted to that.'

Fanny had hated his home at Burnham Thorpe, not least because it reminded her that their five-year stay in his father's Norfolk rectory had been forced upon them by Nelson's lack of employment and the consequent shortage of income. But there were other factors: biting east winds that came straight from frozen Arctic wastes, barren trees that sighed even more than she did as she pined for the warm Caribbean sunshine in which they had been betrothed. With no childhood connection to Norfolk she could not be brought to love it, nor accept people she thought of as rustics, even when the sun shone on a warm summer day.

'You do know that I called at Roundwood?'

'No,' Fanny replied, surprised but still poised.

'With my travelling companions,' Nelson added. 'I was quite put out not to be able to offer them hospitality after all that they have done for me.'

'They would have frozen, husband,' Fanny said vehemently, 'especially in the present spell. Why, even in here the howl of the wind is audible.'

'The weather is exceptionally foul,' Nelson replied. 'Somehow I had always seen myself return in sunshine.'

'When common men stir no sight is seen, the elements themselves trumpet forth the arrival of heroes.'

The paraphrase of Shakespeare's line on the birth of Caesar had clearly pleased him, because Nelson grinned at her, allowing Fanny to relax and do likewise.

'I do not recall that Halley's Comet was seen on the day I was born.'

'It should have been, husband, given what you have achieved.'

'Thank you for that, Fanny.'

'It is hardly fitting that we perch thus, Horatio,' she said. 'Will you not sit with your wife.'

Tempted to refuse, Nelson could not, and as he sat closer to her he experienced a feeling of warmth. When she held out her hand, he took it, and he could not avoid the direct look she gave him. Was she questioning him? Again he smelt her lemon scent, which conjured up some of the better moments of their joint past.

There was still something in her face of the handsome woman she had once been, and it could be said with certainty that she comported herself in exemplary fashion as the wife of a naval hero, both in her carriage and her manners. Everyone who had mentioned her in his correspondence had nothing but praise for Fanny. She was as kind as he would be himself to an itinerant sailor, of whatever rank, and utterly at home in the layer of London society in which she moved.

She kept her social obligations assiduously and there was not a senior officer or politician born who could complain of being ignored by Lady Nelson. She had taken on the care of his father without ever once alluding to it as a burden. In short, she was a good person, and he knew that he had no desire to hurt the woman for whom he still carried a high degree of affection. Nelson prayed she could be brought to see what good Sir William had seen: that his love for Emma was too strong to withstand.

'You are healthier than when I saw you last,' Fanny said softly.

'Yes.'

It could hardly be otherwise, although he knew that two and a half years in the Mediterranean had taken its toll, the wear and tear of battle and command. Fanny was referring to the period after the failure at Tenerife and the loss of his arm, a troubled time of constant worry and pain: worry that he had sent men to die to no good purpose, pain from a wound that would not heal. Nelson could not help but recall how supportive Fanny had been, always there when required, quiet, elegant, keen to reassure him that the way his attack had been rebuffed added lustre to his name for the heroism of the action. She insisted all blame for the defeat had fallen on the deficiencies of the political masters who had sanctioned the attempt without providing the means to guarantee success.

Fanny put up a hand to stroke Nelson's cheek. 'Yet you look tired.'

Nelson didn't recoil. Her touch felt as natural now as it had in the past. 'I was a perfect wreck four months ago. I would not have said it before, but being on land restores me, that and good company.'

Nelson knew that by alluding to his travelling companions once more he had set out to shatter any intimacy between Fanny and him, and it was plain that she saw it to. She didn't snatch away her hand but let it fall gently to her side. But there was hurt in her eyes, much as she sought to disguise it.

'I so want you to meet them, Fanny,' he said, 'for they are the kindest people on earth.'

'You often wrote to tell me so,' she replied, her voice soft.

'And now, my dear, you are to meet them in the flesh, for I have arranged that we shall all have dinner together this very evening.'

20

When Emma first met Fanny it was a moment for sharp observation, and what she saw was in a large measure what she had expected. Fanny's face was long, thin and solemn, her nose prominent with skin that seemed dry. Around her set mouth Emma could see the vertical wrinkles that rose over the thin top lip, which was downy with hair. Her blue eyes were pale and lacklustre, with generous bags beneath them. Her hair was pepper and salt and, though held by a blue silk bow, several untidy curls had escaped at the nape of her neck. Not tall, her body was more hips than shoulder, she lacked a waist and had no bosom to speak of. She wore a dun-coloured dress, cut high, with added lace arranged scarf-like to show little neck. The whole image was one of overwhelming respectability, of a woman comfortable to be sinking into dull middle age.

'Lady Nelson,' Emma said, stepping forward, 'how pleased I am to make your acquaintance at last.'

What Fanny Nelson saw was a woman a good deal larger than she had expected, but one who had been and still thought of herself as a beauty. The hair was so rich in colour that she a suspected dye, but the face was warm and smiling, with round rosy cheeks and a high forehead above large green eyes. Dressed in a deep burgundy-coloured gown Lady Hamilton was not afraid to show a great deal of neck, though her ample cleavage was masked by a sparkling silver cross studded with gemstones.

Was she a harlot? Emma Hamilton was certainly fulsome and forward, at home in company, lacking any hint of shyness. But the shock in the meeting for Fanny was that her husband, who had pledged his love to her, could find attraction in one to whom she was so contrasted. There was no refinement in Emma Hamilton that Fanny Nelson could see.

Still, she would reserve judgement, keep her own counsel, give no cause for offence and let matters take their course. She would avoid any situation in which a precipitous decision could be made. All the parties needed time to adjust to the more rigorous social climate of London. That applied to her and her husband when alone, and even more so in this company.

'Allow me to name Sir William Hamilton to you, Fanny.'

The old man stepped forward on his stick-like legs to take her hand, execute a deep bow over it, and brushed it gently with his lips. It was the act of the perfect courtier and that impression underlined her appreciation of his features when he stood again: a prominent nose, which denoted activity, under a broad forehead, which implied intelligence. The blue eyes still had in them enough sparkle to indicate devilry and the way the man held himself, in expectation of elegant conversation, was attractive.

'I have long wanted to meet you Lady Nelson,' he said, 'for I have been in receipt of much correspondence lauding you. I see now that those who wrote to me were not mistaken.'

Fanny executed a little curtsy, then, since the clock had chimed five o'clock, allowed Sir William to seat both her and his wife at the table. There she sat, opposite Emma, trying hard not to look that lady in the eye, knowing that to do so would incline her to be angry and disputatious.

The curtains were closed to keep out the dark cold night, though the wind could still be heard as it gusted at the creaking windows. Everything seemed to shrink to the table, which was well lit with double candelabra reflecting off white linen. The only other light stood in a corner by the sideboard, which was used by the servant to transfer food from chafing dish to plate, and wine from bottle to decanter.

That the woman was so different was initially surprising, but Fanny was now inclined to look on it as a good thing. Warm sunshine and loose Italian morals might suit this Hamilton creature, but that bloom would struggle in cold winter London. Nelson had been absent from her side too long: he had forgotten the asset that she was to his name and station. Once reminded of that, Fanny was convinced he would see sense.

Over the soup, conversation turned to Nelson's success at the Nile, and Fanny noticed the excessive level of mutual praise between this trio with whom she was dining. Modesty was her watchword, as it was to all right-thinking folk, and she longed to remind them of this, but, true to her strategy she bit her tongue.

Nelson praised Sir William as an ambassadorial rock whose thirty-seven years of service had laid the foundation for all that followed, only to hear a paean to his own character from the ex-Ambassador. And if his approbation of Sir William was fulsome, that for Lady Hamilton was extravagant. It seemed to Fanny that her husband would not have stood any chance in battle without the woman's aid.

'I did my duty,' said Emma, in a rare attempt at modesty.

'And I say bravo to that.' Nelson cried, beaming at his wife. 'I did try to get the government to recognise Lady Hamilton's contribution, my dear, but they were deaf to my entreaties. Fortunately the Tsar of Russia was not so tardy, as the cross at Emma's neck will testify.'

The use of her name, and the intimacy it implied, had everyone spooning their soup with concentration. Nelson was blushing at his gaffe, Fanny was seething, but she maintained her *sang froid* as the soup plates were replaced with a the fish course.

Emma was determined to pick up the conversation and root it firmly in the triumph of the battle. 'I cannot describe to you, Lady Nelson, the joy that attended the news of Lord Nelson's victory. Naples was *en fête* for weeks.'

'I have never been to so many balls and entertainments in such a short space of time, my dear,' added Nelson. 'Damn me if I wasn't closer to expiry in Naples than I was at Aboukir.'

Fanny shot her husband a sharp look for employing such shipboard language in her company. How far had these people corrupted him? Then she replied to Emma, 'There was much joy in London too, Lady Hamilton.'

'I am sure it could not have compared to Naples. Even the King and Queen danced for joy.'

'Is that not unseemly behaviour for a monarch?' asked Fanny, archly, before adding. 'Though I daresay the removal of a guillotine blade from a royal neck is an occasion for some vivacity.'

'Take my word for it, Lady Nelson,' said Sir William, quick to cover another chill in the atmosphere, 'I saw our own sovereign dance many a jig when we were lads together.'

Fanny grasped at that, aware that she had forsaken her planned approach. 'You were a boon companion, I believe.'

'We shared a nursery, George and I, and much more besides as we grew up. I fear now, though, that he has become too serious for his own good.'

'He has much to make him so,' said Fanny.

Sir William smiled at Fanny, thinking that she was without doubt a good woman, no beauty but with a fine sense of refinement. In some ways she reminded him of his first wife, Catherine, who had been cut from the same mould. Respectable, with a determination not to see that which was otherwise; musical without too much talent, good at embroidery and all the other domestic talents; an excellent hostess who was a boon and close companion. She had made him very happy. But was Fanny Nelson like Catherine in any other way – for instance in the matter of turning a blind eye to her husband's peccadilloes?

'Would that King Ferdinand of Naples,' Sir William added, 'was a little less frivolous and our own dear sovereign a little more so.'

'I have heard much of this Ferdinand,' Fanny replied, enquiringly.

Not the half of it, thought Emma.

Ferdinand might be a lecher and a boor, but Sir William was happy to make him sound a harmless and amusing booby. He related to Fanny Nelson a number of the Sicilian king's oddities without referring to anything salacious that might embarrass her. The subject of sovereigns and their foibles being safe ground for all four diners the conversation flowed in a way that allowed Nelson to relax, moving easily on to commoners and recent events with Sir William at his most urbane.

Fanny was happy on the safe ground of a general conversation led by Sir William, who ranged far and wide with ease; the masked condemnation of this person or that, usually someone in government, carefully wrapped in what sounded like praise; the excitement for him of a dig and the discovery of some ancient artefact, the disaster of the sinking of the ship bringing the bulk of his treasures home, which earned vocal sympathy from Fanny.

'I am not entirely bereft, Lady Nelson. I kept back my best pieces to travel with me. They are being brought by separate conveyance from Lowestoffe where we landed.'

He didn't add that he would be obliged to sell the things he cherished, vases, coins and statuary, which he had intended to keep, and he felt sad as he described them in some detail to Nelson's wife.

The servants had just set before them the meat course, thick slices of fine, rare roast beef as befitted a British hero. Nelson, tasting the claret, was too busy to notice that the ladies saw food with which a one-armed man would struggle. Both Emma and Fanny moved simultaneously to cut up his beef, each noticed the other do it, and froze.

There was no avoiding difficulty now. They sat, eyes locked, as if daring the other to undertake the task. It was a defining moment for both women, a duty that only one should perform. Fanny, when her husband had come home from Tenerife minus his arm, had become accustomed to beg anyone who invited them to dine to be allowed the unusual privilege of sitting beside her husband for just such a purpose. That Lady Hamilton should assume it with Fanny present was outrageous.

Sir William, quick to react, called for a servant, 'Will you cut Lord Nelson's meat for him?' The servant whipped away the plate away as Sir William added to Fanny, 'It was a task my wife kindly undertook for him on our journey.'

'For which I thank you, Lady Hamilton,' said Fanny icily. 'But now that my husband is home, I will do it for him.'

Emma was silent for one reason; she expected her lover to say something – not to put his wife in her place, that would be asking too much, but to inform her, somehow, that she no longer had sole rights to such intimacies. Nelson said nothing: he waited until his meat was put in front of him, then proceeded to eat it.

The rest of the meal passed in near silence, with Fanny stiff. Nelson red-faced, drinking more than was good for him, and Emma seething.

'I must tell you,' said Nelson, trying to keep the conversation between him and Fanny formal, 'that I have made an appointment to be at the Admiralty by seven of the clock.'

They were back in the parlour, the meal over, the Hamiltons departed, man and wife alone, standing, not sitting, both fearful, both determined.

'And I must tell you, husband, that the meal I have just consumed was one of the least pleasant in my life. Did you deliberately set out to discomfort me?'

That was the opposite of what he had wanted to do. 'I wished merely for you to meet my friends, Fanny, to get to know them and to esteem them as I do.'

'It is a matter of some conjecture just how well you know your friends, husband, especially Lady Hamilton. Do you think me blind? Do you not know that half of the people who have written to me from Naples have alluded to a connection with that woman that goes way beyond the bounds of friendship.'

Nelson didn't want the truth to emerge with Fanny in such a mood. 'And what do you believe?'

'Since I do not know what to believe I require that you tell me from your own lips whether such assertions are true or malicious.'

Still he felt the need to procrastinate, still the hope that there would be no need for a confrontation. 'Do you believe that certain things are preordained?'

Fanny didn't reply, and Nelson took her arm to sit her down, which she did reluctantly, perched upright and rigid as he began to pace back and forth.

'You know that I do, Fanny, for I have told you often enough of the dreams I had regarding my destiny.' He stopped and looked hard at her. 'I knew I would be a hero. Before I was even a lieutenant I knew I would command fleets and win the kind of victories that are now attached to my name.'

She could not deny that, though even now she would not admit that the way her husband had talked about 'his visions' had sometimes troubled her as being almost blasphemous. Fanny felt it was not for mere mortals, however convinced they were of their attributes, to forestall the Almighty. She had thought her husband sometimes a touch deranged when he talked of such things, near penniless in a Norfolk Rectory. The light in his eyes had been as it was now: absolute certainty about the future, which to Fanny, as it should be to any God-fearing person, was sacrilege.

'I have heard enough of your victories on this occasion, husband,' Fanny snapped. 'And, I must say of the attributes of your friends. Rarely have I heard such vanities. If that is what passes for proper behaviour in Naples it will scarce pass here. Strutting peacocks would blush to hear the acclamation you granted each other.'

'You would want me humble?'

'I would want modesty, husband, which is a quality, not a crime.'

Nelson's eyes were suddenly sad, the light of destiny gone to be replaced by gentleness. He realised there was no course open to him now but to tell the truth. 'Would you believe me if I told you that I have no desire to cause you any hurt?'

Fanny knew the meaning of that, and knew that if she responded she would hear words she dreaded. She also knew there was no alternative but to speak, though she left it open for her husband to pull back from the direction in which he was heading.

'Nothing would please me more than that you should convince me of it.'

Nelson wanted to tell her she had been a dutiful wife, a sterling companion and a great support. Yet he knew that was not what he felt. It would be too much to say that she had betrayed him, thus allowing him to do the same. He knew that it had been his enthusiasm that had got them to the altar, but she must have known his needs and desires. Had she set out to fulfil them only to find she could not, or had she never had any intention of satisfying him?

'What do you want of me, Fanny?' he asked, temporising.

'That you should lay the ghost of this gossip, husband.' She looked around the small parlour, almost with distaste. 'That you should leave this place with me at once, and let all London know that on the hero's return he has come back to his family as well as his nation.'

Nelson spoke softly, almost with sadness. 'That I cannot do.'

Fanny dropped her head. 'Am I to be told why?'

'You know why.'

'Lady Hamilton?'

'Emma,' said Nelson, with some force.

'Such familiarity,' said Fanny, 'A friendship must be very deep for that.'

'Emma is more than a friend, Fanny. I am in love with her.'

'You have . . .' Fanny paused, '. . . taken matters beyond mere mutual regard.'

'Yes.'

She had one defence left, that the sun and his fame had turned his head, and there to take advantage of his state of mind had been a woman who had once been a whore, and had turned into a climber, latching on leech-like to a hero.

'You are sure, husband, that this is not mere infatuation?'

'I thought that on first meeting Emma seven years ago.'

'Seven years,' gasped Fanny. 'You have kept this from me for seven years?'

Suddenly the continual references to the good Lady Hamilton in all those earlier letters made sense. How could she have been so blind? Later reflection would tell her that she could not have known: that Nelson had said as much about others, including women, as he had about Emma Hamilton.

Quietly Nelson explained that it had not all been deceit. He could honestly say that he had doubted his own feelings for five years and that it was only seeing Emma again that had brought them to the fore. Fanny listened in silence, her fingers knotted around a handkerchief, determined not to give way to tears.

'If you say you do not wish to hurt me, husband, that must mean you still have some regard for my feelings.'

'I do,' replied Nelson, truthfully.

'Then I demand a chance. I have that right.' She looked up at him for the first time in an age. 'You and I have had so little time together these last seven years it is scarce to be wondered that you have forgotten what it was that attracted us to each other in the first place. I ask that you spend some time with me, give me the chance to rekindle in your heart some of the tender feelings you have expressed so eloquently in your letters.'

'Fanny.'

'A chance?'

Now that matters were out in the open he wanted to say no, to draw a line. Yet good sense prevailed: if Fanny could be brought to see that there was no alternative a fourth might be added to the trio of himself, Emma and Sir William. Not a happy quartet necessarily, but a tolerant one.

'And if it should come to naught?'

'You will be late for your appointment,' said Fanny with some force, pointing to a wall clock showing it was nearing seven. 'And since you are calling on Lord Spencer, I will take the opportunity of calling on his dear wife.'

Nelson, still pondering that conversation with his wife found it hard to concentrate on what Spencer was saying to him. The First Lord was embarrassed, that was plain. He wanted somehow to have Nelson see his admonition in the despatch as having been required officially, but which was a thing personally regrettable. He manifested this in an openly stated willingness to listen to any ideas his visitor might have about future postings. He also insisted that everyone on the Board of Admiralty was eager to hear Nelson's appreciation of what should happen in the Mediterranean. That wasn't true: some still thought Nelson no more than a lucky individual, who had found himself in the right place at the right time, with the right weapon to hand. Luck was a fickle thing, prone to run out, and certainly no basis for tactical dispositions. And then there were Keith's complaints.

The implication of Fanny's presence in the same building was clear: that as Lord Nelson's wife she, not Lady Hamilton, could expect to be received in such a setting. And, naturally, with both she and her husband in such close proximity, when it came time for him to leave they would return to their own home together. In the latter she was both disappointed and embarrassed, for on enquiring about Nelson's whereabouts, Fanny was informed that having discussed the possibility of some new postings with Lord Spencer, he had left for his hotel.

For the first time Fanny saw masked sympathy in the eyes of a member of her social circle, which she had dreamt of and dreaded.

Lady Spencer knew as much as anyone about what had gone on in Naples. She was her husband's main support, with whom he discussed all the problems of an office he felt himself unqualified to fill. To make matters worse, Lady Spencer had issued an invitation to dine on the next but one night, as eager as the rest of London to capture Nelson as a guest. Fanny had accepted on behalf of them both, only now to be faced with the possibility that her husband might refuse.

Indeed that was his first reaction on receipt of Fanny's note, which arrived before he retired for the night, telling him of the engagement. Nelson was sure he could smoke her game. Fanny would enmesh him in a round of social obligations that would keep him away from Emma. She would parade their marriage in a way that would make it impossible for him to break free of her clutches.

'I would do much more than that, Nelson, if I feared to lose you.' Emma laid her head on his chest, having listened to her lover's report of what had transpired. Her reflection on the evening was confused. At one moment she saw it as having gone horribly wrong, at another quite well. If Nelson had not spoken to support her over the incident with the meat he had not defended his wife either, which Emma had feared: she had been only too aware of the time they had spent apart, and that seeing Fanny again might cause him to pause.

Nelson stroked her hair away from her eyes. 'You must never fear to lose me, Emma. You are the keeper of my heart.'

'Then I must purchase a silver casket in which to carry it.'

Nelson slid down under the coverlet, pulling Emma's shoulder until they were lying head to head.

'You already have a casket, my love.'

Emma laughed, and pressed herself hard against him as his good hand rucked up first her nightdress, then his own bed gown. One leg was pressed without resistance between hers and a slight roll allowed Emma to push herself under him. His lips were at her neck, her lips close by his ear as she whispered, 'That is not made of silver, Nelson, and what you propose to place within it is not your heart.'

21

Nelson was still basking in the glow of the previous night's City of London banquet as he and Sir William set off for Windsor Castle. The accolades from the city merchants had been loud and continuous, though they had listened to his short speech of thanks in respectful silence. This body had already gifted him ten thousand pounds for the Nile, a tidy sum but small given the million they must have saved on insurance claims. Now they had added a commemorative sword with a jewel-studded gold hilt, as well as their personal appreciation.

Sir William, presenting himself as was his right as a retiring ambassador, was wondering if his sovereign remembered the last time they had spoken, just after his marriage to Emma nine years previously, before he had returned to take up his duties in Naples. It had not been a happy parting. King George had declined to receive the new Lady Hamilton, causing his old friend to remind him that he ruled only by the consent of his subjects – not a cheering thought for the likes of Farmer George, who became fractious at any mention of the French Revolution.

Since the levee had been gazetted and Lord Nelson was known to be due, knots of people anxious to see him lined the route to Windsor. This reassured him that if some at the Admiralty doubted the virtue of his conduct, there was nothing but affection for him from the populace, whether rich City bankers or these good folk on the road. Within minutes of his arrival the King had disabused him of this idea. Having formally, and somewhat brusquely, accepted Sir William Hamilton's letters of retirement, he turned to the Hero of the Nation.

'How d'ye do, Lord Nelson?' barked King George, in his abrupt staccato manner. 'How's your health?'

'Much improved, Your Majesty,' replied Nelson, finding himself fixed by bulbous-blue Hanoverian eyes. The face was red and fat, the lips thick and glossy with saliva.

'And Lady Nelson?' demanded the King.

'Is well,' Nelson replied, after a short pause.

That delay was enough to allow the King to turn his back on Nelson and immediately engage an army officer in deep conversation, leaving the Admiral in the embarrassing position of staring at the royal back. Everyone in the room had witnessed the royal snub, and this from the man to whom Nelson had devoted his service life. Sir William, nearby, shook his head in despair, and his friend was left with nothing to do but blush. Nelson noticed that those who had been eager to speak with him when the King was finished were now edging away. None would dare to offend their sovereign by speaking to a man who was only present on sufferance.

What was more depressing to Nelson was the presence of several of his service superiors, even one or two who had in the past been members of the Board of Admiralty. And it was clear from the attitude of some that they thought Nelson was only getting his just deserts. What for? he wondered. His love of Emma or his defiance of Lord Keith? For the first time he realised the depth of the enmity against him that existed in some quarters.

It remained like that for half an hour, with King George totally absorbed in his conversation with the soldier. Nelson could not leave – no one could until the King departed; that was the protocol. Only Sir William conversed with Nelson, making him feel like a pariah as he waited for the King to turn round again. Farmer George did nothing of the kind: as soon as he finished with the soldier he marched out of the audience chamber, leaving behind a buzz of speculative conversation.

As they made to leave, a liveried servant handed Sir William a note. He opened it and his bony face took on an angry look. He passed it to Nelson who saw it was from the head of the Queen's household, the purpose to inform Sir William, curtly, that his wife would not be welcome at Queen Charlotte's Drawing Room the following day. Emma, Lady Hamilton, was not going to be received at court.

'After all she has done,' said Nelson.

'The King has treated you just as badly, my friend. I wonder what he found so interesting about that soldier's conversation.' Sir William then added in a wry tone, 'I'm sure they were not discussing his successes.'

Nelson had a more pressing concern and waved the note. 'I do not envy you, breaking this news to her.'

Sir William did not relish the prospect either, and it was a silent pair that coached back to London.

Nelson had no desire to take dinner with the Spencers. First, Lady Spencer, though a sparkling conversationalist, was not noted for the quality of food or wine at her table. Second, it was very much a service affair attended by some of the admirals who had been at Windsor that morning and witnessed his humiliation by the King. Third, Lady Spencer had enquired of him if he wanted to be placed next to Fanny, as he had on a previous occasion, so that she could help him with his food. He had angrily declined.

As if to add insult to injury his hosts had seated him opposite Admiral Sir Richard Hughes, an old adversary whose conversational gambits, and fawning respect for Fanny, seemed designed to make Nelson feel uncomfortable. The only saving grace was that Lady Hughes, his battle-axe of a wife, was seated far enough away for her overbearing voice and manner to be inaudible.

Now a vice-admiral of the White Squadron, Sir Richard had only one more rank above that to achieve. If he lived, and others died, he would end up as an Admiral of the Fleet, doubtless with the necessary peerage, although he had not been at sea or held anything other than shore commands for fifteen years.

To Nelson he was the worst kind of officer, a trimmer and time-server. They had clashed in the Caribbean when, as second in command to Sir Richard, he had insisted that he enforce the laws relating to foreign vessels trading into the sugar islands. His then commanding officer had concurred with him only to rescind that agreement as soon as Nelson's ship was out of sight over the horizon. The result had been a lawsuit against Nelson, which, had it been successful, would have ruined him.

But Sir Richard was powerful, not because of his innate gifts, but for his connections. He came from an extended naval family of many generations standing. Several, including this one, had served on the Admiralty Board and were famous and active officers with whom Nelson would have been proud to serve. But the family connection made no distinction between the worthy and the ineffectual. When not at sea the Hughes clan were of the type to ensure that their voices could be heard, because they spent a great deal of time cultivating their fellow officers. In Sir Richard's case, this was with a view to feathering his own nest, a task at which he spent much more time than he ever did in confronting the country's enemies.

Now he was busy telling Fanny about the splendid success Lord Keith had enjoyed in taking Genoa from the French. He had lost ships and men in the process, but even Nelson had nothing but praise for his actions: although they disagreed about many things, not least about the tactical distribution of the fleet, Keith was an active officer and an inspiring commander. But he was no genius, which was what Sir Richard was implying to Fanny.

It was with more sorrow than anger that Sir Richard turned to the difficulties of a divided command, the opinion that the presence of more ships and greater application at certain vital junctures might have ensured another Nile. It was all carefully couched not to name Nelson, but sharp enough to let him know that Hughes, who had reckoned him insubordinate as a Caribbean post captain, still thought him so.

Fanny took a while to pick up her husband's mood and to realise what lay behind Sir Richard's subtle barbs. That she had let him burble on infuriated Nelson, who wondered if in his absence anyone could say anything they liked about him to his wife and not be checked. The thought that he was being unfair to Fanny lay at the back of his mind, but his annoyance was so great as to disallow any possibility that it might surface.

In truth, he was still smarting from the treatment meted out to him by King George. For a man who prided himself on representing his subjects Farmer George had missed the mark by a mile, proved on his return: the route from Windsor was still lined with well-wishers few of whom, Sir William assured him, would turn out for the King himself.

Fanny had been shelling walnuts for him, one of the many tasks that had been beyond him since he lost his arm. She filled a small glass dish and pushed it across to him. With his left arm he swept them to one side, glaring at Sir Richard. The dish smashed on a candlestick, killing the conversation. Every eye turned first to Nelson, then to his wife. Across the table, Sir Richard Hughes allowed himself a slow smile.

'Mr James Perry, milady.'

'Thank you,' said Emma, still fingering the calling card that had preceded her visitor. Quickly she tidied up the materials left by the

213

dressmaker for her approval, silks of various colours and lace of such fine quality it must have been smuggled in from France.

Perry entered, tall, a bit stooping now, but still with something of the looks he had had as a young man. He was a newspaper editor now, of one of the most important titles in the capital, the *Morning Chronicle*. But more than that he was an old acquaintance of Emma.

'Mr Perry.'

'Lady Hamilton,' Perry replied, an enigmatic smile playing on his lips. 'You look to be blooming.'

It was a strange word to use, but Perry did not elaborate, leaving it in the air for his hostess to decipher. Not that she had much trouble with it. Perry was one of the best-informed men in London: he knew what was going on everywhere, had well placed informants all over Europe, probably had secrets in his desk drawer that would destroy half of society. But he was also discreet, especially with those to whom he was well disposed. Emma Hamilton was one of those people.

'My very favourite housemaid,' Perry added.

It was a well-worn joke between them, given that that was what Emma had been on their first meeting at a Southwark fairground. Emma had led him a merry dance that night, a recollection that Perry was always willing to see in an amusing light. When she had been mistress to Charles Greville they had come across each other frequently, given that he and Sir William Hamilton's nephew moved in much the same social circles. Perry had watched Emma develop with a distant but paternal eye, and had rejoiced to see her wed to old Sir William, in the certain knowledge that a girl who was lively, good-humoured and kindly had found some security.

Emma had asked him to call because she was in a quandary. The stumbling way in which her husband had informed her that she would not be received at court had hurt deeply. She was well enough aware of her own past to see why that should have been when she and Sir William had first been married. The King had disapproved of the match and only assented because his ambassador had come to him with a request from Queen Maria Carolina that it should be sanctioned.

But her efforts on behalf of her country in Naples must surely count for something. The British royal family and the government surely could not be unaware of how hard she had worked, and how much she had achieved on their behalf. While acknowledging that she had not been alone, Emma felt that it was mostly by her efforts, as a close companion to the Neapolitan Queen, that Naples had stayed true to the alliance with Great Britain.

Emma wanted to know what obstacles lay in her path, because only then could she work to remove them. She felt she could not ask Sir William because he would evade any answer that would cause her discomfort. Even less could she seek reasons from Nelson, for that might open the casket of worms that was her past. Perry was perfect; he knew her history, knew everyone who mattered and was something of a friend. She put the question to him.

'Ah, Emma,' Parry said, seated now, twirling a wineglass.

'With respect, James, that does not tell me very much.'

'I wonder what you would like me to say?'

'The truth.'

Perry felt sorry for her. Chequered past or not Emma was a good woman. If not without her vanities and a sense of humour sometimes hard for the prudish to appreciate, she knew how to be benevolent, as in the example of Cornelia Knight, a woman without either fortune or prospects whom Emma had nurtured as a friend and accepted as a responsibility. Within twenty-four hours of arriving in London that bosom friend had fled from any connection with the Hamiltons. She was now trying to persuade society that, despite her long association with the couple, she had had no idea of the any untoward connection between Emma and Lord Nelson.

'The first thing,' Perry said, 'is that you are with child and, given the length of your relationship with Sir William, it is unlikely that he is the father.' Emma blushed, which Perry found enchanting.

'Is this common knowledge?' Emma asked

'I have it, though I have told no one. Nor will I. But you must understand, Emma, that if I have it, then it is highly likely that others are informed. I am not the only newspaper editor, and I am certainly not Billy Pitt or the King.'

'They will know too.'

'It would surprise me if they did not,' Perry said sitting forward. 'Governments need to know the minds of others, much more than mere newspaper editors, thus, just as I do in a lesser way, they garner intelligence by fair means or foul. The Prime Minister is bound to share what he knows with the King. Let us take one example. How do you think your time in Naples has been viewed here in London?'

'Positively, I hope,' said Emma. 'I tried my best, and I believe my service had a great effect.'

Emma went on to list her achievements, not forgetting to show

Perry her jewelled Russian cross. He listened, helping himself to more wine, his face betraying neither agreement nor dissension. Could he tell her that what she had seen as service, helping her husband to be an effective ambassador, others had interpreted as interference? Could he tell her that what had come back from Naples was not tales of her effect upon the Queen, but of her extravagance? Many a guest at the Palazzo Sessa had flattered Emma, drunk deep at the trough of Hamilton hospitality, then written home to damn her as a whore risen too high and her husband as an old fool. Others, who had sat and applauded her Attitudes, had penned reports to relatives in London, excoriating them as lewd.

Perry thought he knew the truth, and though it was not, he suspected, as elevated as Emma would have liked it to be, it tended towards the positive. She had been a valuable asset and helpmate to Sir William. Certainly Emma was extravagant, certainly she was spendthrift, certainly she was given to exposing too much flesh in her performances, certainly she was married to a man far too old for her, but she was a joy to be with, famous all over Europe, and a linguist. In short, Emma was exceptional, and many of those who had met her in Italy were eager to say so.

And her effect on policy? She had been received by the King and Queen of Naples, the latter valuing her so much that she had breached the protocol that no foreigner could be received at court who had not enjoyed the same privilege from their own sovereign. Maria Carolina, a dour woman by all accounts, had gone out of her way to honour her friend. And every report Perry had was full of the regard that existed between Emma and the royal children. On balance, Emma's star should have been in the ascendant. But then there was Nelson.

'How long will you be staying here?' asked Perry.

'Lord Nelson is going to take a house, and as soon as he does we shall move there.' At this Perry made no attempt to mask his feelings: he looked disapproving. 'I can tell you, James – although my husband would hate me to do it – that we are utterly dependent on Lord Nelson for everything. The cost of Sir William's office has fallen so heavily on his purse, and he has lost so much, that we cannot meet our bills.'

The glance Perry aimed towards the piles of expensive silk and lace said more than any words he could have used. If Sir William was not paying for them, only one other person could be.

'Emma, how close are you to Nelson?'

Emma looked at her hands. 'Dare I tell you?'

216

'I think you just have.'

'You will be discreet?'

'Have I not been so already? And I am bound to add that as long as that association is suspected you will whistle for a reception at court. He will not tell you this but the King was exceedingly uncivil to Nelson at today's levee.'

'Because of me?'

He left the question unanswered. 'Do not move into any house Nelson takes, Emma. Rumours are rife enough without you fanning them.'

'That may be sound advice, James, but I fear we may have no choice.'

'Thank God,' cried Sir William Hamilton. He read again the letter from his old friend William Beckford, offering him the use of his town house in Grosvenor Square. Near to a palace in size, it was the kind of establishment Sir William could never have afforded, and here was Beckford not only offering it to him for free, but telling him to avail himself of his food suppliers and cellar as he wished.

Though he could never say so to Emma, he wished to be free of the constant presence of Nelson, because he hated to be dependent on him. The man he was happy to call a friend had never by word or deed intimated that he minded paying the Hamilton bills, but it was galling for a man of Sir William's breeding to be always at the back when settlements were required.

Beckford, a noted pederast, was as rich as Croesus, and half of London society loved him for his proclivities, his gaiety and his extravagance while the other half avoided him like the proverbial plague. The author of the famous novel *Vathek*, Beckford had been forced to flee the country for several years because of his very obvious sexual preferences. He had not been discreet on his return, lavishing his millions on a new country house at Fonthill in a style that the prudes found shocking.

Right now Sir William loved him for his generosity, and using Grosvenor Square as a separate establishment from Nelson's would go some way to dampening speculation about the relationship between the trio. Sir William was not troubled that his reputation would suffer – his wife having a lover would not raise an eyebrow – but Emma was different; the way she had been denied an appearance at court was ample proof of that. She had a reputation, and too much propinquity in the case of her and Horatio Nelson would not do it any good. He still had enough love for Emma to want to protect her from her headstrong self, and the complications attendant upon her giving birth under a roof provided by Nelson were incalculable. Beckford had solved that too.

Happier than he had been for a while, Sir William went in search of Mary Cadogan, passing as he did so the departing figure of James Perry.

Fanny knew she had lost her husband for ever the next night, when the whole *ménage* went to the opera. She would have preferred not to go in the company of the Hamiltons, but Nelson had insisted and included his father in the party. Since the Hamiltons had moved out of the hotel, Fanny felt there was a slim chance that her husband would escort her and his father home. He could hardly do that and refuse to cross the threshold. That was where she wanted him to be. Only there could her presence have the desired effect – no amount of meetings at social gatherings or in hotels would aid her cause. She was prepared in every respect to oblige him, and to admit that in the past she might have been less a wife to him than he required, so she dressed carefully, in a turban and a fetching silk dress, and paid careful attention to her toilet.

The usual crowd followed them through the streets, so the news that the Nelson party occupied a box overlooking the stage could not be kept from the rest of the audience. All stood to cheer as the Admiral entered, obliging him to come forward to wave to them while the orchestra played 'See the Conquering Hero Come', and Emma's favourite, 'Rule Britannia'.

Emma took a bow, Sir William took a bow, and so did Fanny, for once included in the adulation. Flowers that had been bought to toss at the performers were instead flung at them and for once Fanny felt, standing next to her husband, that she was in the right place. In such an atmosphere she could block out Emma Hamilton and imagine that they were a couple receiving what was their due. She had heard of the royal snub at Windsor, which was another problem that only she could solve. Let Nelson take her to meet the King and his reception would be different.

It was a full twenty minutes before they could sit down and the strain of standing had made Emma feel uncomfortable. In the womb the child was stirring and kicking. She knew her lover would want to feel this, so in the semi-darkness she took his hand and pressed it to her belly. Nelson felt a kick and his face lit up in a huge grin.

Then he heard a loud gasp, and lifted his head to see Fanny looking first at his hand, then at Emma, then at him. The knowledge that this was something with which she could not compete was in his wife's eyes. She had failed to give Nelson the child he craved.

Fanny came half out of her seat, letting out a loud cry, which caused the crowd to look up. Then she collapsed.

22

For the first time in his life Horatio Nelson was less than happy to be going to sea. Having spent Christmas in Wiltshire at Fonthill, the country home of William Beckford, he had experienced something that, apart from the weather, was almost like a return to Naples. There had been no Fanny, just himself and the Hamiltons, the *tria uno in juncto*, enjoying the company of a fabulously wealthy host, in a mansion on which he had lavished a quarter of a million pounds, and which he filled daily with amusing and admiring people.

To call Beckford 'a knowing one' or a Jemmy Jessamy was an understatement. He was flowery to the point of caricature, every gesture an exaggeration, a man who could make a drama out of even the most innocent statement. When he talked it was in a breathless way, his mind skipping from topic to topic. Over-dressed, foppish, given to studied alarm at any unpleasantness, yet generous to a fault, a man to whom kindness and consideration were an obligation not a pastime.

That he was a shameless pederast bothered Nelson not one whit. Having been at sea as long as he had, and having visited ports aplenty, there was not much of a sexual nature that was a mystery to him, nor did his nature run to condemnation. Yet it was true that others disapproved mightily of Beckford, and were wont to berate as less than suitable anyone who socialised with him. Sir William's view was simple: those who were worth knowing and talking to loved Beckford: those who did not, who hated or feared him, were to be avoided.

Nelson's own wife was among the latter. He had invited her to accompany him to Fonthill, but she had declined in shock, pleading with her eyes that he stay in London with her and his father. He could not agree to that. The prospect of even the shortest separation from Emma was not to be borne, and a cheerless Christmas in London had no appeal. But more important to Nelson was that Beckford adored Emma. And she loved Fonthill and its host.

When Emma and Sir William headed for London in the January chill, Nelson made his way to a meeting near Torbay with his old commander-in-chief, now likely to be his new one, Admiral the Earl St Vincent. Promoted to Vice Admiral of the Blue Squadron on New Year's Day, Nelson felt he could look his old chief right in the eye if he mentioned their ongoing dispute over prize money, which was near to coming to court and, hopefully, resolution. But St Vincent had more important matters to discuss, like a proposed expedition to the Baltic.

Tsar Paul of Russia ruled the greatest power in the northern region, which his neighbours had every reason to fear. Reputed to be as mad as a March hare, murderous with it, and enamoured of Napoleon, he had created a federation of four kingdoms: his own, Denmark, Sweden and Prussia, called the Northern League. Its object was to deny Great Britain access to the Baltic and the naval stores on which her fleet depended. In the straits between Sweden and Denmark, the Skagerrak and the Cattegat lay the entry to the seas beyond. It was paramount that it must be of free passage to the Royal Navy and to British mercantile trade. To leave them in the hands of those who were, in all but name, enemies of Britain, would cripple the fleet on which the nation's security depended.

Negotiations, especially with Denmark, had failed to resolve matters. The Danish king was more fearful of Russia than Britain, while voices in the British government were split between those who would keep talking and those who reckoned the only way to make the northern nations see sense was to pound it into them with cannon. Whatever course was adopted, a fleet must be sent to the area – no point in diplomacy if it was not backed up by force.

St Vincent was adamant that it was an operation for soldiers: that the Danish capital, key to the procedure should be taken from the landward side. The strait known as the Sound, the approaches to Copenhagen, was at best some four miles wide: it lay between Elsinore and the Swedish fort of Helsingborg. This, in St Vincent's opinion, constituted a graveyard for warships. And that was before naval vessels got anywhere near the main Danish defences. Just where the government was going to find the ten thousand troops required St Vincent had not ascertained, and, in truth, with no standing army to draw on, it would be a naval operation because there was no choice.

'They are planning to give the Baltic command to Sir Hyde Parker.'

Nelson was happy to see St Vincent so sprightly, more so than he had been on their last meeting two years previously off Cadiz. There, the wear and tear of endless years of sea time had undermined his health. There had always been something slightly odd about their relationship. As Admiral Sir John Jervis, St Vincent had been famous as a strict disciplinarian, who never suffered fools and was barely polite even to his most intelligent and active captains. On first meeting him, and well aware of his reputation, Nelson had expected to be treated in a like manner only to find the old and confirmed bachelor treated him as he would a favourite son.

Nelson knew that St Vincent had indulged him as he had no other officer under his command, giving him freedoms and responsibilities way above his rank, much to the chagrin of others, but it had paid handsome dividends at the battle from which St Vincent had earned his title. The Spanish fleet would have got away to the safety of their Cadiz base had Nelson not disobeyed the standing Admiralty orders contained in the Fighting Instructions and pulled out of his place in the line. It was he, risking court-martial and disgrace, who had brought them to battle, he who had boarded two Spanish ships in succession.

Nelson had become a hero to the nation and his Admiral had become Viscount St Vincent and a rich man. This had not dented his irascibility with others, or his determination to demand as much of the available prize money as he thought he could get away with. Nelson wasn't the only officer who had served under him who was keeping the lawyers busy.

Clearly a stint ashore and the waters of Bath had restored the old scoundrel to something of his former self. And the dispensation that allowed him to exercise his command from a shore base overlooking Torbay meant that he was not constantly at sea, which would only cause a relapse in the state of his health.

St Vincent was too discreet to stare openly at Nelson, but he saw the cloud on Nelson's brow at the mention of a command going to another admiral. It was one of the traits he loved about the man, that what he thought was imprinted on his face. In a world where most men hid their true opinions Nelson was an exception. St Vincent always felt he knew where he stood with him, a rarity indeed. If Nelson disapproved of a plan of action he said so, and his approbation was just as open and honest.

In near sixty years at sea, with a high measure of success, St

Vincent had never met Nelson's like. In his knowledge of his trade the man was a genius, who had the appealing trait of being unfazed by his gift. Nelson could dissect and explain an idea in a way that made it both clear and dramatic to whomsoever he spoke: seaman, officer, captain, and admiral. He had a healthy disrespect for rigidity in tactics, allied to an almost encyclopaedic knowledge of sea warfare through the ages. Show him an enemy, singly or in the mass, and he would, by some uncanny endowment, have the measure of them, their power in gunnery, their seamanship, their morale, in seconds.

Nelson knew his trade as well as any officer St Vincent had ever commanded: he was a first class seaman, a brilliant navigator, a master of every task on the ship that fell to every different trade or function. But it was his leadership that was most impressive. St Vincent had once wanted to be loved by his men, but had settled instead for their respect. To an orderly mind like St Vincent's, Nelson ran his ships like a Barbary bazaar. In any course of action there was too much opinion-giving by junior officers, while warrant officers felt free to publicly moan if they felt slighted or overworked. Even a common sailor would look Nelson right in the eye and dare to smile at him if the mood took him.

Yet a Nelson ship sailed better and fought harder than any other vessel in the fleet. If there was some difficult and hazardous duty to undertake Nelson was the man to send. Some said he was a chancer, but St Vincent knew differently. Nelson was merely the supreme master of the fighting sailor's craft. He knew instinctively what others would spend hours agonising over.

'Sir Hyde Parker?' said Nelson, his face screwed up with uncertainty.

'It's seniority, Nelson,' St Vincent replied, although he knew that there were other reasons for not giving Nelson the post.

'I cannot imagine that particular gentleman in an active role.'

'He's more active than you think, Nelson. The old goat is about to wed Sir Richard Onslow's daughter, a lady over forty years his junior. A batter pudding of eighteen with no brains, to my way of thinking, but she's bound to be sprightly at that age.'

St Vincent was thinking that if only Nelson had not shown such disregard for Keith's orders then the voices against him at the Admiralty could have been silenced. Not privy to the truth about what had happened in the Mediterranean, when the public and the press heard about the Baltic expedition they would clamour for England's best admiral and the Board might bend. But there again, maybe it would not: the man's attachment to Emma Hamilton had further soured his reputation, even if his adoring public knew even less of that.

Given the choice, the Board would probably have left him on the beach, but the John Bulls of the shires, to whom he was the greatest hero since Drake, would not stand for it. St Vincent had even heard it said in some quarters that to treat Nelson badly was to risk bringing down the Government. Exaggeration, of course, but it showed how Nelson stood with both those in power, and those who had to put them there.

Nelson knew Sir Hyde Parker. He had been third in command to Hotham at the action off Genoa and just as supine as the titular commander, a trimmer who would always take the easy route out of any problem.

Then I predict,' he said, 'that Sir Hyde Parker will sail to the Skagerrak, look at the Danes, think of the comforts of a young wife and sail straight home again.'

'Not if they send you with him,' St Vincent added, with a wicked grin.

That made Nelson sit up. 'There is a possibility?'

St Vincent chuckled. 'You think the Board of Admiralty is stupid, I know, but occasionally they can be counted on to show some sense, provided they heed the right advice. Parker is a lover of comfort not war, of his new wife and her charms in the bedchamber, not life aboard a ship in the North Sea. He has the seniority for the command, but not the stomach, unless you count its size. I have been asked my opinion and it is that they must send someone active with him. I intend to recommend you.'

Lord Spencer was aware as a civilian that the service members of the Board of Admiralty and permanent officials had an agenda that was not entirely attuned to his. The First Lord was a politician, and his appointment stemmed from that, though that was true of all the other members: no sensible government peopled such a vital controlling body with opposition supporters.

The exception was Evan Nepean. The long-serving Admiralty secretary was possibly the most important person in the room. He had in his hands all the details of the greatest fleet in the world: ships, numbers of men, monies available to support that huge enterprise and the areas in which weaknesses existed. In appearance he conformed to what a secretary should look like: grey-faced, with heavy lidded eyes under an old fashioned full wig.

Admirals and secretaries had a loyalty to the Navy and the way it was run that transcended politics, and Nelson's behaviour as a junior admiral to Keith had caused much disquiet. It had also given those who resented his success a grievance to work on. Spencer had letters from high-ranking officers, Sir Richard Hughes among them, who thought Nelson an upstart and a swell-head, and advised that a period of inactivity would remind him of his place.

Before the convening of the Board, Spencer had a meeting with Sir Hyde Parker to discuss chastising the Danes in a way that would reopen the Baltic to British merchant shipping. For all Parker's imposing bulk and handsome profile, Spencer had sensed reluctance in the man. He had just returned from the West Indies with a fortune estimated at three hundred thousand pounds. To Spencer, he had seemed more interested in where he was going to locate his country house than in forcing a defended passage.

Asked who he wanted as his second in command, Parker had demurred, showing some skill in the way he avoided commitment, keen to imply that he would work with whichever officer the Board of Admiralty wished to send to him. Yet Spencer knew from his social informants that Parker was dead set against Nelson and had said so to several influential friends.

Had Spencer been wholly a Nelson partisan then the conclusion would have been foregone. But his opinion was variable, high when he recalled the relief he had felt at news of the Nile, less so when his wife reminded him of the way the Admiral was treating his noble wife. Then there was the distinct possibility of a scandal becoming public knowledge at any time, which bothered the King nearly as much as the subject of Catholic emancipation.

As he looked down the long, highly polished table, Spencer knew that in the event of failure in the Baltic he was most at risk and, through him, William Pitt and the government. They were on rocky ground anyway, Pitt trying to force through an Act of Union with Ireland, freeing the papists from the debarring articles of the Protestant faith, with the intransigent King dead set against it. The way things were shaping Spencer was unsure if he would be in his chair for another week.

That applied to the other appointed Board members though they seemed unaware of it. Nepean would survive, but the rest must know that there were other political problems, not least the clamour for peace. After seven years of war the nation was weary. So, to a political mind, success in the Baltic was of paramount importance.

Yet it seemed that nobody at this table was going to mention

Nelson's name. He was like Banquo's ghost, there in everyone's thoughts but absent from the discussion because merely to mention him would precipitate remembrance of his exceptional abilities. Nepean did not want him because Nelson had been just as high-handed with the Admiralty as he had with Lord Keith, a slap in the face to a man who was sure that, to the Navy, he was more important than any serving officer. The serving officers didn't want him because they were advancing the interests of others to whom they were attached by blood or years of service.

This admiral was proposed and that captain, each a paragon in the eyes of the sponsor, each with a fatal flaw in the opinion of another, until Spencer was sure that they would be there all night. With that in mind he pulled a letter from his pocket. 'I have here, gentlemen, the opinion of Earl St Vincent. You will readily understand why I canvassed it. He is, after all, commanding our most important fleet. He says that, "when appointing an officer to a difficult task it is as well to look for one who fits the bill. If caution is required then root out your diplomat, when zeal is the nub of the duty, then fetch forth your warrior".'

'We have any number of both,' said Nepean, sensing where this was heading.

'Yet you will agree with the sentiment expressed?' asked Spencer. Nepean nodded. 'Our intelligence tells us the Danes are fortifying Copenhagen. They will not come out to fight us. Rather they will invite our fleet to attack them.'

'Or invite us to talk,' insisted Nepean.

'Quite,' said Spencer. 'Lord St Vincent feels that Admiral Sir Hyde Parker, given suitable envoys who speak Danish, will fulfil what-ever need we have for diplomacy. He therefore suggests the second should be a fighter, and tells us what we must already know that the best in that department is Admiral Lord Nelson.'

The name was out, up there to be damned and discarded. But Spencer noted the reluctance to voice such an opinion: his colleagues were as aware of Nelson's standing with the public as he was. What St Vincent was saying to them was that if Nelson failed the task would be seen as having been impossible. If another failed the public would want to know why the Board had not sent Nelson.

'I fear gentlemen, the case is made.'

The boy who entered the Admiral's day cabin on HMS *San Josef* and smartly removed his hat had his antecedents stamped on his face, or more precisely in his ears. Young James Frears had his grandfather's lugs, more prominent on his gaunt young head than they were on the old lieutenant.

'You will have a letter for me young man?' Nelson asked, and was amused by the panic with which James Frears fetched it out of his pocket. As he handed it over, Nelson pointed to the other side of the table. 'Thank you. Now you will oblige me by sitting down.'

Frears obliged, hat held tightly on his lap, and Nelson laid down the letter preparatory to slicing it open. He had become practised at this over the last years, a well placed finger and a sharp knife flicked to break the sealing wax. But the youngster was as stiff as a board, and Nelson hesitated. 'I have another favour to ask of you, young sir. As you can see I am a one-winged bird. I would ask you to take this knife, break the seal and open your grandfather's letter for me.'

The boy's hands shook as he obliged, more so as he laid the creased paper before the Admiral. Nelson read it, and was pleased to hear that old Frears had given the boy a grounding in matters nautical, a bit of small boat experience, some basic knowledge of the night sky, skill in ropes and knots.

'I see you have some experience of sailing, sir.'

'Only in wherries, milord.'

Nelson grinned at him. 'All naval officers start in small boats, Mr Frears, and some who are lucky get to sail ships such as this. Captain Hardy, who will be your captain, was like you once, as was I.'

'Milord,' Frears replied, as he tried to digest that notion.

'We do hard service, but if you are the type you will come to love it as I have. But a knowledge of ships is not enough if one day you are to be an officer. Manners, too, are important. How are your manners, Mr Frears?'

'Tolerable, sir, though my mother has cause to chastise me.'

How lucky you were to have a mother, thought Nelson, and immediately buried the thought as unfair on his father. Frears was so like him, so like the boy his grandfather had rescued from the wet misery of a strange naval port.

'Then I require you to be on your mettle, sir, of the kind that would please your mama. I am dining today with the Mayor of Portsmouth and it has always been my habit to take along to such occasions some youngster. Since your dress is new and smart, I shall take you. That is, if you don't wish to decline.'

'No, sir,' protested Frears, in clear contravention of the look in his eye.

'Have you met with your messmates yet?'

'Yes, sir.'

Another flash of memory, of his uncle William telling him on their first interview that the proper response was, 'aye, aye sir', which he told Frears now. He also remembered that it had taken him an age to find out why. 'In a gale of wind Mr Frears, or a battle, it is often hard to hear what is being said. The double positive is for that purpose, working even in the reading of lips.'

'Aye aye, sir,' said Frears cautiously.

'Right. Report to the officer of the watch, tell him you are to accompany me, then ask my coxswain, Giddings, to get the barge ready for one of the clock.'

The reply was more brisk this time. 'Aye aye sir.'

'And Mr Frears,' Nelson added, as the boy stood up, 'I look forward very much to serving with you.'

The 112-gun HMS *San Josef* was one of the ships Nelson had captured at St Vincent. He sailed her from Portsmouth to Torbay to have another meeting with the earl of that name, temporarily his commanding officer, there to be told that his appointment to the Baltic was a certainty. It was a convivial evening at the family home of the old admiral's cousins, and over dinner they discussed the problems Nelson might face, a talk that went on long after the cloth had been drawn, leaving Nelson and his barge crew a two-hour pull against the tide and in darkness, to get him back to the ship.

The letter was waiting for him. It was a coded note from Emma, to inform him that he was a father: she had been delivered of a daughter two days previously. Tom Allen entered to find his master weeping and laughing, pacing the cabin as if there was no position, seated or standing that would provide comfort. Eventually Nelson went to his desk to write a reply, something in which he knew he had to take care.

He couldn't use his own name, given that letters taken by post had been known to go astray. Besides, there were the naval censors, who had the power to read even his mail. He and Emma had devised a stratagem whereby he would claim to be acting on behalf of a sailor called Thompson. This poor fellow had, in their fiction, just become the father of an illegitimate child, for the girl he loved and who was the mother had been denied the right to matrimony by a cruel uncle. Both girl and infant, thanks to the intervention of Admiral Lord Nelson, were under the care of kindly Lady Hamilton. Thus he could write as Thompson, and in that guise tell Emma of his joy and his love for her and the child he had yet to see. It was flimsy to be sure, but the censors were not noted for deep erudition, or for much zeal in the performance of their duties, and Nelson was well known to be soft regarding the men who served under him.

There was much about the way in which he and Emma behaved that Nelson expected people to understand, but he knew the birth of his child to the wife of another man to be beyond acceptance. That would have caused a scandal in Naples, let alone London. Emma's reputation, already fragile, would never recover from it.

'Get this to the post, Tom,' he said, as he finished, 'and then prepare to pack.'

'Your honour?' demanded Tom, in a shocked voice.

He had been up to his eyes getting this cabin shipshape and as yet it was still to be painted. The notes that had flown between Lady Nelson and her husband about the state of his stores and possessions were no-one's business. He could not yet be said to have settled.

'We are bound for the Baltic, Tom, to teach Frederick of Denmark and Paul of Russia a lesson, and this fellow we sail in now has too deep a keel for the kind of work we will be doing.'

'Not a frigate, your honour,' moaned Tom, who hated the confinement on such a small vessel. 'Tell me it ain't going to be a frigate.'

'I'd go in a sloop if I had to,' said Nelson.

'You would and all,' said Tom, softly as he left.

The news was all over the ship in minutes, with men clamouring to transfer with the Admiral in such numbers that the *San Josef* would have been unable to raise her anchor. The news that he would come back to her after Baltic service stilled some requests, but it was a hefty bunch who looked to pack their ditty bags the next day.

23

Fanny Nelson was reading the *Morning Chronicle*, which told her, with what she thought must be mock alarm, that Lady Hamilton had suddenly and most unfortunately become indisposed, victim of a severe cold that had confined her to bed for several days. On those few occasions that she had seen Emma since that night at the opera, Fanny had kept an eye on that burgeoning figure, and she had come to the conclusion that the pregnancy was nearing its term.

The same could be said of the Nelsons' marriage, after the embarrassing scene in the lawyer's office before Christmas. The mere mention of Lady Hamilton grated on Fanny's nerves and the way Nelson had praised her on that day, with his lawyer present, had been so indiscreet as to drive her out of her normal self-imposed reticence.

She had snapped, and protested, 'I am sick of hearing of DEAR Lady Hamilton, and I am resolved that you give up either her or me.' She had the right to expect that in his reply Nelson, because of the presence of a stranger, might spare her feelings. This turned out to be foolish. His voice had been cold and unsparing.

'Have a care Fanny. I love you sincerely, but I cannot forget my obligations to Lady Hamilton, or speak of her otherwise than with affection and admiration.'

It was the word 'obligation' that had made her leave the room and she had not seen him since that day. Now the newspaper report made her feel a degree of despair deeper than any that had gone before. Fanny could not understand what had prompted her God-fearing husband to spend the Lord's birthday with that disgusting fellow, Beckford. She had no doubt that Fonthill Abbey was a magnificent house, just as she had no doubt that it was home to the most vile carnal practices. She would rather be seen dead than accept hospitality from its owner.

Christmas had been cheerless and cold, the hardest task had been to animate the Reverend Edmund Nelson, who, though he pretended he had no knowledge of the state of affairs, could not have missed what was happening. He loved his son, and could not bring himself to condemn his behaviour to his face. Fanny had enough faith in Nelson's love for his father to believe that he alone might bring him to his senses. Instead Edmund Nelson tried to avoid the subject, though she had caught him looking sadly at her when he thought her attention elsewhere. And it was galling that he took a certain delight in Emma's company. For a woman who knew she was competing with a serious foe for the soul of her husband, it was annoying to hear the dour Edmund Nelson laughing at one of Emma's sallies, only to look guilty if he saw her glaring at him.

In some ways she would have been happier if Nelson had hated her: that, at least, she would have been able to comprehend. But he did not. He constantly told her that he thought of her kindly and wished her no harm. It was as if she had been relegated to the status of a sister who was supposed to like her brother's new wife.

There was no absolute breach. They still wrote to each other, at times angry letters in which she was blamed for some missing article of furniture, clothing or provender. He still paid her household expenses, and before going to join the *San Josef* he had taken pains to ensure that she had money for continued support. And Fanny wondered if the care she took never openly to criticise or refer to his affair, her way of guarding her position, was replicated in his letters, which, though brief and pointed, were always signed with an affectionate postscript.

Here was the last straw. He had the child for which he had craved. Perhaps if she had explained to him he might have understood: physical love to her was loathsome, a duty not an inclination; that having had Josiah in excruciating pain, the notion of a second *encouchement* scared her witless. But Fanny could never have discussed such a thing with her husband. To refer to things so intimate was as beyond her as to take pleasure in them.

Right to the end Emma had kept to her social calendar, the gown she wore ever looser, her bulk greater. She knew that it had not escaped attention, because Gillray, the cartoonist, had been at his satirical work, and someone was always willing to show her his efforts. To coincide with Nelson going back to sea he had drawn a vast Dido despairing at the departure of the fleet. Another featured a spindly Sir William surrounded by lewd statuary, peering through a lorgnette at a Venus bearing a cuckold's horns. They annoyed her intensely.

But care, and the kindness of such as James Perry had kept her condition from becoming too widely known, and it needed some social skill to read between the lines of what the newspapers recorded to discern what was going on in the lives of the Hamiltons. Nelson being absent at sea helped, though both he and Emma had acknowledged that in any case a separation would have been essential.

Every movement of Emma, her husband and Fanny was reported. Lady Nelson called today on so and so: Sir William and Lady Hamilton attended this function or that play or opera: Sir William and Lady Hamilton have moved from Grosvenor Square to a house at number twenty-three Piccadilly. Nelson was reported as being at Portsmouth or Torbay; that he had shifted his flag to the *St George*, an item that allowed the more military-minded to read between the lines.

The birth itself had been handled with discretion, Emma's mother acting as midwife while Sir William had found good reason to be absent for a few days. Emma had sold her jewels so he was solvent once more and the five thousand a year he had from his estates would whittle away at his debts. His claims upon the government had been acknowledged and were being processed, so he was no longer reliant on his wife's lover for support.

Outwardly Emma behaved in London as she had in Italy, so that no one observing her and Sir William could be in any doubt that she was attached to her husband. Nelson was careful too, never intimating that anything other than the deepest friendship existed between him and Emma. It was in private that the affair rankled with Sir William: even when the third member of the trio was absent he was a constant topic of conversation, his exploits, his prospects, his wonderful nature. Emma had even installed a Nelson Room in the newly rented house in Piccadilly. Sir William felt himself and his needs being increasingly ignored, and occasionally the annoyance that engendered was allowed to surface.

Mary Cadogan played her part to perfection, only the twinkle in the brown eyes letting Sir William know that it was a shared joke.

'A foundling child, Sir William, right on our own step scarce three days past. I daresay some poor soul heard what a kind nature my daughter has and thought to entrust to her the future of a bairn that would otherwise starve.'

Sir William had had a couple of bottles of claret in a St James's establishment, and was tempted to blow this fiction out into the open. But he checked himself with the worrying thought that what would be out in the open was his old bones. Emma had rarely played the termagant with him in all their years together: but he knew she had a temper and had no wish to expose himself to it.

'My wife must have been shocked, Mrs Cadogan.'

'Quite bowled over your honour,' Mary Cadogan replied, sailing mighty close to the truth.

'It is enough to make anyone take to their bed,' Sir William responded sarcastically.

'Thank God Emma is made of sterner stuff.'

'She is not abed?' he asked, much surprised, since a confinement of several weeks was usual in the circumstances.

'Why would she be?' Mary Cadogan enquired mischievously.

Sir William knew he was being teased. Mary Cadogan might no longer be the beauty she once was, but she possessed a ready wit that had grown more pointed over the years. What he did not know was the ease with which Emma had delivered, her second child emerging as easily as her first. Far from being prostrate and weak, Emma was up and about in two days, if moving with caution. She was much occupied with sorting out pillows of a diminishing size that would, over the following weeks, help her bring her figure back to what it had been without anyone being aware of the delivery.

'We have looked after the mite as best we could, but it will need to go to a wet nurse soon. Emma is certain that it must suffer from inattention if it is to stay in this house.'

'And *she* will suffer from too *much* attention,' thought Sir William angrily.

'Besides,' Mary Cadogan continued, 'can't have a little 'un in residence, howling the night away and keeping all and sundry awake.'

The first joy of fatherhood had settled in Nelson's breast, mixed with concern that the child might not survive. There was much to worry about besides: whether to give way to Emma, after whom he wanted to name the baby, or agree to her choice, which was Horatia. Then there was the baptism, which must take place as soon as possible. Names would be demanded so he and Emma would have to pretend to stand as sponsors for the real parents: Thompson, the father at sea, with the mother too ill to attend, still suffering from the effects of childbirth.

The child's future and that of her mother must be secured should anything happen to him in the Baltic. Any allowance he made for them would be administered by the ageing Sir William – but everything *he* owned would go to that rascal Greville upon his demise. The fate of Nelson's daughter could not be left to such a scoundrel, a man who had claimed to love Emma and traded her off for that very inheritance.

When he heard that the Prince of Wales had expressed a desire to call on Emma Nelson flew into a rage. The man was a notorious rake with whom no woman was safe and he would not be calling on her for the elevation of her social position: he would visit Emma to take advantage of her lack of it, a chance to flit around a beauty who, when she lived with Greville, had caught his eye. It was rumoured he claimed to have bedded Emma, but he said that about every woman in London, so it was generally held that he lied.

Letters flew back and forth, full of loving sentiments and warnings. Sometimes he wrote as Thompson, at others, as himself when the bearer could be trusted. Edward Parker, a young, sprightly, merry captain to whom he had become attached, was one, and another was Alexander Davidson. The content of all this was similar: any child born to him and the most beautiful woman in the world must have been the work of some divine force, ordained in heaven if not in the married state. He knew his daughter was with a wet-nurse, that Emma in the speed of her recovery had allayed any suspicion that the infant might be hers. Yet still he fretted over discovery.

When Emma sent him a lock of the child's hair he saw in it the fair colour of his own infancy. He felt fulfilled as a man in a way that he could describe to no one but Emma. All the ghosts and worries of his past, that he might not be the man he wanted to be, evaporated. Those who had transferred with him to HMS *St George* observed him to be in a state of contentment marred by the occasional deep frown. Those who guessed why, Giddings and Tom Allen, kept their own counsel. The rest thought of the Danes, Swedes, Prussians and Russians and felt sorry for them. When Nelson was happy, yet tussling with problems, somebody else was in trouble.

An ailing King George, in the grip of his old malady and a political crisis over Catholic emancipation that might bring down Pitt's government, took even the most avid press attention off Horatio Nelson. And in Portsmouth there was a very discreet carriage company accustomed to taking officers to assignations they did not wish to be public. Setting off in early-morning darkness, with only Tom Allen for company, Nelson arrived behind drawn shades in an anonymous hack and, unannounced, rapped the knocker at number twenty-three Piccadilly. Emma's mother spent no time in greetings on the doorstep, but ushered Nelson inside without ceremony.

'Emma?' he asked.

'In such rude good health, sir, that you will faint to see her.'

And that was no lie. Nelson had visited the wives of fellow officers after the birth of a child often enough to know that it gave extra colour and radiance to a woman's face. Emma was no exception. Even her hair seemed to have added lustre.

'Nelson,' she yelled, throwing out her arms, scattering a pile of letters that lay strewn across the coverlet, for he had burst into her room without warning. In his ear she whispered, 'I dream of you and you appear.' Then she said, 'I have been re-reading all your letters,' pointing to the sheaves of paper strewn everywhere, 'and waiting for a knock that would herald a post.'

'I knocked.'

'And I sat here impatient, willing myself not to rush downstairs to see if a letter had arrived.'

'I brought myself. I had to.' Seeing the hint of alarm on her face he reassured her quickly. 'No one knows I am here, and as long as we exercise due discretion they never will. Everyone thinks me aboard ship at Portsmouth and by the time they think me absent I shall be back again.'

'How long?'

'Three days, no more.'

Emma rubbed a hand across his brow. 'You look weary.'

Nelson sighed. 'I am caught between the Scylla of elation and the Charybdis of fear for both you and our daughter.'

It all tumbled out verbally then, the same concerns that were in the letters: worries about financial security, the child's health, Emma's well-being and reputation, the Prince of Wales and his attentions. As he talked Emma slipped off his unadorned uniform coat and loosened his stock. By the time he was talking of the Baltic, of the plans he had already formed and the difficulties he anticipated in taking orders from Sir Hyde Parker he was lying with his head on Emma's shoulder. She spoke little, letting him ramble on, until he fell asleep.

They awoke after nightfall, and Emma asked that supper be prepared for them in the Nelson Room. Sir William, increasingly remote since the birth had removed himself to dine elsewhere, warned by Mrs Cadogan that Nelson's visit was a secret and must be kept so. Thus only the two dined in the room Emma had set aside as a celebration of her lover and hero. Nelson had entrusted to her all the gifts and trophies that he did not wish to take to sea. A portrait of him executed in Vienna took pride of place above the mantel, surrounded by numerous miniatures and his swords, both gifted and surrendered.

There was a painting of the Nile battle and a copy of a more benign Gillray cartoon showing Nelson thrashing about in seawater clubbing crocodiles. Orders of chivalry, both ribbon and stars, were ensconced in a glass case, as well as copies of his medals, the originals of poems, odes and songs dedicated to his victories. The tattered flags of his defeated enemies hung limply in the light afforded by candles and a roaring winter fire.

The table in the middle of the room was set with the crockery given to him by King Ferdinand, made at his own royal pottery, the silver cutlery and accoutrements, cruets, decanters, even the wine coasters, engraved with his coat of arms. The walls were that sea green that looks blue in certain lights, the fabric of the chairs the naval blue of the service embroidered with a golden N encased in triumphal laurel. In the presence of such display, Nelson felt a tinge of embarrassment, but the décor pleased Emma so much that he could not bring himself to ask for it to be toned down.

So they dined, at peace in each other's company, cocooned from a cold winter night and a potentially hostile world. Once dinner was over, they retired to bed, like the married couple Nelson longed for them to be.

Next morning, another closed carriage was needed to get them to the nearby house of Mrs Roberts, the wet nurse. A recent widow, with a posthumously born child of her own, she was caring for the little girl who, from now on, was Horatia Thompson. If the woman recognised the one-armed man who billed and cooed over the infant, and made excessive claims for the regularity and beauty of her features, she felt it unwise to say so. Nor did she remark later to anyone on the look that had graced the face of the lady who had brought the child, the mixture of triumph and affection in a mother who has presented her man with a baby.

Dinner that evening was with Sir William, who, his usual urbane self, kept well hidden any resentment that had grown in his breast. Besides, he found it near impossible to be angry with Nelson present. It was only when he was away, and Sir William lost sight of their mutual regard, that irritation surfaced.

Nelson had his own reasons to be annoyed with Sir William, who had started to auction off his possessions, one of which was Nelson's favourite portrait of Emma as St Cecilia. Alexander Davidson had had to be roped in to bid on Nelson's behalf. Yet that too faded with their meeting. Nelson admired the older man too much to be annoyed with him for long. They talked of many things: the King's health, the likelihood of a Regency, of a new government being formed under Addington, the prospects of peace with France, of Earl St Vincent becoming First Lord in place of Spencer, everything except the matter that filled Nelson's mind.

Alone again in their shared bedchamber, Nelson talked of death. While he was keen to assure Emma that his demise in battle was unlikely he wanted her to know that all things were possible. He would never describe to her what it was like on the deck of a ship in the midst of a fight. The instrument of his destruction might be a cannon or musket ball, a block, a spar or a deadly splinter of wood. It might come from anywhere, to the left, the right, or from above his head.

As he spoke, Nelson was aware that at one time he had almost sought death in battle, seeing it as the ultimate apotheosis of the hero he so wanted to be. His own was General James Wolfe, who had died on the Plains of Abraham above Quebec in the Seven Years War, winning in that one victory the whole of French Canada for Britain. That was the kind of death he had desired.

He did not want that now. He wanted Emma as his wife, and a place where they could both live with Horatia, free from the constraints of his previous attachments. Divorce was out of the question, requiring an Act of Parliament to become legal. Fanny might try it as the wronged party but he doubted that: the shame would kill her. If *he* tried it he would be laughed out of the chamber of peers.

'Brontë, perhaps,' he whispered.

He had never seen the ducal lands that Ferdinand had given him after the rescue from Naples. He knew that they were on the slopes of Mount Etna: that they were in need of investment, that given such they might yield an income on which he could happily exist. But, more than that, they were in a land where he could live openly with Emma and his new-born daughter.

In his heart he knew it to be a pipe dream. He was a serving officer and, though comfortable, he was far from rich. His good friend Alexander Davidson chastised him constantly for his generosity to anyone with even the most distant claim on his purse, his family the greatest beneficiaries. He had an obligation to support Fanny, and to secure Emma and Horatia against future troubles required a great fortune, not a middling one: he could only thank his God that, as a fighting sailor and admiral, he was well placed to acquire one.

For a man on the edge of losing office William Pitt seemed remarkably relaxed. He had been Prime Minister for so long that no one could easily recall his predecessor, and had worked hard to make his nation fiscally sound only to see this threatened by endless war. He was a reluctant combatant, who would have had peace with France if only that nation had shown any inclination to consider it. But he hated their Revolution, and as long as the French made war to further it, his government would spend whatever sums necessary to contain it.

Millions of pounds had gone to other countries – Austria, Prussia, Naples, endless German principalities – to put in the field that which Britannia could not: a mass army to beat the French. All had failed abysmally. Pitt had watched his coalitions founder, the latest just over two weeks previously when the First Consul of France, Napoleon Bonaparte, had signed a treaty that virtually dismembered the Holy Roman Empire, a confederation which had stood since the days of Charlemagne. All the while Pitt had juggled the domestic issues of the home nations: unruly Ireland, a noisy Parliament, a tendentious sovereign so wedded to his Protestant faith that he would see the country in turmoil rather than surrender a single one of the Thirty-Nine Articles. And an opposition party that would sweep into power as soon as that fat poltroon the Prince of Wales secured his inheritance.

Nelson listened as Pitt talked on for a good ten minutes about all the areas of war policy: India, the expedition to finish off the French in Egypt, arguments regarding Malta, and support for Naples and stability in the Italian peninsula, the weakness of the Sultan, an expedition to seize the Swedish and Danish islands in the Caribbean, and other minor operations in various far-flung places.

'The King caught a cold in chapel,' he said, almost wearily, 'which I fear has triggered a reaction.' Then he poured himself another generous glass of claret, although it was well before noon.

Nelson had yet to touch the one he had been given earlier and wondered, given Pitt's consumption, how he managed his duties. He was known as a man who, though he ate sparsely, drank three to four bottles a day, and often turned up for an evening sitting in the House of Commons in a high state of inebriation with his last bottle still in his hand.

'So we seem to have a return of his old malady, Lord Nelson, and as a consequence the wolves hover.'

The King's madness, his talking to trees and uncontrolled behaviour had nearly brought down the government before. Pitt had more trouble than that now, but clearly he had no desire to discuss with this visitor the Union of Ireland Bill.

'But good governance cannot rely on a King's health,' Pitt said, then added with force, 'or his whims.'

'The Baltic, sir?' said Nelson, finally sipping from his glass.

Pitt ruminated for a moment, his curious young-old face in deep study. Not yet forty, he had the smooth skin of youth and the aged cast of long experience. There was a puffiness about the eyes, hardly surprising given his drinking, but Nelson thought him a handsome man, though his thin chest and spindly legs suggested he had somewhat gone to seed.

'Tsar Paul is mad and the Danish and Swedish royals are not much better – too much inbreeding I shouldn't wonder. But it is the superior madness that has brought about the need to send a fleet.'

The Russians' seizure of every British vessel and trader in their waters, then their insistence that the lesser Baltic powers combine against the perceived enemy, had precipitated the crisis.

'Our sources tell us the tsar is quite besotted with Bonaparte, of course,' Pitt said dispassionately. 'Sees him as a modern Alexander. It is an attraction that has cost us dear. But,' he added, sitting forward and at last showing some spirit, 'cut off the head and the rest will tumble, Lord Nelson. Catch and destroy the Russian fleet and the others will fold.'

'I will do my best, sir,' said Nelson, raising his glass to drain it.

Pitt stood up, to indicate that the interview was over, and Nelson did likewise, but before he was out of the door, Pitt stopped him with a question. 'Lord Nelson, what are your opinions on the emancipation of the Catholics?'

'That it should be done, and swiftly, sir. I have served with too many good men of that faith, seen them mutilated and die in the cause of our country, to wish to debar them from any rights.'

Pitt smiled. 'Odd that. Before he fell ill, the King asked St Vincent for an opinion and your old commander said much the same.'

24

⁓

Everyone in Portsmouth had been working double tides to get the fleet ready for Baltic service, not least Nelson's flag captain, Thomas Hardy. Yet it was a telling indication of the effect of Nelson's presence that the work rate rose sharply on his return from London. Colonel the Honourable William Stewart, the bored and frustrated commander of the troops in the tented encampment on Southsea Common exhibited the usual soldier's arrogance when it came to the officers of the Navy. When he was told to get his men aboard their transports at once, he anticipated it would take at least two days. Yet the boats to carry his men arrived half an hour behind the orders, camp was struck and the troops loaded in two hours. He was to say ever after that he had never met the like of Lord Nelson when it came to making things happen.

They were happening aboard the warships as well. Everyone from the ship's captain to the lowliest caulker was admonished to waste not a moment, because, fully finished or not, Nelson intended to weigh within forty-eight hours. Many scoffed at this – it was the mere bravado of a man playing up vainly to his reputation – but were forced to eat their words as the order came two days later to get their anchors up. Every ship was still a mass of unfinished tasks: ropes hung loose, bales and barrels littered the decks while the animals had not yet been transported to the manger.

Land based contractors employed to speed up the work were not put ashore, instead they risked being carried to sea. Nelson's response to their complaints was to tell them to be about their tasks, or they would be obliged to practise gunnery and fight alongside him. He was less amazed than some by how much they achieved within twenty-four hours: before the fleet had cleared the Isle of

Wight the work was finished, the contractors in boats, heading for home.

The journey to Yarmouth to join the fleet assembling under Sir Hyde Parker was nine days of mayhem, but first lieutenants tearing their hair out at the disorder were calmed by an admiral who thrived on chaos. Nelson was all smiles, all advice, with never a cross word to anyone of his own ship's company, or a bellicose flag signal to one of his captains to mind the order of sailing.

He sent a despatch to St Vincent from Harwich congratulating the new First Lord and telling him of his imminent arrival at Yarmouth. He received a gratifying answer as he spied Parker's fleet, thanking him for 'using the spur'. Sir Hyde Parker got an express despatch at the same time telling him, with the topsails of his reinforcements barely visible, who was to be his second. He was also told to emulate Nelson and get his fleet to sea forthwith.

Sir Hyde Parker was surprised to learn the identity of his second in command; he had feared he might get Nelson, but had hoped that his own reluctance coupled with the efforts of his friends would prevent it. He was further discomfited by the haste with which Nelson had arrived. The fitting out of his own contingent had been sedate: to Parker matters taken at haste were regretted at leisure – the enemy would not suffer for having to wait a fortnight to be thrashed, but his ships might.

So it was a pair of very different admirals who met at Parker's shore accommodation. To those watching the pair, Parker's senior officers and his secretary, it was hard to believe the contrast. Sir Hyde Parker looked like a warrior chieftain, with his imposing height, bulk and features. If his face and body were portly that was as it should be, because he looked successful. One-armed Horatio Nelson, with his slight frame, despite his stars and decorations, seemed like a boy beside a grown man.

Nelson expected Parker to be haughty and he was not disappointed. The vain but noble-looking creature he remembered from his Mediterranean service had gone to seed. The care of dress was still there, and so was the determination to strike a noble pose, but both were a cover for the corpulence that came from excessive good living. Parker was a man who fell into a chair and had to heave himself free, likely to be red-faced just making his way from his cabin to the quarterdeck. He was slow, lumbering, and at sixty-two should never have been marrying an eighteen-year-old girl. None of that would have mattered to Nelson if Parker's mind had been sharp, but it was like the rest of him, cautious of effort, slow of deduction, fearful of disgrace, either personal or professional.

Each had a memory of the other: Nelson of Parker, third in command to Admiral Hotham, agreeing with his superior that to pursue the French after the action off Genoa was unnecessary, 'that the fleet had done well enough'. Parker recalled, with equal ease, the tight-lipped Captain Nelson, a man who had stretched what orders he had been given to near destruction, making no secret at all that he disagreed with Hotham's conclusions.

'I am glad to see you arrived so soon, Lord Nelson,' said Parker, 'and you, Captain Hardy.' Nelson saw that the smile on his face was not reflected in his eyes.

'And I am happy, sir, to serve under such a distinguished commander.'

'Obliged,' growled Parker, not fooled by that ritual response.

An uncomfortable silence followed, as Nelson waited for Parker to invite him to sit, prior, he hoped, to a discussion of the forthcoming campaign. Parker had no intention of obliging him, well aware that to do so would only open him up to a torrent of unwanted advice.

'Lady Nelson, is well I trust?' Parker asked, a remark which was greeted with a tight-lipped nod. 'Good.'

'May I ask your intentions, sir?'

Parker was good at mock surprise: He almost looked as if he really believed that no one had told Nelson where they were going. 'Why, to obey my instructions and take the fleet to the Baltic.'

'I meant once we get there, sir.'

'To make the fools see sense, if they have not already done so. It is my opinion that the Danes will come to that as soon as they see our topsails.'

'And the Russians?'

Parker blinked. 'Likewise.'

Again there was an uncomfortable silence, with Nelson waiting for Parker to elaborate, and Parker willing himself to remain silent. Fifty years of naval service and birth into a formidable family had gifted him with the kind of social skills his junior admiral entirely lacked. He could look his second-in-command straight in the eye and, if necessary, lie to him without a blush – which he would do if he felt it was required. This was his fleet to command, his reputation to enhance, not Nelson's. The rewards for success, which he did not doubt would be gifted without a shot being fired, would come to him, not to this over-medalled popinjay before him.

'I must ask the condition of your ships?' said Parker.

This request was aired with the manner of a man deliberately changing the subject. Parker knew that as a matter of routine the information was already in the hands of his executive officer, Dommet, the Captain of the Fleet, who was standing just behind him looking suspicious.

'Ready for whatever service you require of them, sir,' Nelson replied.

'Excellent,' boomed Parker. 'Then it gives me pleasure to issue to you the first of my orders, for I know it will please your ears. We weigh at the first opportunity, Lord Nelson, which means much work for both of us. I must get myself aboard the flagship.'

He was smiling broadly, as if the natural end had come to the meeting and all should be happy at the outcome. It was a full twenty seconds before Nelson took the hint and made to depart, tempted to force the issue, but aware that to try to would achieve nothing.

'Well, Hardy,' he said as they emerged, 'I am no further forward now than I was when we came ashore.'

'We must replenish our wood, sir, being as we are going north.'

Hardy's mind was, as usual, on practical concerns and Nelson wondered if he had deduced anything from that non-conversation. Parker was going to keep his future intentions close to his chest, which Nelson would find frustrating. He had hoped to establish an outline plan before the fleet got to sea. But that was not going to happen, and he would be obliged to meet for any conferences aboard the flagship, HMS *London*, an uncomfortable prospect for a one-armed man, who required to be lifted from his barge onto the deck, always a risky affair on a heaving sea. Contemplating that, he recalled the reported words of his stepson Josiah, who had apparently said, woundingly, 'that he hoped his stepfather would fall off and break his neck'.

The boy had no gratitude to the man who had taught him all he needed to know, and done everything he could to advance his career. Would he be a post captain now if he had not had a connection to Nelson? Probably not, and given his bellicosity Josh would probably have been on the beach. Nelson, however, found time to beg from St Vincent a ship on foreign service for his cantankerous stepson, this to oblige Fanny. Thinking of both Josh and his mother made it impossible for him to smile at the crowd that had gathered to cheer him as he made his way to the quayside, where Giddings waited by the steps that led to his barge.

'All's a fair old bustle, your honour,' said Giddings, jerking his head to the outer roads, to the mass of ships surrounded by boats and water hoys.

That earned him the usual frown from Hardy, who hated to see a seaman address an officer unbidden. But Hardy had reconciled himself over the years to the fact that Horatio Nelson was a lamentable failure in the article of proper discipline.

Nelson saw the remark differently and paused at the top of the steps. He had known Giddings for so long and served with him in so many situations that he could almost read his mind. His coxswain, a proper ferret when it came to finding out things that were none of his business, had words to say. In deference to the presence of Captain Hardy, Giddings spoke softly, as usual his words emerging from the side of his mouth, 'Admiral Hideaway is getting it in the neck from all quarters, your honour, so the word be.'

'Really,' remarked Nelson, as Hardy's eyes rolled in disgust at hearing their commander in chief reduced to a lower-deck tag.

'That young filly he wed was set to have a ball,' Giddings continued softly, 'but an express came from El Vincento tellin' him it were time to sling his hook. Get to sea, was the gist, or I might be finding someone with a bit more fire. Now you knows as well as I do, your honour, that there be one person you don't take issue with and that be El Vincento, and with 'im being First Lord that be double strife. So there's no more of all here sitting on their arses taking a pipe. Ball cancelled, invitations gone out and Lady Parker's tears notwithstanding, with Hideaway yelling orders like billy-o till you came ashore.'

Nelson did not ask how Giddings knew all this, he just accepted it. When it came to finding out the true state of affairs in a fleet it was better to ask a seaman than an officer. At sea Giddings and his like could overhear a conversation through six inches of solid planking and, for a quid of tobacco, elicit information ashore that would never be vouchsafed to any admiral.

'So, Giddings, when are we to actually weigh our anchors?'

'On the morrow, your honour,' Giddings replied with certainty. 'Had that from Hideaway's own barge crew. The neck of the Baltic Sea is where we're headed, though it's reckoned that the Danes won't fight, so it'll be bang a few guns, then good dinners all round and a barony at least for our valiant leader when we raise home again.'

Giddings' voice dropped even lower as he confided the next scrap of information. 'Weren't expecting you, your honour, nor anyone else for weeks yet, and he is afeart that you'll be after giving him the old eclipse. Swore fit for the lower deck when he made out your flag.'

Nelson nearly laughed at the expression on Hardy's face, which was one compounded of disapproval and wonder. He was tempted to ask Giddings, as he was rowed out to his ship, what Parker's plans were if the Danes elected to fight, but that would be going too far.

The barge had pulled up alongside the *St George* and, since his flagship was still rigged for the open sea there was no gangplank for him to ascend. Nelson was hauled aboard in a chair lashed to a whip from the yardarm.

'All captains, Mr Hardy, if you please.'

There was much to do before the fleet sailed. Nelson wrote to Davidson asking him to add a codicil to his will leaving Emma the sable pelisse and the diamond studded *Chelenk* he had received from the Sultan. Otherwise the arrangements he had made for her welfare and that of the child should remain as of his last will and testament; proper distribution to family etc.; enough to provide for Fanny, bury me at Burnham Thorpe and take good care of Emma and Horatia. There was a letter for Fanny as well to say that Josiah would probably get a frigate.

He wrote to Troubridge to report that he thought Sir Hyde Parker a trifle tardy, and to tell his old friend, now taken by St Vincent on to the Board of Admiralty, that he had only the sketchiest notion of what they were about. He knew there were diplomatic moves in progress but he was sure that diplomacy without an application of force would achieve nothing. Rumour had it that the new government had offered the Danes twenty sail-of-the-line as a force to protect them against the Russians should they decide to break their alliance. Nelson was left to wonder, and ask Troubridge, where ships and men were to come from when Britannia could barely fulfil the commitments she already had.

His secretary had a mass of official papers for Nelson to read through and sign; impresses for everything the fleet needed to remain at sea, prepared by his captains and needing to be passed on by him to the man who bore the final responsibility, Sir Hyde Parker. Then, sitting beneath a portrait of Emma, which Hardy had kindly had framed for him in Portsmouth, he wrote to his lover. Thinking of her and his new-born daughter, all his cares about the expedition to the north faded. Be it against Danes, Swedes or Russians there would be a fight, and he was resolved to win. He would bring back the laurels of victory to lay at the feet of the two dearest creatures in his life.

This letter was entrusted to that other Parker, known to all as Merry Ed, who had, these last few days, taken much ribbing regarding the libidinous nature of his elevated and elderly namesake.

Captain Edward Parker was the soul of discretion where Nelson's business was concerned, a man the admiral wanted by his side, and a sloop of war was left behind so that he could rejoin him once the fleet was at sea.

Guns banged, flags flew and the band that Nelson had brought aboard at Portsmouth played a brave tune as the fleet weighed, sailing into a real peasouper of a fog that persisted for much of the voyage. When it was not foggy it was overcast and grey on a sea that seemed designed to depress the spirits.

That expanse of the cold North Sea was covered with no sense of haste, all ships relying on the Master of the Fleet, who was no great shakes at navigation, and an admiral who had an overly developed fear of running aground. Parker was for ever heaving to and casting the lead to ensure he had enough water under the keel of his capital ships, turning away from dangers that no one but he could perceive.

In a voyage of two hundred miles, to miss the Skagerrak, his intended landfall, by sixty miles, regardless of conditions was, to Nelson, near criminal. Not that he got any chance to tell Parker: the commander-in-chief issued no invitations to come aboard the flagship and discuss forthcoming operations until they were anchored off the entrance to the Baltic.

The condition of the fleet was not one to raise Nelson's ambitions even when they had anchored and all the stragglers had joined. Fifty-two vessels were strung out over miles of sea, consisting of line-of-battle ships of every size and displacement, 100-gun first rates, 74's and old 64's. They had frigates, bomb ketches, even a converted East Indiaman, not one of which was in prime order. It was a fleet required to cover too many eventualities: a siege and bombardment of the Danish capital of Copenhagen, or a fight in open sea with either Russia, Sweden, Denmark or all three combined.

It was the last prospect that troubled Nelson, the thought that he would be required to take part in an action against the combined fleets of three lesser powers under a commander like Sir Hyde Parker. Nelson's view was that Parker should ignore Denmark and bypass its capital. Likewise the Swedes: intelligence insisted that they were unprepared. The Russians, by far the greatest threat in terms of ship numbers, were ready for action but ice-bound still in the ports of Revel and Kronstadt, which they would leave as soon as the ice melted. Nelson wanted to be off those bases at that moment: let the enemy come out and find a superior British fleet waiting to engage.

He had no doubt that, with proper application, the Russians could be beaten. Then Parker could turn back and take on the Danes and the Swedes, who, with the defeat of their principal ally, would most likely make peace.

Another worry was the quality of the men he led. Fresh from the damp and freezing English winter, the crews had sailed north into falling temperatures that had every man on board subject to a hacking cough and bouts of shivering. The bulk of these were not the men of 1793, volunteers who were seamen by trade. The long war, the commissioning of too many ships, mutiny, death and desertion had culled the best. The ships Nelson commanded still had their sailors, but in the main they were crewed by those who had been press-ganged, many illegally, or petty criminals and debtors offered up as voluntary contingents by the various boroughs and shires responding to a government order to provide a quota of men. There were volunteers, but few robust souls opted for a life in the Navy if they could make their way elsewhere in the world.

In the leeward squadron, his own section of the fleet, Nelson had instituted training, explaining to his captains the dual nature of a beast that would keep the men from boredom and by heating their bodies improve their health. It would also encourage them by increasing competence to perform better in the forthcoming fight. Some had sailed with him before, a couple of Nile captains who knew his methods and required no pressure, but most had not and he was obliged to bear down on them to see his orders obeyed.

Drills were instituted, in gunnery, boarding, sail and rope work, and over the days, in conference after conference, the men who were strangers to Nelson, captains and lieutenants, were exposed to what Nile captains called the Nelson touch. Tom Foley, captain of HMS *Elephant*, an old friend from Nelson's first days at sea, watched him operate with amused detachment, and observed sceptical faces slowly lose their look of doubt.

Before his officers, at dinner or pacing the great cabin, talking incessantly, was a man who could paint a picture of the forthcoming battles, even though he had never seen the approaches to Copenhagen or clapped eyes on the Russian fleet. Using charts and his one good arm he told each of his juniors just how the Danes must deploy, how the Russians would sail, their probable strength in both guns and men, and his own plans to confound them.

Well aware that he would have to sell his ideas to Parker, he advanced his own opinion that the way to beat the Russians was by manoeuvre.

'Always lay a Frenchman close and you will beat him, but with a Russian it must be different. For, gentlemen, they have spent six months bound by ice. They can rehearse gunnery drill at anchor, and they can practise boarding, but a man has to be at sea to have full competence with his sail drill. Therefore I will attack the head of their line as they emerge and test both their cannon and their seamanship.'

Again and again, the gathered officers heard him utter his watchword: 'Waste not a moment.'

Nelson might convince them, and raise them collectively to the pitch of enthusiasm, but it was less easy to carry his superior officer, because he was not invited at any stage to advise him. Over the next few days all Parker did was to move anchorage to take the fleet marginally nearer to the enemy. Nelson suspected he had sent away a frigate carrying an envoy to negotiate. To his mind that was a waste of precious time. He preferred to fight the Russians, but if Sir Hyde was determined to subdue Denmark first, the sight of open gunports, with the muzzles of their cannon threatening their capital city and no friendly fleet prepared to come to their aid, would bring them round.

A certain amount of ship visiting by less elevated officers kept him abreast of what Parker was doing, but it did little to cheer him, especially when it was confirmed that Parker had, indeed, sent people in to try and talk the Danes into peace. Days stretched to a week before the frigate returned, days in which Nelson fretted about the state of the ice off Revel and Kronstadt,

'Seven wasted days, Hardy,' said Nelson, as they watched the frigate, HMS *Blanche*, beat up towards the flagship. 'Pray to God we do not have to pay in blood for such dawdling.'

He and the Ghost were still watching when the flags went up to request that he come aboard.

Nelson picked up the gloom-laden atmosphere as soon as he set foot on the deck of HMS *London*, only to find as he awaited Parker's pleasure that it had been building over the last few days. Everyone wanted to impart to him the depressing news that Copenhagen might be too hard a nut to crack, and this on the flagship of a fleet supposedly preparing for battle!

It seemed that Parker's envoy, Nicholas Vansittart, accompanied by the *charge d'affaires* in Denmark, had come aboard and listed in detail to Sir Hyde Parker the strength of the defences around Copenhagen. For good measure, Vansittart had added those covering the narrow approaches that must be breached before the city and the harbour could be attacked. He had observed and counted fortress guns, anchored warships, armed hulks, gunboats and floating batteries, and described them in terms that had Parker struggling to sleep.

Nelson knew that the cramped nature of the entrance to the Baltic provided natural defences that made an attack on Copenhagen difficult. The city stood on the eastern side of the island of Zeeland, which effectively blocked easy access to the inland sea. Before even approaching the Danish capital or the open waters of the Baltic a fleet had to pass through the Sound. This lay on the northern shore of Zeeland, a four-mile wide passage covered on both sides by the fortress cannons of Swedish Helsingborg and the Danish fort of Cronberg hard by Elsinore. The only alternative was to go south of Zeeland by the Great Belt, a laborious passage through dozens of islands and numerous sandbanks, waters so unsuitable for deep-draught warships that it would take at least three days.

Once through the perils of the Sound, the approaches to Copenhagen ran north to south on a narrow channel between Zeeland and the outer island called Amager, which in turn led to an even narrower channel, really no more than a wide canal, that gave access to the inner harbour. This was the passage used by ships entering Copenhagen from the North Sea.

For ships coming from the east, between those two island shores lay a wide sandbank called the Middle Ground Shoal, which created two channels, the southernmost of which, known as the King's Deep, narrowed the eastern approach to Copenhagen to less than a mile in width. On the other side of the Middle Ground Shoal was a second navigable passage called the Holland Deep, the usual route for shipping bypassing Copenhagen going in either direction.

Unfortunately for an attacker, the city was out of range of bombardment from the Holland Deep. Only in the King's Deep could an attack have any effect and that was where the Danes had sited this powerful defence. Thus the option of choosing when to come in range of enemy guns was not available to the attacker. He had either to take the defence on in its own terms or risk running aground.

A squadron of warships blocked the head of the channel that led to the city. These were covered by two strong forts sunk on piles in the shallow waters of the approach called the Trekroner and Lynetten Batteries, between them mounting some one hundred cannon.

Behind lay the city walls, with the Quintus and Sixtus batteries to the east of the harbour. This was protected by a boom across the entrance thick enough to stop any warship breaching the defence, and covered by the Castellet battery that lay within the city walls. This would leave at the mercy of the Danes any vessels caught on that boom unless all their batteries had already been silenced. Running east from the Trekroner fortress lay a line of warships, backed by batteries both land-based and floating, which covered the city itself. Copenhagen lay over a narrow neck of land to the south and west.

Nelson had known even before he left England that capturing the harbour was impossible. But it was not necessary: all that was needed was a fleet in the King's Deep channel powerful enough, and close enough, to threaten to bombard the city and thus force the Danes to surrender or see their capital destroyed. Especially dangerous to the inhabitants would be the bomb ketches with heavy mortars capable of lobbing in shells to do awesome damage, but they were vulnerable to counter battery fire unless supported by ships that could subdue the response.

But how to get capital warships, the shallow draught 64-gunners and a few of the 74's to that point without risking destruction? They would have to pass each ship and heavy land battery in turn, surviving endless cannon fire, and still be in a fit state to take on the defences, all the while with a sandbank on their larboard quarter, which would leave them defenceless if they ran aground.

Thus the gloom on the flagship had a sound basis, but to Nelson that was only true if you accepted everything you were told at face value and stuck rigidly to tactics and stratagems as laid down in the Fighting Instructions. All his life he had held such a set of orders to be foolish: how could a committee sitting in a room at the Admiralty decide what should and should not be done by a fighting commander at the scene of a battle?

Probably it was the same set of mind that had Sir Hyde Parker in a funk: the fear of losing ships. Nelson hated to lose men and vessels as badly as the next naval commander, but he also knew that no one could ever hope to make successful war without risk. And he had supreme confidence in his ability to balance the advantages against the potential for loss.

Another thought occurred to him; that Parker's reservations might work in his favour. Nelson still saw the Russians as the greatest threat, and as far as he knew they were still stuck in the ice. If his commander in chief was reluctant to risk his ships, Nelson would only need to steel him to make the passage of the Sound then bypass Copenhagen and proceed to the Russian shore.

What was worrying was that he was being told Parker feared even that.

25

In the great cabin of HMS *London* Sir Hyde Parker sat in uncomfortable contemplation. All his life he had sought a command like this, even when he had been in the West Indies. There, watching his wealth grow by leaps and bounds, he had prayed that the French, as they had in the American War, would send a fleet to the area. His rise in the service had been seamless, yet that acme of professional success, a victorious fleet action, had eluded him.

There had been any number of alarms and excursions, yet no enemy topsail had appeared over the horizon to fulfil his ambitions to fight a major enemy as a commanding admiral. Action with Hotham in the Mediterranean as third-in-command signified little; some prize money, congratulations, but little in the way of public esteem: no title, no thanks from the City of London, no special sword or medals struck in his honour.

The man waiting to see him had all that and more. Parker had observed the crowd on the day Nelson had arrived off Yarmouth, the news having spread that the Hero of the Nile was coming ashore. He had sneered at such adulation and pronounced it the province of addle-headed fools. But even as he had treated the officers present to his views, encouraging their laughter, Sir Hyde Parker had felt a stirring of jealousy. Never mind the mob, he wanted desperately to see the light of such adoration in his young wife's eyes.

There was no doubt in Parker's mind that as soon as Nelson entered his cabin he would want to discuss some form of action. It was the nature of the man: it had been so when he had HMS *Agamemnon* and it was probably more so now that he was John Bull's darling. Parker, too, wanted action and success; the only problem was that he had no idea how achieve it. Every avenue open to him carried with it great dangers.

If he suffered defeat he would be ruined and that appeared a distinct possibility. Success was a Danish offer of peace without a shot fired, which was what he had anticipated, but the Danes had rejected the last overture presented to them. Success thus moved to the need to compel them. As it stood from the papers that had been delivered to the Danish Crown Prince, regent for his mentally enfeebled father, war would be declared the moment Parker, as admiral of the aggressive fleet, fired the first shot.

To get to any of his potential opponents he still had to pass through what he now referred to as 'that damned Sound', which the pilots he had brought from England told him was extremely risky: shallow water at either side of narrow channels, little chance to manoeuvre, cannon that grew more threatening every time he contemplated them – and a vision of ships under his command set afire and drifting on to an enemy shore. Or worse, sunk in shoal water that would leave their upper masts still visible to mock him and act for decades as a monument to his failure.

Inactivity seemed attractive until he reread his orders, which were quite specific: he was to offer terms to the Danes, and if they were refused he must compel them to make peace by all means at his disposal before entering the Baltic and applying the same treatment to Russia and Sweden. Compel! An easy word for an Admiralty secretary to write, even easier for St Vincent to approve and to sign. For Sir Hyde Parker, anchored in the Cattegat with Sweden to the north, Denmark to the south, and the fleet of mad Tsar Paul further east, compel was anything but easy.

'Show Lord Nelson in,' he said to his flag lieutenant, 'and ask Mr Vansittart to join us.'

Nicholas Vansittart, sent by the British government to negotiate with the Danes, was an experienced diplomat, a handsome man of easy manner and fluidity of speech. He reported the failure of his mission, then outlined for Nelson's benefit, using a chart spread out on Parker's table, the defences they faced.

Carefully, Nelson began to question Vansittart in more detail about them, and was impressed by how observant the diplomat had been – he had listed each of the vessels in the whole Danish line. Naturally the Danes had concentrated their most powerful ships, under the command of Commodore Steen Bille, at the point where an attack would come: at the entrance to the harbour, between the Trekroner and Lynetten fortresses, to face a fleet sailing south to engage. The rest of their active fleet, under the orders of Commodore Olfert Fischer, plus all the ships in the dockyard that could float and bear cannon, lay ranged along the northern shore of Amager Island, covering the neck of land that cut off the city from the waters of the Baltic. With floating batteries in between the capital ships and shore batteries behind them, their unprotected sides close to shoal water probably too shallow for the British to sail through, the Danes presented in the King's Deep a staggered front of cannon ready to smash their enemies. Vansittart had counted both guns and men at these points too, and noted that they seemed eager for a fight.

No wonder! They expected to face warships that had already suffered from having to sail past the squadron and guns protecting the harbour entrance. Their aim would be to compound that damage, to sink or render useless what remained of an attacking fleet seeking to escape eastwards and drive them as hulks on to the shallow sandbanks of the Middle Ground Shoal. At the very least they would expect them, wounded and unwieldy, to withdraw.

Then Nelson turned to the situation at Elsinore, covering the four-mile wide Sound between Sweden and Denmark. If Vansittart was gloomy about the defences around Copenhagen, he was even more so about the chances of breaking through the Sound. Before Elsinore stood the fortress of Cronberg, and opposite that its Swedish counterpart, Helsingborg. He had counted every gun on the Danish side and pronounced as near suicidal the notion of entering the Baltic by that route. But as Nelson probed he felt more and more confident.

The command at Copenhagen rested in the untrained hand of Crown Prince Frederick. He had no experience of either naval or land warfare, yet proposed to lead his fellow countrymen in a defence against elements of the most efficient fleet in the world. And those men, what of them? Sailors, yes, gunners too, but never enough to man such defences! They must be augmented by untrained artisans and labourers, as well as young, enthusiastic gentlemen.

Nelson watched Parker's expression grow more fearful by the minute, but he was less convinced than his chief that an approach by the Sound was so hazardous, even less that the defence of Copenhagen was so formidable. First, those who had described the artillery of Cronberg were civilians, and thus their information was suspect. Where had the Danes, a nation that had been at peace for seven decades, got all these cannon? Again, when it came to calibre, condition and the age of the weaponry, Vansittart was at a loss to give a proper description and the range of the guns was to him a mystery. Very likely the Crown Prince had scraped every fort and bastion in the land for weapons that had not been fired in years, more useful for ceremonial than battle.

Nelson had studied the charts and knew that even if all the cannon were modern and forty-two-pounders, they could not command the whole width of the Sound, having a maximum range of some two and a half miles. So by standing to the north side of the channel, the British fleet could, apart from a few points where sandbanks threw them south, sail through without threat from Cronberg. Thus the danger lay with the Swedes at Helsingborg, and even Parker knew from intelligence reports that the fort was in poor repair, that they had fewer cannon than their Danish allies and that which they had were in poor condition. And of all the nations in this Northern Alliance the Swedes, with their well-known and long-standing antipathy to Russia, were lukewarm in their support.

As soon as he had finished quizzing Vansittart, Nelson was up and pacing: he could never run down an idea or fully explain a tactical notion when seated. It struck him as odd that none of Parker's executive officers was here, his own flag captain, Otway, or the Captain of the Fleet, Dommet. Neither was Rear Admiral Graves, the third in command. That could mean only one thing: inaction, which was anathema to Nelson.

'Sir, might I ask whom you see as the greatest enemy?'

Sir Hyde Parker was thinking at that moment that the greatest enemy he faced was probably his own government but he could hardly say so. And since he had no other point to make he merely turned sad eyes on Nelson knowing that any silence he left would be quickly filled.

'If I may make so bold as to speak, sir?' Those sad eyes did not flicker, never showed the thought that he had rarely known Nelson to shut up. 'My appreciation of our situation is that the greatest danger we face is a simultaneous action against all three of our enemies.'

Parker reckoned he feared that more than Nelson.

'We must take them piecemeal, and since the Danes have obliged us by tying their ships to the defence of their capital, and our intelligence tells us the Swedes are unprepared, it is my suggestion that we proceed at once to attack the Russians.'

Again Parker stayed silent, listening as Nelson repeated what he had said to the officers of his own squadron, trying to impart to his commanding officer the need for haste: that the Russians were the main enemy, the unprepared Swedes not really a consideration, that

255

the Danes would collapse with no hope of help from the Tsar, until he came to the point at which Sir Hyde felt he had to intervene.

'The Russians, Lord Nelson, are on the other side of Copenhagen.' What he meant was that they were on the other side of that damned Sound. There was another route, of course, and that was undefended. 'Tell me, what is your appreciation of the fleet entering the Baltic by the Great Belt?'

Nelson had to stop his immediate negative response, which was hard. Impulsive replies, however accurate, would not serve. His aim, based on a reading of Parker's state of mind, was to get the man moving, because everything about him suggested he wanted to stay put. To go by the Great Belt, with its treacherous, shifting sandbanks and no guarantee of a wind to carry them through might take a week if things went badly. But that was better than doing nothing.

'You are faced, sir, with a series of choices that I hardly need to outline.' Nelson was thinking of whom to fight, Parker of how to get to them at the least risk. 'Let me say sir, that if it was my task to choose, I would not attack the Danish defences directly.'

Nelson pointed to the chart showing the Copenhagen approaches. 'They have arranged their ships on the assumption that we will sail from the north, our objective being the harbour. Thus their strongest vessels, well manned by proper sailors, their best-manned forts and, I dare say, the most modern cannon, are concentrated thus.' Nelson finger was on the channel leading into the harbour. 'It is therefore obvious that the weakest vessels, the less useful cannon, and very likely the least trained men, are ranged here, along the King's Deep.'

Nelson's traced the line of that channel until he reached the open sea at the eastern end. 'And if that is the case, then the very least in terms of ability to withstand us lie here at the end of the Middle Ground Shoal, where the King's Deep joins with the Holland Deep.'

Parker nodded. He still remained silent because he had yet to deduce what Nelson was getting at.

'That, therefore, sir, is where we should begin any assault. If the Danes have set themselves to face an attack from the north, we should come at them from the south. Whichever way we assault their line we will be engaging in a close quarter artillery duel, and in that, even if I were to grade the Danes as good fighters, I would back our men for rate of fire. Accuracy will mean nothing compared to the ability to get off more broadsides than our opponents. I anticipate that the attack could be pressed home with some ten ships-of-the-line, naturally those with the shallowest draught.'

Several thoughts were chasing themselves round Parker's head, the first being that what Nelson was proposing was not something he would be in a hurry to try. To come from the east up the King's Deep was hazardous to say the least. It wasn't all plain sailing between the Amager sandbanks and the Middle Ground Shoal: there were plenty of treacherous sandbanks known only to the local pilots – no merchant vessel would sail through that approach without one aboard. Knowing the dangers, the enemy had removed all the buoys that marked the deep-water channel, so the risk of running aground, even for ship without great depth of keel, was high. Again he had that vision of ships on fire . . .

In his mind's eye he could envisage Nelson's artillery duel, and appreciate how damned hot it would be. The land batteries of Quintus and Sixtus were manned by soldiers, and on *terra firma* their rate of fire would match and might exceed that of a ship rolling, even on a gentle swell. And as ships entering the east of the King's Deep encouraged their predecessors on, they would be pushing them into the maw of the enemy's greatest strength.

But there was a positive thought too: if his fleet were to attack from the south there was a relatively risk-free way to get there, and that was by the Great Belt, which would put his ships where Nelson claimed he wanted them.

'What you propose carries great risks, Lord Nelson. Here we are, east of Zeeland, in open water. What happens if, while we are preparing to subdue the Danes, a Russian fleet appears?'

'Excellent, sir,' Nelson cried. 'The more the merrier, I say.'

Even Vansittart, who had been a silent witness to his tactical suggestions, raised an eyebrow at that point. But Nelson knew of what he spoke. 'Give me my ten ships of the shallowest draught, and I will undertake to get them down the King's Deep. The winds are variable enough, blowing east one day, south or north on another, and very likely west the next, so we will attack as soon as it is favourable.'

'Combined enemies, Lord Nelson? You said yourself that presented the greatest danger.'

'Naturally we would have a screen of frigates to the east, perhaps even a fast vessel off Revel to tell us when the ice melts. As to the Danes, it is my opinion that they will not dismantle a carefully constructed defence to come out and attack. If the Swedes emerge, we can interpose ourselves between them and the Russians and choose whom to do battle with first.'

Parker suddenly realised, and it was underlined by the way that Vansittart was looking at him, that he was behaving like the junior officer and Nelson like the commanding admiral explaining his aims.

For a man so proud, the consciousness of that reversal of roles came like a slap. Yet with his mind still in a tactical fog he was at a loss to know what to do about it.

Nelson was thinking that it was a wearying business being second-in-command, that he had suffered the same problem up to a point with Lord Keith, though he would grant that his Mediterranean commanding officer had been a fighter. Parker was not that now, if he ever had been. He was more like a rabbit caught in the open, unsure whether to bolt for his hole, or to seek invisibility with stillness.

Parker's finger shot out and jabbed at the chart right at the point where the King's Deep met the Holland Deep at the eastern end of the Middle Ground Shoal. He then traced his finger south-east to the southernmost point of Zeeland, before it headed west through the Great Belt. It was with the voice of command that he said, 'I approve of your notion, Lord Nelson, but I do not think our cause would be aided by risking the ships we might need against the guns of Cronberg and Helsingborg. A passage by the Great Belt will bring us to the position you desire to be in, here at the eastern end of the King's Deep.'

'By the Sound or the Belt, sir, I do not care, as long as we get there.'

There was a flaw in Parker's appreciation that immediately became obvious to Nelson. It could take at least three days, if not a whole week, to get the whole of his fleet through the Belt, time enough for the Danes to shift the focus of their defence to what would be-come the obvious point of attack. But since he wanted to take on the Russians first, sure that the Danes would not remain bellicose with-out support, he cared nothing for how they would react. All he wanted was movement, action, a chance to do battle, instead of sitting in the Cattegat doing nothing.

Parker had stood up, swelling out both chest and belly as if determined to impose himself physically in compensation for his mental inferiority. 'Mr Vansittart, do you anticipate any good will come of further representations being made to the Danish court?'

'I fear not, Sir Hyde.'

'Then I require you to take for me a despatch back to London. In it I will tell the government of my intention to sail my fleet through the Great Belt. Once in the Baltic, I will make my dispositions to respond to whatever threat then presents itself.' He turned to his second-in-command. 'Lord Nelson, thank you for your contribution. My orders will be with you before first light tomorrow.'

In his barge, rowing back to *St George*, his mind ranging over what had just been discussed. Nelson was troubled. Even strapped in his chair to be hauled aboard the thought nagged at him that Sir Hyde Parker might be in a quandary about what action to take, but also that he did not trust him. His commander was evincing the same opinion he had had of Nelson when he was in command of HMS *Agamemnon*, that he was a glory-seeker who cared nothing for the reputation either of his country or his superiors, only for himself. That nothing could be further from the truth made no difference. He resolved at once to write to Parker in the hope of changing that opinion.

The following morning, on board HMS *London*, the atmosphere was still gloomy, but topped with anger. A whole day had gone by with the ships inactive, the wind too strong to allow them to lift their anchors. But the course they were going to sail was no secret, since the Master of the Fleet had told anyone who cared to listen of his concerns regarding his own ability to get them safely through the Great Belt.

Parker had consulted the men he had brought to the Baltic as pilots, the masters of merchant vessels involved in the northern trade who sailed the routes of both Sound and Belt frequently. He did not confine himself to their opinions on that, but asked them for their thoughts on the approaches to Copenhagen, and the possibilities and dangers of taking warships down unmarked channels between encroaching sandbanks.

That explained the gloom, for these 'pilots' made it clear that the prospect horrified them. They did not mention that what horrified them most was being on board ships under fire even should they succeed in getting them to where the fighting sailors wanted them to be. There was not a warrior among them: they were tradesmen from Leith and the ports of eastern England whose stock in trade were manifests not men o' war.

The contrary emotion stemmed from Parker's executive officers. His Captain of the Fleet, Dommet, the man responsible for the smooth running of the ships under his command, was an experienced officer. He had held the same office under Lord Howe at the battle of the Glorious First of June in '94 and reckoned that he knew a bit about fleet actions. Otway, the captain of HMS *London*, was also an experienced officer, who expected at the very least to be informed of any course of action and to have his views on the efficacy of any proposals receive proper due. It was they who were angry.

Vansittart, his despatch for Earl St Vincent written and safe in an oilskin pouch, was gone, sent off in a fast frigate to carry the news of Parker's intentions to London without either of these officers having had any say in the contents. Subsequently it was made obvious to their commander that they took great exception to the way he kept asking civilians, diplomats and non-naval sailors about military matters while ignoring those aboard who had the experience properly to advise him. Then, in the midst of Parker's solitary dinner, with his secretary scribbling away in one corner of the cabin, Nelson's letter arrived.

Parker read it more than once, long as it was, although he was as aware as the writer of most of the points it made. But certain passages received more attention, causing knife, fork and wineglass to remain untouched, not least the passage that reminded him of his position . . .

> . . . *you have the honour of England more entrusted to you than ever fell to any British officer. On your decision depends whether our country will be degraded in the eyes of Europe, or whether she shall rear her head higher than ever.*

There were the 'what ifs?'. The idea that should Parker not go through that damned Sound, the Danes might take their seven seaworthy capital ships out to join the French. That Nelson discounted it did not stop Parker worrying about it.

It was all very well for Nelson to say that it was acceptable for ships to be crippled and lost, for he would not be obliged to account for them. When appointing a commander the Admiralty did not give him ships to keep or lose, they entrusted the vessels and men to his care, certain that that officer would know just how much the country's well-being depended upon their safe return. It was all attack, attack, attack in this letter – typical of a man like Nelson who could easily hide behind his inferior rank while the blame for failure rained on Parker's head. And could he believe the closing paragraph?

> *The measure may be thought to be bold, but I am of opinion that the boldest measures are the safest: and that our country demands the most vigorous exertion of her force, directed with judgement. In supporting you, my dear Sir Hyde, through the arduous and important task you have undertaken, no exertion of head or heart shall be wanting from your most obedient and faithful servant,*
> *Nelson and Brontë*

'Obedient, by damn!' growled Parker. 'That, sir, you never are. And as for faithful that has yet to be proved to me.'

He realised he had spoken aloud in the presence not only of his secretary but of his cabin servants, and in a voice that must have sounded close to that of a spoilt infant. And he realised his food had gone cold. With the wine now tasting somewhat sour he abandoned any pretence of enjoying the meal. He dismissed everyone and sat in solitary unhappiness, gazing out at a northern sky that seemed to darken so very slowly, ranging again and again over all the tactical and strategic alternatives, and the possible consequences.

Captains Dommet and Otway finally saw Sir Hyde Parker at first light the following morning, just as the fleet weighed, as per orders, and headed south for the Great Belt. It was an uncomfortable interview for all three. Against his will, Parker was forced to relate to the two officers what had taken place over several days. His rank gave him many privileges, but that did not include discounting the thoughts of these men.

True, he could issue orders and demand that they were obeyed, but that would not protect him from written submissions of disagreement, with copies kept by the originator to be produced at a future hearing. The two captains became increasingly tight-lipped the more Parker prevaricated, and it was clear from their faces that they profoundly disagreed with the conclusions he had reached. Then Dommet asked what Nelson thought and Parker, in a move he instantly regretted, handed over Nelson's letter.

The Captain of the Fleet lacked a sense of humour, and he had the face to go with that. Everything about him seemed squashed, the eyes too close, the nose too sharp, the mouth small over a jutting chin. Yet even he, who had expressed little love for the writer, as he read the letter, gave a look of such deep disgust that his admiral was in no doubt of his opinion. As Otway read it, Dommet quietly questioned his commander.

Parker had to restate his reasons for his actions, reiterating Vansittart's opinions, those of the merchant captains he had engaged as pilots, and last his own inclinations that the losses might outweigh the gains in any action undertaken by the fleet. That the task was to get into the Baltic and there decide what future course of action to adopt.

Parker was unaware that he was creating exactly the same impression with this pair as he had with Nelson: namely that he would prefer to do nothing; that in sailing by the Great Belt he was

261

merely buying time in the hope that some peaceful conclusion might present itself.

'You do not feel, sir, that Admiral Lord Nelson's letter answers those points?' asked Dommet. He then turned to Otway, who was gazing at his commanding admiral with barely disguised repugnance. 'Captain?'

'Sir,' said Otway, addressing Parker, 'you are aware that I dissented from your opinion to send Mr Vansittart to negotiate, thus wasting a whole seven days in which, it appears, the Danes have merely made more difficult an already formidable defence.'

Parker could remember nothing of the sort. Neither Dommet, who was nodding agreement, nor Otway had expressed a contrary opinion regarding that course of action. Yet he could see from their expressions that they would swear blind, if asked, that they had. No stranger to naval politics Parker realised that these two men were preparing to detach themselves from him if the situation demanded it.

'Lord Nelson says,' Dommet added, 'that the boldest methods are often the safest. As someone who has fought in a wholly successful and undisputed fleet action, I can only say that I am inclined to agree.'

Then Otway spoke. 'Another four to five days while we crawl round Zeeland by the Great Belt will alert the Danes to our line of attack. They may well alter their defence to thwart us.'

'And since Lord Nelson had advised the actions he has outlined, and put them in writing . . .'

Dommet stopped, leaving Parker's mind in turmoil. What where they saying, this pair? That he was wrong and Nelson right? Or that with Nelson's letter he could afford to give the man his head and claim as a success anything he achieved while escaping any responsibility for failure?

As he looked at the two captains Parker realised that he would never know their true motivation. Professional pique at the lack of consultation or a genuine belief that he was wrong? Faith in Nelson, or a deep seated concern for their own reputations? There might be a multitude of explanations but the real reasons would never be stated, since Otway and Dommet were too well versed in naval politics to ever voice them. In contrast was the naïvety of Nelson, in so openly writing to him regarding the alternatives. Could he really so naïve, or was it possible that his sentiments were genuine?

'Your suggestions would be most welcome, gentlemen,' said Parker, who felt he could play politics as well as the next man, 'and I would appreciate that you give them to me in writing.'

26

Nelson, pacing the windward side of the deck, was relating to an enthralled Midshipman Frears the tale of the ancient battle of Actium when the first of the two signal guns banged out from HMS *London*, sending a puff of white smoke racing away on the breeze. The wind was stiff and invigorating, and the *St George* was pitching and rolling on a choppy sea typical of the narrow channel between the North Sea and the Baltic.

'You must always stand to the fore, Mr Frears, and accept the prospect of death or a crippling wound if you wish to lead men into battle, and it is best to stand out to sea, for sailors only become good hands in open water. Keep them idle in port and they go to seed.'

'Mark Antony did not do that, sir?' asked Frears, as more guns boomed.

'He did not, Mr Frears. He kept his ships idle at their anchorage.' Nelson stopped then, conscious of the second gun, not wishing to mention that the great Roman general was more interested in dallying with his mistress, Cleopatra, than going out to meet Agrippa, the commander of the rival fleet. 'Marcus Antonius had heavier vessels, more numerous than those of his enemies, reports say twice the number, but Agrippa, just like the fleet of your own country, had the better men. So when Antony emerged, he was outmanoeuvred by swift sailing ships and forced to flee the battle. He was, of course, like that devil Bonaparte, a soldier not a sailor.'

'You would never flee a battle sir?'

Nelson smiled as the first lieutenant approached, throwing a frown at Frears who, like all the mids aboard, was far too familiar with the admiral.

'I hope not, Mr Frears.'

'Sir,' said the first lieutenant. 'A signal from the flag to wear round on a course north-north east.' Nelson turned to look at the flag streaming from Parker's masthead, as he continued, 'and HMS *London* has put off a boat, which is heading for us. We think it is Captain Otway.'

Nelson dropped his gaze to the grey, uninviting water, criss-crossed with white wave tops. 'Poor Otway boating in this sea. May I borrow Mr Frears?'

'Sir,' said the First Lieutenant, nodding, still surprised, even after weeks of sailing with Nelson, that he should he asked.

'Please go to my cabin and ask Tom Allen to prepare a hot punch for Captain Otway.'

'It may not be him, sir,' the first lieutenant insisted. 'We only had a fleeting glimpse.'

'Whoever it is will be wet and cold, I daresay,' Nelson replied, as Frears ran off. 'Even a midshipman needs a warm drink in these waters.'

Otway was both cold and wet. Even in a dreadnought oilskin boat cloak the choppy freezing sea had penetrated to his uniform. By the time he made Nelson's cabin the fleet was on its new course, which Nelson was informed was to take them to a new anchorage off the Sound.

'Sir Hyde has been mulling on your suggestions, Lord Nelson, and feels, like you, that to waste time only aids the enemy.' Otway had an open, honest looking face, but perhaps because he was shivering his words lacked verisimilitude. 'Captain Dommet and I, when finally asked our opinion, could only concur with the sentiments you expressed in your letter.'

'Admiral Parker showed you my letter?'

'Yes, sir,' Otway replied. He said this as if it was the most natural thing in the world. It was not so to Nelson. That letter had been intended as private advice. 'Sir Hyde wishes me to tell you that he will abide by any suggestions you make regarding the dispositions of the fleet. He also asks if you are prepared to agree that Copenhagen should be the primary target.'

'Not the Russians?'

'No, sir.'

There was something not quite right about all this. Nelson was prepared to accept that a man like Parker might both dislike and distrust him: he came from a school of old-fashioned thinking with which Nelson had no truck but old ideas were hard for those raised in their shadow to throw away. That letter had been designed not to dent Parker's *amour propre*. But even a dolt could see, reading between the lines, that it could only have been composed in the face of Parker's total lack of authority. To show it to others, to risk opening it up to public scrutiny, struck Nelson as odd.

He knew enough about flagships to be aware that they could be many things, depending on the admiral in charge: happy ships, setting an example to the fleet, which he hoped was the case on his own vessel, or a floating hell when an admiral wanted to show how much command he had over his captains. Or they might be gossip parlours, which was the impression he had gained on going aboard *London*, leaderless three-decked hotbeds of rumour and chatter, with plenty of slander and calumny stemming from the lack of positive leadership.

Now, all of a sudden, there was a definite air of that most necessary commodity. Who had engineered it? He was not vain enough to believe that his letter had been sufficient, nor did he truly suppose a sudden conversion in Parker from timidity to bellicosity. If Dommet and Otway had been the force of persuasion, what words had they used that he had not? Why did he feel, for no apparent reason, that what had happened might threaten him? Nelson forced himself to bury these speculations. It mattered not a jot why the change had occurred, it was enough to rejoice in the fact that it had.

'Sir Hyde,' Otway added, with just a touch of nervousness, 'particularly wished to ask if you still inclined towards the Belt.'

'I say to you what I said to him, Otway, the Belt or the Sound, it makes no odds.'

'But the Sound for preference?'

'Yes.'

'Then Sir Hyde requests that you proceed on that assumption.'

Otway did not know Nelson except by reputation, but as he warmed his hams against the stove he was treated to a view of the man in action. And seeing the orders that flowed from him he could not help but contrast it with what he had observed of Sir Hyde Parker. With no reference to a single sheet of paper Nelson reeled off to his secretary the order of sailing for the entire fleet. At the same time, almost, he planned boat exercises that had a succession of midshipmen scurrying from the great cabin on to the deck, where a harassed signal lieutenant sought to keep pace with the raft of instructions.

He and Otway returned to HMS *London* where, with Parker present, the difference was even more marked: an excited Nelson made absolute sense while the occasional words of caution Parker interjected sounded a false note. In a *tour de force* of explanation, Nelson outlined how he would get the fleet to Copenhagen and, since that was the nub of Parker's orders from the government, how he would go about subduing the defences, provided no other threat appeared to prevent it.

Nelson was in seventh heaven. He had what he wanted, a fleet to organise and a target to attack. As he paced up and down, he felt sorry for Parker, which tempered his ebullience. The man had not been born to this situation: that he was here was the fault of the system and of a government too weak at the time of his appointment to risk alienating any of their political allies. No good would come of humiliating him, so what would have taken time anyway took much longer as he nudged Parker into pronouncing obvious conclusions.

'I do feel it necessary, sir,' Nelson concluded, 'that you personally explain our plans to all captains.'

Parker put his hands under his double chin as if in prayer. He was thinking this was Nelson's plan and not his. His mind was in the same turmoil he had gnawed on for weeks – victory with laurels or defeat and disgrace – but his junior was so anxious to lead that he could operate at one remove. This might gift him the victory without effort or temper any odium.

'Lord Nelson, since you are appointed to lead the fleet through the Sound and the attack on Copenhagen, I think that is a duty better left to you.'

'Thank you, sir.'

'Meanwhile,' Parker added, spoiling the air of martial endeavour, 'I shall send a message to Colonel Strickler, the commandant of Cronberg fort, asking him what his intentions will be if we attempt to make the passage through.'

None of the others looked at him then, but they were all wondering why he wanted to alert the Danes to his intentions.

Prior to the captains' meeting Nelson watched the result of an order he had issued when Otway was warming himself by the stove. Every flat-bottomed boat in the fleet, each with an officer or midshipman in charge, and half a dozen marines and a cannon in the bows, was required to wheel and manoeuvre round *St George*. Even young Frears had a command, though several experienced hands were in his launch to ensure he made no cardinal errors. Formed into squadrons, the boats mounted mock attacks on the side of the ship only sheering off once contact had been made.

'There, Hardy,' Nelson cried, pointing as another section of a dozen boats surged in. 'Let any one of those fortress gunners fire on us and I will send our brave lads ashore in their boats to singe their tails.'

Hardy responded to this in his usual manner, which left Nelson wondering if he was happy at the idea or thought it madness. Not for the first time he realised that this man would never do in high command: he would get there, of course, if he stayed alive and enough admirals before him died. Competence had little to do with the system of promotion: once on the captain's list you rose inexorably to become a flag officer. God forbid the Ghost should ever have to fight a fleet action!

'Make an order, Captain Hardy,' Nelson said, with just a trace of a sigh. 'Boats to break off and return to their ships.'

The conference of captains was not as Nelson expected. Instead of the enthusiasm to be at the enemy that he had anticipated, he heard many objections to his plans. These men had not sailed with him before, although he had met many of them in his years in the service, some a long time ago, like Thomas Bertie who, as a brand new midshipman, had journeyed with him and Troubridge in HMS *Seahorse* on the voyage to Calcutta in '76. Now he commanded HMS *Ardent*, which had fought and suffered against the Dutch at Camperdown.

Those who had previously been under his command, like Freemantle and Foley, posed pertinent questions and accepted his answers, showing trust in his judgement. But most did not, and Nelson was forced to admit that not only had he been lucky in the quality of his Nile captains, but that he had had the time to introduce them to his mode of thinking. Here in the Cattegat, he was trying to do in one day what had taken three months in the Mediterranean, and to a far more numerous body of men, over thirty officers of post rank.

Why did he have to explain to professional naval officers, not once but several times, that in a four-mile wide channel the largest Danish cannon, now known to be thirty-six pounders, with an effective range of less than two miles, could not even command the middle of the Sound? Why did they doubt his assertion that the Swedes manning Helsingborg would do nothing, and that if they dared he would not only bombard them into submission, but send in his flat bottomed boats to assault what was an under-manned fortress.

'Gentlemen, we face two nations who have no recent experience of war. Even should our ships be forced by wind and current into the extreme arc of their fire, where are the gunners who can hit moving targets.'

Regardless of the truth of that remark – that for a shore-based gunner to employ deflection gunnery required a high degree of skill – it was met with demands to know what would happen if they were becalmed or the wind backed so that the fleet would have to come about in narrow shoal water. He answered that the former, in these seas, was a near impossibility while the latter would see them anchor rather than run. He wanted to say that this was war and not for the cautious or cowardly, but he must carry the doubters with him – no good would come of ruffling their pride.

'Captain Mosse, you will lead the fleet through the Sound in HMS *Monarch*.' Mosse nodded, but in a way that told Nelson nothing about his opinion of the honour. 'Captain Murray, you will take under your charge the bomb ketches. You are to take *Edgar* into the Sound and anchor, here, to the north-west within range of the fortress of Cronberg, your task to play on Colonel Strickler's gunners and unsettle them should they open fire on us.'

George Murray had lost HMS *Colossus* off the Scilly Isles, the ship that had taken down with it most of Sir William Hamilton's fortune. Despite that, he was not one to demur, nor had he objected to Nelson's plan. A sailor of great experience, he had fought in the Far East against the great French admiral Suffren. He had also been with Nelson at St Vincent, so was no stranger to fleet actions. He was the only officer in the entire group who had made the passage of the Sound, albeit in peacetime, so could claim to know the waters.

'You will not be a target to them while the fleet is in view, but you must be prepared to win your anchors quickly as soon as we are through, or risk facing the whole barrage once they have levered round their guns.'

The whole table had gone quiet now. Orders were being issued to be accepted with good grace or ill-will. There was no doubt that they would be obeyed, since they would carry Parker's signature, but Nelson knew that the way in which they were taken on would have a bearing on individual conduct. Thinking of his talk with young Frears he wondered how many Mark Antonys were in this cabin, and how many Agrippas?

'And now, gentlemen, you are aware that Sir Hyde has orders to attack Copenhagen and bring the Danes to sue for peace.'

Some nodded, other faces remained blank and one or two shook their heads, as if wondering at the folly of such a notion. What Parker had heard about the Danish defences had wormed its way round the fleet and along with it, Nelson suspected, a good dose of the commander's pessimism.

The charts of the Sound were replaced by those of Copenhagen Roads, and the north and south approaches to the harbour. Each captain was given a layout of the Danish defences, which the master of the *St George* and his mates had spent half the night drawing. Again it was instructive to watch each face as they perused details they had heard only by word of mouth. Again a mixture: an amused smile here, a sucking of teeth there, some peering, others barely looking as if to imply that if the others were in ignorance they were not. And then Nelson called for their attention.

First he gave them his impression of Danish thinking, which was that if the British fleet wanted to dictate peace terms, it would need to take the harbour and with it the arsenal and the navy yard. Command of the harbour would also give them absolute command of the city, the royal palaces and all the official buildings, though the Castellet battery, set so close to the city, would seem safe from anything other than an assault by soldiers.

'So you see, gentlemen, the Crown Prince has only one question he feels needs an answer. He knows that it is possible to take the harbour, but will we be prepared to pay the high price such an assault would entail?' That brought forth much agreement. 'It cannot be done without severe damage to several ships, perhaps half the fleet, and perhaps fatal damage.'

A buzz of assent, and even more worried looks from the captains of shallow draught ships. These men were not cowards. But when a man suspects he and his ship's company are about to be sacrificed, he has the right to enquire of the necessity.

'That north-south channel is too narrow to deploy the whole fleet, so we would be required to throw ships piecemeal into the maw of the Danish defence, trading our damage for theirs, trying to wear them down. I do not doubt that we could carry that objective, gentlemen, we have the men and the courage to do it, but at what cost?'

'He has obliged us by arranging his defences for that very possibility, his strongest ships, his best gunners manning his most modern ordnance, covered by the two forts mounting over a hundred pieces of ordnance, all there to greet us as we attack. So, as a responsible commanding officer, Sir Hyde has wisely decided not oblige him.'

Smiles from different people now, yet surely everyone knew these were Nelson's orders they were about to hear, not Parker's.

'You will observe, gentleman, the passage to the east of the Middle Ground Shoal known as the Holland Deep, which is the route taken by merchant vessels bypassing the port of Copenhagen. It is my intention, with ten sail-of-the-line, those that draw the least under their keel, and all the bomb ketches, to sail down that channel, then come about at the eastern end of the Middle Ground Shoal and attack the Danes from that point. There they have nothing like the strength that they can muster at the head of the King's Deep. The aim will be to subdue those forces ranged along the sandbank that abuts before Amager Island so that we can take position to bombard the city at will. Our aim will be to force the Danes to sue for peace or see their capital city reduced to rubble. In order to lead this attack, I will be shifting my flag to HMS *Elephant*, since *St George* draws too much water.'

Hardy looked crestfallen. Dull he might be, but he loved the idea of a fight. Nelson's old shipmate Tom Foley of the *Elephant* looked mightily pleased. If anyone believed in the Nelson method it was he, the man who had led Nelson's fleet into Aboukir Bay, taking the French on their unprotected inside flank without bothering to ask his admiral for instructions.

'The rest of the fleet will stand off in Copenhagen Roads ready to lend what support we require.'

Then the questions started, and over the next five hours, Nelson was able to sort out the meek from the strong, the eager from the cautious, those keen to fight from those who cared more for what they had than what they might gain. There were those who enthused so much he suspected they secretly harboured an opposite opinion, and others, like William Bligh, in command of the converted East Indiaman, *Glatton*, who hid behind his dour nature and ponderous features the dogged determination that might win the day.

Some, like Captain Bertie, had genuine concerns and had to be reassured. HMS *Ardent*, an old 64, was slow, unwieldy and given to falling off at the slightest excuse, so any narrow channel held a greater terror for Bertie than for others. Added to that, *Ardent* had the residue of a crew that had been decimated at Camperdown, and might balk at a similar battle. And there were those who, as they consumed too many glasses of his wine, went from caution to braggadocio.

Tom Allen had already packed Nelson's sea chest and Midshipman Frears had been alerted to stand by to accompany his admiral. As a tired Nelson explained to Tom Foley, just before he was hauled up and over the side, he owed a duty to the boy's father.

'To take him into the thick of a desperate battle?'

Nelson smiled. 'Neither father nor son would ever forgive me if I did not. Young Frears comes from a family that could use a bit of glory.'

Deciding to sail through the Sound and achieving it depended on the right wind and an eastward running current, so that any damaged ship could be taken in tow and got to the safe anchorage in Copenhagen Roads. Nelson spent a frustrating twenty-four hours, not aided by the attitude of the pilots he had had brought aboard from HMS *London* so that he could quiz them himself. If some of his captains had been less than enthusiastic, they were paragons of vim and fire compared to the pilots, not one of whom would do other than issue dire warnings. To hear them moan, it was as if the Sound was unnavigable, the Holland Deep a graveyard for ships and the King's Deep ten times worse. Nelson sent round the fleet to ask if any of the masters had Baltic experience.

The next day the wind turned northerly, which was perfect for square-riggers, and the main current, which might have been dead against them even with an opposite wind, obliged the fleet by setting to the east. HMS *Monarch*, the lead ship, had taken station at the entrance to the Sound, there to wait for the rest of the fleet. Murray, with the bomb ketches like a flock of ducklings about their mother, had got off early too, and taken station to enter the narrow passage on a course just south of the main body, preparatory to anchoring and running out his guns.

Aboard HMS *London* Parker sat in his cabin, alone, before a stiff glass of brandy, contemplating for the last time what he was about to do: commit a whole fleet to action that, once joined, could not be called off. He was lonelier than he had ever been in his life. Above his head, everyone was waiting, so sinking the spirit in one gulp he stood up, grabbed his hat and made his way to the quarterdeck.

Dommet and Otway were already there, and there was a light in the eyes of all the others present, which lifted his mood. He turned to Dommet and gave the order to weigh. Flags streamed up to the masthead, fluttering on the stiff breeze carrying the order. As soon as they were in place the signal gun banged out its message that all should look. It was superfluous: it was clear from the speed with which sails appeared and the ships were hauled over their anchors that every sailor had been at his station in readiness for this moment. And much as Sir Hyde Parker had his doubts as to the outcome of this adventure he could not but be uplifted by the sight of so many noble ships making sail. There was a catch in his voice as he issued the next order, 'To all captains, Dommet, form line of battle.'

Nelson stood easily on the quarterdeck of HMS *Elephant* with a proud Midshipman Frears, appointed the Admiral's special messenger. In front of them stood Tom Foley and his officers, the former silent while his lieutenants got the ship under way. There would be much backing and filling as ships got into their order of sailing and no doubt the odd yell through a speaking trumpet for some bugger or other to sheer off and damned quick, but it was impressive nonetheless.

Monarch was already under way, with *Edgar*, and the bomb ketches heading for the gap between Kullen on the Swedish shore and Gilleleje on the Danish, both ships with leadsmen already in the bows reeling off the depth of water under the keels. Ahead of Captain Mosse, clear in the late afternoon light, the channel narrowed all the way to that vital gap between Helsingborg and Cronberg.

'Mark this moment Mr Frears,' said Nelson, 'for it will live with you for the rest of your life. No matter what you do nothing will ever outweigh the first time you go into battle.'

As soon as the Sound began to narrow Murray and his bomb ketches pulled away to anchor. Nelson watched, and pointed out to Frears the way the 74-gun ship positioned herself. 'See, he drops the stern anchor, and below decks his men have prepared a spring, a hawser that, fed out the front ports, will be attached to that anchor cable so that *Edgar* can be hauled round and have all her cannon facing the castle. The bomb ketches will use twin anchors and their capstan not only to position themselves but also to adjust their aim.'

Nelson was talking, he knew, to allay his own late doubts. It was a common thing, this series of afterthoughts about what might go wrong, made worse by the length of time that the whole adventure would take. Behind him the fleet was strung out and he knew it would be near nightfall – a late darkening indeed in these northern climes – before the last ship cleared the danger.

All eyes were on Helsingborg, telescopes adjusted constantly for a clearer picture of the battlements. There were men there for sure, and a sharp eye through a long glass could see a trace of the smoke from the tubs of slowmatch set behind the guns as an insurance in case the flintlocks didn't fire. But there was no great activity, no sign that the cannon, so much closer to the fleet than those of Cronberg, were preparing to open fire.

It was about an hour later that *Monarch* got abreast of both fortresses. Nelson pointed as Mosse raised his colours and the great battle flag streamed out from the masthead. It was as if Colonel Strickler, the officer in charge of the Cronberg gunners, had been waiting for that: the signal that battle was about to be joined. Before it was half way up to the peak, a huge jet of smoke appeared from the walls. That beat the sound of the cannon, and the sound beat the black heavy ball that arced through the air towards HMS *Monarch*. Hitting the water it sent up a huge plume of white spray that shot forward and smashed into the side of the ship.

'Make a note of the time,' said Sir Hyde Parker, 'and signal Captain Murray to open fire.'

Aboard *Edgar* and the bomb ketches they had been waiting too, bent over their ordnance, every gun at maximum elevation to make the range. Hyde Parker's signal was also half way up to the mast when those guns spoke, no single weapon now but everything they had aboard. Even in the rolling heavy smoke from *Edgar's* broadside Nelson could see the way the bomb ketches dipped and reversed as their great mortars fired. Those balls, ten times the size of that from Cronberg, seemed to fly so slow it was a wonder they stayed in the air. But when they came down, they did so with awesome power, sending up great plumes of earth and stones, part of the escarpments in front of the fort.

'Now our friend Colonel Stricker has a conundrum Mr Frears. Would you care to outline for me what that is?'

Frears gulped, but even to a near child the answer was obvious. 'Does he direct his fire on to the *Edgar*, sir and ignore the fleet? Or does he seek to damage us?'

'Well said Mr Frears. And what would you do?'

It was with no pleasure that Frears replied, 'I would concentrate on us sir, since his object is to prevent us making Copenhagen Roads.'

Nelson watched the water around *Monarch* start to boil, as Strickler opened up with his entire barrage. Some balls fell well short, the odd one made the range but did no damage, the majority landing between the stern of one ship and the bowsprit of the next in line. And Helsingborg, more than a mile distant, stayed silent. The following ships reached the point of maximum danger, but before that happened to HMS *Elephant* Nelson announced his intention of going below. While most on the quarterdeck were astonished, Captain Foley was not. He had known Nelson since they were boys together, warring with the senior midshipmen aboard their first posting. What he was doing was typical. The message was simple: we are in no danger.

'I think Mr Strickler will need to be damned lucky,' Nelson said, just before he disappeared down the companionway. 'The Swedes, it seems, prefer caution to war, and unless he sinks one of our ships in the deep water channel, he is doing nothing but waste his powder and shot.'

As the fleet sailed on *Edgar* kept up a steady barrage, doing little damage, but the shots obliging the Danish gunners to keep their heads below the parapet lest some ricocheted stone from the exploding ramparts inflict a serious wound. Nelson had left Frears on deck, his task to tell his admiral when the last ship had cleared the narrow part of the Sound. The sky was the azure blue of approaching night, the gun flashes, from both fort and ships orange tongues of flame that darted into the clear icy air, before the boy came down to find his admiral calmly writing letters.

'The Cronberg shot is to the stern of *Glatton*, sir. Captain Bligh is through. The flag has sent a signal with HMS *Edgar*'s number to discontinue the action.'

The first part – the easy part to Nelson's way of thinking – was over. Now he had to turn his mind to the much more difficult task of subduing a whole nation.

27

HMS *Amazon* had enough gold braid on the quarterdeck to light up a ballroom, mixed with the red coats of artillery officers and Colonel Stewart, commander of the contingent of soldiers. Nelson imagined it was the kind of scene that a figurative painter might appreciate. The frigate was inching along the King's Deep, through floating ice and the detritus of the rivers that fed the Baltic, sailing north to south, with the spires of Copenhagen and the grey, green and red tiled roofs of the buildings easily visible in the light of the piercing northern sun.

The master was making observations and marking off distances, using his quadrant and the many spires of the city, hastily scribbling notes into a book held for him by one of his mates. Two leadsmen were fully active in the bows, calling out the depth of water under the keel to an anxious officer in the waist, one that Captain Riou, the commanding officer of *Amazon* could see from the quarterdeck. Men stood ready to back the sails at a moment's notice and take the way off the ship. With no buoys to mark the safe channel, it was essential to be able to take the way off the ship quickly, though being stationary might expose them to some gunnery.

Parker, Nelson, Rear Admiral Graves and Captain Dommet would not face capture, but Nelson suspected that being forced to take a boat back to his ship would do nothing for the fire in Parker's belly, which showed every sign of dying out. Nelson tried to avoid embarrassing his superior, positing suggestions in such a way that any conclusion seemed as if it had come from him. They had sailed south from the fleet anchorage, passing the main Danish defence, the forts and warships at the head of the channel between Zeeland and Amager, using the frigate's shallow draught to stay at the furthest possible range. Yet it was close enough for both sets of officers to examine each other.

One of the lieutenants from HMS *London* read the enemy strength. *Iris*, frigate, 36 guns, believed to be 24 and 18-pounders. *Trekroner* 74 guns, 36-pounders on the lower deck, 24's on the upper, with the Lynetten fort to the rear. Steen Bille's flagship, *Danmark* 74, was next, set quite properly in the centre of the defence. In front of the Trekroner Fortress, built ten feet high on piles driven in a protruding sandbank, with earth packed redoubts, lay two brigs of 18 guns.

According to Vansittart over five hundred men manned the fort behind these brigs. It mounted sixty-four heavy calibre cannon and one huge 94-pounder carronade designed to smash ships at close range. Then came *Mars* 60, and *Elephanten* 74, both two-deckers lacking masts, vessels once proud, now relegated for use as blockships.

Sailing into King's Deep what they saw was even easier to identify. They examined Olfert Fischer's defence line along the northern shore of Amager. Though more numerous in terms of vessels and guns, it was weaker because of lack of depth and no fixed target, like the canal entrance to the main harbour, for an enemy to assault.

Each observer carried in his mind a view of the whole layout of the city behind the defences and there were sharp eyes in the tops to remind them of what, from sea level, they could not observe. The round moated walls that encased the pocket capital, the numerous harbours that ran off the main channel, the wide canal that ran between the two islands on which the city stood. At the end of that canal, less than a third of a mile from the royal palace of Amelienborg, sat the Castellet fortress, bristling with guns.

Nelson was busy calculating ranges, noting that if he entered the King's Deep at the southern end then he would be out of range of the fixed fortifications of both Trekroner fort and behind them, on the city walls, the Quintus and Sixtus batteries. There was a battery of guns behind a low, newly thrown up rampart near the northern tip of Amager, but he saw that as a readily acceptable risk since it mounted fewer cannon than any one of his line of battle ships.

The lookouts calculated less than ten cannon, probably 36-pounders and a couple of mortars. The latter were deadly to a ship if accurate, but were notoriously difficult to aim, and the charge of powder firing the ball had to be measured correctly to a fraction of an ounce to hit a stationary target, never mind a moving one. That meant his intended entry in the King's Deep from the south would start virtually unopposed.

But even as he sniffed the freezing air, and watched the floating ice and bits of trees ease by the side of the ship, he could not help but be aware that his opinion about subduing these guns was not shared by his fellow admirals. By the look on Parker's face he was seeing problems where Nelson was seeing solutions. Rear Admiral Graves was pointing out, with increasing despondency, the armed hulks, pontoons, gunboats and wood-stacked fire ships that lined the shore, observations that were having just as morbid an effect on Sir Hyde Parker.

If Nelson had been in command of that defence, he would have opened fire, attempting to sink or send packing what was obviously a reconnaissance. Parker ascribed the lack of that reaction to a general regard for the better rules of polite warfare. Nelson, though he didn't say so, made an entirely different deduction. To him it meant that powder and shot were not in generous supply and that the guns that Fischer had at his disposal were not of the best. He might look at this deck and wish to remove the odd braided head, but to try would waste ammunition and would tell the enemy the nature of both his cannon and the quality of the Danish gunnery.

Did neither of them look, like he had, at that flotsam and ice floating by? That could only have come from further north, a clear indication that the ice and the muck of the great rivers was breaking up. The Russian Fleet could be free of frozen water now, and already sailing to the relief of their Danish allies. In his head he was repeating to himself, over and over again, 'waste not a moment'.

'Gentlemen,' said Hyde Parker, addressing the assembled artillery officers, and the lieutenants from the bomb ketches. 'You have seen what lies beyond these defences. Our object is to bring the Danes to their senses by threatening the city. Can you bombard it effectively from this channel?'

The group trained their telescopes back up the channel, dipping occasionally to the defence line, calculating where to anchor, trajectories and range, discussing targets – the Arsenal and the Navy Yard, as well as the royal palace, seat of the Danish government. With so many spires they had easily visible fixed points from which to deduce the fall of shot. There was a minimum of a huddle before the most senior gunner spoke.

'Provided the guns before us are silenced or subdued, and we can anchor close to the Amager sandbanks then we can threaten most of the city. Nothing of importance would be left whole if we had a week of activity.'

Parker nodded, then turned to the commander of the *Amazon*, 'Captain Riou, you may go about as you feel convenient.'

Nelson watched Riou with professional interest, noting that he handled his ship well and that his men obviously trusted his seamanship. It felt like a happy ship, and Nelson was sure the man who commanded it was a seaman to his fingertips. It was in the way Riou carried himself; assured, confident, happy to be on a deck. Very gently he let the way come off the frigate leaving just enough forward motion to turn the bow. The hands hauled hard to bring round the yards and with what seemed like a whisper the ship was facing north, with yards being braced to beat up the channel into the wind, no easy task since there was little room to tack and wear.

Back aboard HMS *London* the senior officers gathered in Parker's cabin; Nelson, Graves, Dommet, and Colonel Stewart. The latter had little to say, and nothing to impart, since he would only come into action when a great deal had been achieved by the Navy. But Nelson noticed that he took a keen interest in the naval deliberations, and he could see by the changes of expression that he inclined towards aggression rather than circumspection.

'Captain Dommet,' Parker asked, 'your opinion?'

'I feel we must attack, sir,' Dommet insisted. 'It is at the core of our instructions and nothing I have seen today makes me fear the outcome, as long as we do not attempt to take on the enemy where he is best placed to thwart us.'

'You have seen the strength of the defence yet you still feel that is true?'

'I do, sir.'

'I trust you would be prepared to put your opinion in writing?'

There was a moment when their eyes locked, the still smarting Captain of the Fleet, previously ignored, and the commander-in-chief who, by asking Dommet for a positive written submission, was looking to cover his back in case of failure.

'Most certainly, sir,' said Dommet, with a look that was close to a glare.

It was a wasted stare, because Parker had already turned away to talk to the next up the ladder of seniority. 'Admiral Graves?'

'A most hazardous endeavour, sir.' Graves had a long face, and a sad look to go with his grim forecast. 'I cannot see how we can attack such a solid defence without major damage to our ships. We have no real knowledge of the depth of the channel, only that there is one somewhere deep enough to take line-of-battle ships. Please remember that what is being proposed will put us opposite the defence at pistol-shot range.'

'I am aware of that Admiral Graves,' said Parker, but it was not a rebuke for stating the obvious, more of a thank you for airing a thought he had hesitated to make himself.

'We know that the water close to our enemies has the required depth,' said Nelson. 'If they are there, we can be there too.'

'A point, sir,' Graves acknowledged. 'But we must first get to them, and I for one would be reluctant to sail close down their line when they are as well prepared as they are. The lead ships would suffer terribly. That means we must hog the middle of the channel until we are opposite our chosen targets before easing in to engage. What happens if a ship runs aground, with the Danes having oared gunboats that can manoeuvre where we can not?'

There was more, much more, so detailed it seemed as if Graves had stared down every muzzle, and liked less and less what he saw. What use fire ships when the floating batteries had several inches of water over their planking as protection against ignition? The Amager defence ships were old hulks, which the Danes would happily trade for usable warships, weakening the British fleet at no real cost to themselves. Even sunk, sat on the mud, the top tier of guns on such hulks might still be able to fire, the conclusion an unnecessary reminder that Graves was against the enterprise.

'That too, I would like in writing,' said Parker.

'And you shall most assuredly have it, sir.'

'Has your opinion altered at all, Lord Nelson?'

Nelson knew that his opinion would swing the meeting, whether it was positive or negative. Parker was not going to make the decision; this council of war would. Nor would he personally cast a vote. He would use the advice he was given to justify whatever action was taken.

'I am more sanguine than ever, sir.'

Even Parker, who was using all his guile to remain stony-faced, reacted to that with some asperity. 'You do not see obstacles to your proposed plan?'

'None! I repeat to you, give me my ten sail-of-the-line, as well as all the small vessels and let me deploy them as I see fit. I will hand you Copenhagen the day after the wind obliges us.'

'Admiral Graves's reservations notwithstanding?'

'A channel approaching a trading harbour must, for all love, oblige ships sailing both in and out, and I cannot see that such vessels would brush their yardarms in passing. The trench must be deep enough and wide enough for half a dozen keels. We are at risk, of course, and our ships will suffer some damage, but the Danes will suffer more, for we are better at gunnery than they are. I will also say that the way Captain Fischer has deployed his ships and floating batteries gives them an inherent weakness. The ships are in deeper water moored by twin anchors square on to the Amager sandbank, which means that they cannot provide mutual support but can only fire on ships that lay in the limited arc of their guns. And having deployed the floating batteries further inshore any attacker is masked from their fire by the ships further out. Therefore it will be a one against one contest. I am confident that in a close quarters duel, they will be beaten, especially if we come at them from the south.'

Parker picked up a pair of dividers and twiddled with them, as though he was weighing matters in his mind. But because of his own insistence on written opinions the decision had been made. Dommet was looking quite belligerent, and there was no point in asking Nelson if he was prepared to put his view in writing as he already had done so.

'Mister Osborn,' Parker called, and his secretary entered. 'Please be so good as to take down the following orders.'

Nelson continued to pace about as this took place; he to have the ships, frigates, bomb vessels, fire ships named in the margin and guns therein under his command etc etc. Captain Freemantle, with a pair of lieutenants to have command of the flat boats, which would carry the soldiers to their assaults once the fortress guns had been neutralised. Gun brigs to this officer; signals and passwords as follows . . . Osborn scribbled while Parker dictated, with the commander-in-chief looking like a man who, trying to commit suicide, had jumped off a cliff and was wondering if, halfway down, he had made the right decision.

'With your permission, sir,' said Nelson, 'I will return to *Elephant*. We must buoy the Holland Deep tonight, for I have an instinct we may have the wind we want on the morrow.'

'Carry on, Lord Nelson.'

The dripping wet men who stood before him in the pre-dawn glow looked as though they had been dragged through a soaking hedge backwards. A night spent in the Holland Deep, anchoring barrels to mark one side of the deep-water channel, was a wearing activity. Nelson could see chapped hands, red-rimmed eyes and a general air of exhaustion. But these men had done what was asked. He could take his ships to the southern edge of the King's Deep in safety.

They hadn't slept and neither had Nelson. In passing the task to him Parker had also handed over executive control. So it fell to

Nelson to take the general orders and apply them to each individual officer and ship. He was not one to leave a battle to chance: each captain must know their role, and be aware of the general outline so that they did not foul one another's progress, and a comprehensive knowledge of the overall plan allowed them to know just how far they could vary their orders.

Every line-of-battle ship must be prepared to anchor by the stern, relying on the current to keep their heads round and their vessels broadside on to the enemy. Another party would have to go out the night before the attack to try to buoy the King's Deep, using the same method as had been used on the Holland Deep, empty, sealed water barrels anchored to the seabed with four lashed roundshot. With his own ship denied the battle, Hardy undertook to oversee that task, well aware that Olfert Fischer would have armed parties out in boats to stop him.

HMS *Amazon*, HMS *Cruiser*, and the sloops *Lark* and *Fox* were to proceed into the channel before the main attack to act as markers off the Middle Ground Shoal. Sir Hyde had added two ships to his squadron to boost its strength and these two vessels had to be fitted in to the overall scheme. Tirelessly Nelson had worked and fretted, never once forgetting to sniff for the wind he required, once more obliged to bless the gods of battle who so favoured him, because when dawn broke he had it.

Tom Allen's insistence that his master should rest was ignored. Nelson was in a high old state, jittery, nervously starting at any sharp noise, but alert and his mind on fire. He fretted over every detail, only calming down when the ships were under way, hierarchy demanding that the order to do so come from Sir Hyde Parker. The flags flew up the mast at three in the afternoon, Number 66. 'All ships to weigh' Captain Riou, who had so impressed Nelson on the reconnaissance, took the lead in HMS *Amazon*, with the other frigates, the line of battleships, and even the bomb ketches, thirty three ships in all, sticking rigidly in his wake. There was one moment of anxiety, as *Amazon* touched on a shoal, checking very slightly. But Riou proved that Nelson's confidence was well founded, since the sailors standing by to the back of the ship were switched to putting on sail with such speed that the frigate was carried over the sandbank. Naturally the rest of the van squadron steered well clear as HMS *Cruiser*, another frigate, took up the lead position.

'That gentleman,' cried Nelson to Foley and Hardy, standing close by, 'is my kind of seaman.'

Foley and the Ghost exchanged a glance and a smile, well aware of

Nelson's habit of adopting and favouring officers that took his fancy, merry Ed Parker was one, much cosseted by his admiral, who loved him for the cheerfulness with which he always undertook any duty. Clearly Riou was a candidate for the same sort of intimacy.

Nelson was almost dancing by now, itching for a battle while gnawing on potential upsets. Both Foley and Hardy knew he would be like this until the action was won or he was dead, and no words of theirs would calm him. It was left to Tom Allen to fret, to make sure he ate, to try to get him to sleep, lest he collapse from sheer exhaustion.

Within an hour and a half Nelson was making the signal to *anchor as convenient*, and he was where he wanted to be, surrounded now by a group of admiring mids all of whom had, at some time in the passage, pestered him with a question. Now, as HMS *Elephant* came up on her anchor, he beamed at the group, his eyes fixed on those of young Frears.

'There we are,' he cried, pointing up the King's Deep, to the beginning of the Danish defence line, no more than a mile and a half away. 'We have humbugged the Crown Prince. We are where he did not expect us to be, with a powerful fleet still to the north so that he has no idea if this is a feint or the point of attack. That means, gentlemen, we have the one commodity that is worth more than anything in war. Surprise! A signal for all captains if you please.'

With a smaller group to talk to, and this being in the main his own van division, enthusing his officers was easier than it had been on the other side of the Sound. There was the odd doubter, of course, but in the main Nelson felt he was carrying the group, imbuing them with his beliefs and methods.

'The only beaten enemy, gentlemen, is an enemy destroyed. We have been raised to praise commanders who have enjoyed a few captures and the sight of an enemy breaking off an action. I intend no insult to them, men of an older generation, when I say that in these times that will not do.'

He stooped to look into their faces, enough of which shone with anticipation to make him happy. If Nelson loved anything he loved this, and he wished that his beloved Emma could see him now. As he spoke he could feel the mood of the meeting getting more and more excitable, while he became calm. They were not all officers he would have chosen, but there were several here he would not wish to be without.

Freemantle, who had brought *Ganges* in as one of Parker's extra

74's, The Ghost, Hardy, without his ship but reassuring by his presence; high command might not suit him but bloody battle was meat and drink. Foley, who had teased and fought alongside him when they were but boys, Murray of *Edgar*, tough calm and full of experience. Even Admiral Graves in HMS *Defiance*, the other extra line-of-battle ship, who despite his reservations had bowed to the decision, asked for the duty, and was now all for a swift assault. That marked him as special to Nelson.

Dour, uncommunicative William Bligh, he of the Breadfruit Mutiny, spoke little and glowered much. He was a man who suspected his fellow officers of motives to do him down that, in reality, they were to busy to hold. Nelson had him marked as a fighter, a yardarm to yardarm hard-pounder who had the good fortune to be in a ship, HMS *Glatton*, that had been designed for the purpose. A bought-in former East Indiaman she was not sleek. But she was armed with nothing but forty-two-pounder carronades, a weapon known as the smasher for its ability to fire a very large ball at high velocity over a short distance.

'When we enter yonder channel, the object is the obliteration of the defence. It is not a gunnery duel that will be taken up over several days. It will last for one day only.' A few eyebrows lifted at that, from men who knew what they faced. 'In that one day we will lay our ships alongside the Danes, and pound them into submission. I wish to see a British flag above every masthead before nightfall. I wish for the inhabitants of Copenhagen to fear the morrow, to know that the very roofs of their abodes are about to cave in upon them. And I tell you gentlemen, it is my intention to gift to Admiral Sir Hyde Parker the ability to sail for Revel within the week, and crush the Russian fleet.'

Thomas Hardy was never happier than when he was in some form of danger. That irritatingly sedate nature and expressionless countenance, which could infuriate on the quarterdeck, was exactly what was required for his present service. Danger could not make blood race in a man poorly conditioned for such a thing. In an open boat, with muffled oars, he had found the bearing for the southern end of the Middle Ground Shoal. From there, in bitter cold, he worked his way along the sandbank, noting that water close to the shoal was shallow; that the deeper water lay close to the other bank where the Danish defences lay.

Having worked his way silently along the shoal he headed out in to deeper water, casting his lead every few yards, marking the depth from the knots counted off the recovered line. Every ear aboard was alert for the sound of other oars, an enemy boat, which would be full of armed men and probably mount a cannon in the bows. If they were caught they could be sunk, and in pitch dark and in water so cold, death would swiftly follow.

The thin skein of cloud obscured whatever light the stars might have provided, so there was no reflection off the water. Fearing discovery from the noise of a splash, Hardy substituted a pole for his lead line when he thought they might be near the enemy. To the consternation of his boat crew he took them so close to the nearest Danish ship that they could hear men talking, all the time Hardy dipping his pole and finding no ground to touch. The sighs from his men, who saw themselves as ordinarily brave instead of foolishly so, as he ordered them back to HMS *Elephant*, was audible enough to require from him a whispered command for silence.

Nelson was up all night again, on deck in a boat cloak, sat in a chair, there better to see and hear what was going on, Foley beside him, Merry Ed close by waiting to carry an order. He had one ear cocked for a sudden burst of gunfire that would tell him that his greatest fear had been realised: Hardy in his surveying boat had run in to a Danish patrol. And that nose of his sniffed for the wind his god of battles should provide, a south wind strong enough to fill his sails and create a current that would make the entry into the King's Deep easy.

Foley knew that Nelson was near to collapse, because he wanted to cover every possible avenue of how the battle would develop, what his captains had to know exactly, and what to do in any given development. Foley had suggested that he fetch his cot on deck, only to be told to belay such nonsense. But as a member of the Crocodile Club he knew Nelson as well as Nelson knew him. He sent Midshipman Frears, still present as the Admiral's on board messenger, to fetch Tom Allen.

'You will take to your cot, or your grave, which is it to be?'

Tom Allen had arrived on deck minutes after Foley's request, and it was edifying to watch Nelson's servant deal with his black looks and harsh remarks. What Foley did not know was that Tom, at one time a bit timorous, had become more forthright following on from Nelson's affair with Emma Hamilton. Like the man who had served Nelson before him he now felt he had something on his master, and that made him bolder.

'If you think I am going to face your dear old Papa, and say you passed on 'cause you was foolish not brave then you have another thing coming,' barked Tom. The 'your honour', was tacked on as an afterthought.

'Tom,' said Nelson wearily, 'go back to your pantry or your bed but leave me in peace.'

'I will not,' Tom replied. 'I shall fetch that damned cot on this here deck and see you into it if it be the last thing I do.'

'Oh very well.'

He was lying down, still dictating orders when a cold and wet Thomas Hardy came back on board to tell him the results of his survey. Nelson was surprised at the findings; that the deep water was away from the Middle Ground shoal, which was contrary to what he had been told by the merchant captains.

'Those damned pilots are useless,' he barked, 'give me a warranted navy master any time.' Then his voice softened. 'Get out of those wet clothes, Captain Hardy, I need you fit and well.'

Hardy's information led to another flurry of ordering and writing as these details had to be communicated to every commanding officer, including the notification of such to Dommet aboard HMS *London*. Naturally he kept up a communication by boat with Sir Hyde Parker. He had remained at his anchorage well north of the Danish defences, and had told Nelson of his intention to weigh and join in as soon as the attack began. Parker seemed unaware that any wind which favoured Nelson would be dead foul for him if he maintained his present position. This was something the Ghost took the liberty of reminding him of.

'You can ask, sir, indeed demand, that he move closer to the enemy so he can be of assistance. There's deep water within three miles of Steen Bille's line. Otherwise you will be attacking without even the threat of support.'

Nelson answered quite snappily. 'If he cannot see it himself Hardy, then Captain Dommet would certainly have done so. I can only assume he has had that advice and chosen not to take it.'

Faced with such a rare public rebuke, only an officer who knew him as well as Hardy would have dared to continue. He chose to remind a man who was a far better seaman than himself that Parker's ships, beating up from the present anchorage eight miles from the Danes, would have to sail as much as twenty miles, tacking and wearing, to get into action. This compared to the van squadron's one and a half miles.

'He has promised me his 74's will weigh as soon as we do,' Nelson replied.

'They will achieve nothing, sir,' said Foley, supporting Hardy. 'And the Danes will ignore them.'

'And so shall I, Tom,' Nelson insisted. 'I have no need of Parker and his ships. Let them do what they will. The battle will be won at this end of the King's Deep not from the north. It falls to us on our own to win this, and once let it prey on our minds that we require assistance and the zeal we need will diminish.'

28

Although he was not in command of a ship taking part in the action, Hardy was amazed at the detail of Nelson's orders. The last notes had been made at one in the morning, the final parts of a plan that relied on tidal flows, depth of water and the strength of each enemy number from one to twenty along the Danish line.

It was as if Nelson wanted to be on the deck of every vessel, personally directing both men and guns. Every captain was told which of their enemies to engage, and what they had to undertake while proceeding to their station. The frigates had detailed orders for their support and harrying role, prior to their engagement with the Trekroner fort. Hardy knew he could never have written these up, and even after perusing them a dozen times he could not fault them.

Though Nelson was exhausted, he was no longer fretting for anything except that wind to turn these written instructions into a reality. This was not like a naval battle in open water, with a hundred variables. He had an enemy in place, and even as he saw that Olfert Fischer had moved his floating batteries out from the shore to form a continuous line with his ships, thus creating a single defensive line, he knew that to be a minor alteration. Major change was not an option for his opponent. That was the beauty of the surprise he had achieved, so complete that Steen Bille, at the northern end of the King's Deep, must stay moored in his present position in case this southern squadron was just a feint. Parker had the major portion of the fleet to the north of the Danish commodore and even if Nelson doubted that Parker's ships would pose a serious threat to the enemy, they were a visible reminder of what had to be guarded against.

In essence, though it might look complicated on paper, the plan was simple. Nelson's object was speedily to destroy the ships at the southern end of the line by bringing to bear overwhelming fire on them, then to work his way up the King's Deep, each ship-of-the-line, as it became free, leapfrogging its compatriots to engage new opponents. Being moored, the numerical advantage enjoyed by the Danes would thus be nullified.

He had been tempted to try a repeat of the Nile, sailing some of his ships inside the Danes and doubling up on them in a way that would guarantee total destruction. But among many other imponderables he had no idea of the depth of water under the keel on the landward side of the defence line, the Amager shoal, and no way of finding out. He did know that the tactics he had used in Aboukir Bay two years previously were now common knowledge, and he had every right to suspect that the Danes knew that he, the commanding admiral of that battle, was present – just as he knew that, were he the defender instead of the attacker, this was something he would have taken steps to guard against.

It was around six a.m., just as hammocks were being piped up, that Nelson noticed the wind was shifting. This he confirmed with the *Elephant*'s master, slightly irritated that he had felt it and had had to call for verification when he should have been informed.

'Maundy Thursday,' said Tom Foley, who had been with him all night. He and Nelson had walked to the windward side of the ship, from where they could feel the breeze freshening on their faces.

'We'll gift the Danes more than a Maundy sixpence,' Nelson replied, conjuring up the image of Farmer George – if he was well enough – handing out sixpences to the poor specially assembled to receive his largesse.

'Have you had occasion, Tom, to observe Captain Riou?'

'Only socially, though I believe him to be a competent officer.'

From the best cut of cloth,' replied Nelson, his voice enthusiastic. 'He handles *Amazon* brilliantly and his lead through the Sound was exemplary.'

'I do believe, milord, that you remarked on his seamanship at the time.'

'Am I milord to you, Tom?' asked Nelson, sadly

'It is a mode of address I am proud to use,' Foley said, adding a smile that had never failed to disarm Nelson.

'I want to give Riou a chance to distinguish himself.'

Foley knew it was part question, but there was a hint in it that he expected any preferment to be questioned. It always happened when Nelson adopted an officer. Foley wondered if he knew more about Riou than he was saying, perhaps that the man lacked influence, or was under a cloud for a previous act. Whatever, Nelson liked and admired him – he had misplaced his trust in young officers in the past, most notably his own stepson, but his opinions of competence, bravery and zeal had generally been proved correct.

Enthusiasm for the advancement of younger men was common-place in a Nelson command. It wasn't just Riou, there was young Edward Parker as well and Midshipman Frears. Foley thought Nelson almost feminine in the way he took up the careers of those who caught his eye. Malicious tongues in the service questioned his motives, but Foley had known him too long to ascribe to it anything other than innocent admiration.

'Mr Frears,' Nelson said, as if he had read Tom Foley's thoughts.

'I sent him to his berth, sir,' said Foley. 'The boy was on his knees.'

'Thank you, Tom,' Nelson replied, rubbing a hand across his brow, thinking that he, too, was on his knees. 'That was kind of you and inconsiderate of me. Oblige me by sending a signal.'

That brought on board Nelson's ship the captain of HMS *Blanche*, with orders to take his vessel to the southern end of the channel, by the first of Hardy's markers, to stop the larger vessels from going aground. Foley sent another mid to rouse Frears and as the boy emerged and trotted after Captain Foley's messenger, he found the whole ship a mass of activity.

What few bulkheads remained were swung up on hinges to be lashed to the deckbeams. The red-painted decks were being wetted and sanded so that no one plying a gun, or serving it powder should slip on spilt blood. As they passed the surgeon and his mates, who were setting up their temporary place of work, the other mid shouted, 'Damn you Doctor, if you don't handle me and my wounds tenderly, I'll never forgive you.'

It was a purple-veined and ugly face that turned to reply that, 'now was his chance to settle old scores, with all them who had black-guarded him these months past for being too free with the bottle.'

Frears stopped dead as the other mid traded insults with all and sundry, looking in horror at the table covered with saws, choppers, sharp, evil-looking knives, curved and straight. The other table, stronger, with huge square legs, looked in the light from the overhead lanterns to be deeply stained with something near black. Frears realised that it was blood, that being the table for amputations.

'Make haste,' shouted the other mid to Frears, 'or they'll lop off a leg for practice.'

He came on deck to find the crew craning the flat-bottomed boats over the side, with the *Elephant*'s contingent of soldiers parading on the deck in preparation for boarding them. If the surgeon's table was evidence that this was the day of his first battle, then this underlined it. He found Nelson in a chair, his face lined with fatigue, the one good eye, under a green shade, red rimmed from reading and writing.

'Mr Frears,' he said looking up with a wan smile, 'you are just in time. Oblige me by asking the signal lieutenant to hoist a request for all captains and ship's masters to repair aboard.'

'Sir,' replied Frears crisply.

'And Mr Frears,' added Nelson, as the boy turned away. Frears did a sharp turn to face him again. 'When I say that your linen is grubby, it is not that I do not know why.'

'Sir,' said Frears, blushing, though he thought himself no more a disgrace than the other youngsters aboard.

'It is because of attendance on me, I daresay, but I must tell you that it is a very bad notion to go into battle with an unclean shirt. A ball, should you receive one, will carry a portion of linen into the wound, and I have witnessed many times that such a thing can cause corruption of the flesh. If you do not have a clean garment, tell Tom Allen to give you one of mine.'

'Sir,' replied Frears.

'All captains?' Nelson reminded him, which sent him rushing away.

As that order went out, HMS *Elephant* continued to clear for action like every other ship in the fleet. Within minutes the sea was full of boats hauling for the flagship as the captains came aboard to be greeted with all ceremony by pipes and stamping marines. Again they crowded into the rear of the ship, into what had once been Nelson's cabin but was now devoid of anything other than the table, a few chairs, and several cannon. Behind them lay a clean sweep fore and aft, and anyone turning could look straight forward along the whole length of the deck to the forepeak, past rows of guns and their crews, the whole illuminated by what morning light came through the triced-up gun port lids.

Before their admiral stood the men who, if they acted as Nelson wanted, would most certainly bring victory today: the ships' captains and the army officers who would man the flat boats that would go ashore once the Danes had struck their colours. The commanders of the bomb vessels who would disrupt the enemy before taking station to bombard Copenhagen.

Each came to receive their detailed instructions as well as the overall order of attack. Nelson had had the former copied out on to cards, the easier to carry around and read. He let them ingest that which was particular to each ship, and answered the few enquiries from men seeking clarification. Though tired, he was feeling in good spirits. Then he made a speech that afforded him great pleasure; few things were so fine to Nelson as to single out an outstanding officer publicly, and make it plain, to both him and his fellows, that Nelson had faith in his ability and his judgement.

'Captain Riou, you and you alone have no detailed orders besides a general instruction to distract the Trekroner battery. In addition to your own ship you are to take under your direct command, *Alceme*, *Arrow*, *Dart*, *Zephyr* and *Otter*, with *Blanche* to join once the fleet has entered the King's Deep. With those vessels you are to act as circumstances might require.'

Riou could not blush, his skin was too swarthy for that, but he seemed to swell a little, and his black eyes flashed with pride. He had nothing less than a squadron of frigates and sloops to act independently of the main order of attack. Given the number of senior officers present, any one of whom had a better claim to this command than he, it was a stupendous honour.

'And now, gentlemen,' said Nelson, pointing towards the table where Tom Allen had poured each a glass of wine, 'I think a toast to victory.'

As soon as they had gone Nelson called forward the masters of the fleet, as well as the pilots who had come aboard from HMS *London*, and showed them the order of attack. Hardy appraised them of what he had surveyed the night before, pointing out that the water was deeper towards the Amager bank than near the Middle Ground Shoal. He was fully expecting at least one of the supposed pilots to say that this was so, and that the fleet should be safe in mid-channel. In that he was sorely disappointed.

So was Nelson as he tried to get them to give him some clue as to what he might face once the ships had got past the point Hardy had reached, which was, after all, only the beginning of the Danish defence line. Given the high state of excitement aboard the fleet, which was only to be expected when they were about to go into battle, the attitude of the pilots was, to Nelson, a disgrace. So much so that he was tempted to ask them if they had ever, as they claimed, sailed this stretch of water. What he did say, as he dismissed them, was larded with sarcasm: 'Gentlemen, you stand as a credit to the maritime glory of our country.' As soon as the last one was out of earshot, for the benefit of the ships' masters who had stayed behind, he added, 'I find it galling to have the honour of our country confided to the opinion of such men.'

One of the masters spoke up in their defence. 'If you will permit me, Lord Nelson, it is the nature of the pilot's trade. They have no other thought than to keep their ships safe.'

'They are determined not to get their silly heads shot off, Mr Briarly,' snapped Nelson. 'I think they fear more for that than anything.'

'I am honoured that you remember me, sir.'

'Of course I recall you, Briarly, first name Alexander if I'm not mistaken, You were with Davidge Gould aboard *Audacious* at the Nile.'

Briarly puffed up like a pouter pigeon, proud to be recognised by such a man. 'Master of HMS *Bellona* at present, milord.'

'Then perhaps you will tell me what I am to do.'

There was a murmur of astonishment from the assembly. Nelson's reputation as a sailor and navigator was well enough known to make all present doubt that he needed advice from a ship's master. But Alexander Briarly answered. 'If, as Captain Hardy says, there is deep water from mid to the east of the channel, that is likely to continue, though it will swing north near the Trekroner fort.'

'Go on,' demanded Nelson.

'The deep water is there, milord, in that navigable channel, because it is scoured out by the current exiting from the Baltic Sea, and that sometimes must be as fierce as a tidal race. If we have a following wind and a helpful current, the state and direction of the flow should tell us, once we are in deep water, how we are to proceed.'

'No sandbanks?'

'Bound to be, milord, and they would try a Dane as well as they would us. Sand is given to shifting and there's nowt to do about that outside constant use of the channel.' Nelson's eye was on Briarly, and still full of the pride of recognition, he plunged yet deeper into the pit of certainty. 'That fact notwithstanding, if your honour will agree it, I will undertake to get the fleet to where you require it to be.'

'So be it,' Nelson agreed, giving Briarly no chance to temper his offer. But he came close to take the man's hand, his smile the one that made the person receiving it feel immortal. 'My orders are that you repair aboard HMS *Edgar*. To you, Alexander Briarly, falls the honour of leading our fleet into action.'

Briarly gulped, his Adam's apple bobbing up and down, as he realised the enormity of what he was taking on. But having spoken could not withdraw, and it was with a croak that he said, 'Aye aye, sir.'

✻

Nelson was back on deck to see the vital signal raised, now in full dress uniform, like every other officer in the fleet, the stars of the Bath and the Crescent, as well as his epaulettes, flashing in the sun. Despite Nelson having only one arm, Giddings had been told to stand by with a cutlass and a pistol, for if the chance arose, Nelson was determined to board an enemy ship, even if some of his sailors, including his coxswain, had to carry him.

'How will we do, milord?' Giddings asked.

'We will do very well, Giddings. They say the Danes are good brewers. I hazard you will be at their beer in a day or two.'

'Glad to hear it,' replied Giddings, who was thinking more about the women than the beer. 'I'll pass that on.'

'Do, Giddings.'

Merry Ed Parker was suddenly by his side. 'Signal lieutenant has sent to say that all is ready, sir.'

'Then let us proceed.'

It was precisely eight a.m. when the knotted signal flags shot up the halyards, to burst at the top and alert the fleet to prepare for battle, a mere acknowledgement of a truth that had been known for hours. Each captain knew where he had to anchor, knew he should have ready a spring on his cable to haul him round broadside on to his chosen enemy. Below decks the fighting men were already sealed in, with a marine sentry at each companionway to ensure that no one other than an officer, midshipman or one of the powder monkeys employed to serve the guns could pass.

But Horatio Nelson rated them unnecessary. He might not know the men on Tom Foley's ship as well as he had known some, but he knew his British tar. The men on the two decks below him would ply their guns with gusto, just as they were trained to do. They would be looking at each other now, exchanging jokes, having already settled who would look after whose possessions, and who would take the news of death to a wife, child or sweetheart. Nelson's last will, really only an addition to what he had left with Alexander Davidson, lay on his desk now, alongside the letter to Emma telling her once more that she was, to him, in all respects, his true and only wife.

'*Edgar* getting under way, milord,' said Tom Foley.

Nelson knew the tensions that filled the breast of every man, especially young Frears standing beside him, trying hard not to tremble. A look around with the small pocket telescope, which he could jab open one-handed, showed him a faint outline of Parker's topsails on the other side of the water-covered Middle Ground Shoal. To the west of that, on the eastern side of the Holland Deep, lay the

Swedish island of Saltholm, with the mainland a hazy shoreline further on.

'Have you ever heard tell of Charles the Tenth of Sweden, Mr Frears?'

'Was he not a great general, sir?' croaked Frears.

'One of those so accomplished Mr Frears, that he was said to rank with Alexander the Great. Born some hundred years ago, I seem to recall. He fought so well and successfully that he raised Sweden over yonder to the heights of a European power, and won many a battle against the barbarous Russians, though the Great Peter of that nation did defeat him at Poltava.'

Frears would have preferred not to continue the conversation but, with Admiral Lord Nelson looking straight at him, that was not an option. He felt the warmth of his blood rushing to the tips of his prominent ears. 'I recall him now from my schooldays, sir.'

'They say he won his fights by always being to the fore of his men. The chroniclers say that he inspired by personal example, and killed more of his enemies than any soldier in his army, that he seemed to be without fear and was so skilled in arms that he cleared a path before him wherever he fought.'

'Indeed, sir,' said Frears, who had no idea how to respond.

'An example, would you not say, to any young fellow like you contemplating a martial career?' Frears just nodded, hoping that Nelson could not see the shudder those words produced. 'Yet in his first battle, young Charles the Tenth, no more than a prince then, of course, and no more than the age you have now, ran away.'

Frears looked astonished as Nelson lifted his little pocket spyglass to look once more at the Swedish mainland. 'Which only proves, does it not Mr Frears, that even the greatest of heroes are prey to the fear of death or disfigurement?'

'Sir.' Frears gulped.

'So do not rate yourself alone if you tremble,' Nelson added, smiling at Frears. 'There's many a man aboard this fleet doing that same thing now. And I reckon it a good thing, for a man who trembles before a fight, in my experience fights very well.'

'Did you tremble, sir?'

Nelson laughed, which raised the head of every man who could hear it, causing them to smile and their spirits to lift. 'I did, Mr Frears – and was I not wearing such a heavy coat you would spy me doing it now.'

Hardy was right about Nelson: he did want to be everywhere, to send out every broadside and reply to every shot. Right now he was mentally with Murray aboard HMS *Edgar* as Alexander Briarly, under topsails only, eased the 74-gun ship past the marking frigate, HMS *Blanche*, the towed flat boats strung out behind her, full of Colonel Stewart's soldiers. To the rear of *Edgar* the rest of the squadron was backing and filling their sails to get on station prior to entering the King's Deep in her wake.

There were worries about the sailing qualities of the next three vessels, *Ardent*, *Glatton* and *Isis*, but the first real problem occurred with the ship Nelson loved best, his first line-of-battle command, HMS *Agamemnon*. Under double-reefed topsails, Fancourt, her captain, was struggling to weather the end of the Middle Ground Shoal. The leeway of the tide that would carry the fleet up the King's Deep, added to that blessed east wind, was driving her into shallow water, and sure enough she lost way as her keel ground into the sand.

Nelson had to suppress certain feelings, the first that Captain Fancourt was a doubter, one of those men who had failed to meet his eye when he had been planning the passage of the Sound and the prospects for this battle. The other was that the dolt was about to ground a ship he knew well, in a situation that he would never have got himself into. Yet he had to temper that with the knowledge that if he had been less busy he would have observed that her anchorage point put *Agamemnon* in that very danger from the moment she dropped her best bower anchor two days before.

And Fancourt was doing what he could, bringing up his boats from the stern and loading anchors and cables into them through the stern ports. These were rowed to the east and dropped so that the men on the capstan, by warping her up the cable, could haul her off. She moved and Nelson felt his heart lift. Then she stopped again and he turned to Frears.

'Please request the signal lieutenant to make the number for *Polyphemus*.'

Designated the last ship in the line, Nelson ordered her to take *Agamemnon*'s place, just as the first Danish guns spoke. For an admiral who had started out knowing the numbers favoured his enemy, the loss of a major part of his strength, and an integral part of his plan, seemed to affect him not at all. *Agamemnon* had been designated to engage the last ship in the line, with the previous four of Nelson's line-of-battle ships having already sailed by, giving her a drubbing. Now she was too far from the action to bring a single gun to bear.

At that very moment *Edgar* was drawing ahead of her slow sailing consorts, and if she kept going would be the sole target of the Danish cannon: Nelson had to order her to shorten sail. But even so the Amager battery opened fire and so did the first Danish ship as soon as *Edgar* came in range, a great cloud of smoke billowing from the side to be blown back over the decks and through the gun ports.

Typical of Murray, there was no reply from him. Had he calculated that at his rate of sailing he would only receive one broadside per enemy vessel? Was he going to wait until he came abreast of his own target ship and open up with a devastating rolling broadside, one that would be delivered as if it were a demonstration for some visiting dignitary?

Nelson reckoned, if that were true, he had to admire it. He knew from his own experience that the first broadside, delivered accurately, counted for more than anything that followed in battle. Never again in an action would aim be so careful, the measure of powder so perfect, or the ball better chipped to fit the barrel. Not even the best-trained gunners could reload within the same exact time. A run-up gun would be roughly aimed because, close too, rate of fire counted for everything, so the order would be passed down to let fly when ready, using the superior rate to that of the enemy to overwhelm their gunners and slow them down. He also knew that it took a cool head to withstand fire and not respond.

On went *Edgar* past three more ships, receiving broadsides and sustaining damage, to take up her station opposite the fifth ship in Olfert Fischer's defence line. The smoke from the previous gunnery duels had blown away on the wind and *Glatton*, which had just exchanged a broadside with the first Danish ship, was too far back for her carronade fire to obscure *Edgar*. Nelson thought that good tactics as well. Bligh had smashers that, trading with long guns at short range, could inflict much more damage.

All around him and beneath his feet there was movement as the ships of his squadron formed themselves to enter the channel, but Nelson had only scant attention for them now. His head, heart and emotions were with Murray, who had to drop his anchor with exact timing so that once the veered cable bit, it would haul him up right abreast of his opponent. Too soon, and he would expose himself to a full broadside while able only to mount a partial reply, too late and he would have to warp back on that cable to get abreast, suffering great damage as he did so.

Nelson was trying to make the calculation that would depend on so many factors: wind speed, the rate of the current, the depth under his keel, the nature of the ground that his anchor would have to hold. This would be relayed to him by the leadsman, who would have waxed the end of the lead line so that what was on the bottom would stick to it and tell his captain if it were rock or sand.

HMS *Ardent*, with Thomas Bertie in command, was not going to be as patient as his predecessor Murray – Nelson knew it was not in his nature. The Danish ship had reloaded by the time he came alongside and the exchange of broadsides was awesome, even at a distance, for the noise, the huge clouds of smoke, the orange flashes of the spitting guns and the clear sight of damage inflicted.

All the while Nelson kept up a running commentary for Frears, who was now so enthralled by what was going on before his eyes that he had forgotten to be frightened. He watched as every bit of debris flew from that first Danish ship as *Glatton* pounded her, was confused by the flags that flew as the man next to him trimmed his orders. The boy saw that Nelson was pleased by the way the captain of *Polyphemus* responded to the sudden change caused by *Agamemnon* going aground. She had crowded on sail to get into position, a dangerous thing to do in such waters but one which would help win the day. And Frears tried to make sense of a battle not yet truly joined, which would get harder to understand as the day wore on.

Elephant was on station now, behind HMS *Bellona*, edging along at four to five knots with anxious eyes in the bows watching to ensure that she stayed in the wake of the ship that had preceded her. *Edgar* had just hauled up with perfection opposite her target ship and let fly with a broadside that seemed to remove half her opponent's upper works, when the *Bellona*, right ahead, stooped as if some great celestial hand had grabbed her.

The masts leaned forward alarmingly and looked set to roll out and crash down along the decks, but they righted as the stern, thrown clear of the water, settled down with a great splash. Nelson spun his spyglass, his lips moving as he took his bearings and calculated the range, ignoring Foley who was porting his helm to pass *Bellona* on her larboard side. From one side of the channel, even stuck on the Middle Ground Shoal, *Bellona* could fire on the closest enemy ships, albeit at long range. Once *Ardent* and *Glatton* had worn them down they could sail in his wake to attack the defences further up the King's Deep. That would restore some of Nelson's strength.

'For you see, Mr Frears, it is at the head of the line we must triumph. Succeed there, where our bomb vessels can pound Copenhagen, and these ships at the southern end of the channel count for nothing.'

29

~

Though it might have helped the ships in his wake, Murray, in the *Edgar*, ignored the Danish vessels between him and his designated target, number five in Nelson's order of attack. He withstood several enemy broadsides before finally letting fly, and from then on it was a steady three broadsides a minute, with only a short break when Bertie took HMS *Ardent* between him and his opponent, his task to take on a clutch of floating batteries.

The *Glatton* favoured every ship she passed with a broadside. The guns the ex-merchantman carried not only fired a heavy ball over a short distance, they were quick to reload. So every one of William 'Breadfruit' Bligh's opponents knew he had visited them by the number of dead and wounded, as well as the wreckage of what had been their side timbers strewn over the decks. He went on to take station opposite the Danish flagship, number nine, with Captain Olfert Fischer's pennant flying from the masthead.

Nelson watched and approved, not only of the obedience to his orders, but the initiative shown by several of his captains. Riou had timed his entry into the King's Deep to perfection so that he acted as escort and protector to the fireships and bomb vessels, while ensuring that he would be on his station precisely as required. Walker, captain of the *Isis*, seeing that *Agamemnon*, was aground, had shown good sense in tackling two ships, his own target and that of the grounded 64, until *Polyphemus* came up to support.

There was a worry about the *Bellona*. To ships that had not actually seen her ground it would look at though she was anchored: this because Thompson, her captain, had opened up with his lower-deck cannon as soon as he realised his predicament. Whatever they had struck on was an unknown obstacle, very likely a sandbar protruding from the main shoal ground. Foley's task was to get past Thompson and up the channel, which he achieved to cheers from the grounded ship. Nelson ordered the signal 'engage the enemy more closely' hoisted, then concentrated on getting the rest of his fleet to where he wanted them. As *Bellona* acknowledged that signal, Thompson, stood on a gun for a better view of the Danes, had his leg shot off by a ball from the Amager battery. He collapsed in a heap on his own deck.

To compound the sin of *Bellona* grounding, HMS *Russell*, mistaking the meaning of Nelson's aggressive signal, had crowded on sail, eager to get into the fight. As a result, she ran aground astern of the *Bellona* with her bowsprit nearly over the lead ship's taffrail. Nelson knew everyone was covertly watching him, waiting for the order to break off the action and withdraw. Nothing in his face let them know that he was considering that very possibility. He hated the idea of just carrying on, putting his reputation before that of the men who would suffer and die if he was wrong.

He had lost a third of his strength and the little he had seen of Danish gunnery showed him a tenacity he had not truly anticipated. The enemy would not buckle just because they were being pounded. From what he saw he reasoned that the Danes would take a great deal of beating. Could he do it with what he had left? The enemy would see his problems and be encouraged. But if he pressed on that might turn to despair, in which case he would win.

There was no rational explanation for the decision to press on with the attack, but he knew it to be the right one. Nelson had a clarity of vision denied to lesser men, an ability to take a hundred unrelated facts and distil them into a course of action in which he had confidence. This time his conviction stemmed partly from his feeling that the rigidity of the Danish defence allowed for no alteration.

The bomb vessels, squat, ungainly tubs with their twin mortars amidships, could not have been mistaken for anything other than what they were: the means to lob shells in behind the defences. A child could have seen that they could not protect themselves. So, clearly, his main object, the point from which he could bombard Copenhagen, lay beyond the first clutch of moored ships but no attempt had been made to block it. A pair of those hulks anchored across the channel, hampering his room for manoeuvre, obliging him to destroy them while under fire from the shortened line, would have constricted his options.

But no movement had occurred, even after he had come south through the Holland Deep. Every component of the defence had stayed fixed. The Crown Prince, lacking experience, had made a plan and would adhere to it, while Nelson, was an exponent of flexibility. He had the best men, imaginative captains and a positive offensive goal. Nelson felt instinctively that he had the upper hand, that in this case the power of attack was greater than that of defence.

'Make sure that that signal is kept flying,' he shouted, 'and if the mast is shot away get it aloft on anything that is standing.'

Some smiled at that, others adopted a look of grim determination. But not a head shook in doubt, and that lifted Nelson no end.

Sir Hyde Parker had the best eyes, with the finest telescopes, high in his rigging so, with the wind tending to blow the gun smoke across the defenders and the order of attack on a table before him, he was well aware of the way Nelson's plans were progressing. His line-of-battle ships were tacking and wearing into the wind, still miles from the lead vessels in the enemy line, in a vain attempt to pose a threat that would preclude any of those men o' war cutting their cables to engage Nelson in the open water of the King's Deep channel.

The last communication he had had from his junior had not filled him with confidence, a request that the flat boats and soldiers he was supposed to provide for an assault on the Danish forts be held back. Nelson doubted that they could arrive in time to affect the outcome. Parker's interpretation was that the course of the engagement was in doubt. He had put this to Captain Dommet, to be greeted with stony silence.

Nicholas Vansittart sat opposite the seventy-year-old John Jervis, Earl St Vincent, First Lord of the Admiralty, wondering why he felt like a recalcitrant child hauled before a flogging headmaster. He had dealt with kings and princes in his time, as well as chancellors and prime ministers, and never suffered anything like nerves. He did not know that St Vincent had that effect on practically everyone.

St Vincent was rereading Parker's despatch from the Cattegat, his face creased with fury. Addington, the Prime Minister who had replaced Pitt, had read the very same despatch and pronounced himself satisfied. What could this ancient mariner see in the words that had escaped the most senior politician in the government.

The First Lord was not about to tell him. St Vincent merely raised his eyes, glared at his visitor, and thanked him in a way that left the diplomat no choice but to take his leave. Behind him St Vincent was writing furiously, calling for a clerk and barking for Evan Nepean to get him, damn quick, a list of ships available in the eastern ports. Within the hour the return despatch was being taken by horse messenger to Harwich, as well as orders for a young lieutenant in a fast-sailing cutter to get to the Danish shore with all speed.

The message to Sir Hyde Parker was, 'You have your orders, obey them.'

'*Defiance* has passed *Russell* and *Bellona*, sir, and the frigate *Desireé* has taken station athwart number one.'

'Thank you,' said Nelson. *Elephant* was passing to larboard of Bligh in *Glatton*, who was giving Fischer's flagship a proper drubbing, much assisted by the ship to the rear of him, HMS *Ardent*, Bertie having split his targets. His mind was racing over a dozen imponderables. The ships to his rear still working their way into the channel. On two of the seven bomb vessels: would they take station as ordered and begin to work their anchors to get into position to lob shells into the Trekroner fortress and the brigs ranged before it? The others were to take station to the east of his own ship and concentrate on the arsenal that lay behind the city walls, as well as the Quintus and Sixtus batteries.

The *Elephant* was progressing to her station when Nelson, whose target ship was another 74, realised that the absence of the *Bellona* would leave a gap in which lay three floating batteries and a pair of gunboats. With the amount of smoke billowing about he feared that any signal might not be seen so, while ordering Foley to con the ship and anchor in *Bellona*'s place, he made his way to the side, requesting a speaking trumpet. The next ship in line was captained by Freemantle, a man he trusted.

'Ahoy,' he shouted, his ship slowing as the anchor bit, '*Ganges*, take station opposite number thirteen in the order of attack in place of *Elephant*.'

'Aye aye, sir,' floated back across the water from the wheel.

There were only two ships yet to come fresh to battle, *Monarch* and *Defiance*, both with good officers aboard: Mosse, who had led the way through the Sound, and Admiral Graves who had handsomely volunteered for a duty about which he had had serious reservations. He must hail them, too, as they passed and give them new orders.

'How much a man's fate rests in the hands of others,' he said to the red-coated Colonel Stewart standing beside him. So great was the din that Stewart asked him to repeat it. Below decks the guns, which had expected to engage one target a ship, and were now obliged to split their fire, were hastily being re-aimed.

'We are too far off, Captain Foley,' Nelson called, as the first broadside rolled under his feet, rocking the ship back until the wind on the topsails stopped it, 'a full two cables. I would wish to be closer in.'

The reply from the Danes flew through *Elephant*'s rigging, heavy balls that ripped the top foremast to shreds.

'The pilots fear another shoal, sir.'

'Damn the pilots,' he said, but so low that only Stewart and young Frears heard him. Just ahead was his original target, now being engaged by *Ganges*. 'It does not seem to occur to them that if a Danish 74 can occupy this water so can we.'

Stewart, who knew how to work artillery by land, thought two hundred yards perilously close to the enemy, but he did not know Nelson, who always wanted to lay his ship so close that his shot could pierce the planking. The second salvo rolled out, less disciplined than the first, but good enough to cause damage.

'Mr Frears, take station on the starboard side and let me know when any of our ships come up.'

'Sir,' the boy replied, happy to be as far away as possible from what was coming.

All around Nelson was sound and fury and billowing acrid smoke, as Foley trained his forward guns on number thirteen to help Freemantle, and his after cannon on number nine to assist Bligh, while the central sections pounded the floating batteries. It was in looking at the effect of the second target that Nelson saw *Glatton's* foremast go by the board. Only later would he discover that seven of Bligh's upper-deck carronades were put out of action and men squashed like insects or thrown overboard into the freezing water.

It was bloody work, but all Nelson's battles came down to that. Not for him the stately standing off preferred by elderly admirals, line of ships versus line of ships sailing along, trading regulated fire. At Frears's bidding he called to *Monarch* and *Defiance*, altering their respective stations. He knew that Foley was coping with his targets, suspected that Bligh had begun to use carcasses, combustible shells full of saltpetre, tallow, resin, turpentine, sulphur and antimony, because of the speed with which fire began to consume his opponent. He reasoned that matters must be progressing well when Thomas Bertie sent a midshipman in a boat from HMS *Ardent*, with the information that he had engaged five separate targets and reckoned they were all now useless.

That was the first of a flow of good news that began to arrive, telling him that all his ships were at their stations, that Riou's squadron of frigates and brigs was hotly engaged with the Trekroner fort, that his concerns about the bomb vessels were unfounded. They were in place and hard at their task. Aloft, a lookout could see Sir Hyde Parker and his fleet beating up, and the reckoning was that there was no hope of their arrival for hours.

What Sir Hyde Parker could see, from a distance of four miles, was that matters were at a stand. All of Nelson's ships were now engaged and still those at the head of the line beyond the Trekroner fort were without an opponent to fight, which seemed to him to underline the superiority of the Danes. In near freedom they were playing on the line of anchored British frigates under Riou's command, a squadron fully occupied in firing on the Trekroner forts and the ships in the shallows in front. There was no sign of slackening from the Danish defences, while a third of Nelson's strength, never enough in Sir Hyde's estimation, was either useless or could not properly engage.

'Our man has bitten off more than he can chew, here, Dommet,' he said. 'We are in a fair way to risking being beat.'

'I grant you it is warm work, sir,' Dommet replied, his telescope fixed to his eye, 'but the battle has, in my estimation yet to reach a crisis.'

'I would like an explanation of what you call a crisis. Nelson is outnumbered and I perceive his notion that the mere crash of British cannon would bring the Danes to negotiate has not proved correct. It is four hours since the first shot was heard and if anything the enemy fire has increased rather than diminished.'

Parker failed to add that his own reluctance to shift his anchorage closer to the enemy had contributed to the problem. At a progress of no more than one mile each hour his part of the fleet could not hope to affect the outcome of the battle. The crisis, as Dommet called it, would have come and gone well before then. All the old fears resurfaced in Parker's mind, and now it was not a case of Nelson's success raising him, it was the possibility of a Nelson defeat taking him down and several ships with it. He tried to imagine what it would be like to bring a severely damaged vessel out through the northern neck of the King's Deep. The mere thought made him shudder.

No charts, no buoys, perhaps the best sailing minds on the ships killed or wounded; masts shot away, sails full of holes and a vessel taking in water enough to lower her keel several feet. There was a strong possibility that more than one of the retreating ships would ground on a shoal. Close to the Danes, victorious or at least unbowed enough to continue the fight, those ships would be taken, perhaps refloated, remanned and stuck as hulks in the defences. He might find himself facing his own ships in any renewed attempt to subdue Copenhagen.

And that was before he considered the difficulties of facing the Russians and the Swedes, with perhaps these very Danes sailing to join them for a grand battle in open water. To fail to take the Danish capital was one thing, but the prospect of a defeat in a sea battle suddenly loomed to terrify him.

Parker had a vision that Nelson would escape censure, not just because he was a junior but because the nation loved him too much to blame him. They would call him brave and enterprising for his attempt to overcome the Danish defence line, and laud his zeal for the manner in which he humbugged them. But if it all came to naught, Parker, as commanding admiral, would have to account for the losses in men and ships, for every action that *HIS* fleet had taken, and he suspected, indeed knew, that the British public would not love him for it.

The solution to him was obvious. Better to live to fight another day than to go down in a blaze of futile glory. If he could extricate Nelson's squadron now, while they were still capable of manoeuvre, the fleet would be wounded but basically intact. The grounded ships, he knew, would refloat, either naturally on a rising tide or by towing and warping, and they were capable of defending themselves until that time came.

'I have a mind to ask Nelson to discontinue, Captain Dommet.'

Parker could almost feel every officer stiffen on the deck of HMS *London*. All seemed an inch or two taller, as every ear strained to hear Dommet's reply. The Captain of the Fleet was furious and working hard to hide it, clenching the muscles of his stomach to force out a calm and considered reply. 'I doubt we can tell enough from this distance to make that decision, sir.'

'Captain Otway?' Parker asked.

'I find I must agree with Captain Dommet, sir. I strongly advise that to send such a signal now would be premature.'

Dommet was not sure if Nelson was winning or losing. Like Otway, all he knew for certain was that it was too soon to tell. And Nelson surely had boats coming aboard *Elephant* from his other ships reporting progress. He no longer subscribed to the theory he had held before meeting him, that Nelson was a lucky chancer: having seen him at his conferences, having witnessed his clear brain and sound tactical thoughts carried into execution, having read the comprehensive orders he had issued for this attack, Dommet was prepared to acknowledge that Nelson had a superior mind.

He trusted Nelson to know the state of the battle, trusted him not to pursue a course that would lead to death and destruction for the men and ships he commanded. So far not one of the vessels engaged in the attack had pulled out of the line, and although there was a lot of smoke about it was mainly blowing away from the British ships so it was easy to see they were still firing full broadsides. But Dommet knew that what he saw and what Sir Hyde Parker saw were not the same thing. He also knew that until now his advice had been little appreciated. Yet he was at a loss to know how to stop Parker from doing something he considered precipitate.

It was Otway who provided the solution, addressing Parker directly. 'Might I suggest, sir, that we send a boat to Lord Nelson and ask his opinion?'

'Excellent idea, Captain Otway,' cried Dommet, 'and I, sir, would deem it an honour to be the messenger.'

Parker wanted to say no, to state that as the fleet commander his opinion was what counted: that Nelson, heavily engaged in fighting, could not see the wood for the trees. Dommet did not give him the chance. 'I will need another coat, sir.' With that, the Captain of the Fleet was gone, down the companionway to change from his dress uniform coat to an old and less valuable one.

As soon as he disappeared, Parker rediscovered his voice. 'Am I to see my fleet beaten for the sake of a damned coat?'

Otway stepped forward quickly. 'My suggestion, sir, so I claim it as my duty.' The captain of HMS *London* rushed to the side, and blessed the fact that a boat was passing. He guessed that with any delay Parker would act, so he hailed the boat to come alongside and rushed below to the entry port before his open-mouthed commander-in-chief could stop him.

The navy to which Sir Hyde Parker belonged did not have ships' captains acting as mere messengers, but when he looked over the side, Otway was urging the oarsmen to put their backs into it.

Dommet rushed back on deck in a threadbare blue coat that had seen better days.

'You are too late, Captain Dommet. Look and you will observe Captain Otway is already pulling towards *Elephant* to do the duty you had assigned to yourself.'

Parker expected Dommet to be angry, but the Captain of the Fleet just nodded, picked up a telescope and trained it along the still fighting battle line, leaving his superior once more feeling isolated in a sea of his own reservations.

'Prepare to hoist the signal, "Discontinue the action."'

'Sir,' protested Dommet. 'Captain Otway is not yet with Lord Nelson.'

That was when Sir Hyde Parker lost his temper. 'I must ask you, sir, who commands here?'

For Dommet to answer such an obvious question would have been foolish, so he covered himself with the nod of one who recognised the reality. Not that he would have had a chance to speak anyway, because Parker, who had gone very red in the face, left him no space.

'It is damn annoying, sir, to have everything I say disputed. I do not recall you, sir, or Captain Otway, being given the responsibility for the execution of my orders. That falls to me and me alone, and while I am man enough to be advised I am not such a base fool as to require constant repudiation.'

There was a still, small voice in Parker's head telling him to withdraw, but having put Dommet in his place he could not back down.

'Now oblige me, sir, by preparing that signal, and when it is prepared, oblige me further by having it hoisted. Then I will have it driven home by two guns.'

A shot from one of the floating batteries engaged by HMS *Elephant* struck the mainmast, sending a shower of deadly splinters flying in several directions, although none, fortunately met flesh. Midshipman Frears had spent his time dashing back and forth with messages from the starboard side of the ship, where Nelson paced the deck attended by Colonel Stewart, Merry Ed and a knot of unemployed officers, mostly captains come to see the action. Frears was just passing the base of the mast at that point and the crash made him throw himself down.

Nelson watched as the boy picked himself up, his hands patting his body and his head looking for a wound, his face full of wonder to find himself intact, before he carried on to rejoin his admiral.

'Warm work, Mr Frears, and this day may be the last for any one of us.' Frears looked into Nelson's face expecting to see a worried expression. Instead what he found was a look of contentment as Nelson added, 'Mind you, I would not be elsewhere for thousands.'

The signal lieutenant was right in Frears's wake, to inform Nelson, 'Flag signalling, sir. Number thirty-nine, with two guns.'

That look of contentment was wiped away in a flash to be replaced by a fleeting expression of anger, that, in turn, was masked by forced indifference as Foley approached. Nelson turned away from everybody, pacing toward a gangway before turning to come back.

'Should I repeat it, sir?' asked the lieutenant, as he came close.

That was the correct thing to do, so that every ship in action would know that he, the junior admiral, had received and was preparing to obey the command. But Nelson knew it to be right only in the sense of hierarchy. As far as the battle was concerned he suspected it to be dead wrong. There was a fleeting moment when he thought that perhaps Parker and the officers on *London* could see something he could not.

Had there been a couple of drifting dismasted hulks in mid-channel with blood running out of the scuppers and the decks full of dead and dying the order would have made sense, but if he looked along the line he knew he would observe all his ships in position, all fighting. Captain Olfert Fischer had been obliged to shift his flag from the original position he held, a ship set seriously on fire by Bligh in HMS *Glatton*, to another vessel that was now being reduced to matchwood by Admiral Graves in *Defiance*. That was not the act of a man anticipating victory, and what news he had coming in was positive: Danish fire slackening, through loss of men or cannon, flags hauled down, vessels drifting onshore, boarding parties being formed to take possession of the shattered prizes. On his own deck stood a growing band of enemy officers who had surrendered.

'No, acknowledge it,' said Nelson. There was a brief pause while the signal lieutenant digested the import of that before he turned away. Nelson called after him, 'Is my signal still hoisted?'

'It is, sir.'

'Then mind you keep it so.'

Nelson started pacing again, alarmed, wondering how that would be taken elsewhere. It was another moment when he would have to trust his captains. Those to his rear, unable to see *London*, would not know about Parker's order if he did not repeat it. But the ships ahead of him, closer to the flagship would, and when they looked to *Elephant* they would see his own signal, 'Engage the enemy more closely', still flying.

He knew he was being watched by a knot of officers, the number of which had grown as the battle progressed, and it was to them he spoke, his voice querulous. 'Do you know what's shown on board the commander-in chief?' he demanded. 'Number Thirty-nine.'

The naval officers understood and nodded, but Stewart, a soldier, had no idea what he was talking about and immediately requested an explanation.

'Why, it is a signal to leave off the action.' Nelson's voice rose as he turned to face his old friend Tom Foley. 'Leave off action. Now damn me if I do. You know I have only one good eye, and I reckon I have the right to be blind sometimes.'

Nelson snapped open his pocket telescope and put it to the eye that had been damaged all those years ago in Corsica, his voice showing increasing agitation as he spoke. 'I really do not see the signal. So damn the signal. Keep mine for closer battle flying. That's the way I answer such signals! Nail mine to the mast.'

Sir Hyde Parker had no idea of the confusion and anger his signal caused in the line of ships. The two guns that accompanied the flags had meant that it was no suggestion, the instruction to discontinue the action was mandatory, disobedience a court-martial offence and every commanding officer knew it. But those who could see it looked to *Elephant* for confirmation and, not perceiving it, had a choice to make.

Rear Admiral Graves, who had originally doubted the notion of the present attack, was now wholly committed to action and suspected Parker's signal to be nonsense. Yet he was duty bound to repeat it, as well as the one Nelson was flying. He solved his dilemma by hoisting the repeat in a position where Nelson, and most of the ships engaged, could not see it. Having done that he kept on fighting.

Aboard HMS *Amazon*, Captain Riou, already wounded, had done his best to ignore the flagship of the fleet. He and his squadron had been fully engaged against the Trekroner battery, the three sloops and brigs before it, all this while under fire from Steen Bille's capital ships. But they were doing what was required, occupying the enemy, achieving the kind of success he knew Nelson wanted. But when Graves hoisted the repeat he could see clearly what was hidden from the others, and his two other frigates had already broken off to obey.

Riou was left with no choice but to do likewise, being too junior to flaunt such an order. It was with a heavy heart that he gave the instructions to cease firing, to cut his cable, and to bear away. As *Amazon*'s guns ceased firing, the smoke cleared and, for the first time since action was joined, Riou had a clear view of the target he had been firing at, the fort built on piles driven into the point of the sandbank. 'What will Nelson think of us,' he said.

Seconds later a last salvo was fired from the Trekroner fort. The Danish gunners, with a clear view of a ship hardly yet under way, had both time to aim and a good sight of what they were trying to hit. One ball from that salvo hit Riou in the back, and nearly cut him in half. He was dead before they got him below to the surgeon.

✻

Nelson had the satisfaction of observing that all his capital ships had remained in place. Even the bomb ketches, which had finally anchored mid-channel kept firing despite the order. His instructions outweighed those of his superior, the men of his part of the fleet looked to him not Parker, and Nelson was sure he could detect a diminution in the Danish fire. It was hard to pin down in the mêlée of shot shell and noise, but it was there.

The messengers were flooding aboard in droves, midshipmen and lieutenants, to tell him a ship had struck, boarded and was now in British possession: that another was on fire and a hulk, that yet another's cable had been cut and she was drifting ashore not a gun left firing, that the Danish Commodore's pennant was no longer flying above a ship in the defence line but was on a flagstaff over the Trekroner fort, which could mean that his place on his vessel had become untenable. There were flags and more than enough prisoners to crowd out Nelson's great cabin, and in his own lee were four vessels that had surrendered.

The Trekroner fort, as well as the Quintus and Sixtus batteries – no doubt under the orders of Olfert Fischer, and denied the target of British frigates – decided to open up on the main line, particularly HMS *Elephant*. Most of the shots fell short, landing on a group of surrendered Danish ships inshore of Nelson's flagship, where men were gathered on the decks. The death toll was terrible and the effect on Nelson electric. He knew that only one thing would slacken that fire, and that there was only one way that the men who, having surrendered had become his responsibility, could be kept alive.

The battle was over, Nelson knew that, not fooled by the continuing fire. He also knew that his victory was complete. The Danish defence line had been destroyed, and Copenhagen was wide open to bombardment. To continue the battle would only see good men on both sides killed to no purpose. The task now was to persuade the Crown Prince and his advisors to accept that they had been beaten.

'Mr Frears, to my cabin for paper and pen. Captain Foley, I will need a messenger to carry for me a proposal of a truce to the Trekroner fort.'

The invitation to propose a truce was written on the casing that housed the head of the rudder, Foley's purser making a fair copy from Nelson's scrawl. Sealed at Nelson's insistence with wax carrying the impression of his own coat of arms, it was sent off with Captain Thesiger, a British officer who spoke Danish, the wording really a plea that humanity take over from what could only be carnage.

The Danes were still firing, but the three 74s well out ahead of Parker's division had come close enough to oblige the ships ahead of *Elephant* to strike, which left only the land batteries firing. A Danish ship, the *Danneborg* was on fire and looked likely to blow so Nelson, mindful of Aboukir Bay and *L'Orient*, decided to move his ships out of the north end of the King's Deep to anchor with those of Sir Hyde Parker.

That this turned into a farce showed Parker how right he had been to worry. None of the ships, given the damage they had sustained to sails and spars, could sail efficiently. The *Monarch*, with her captain, Mosse dead, ran aground, then *Ganges* quickly ran her bowsprit amidships aboard the stranded ship. It took an age to separate them, with the Danes still peppering the withdrawing vessels.

The *Danneborg*, grounded on the Amager sandbank, blew up at three thirty, the boom reverberating across the city. Nelson's messenger must have found someone with authority close to that time for a Danish emissary came aboard to be passed on to Sir Hyde Parker and the Danish guns fell silent at around four. In eight hours, Nelson had destroyed the armed might of a whole nation, and as he went over the side of HMS *Elephant*, intent on returning to Hardy's ship, he said to young Frears,

'Well, young fellow, I have fought contrary to orders and I may well be hanged for it.' Then he laughed out loud. 'Never mind, let them.'

30

Emma Hamilton had a great many thoughts to occupy her mind, not least the fact that the man she loved was at war. It was only by roundabout means that she could find any news of his well-being. If he were killed or wounded, at least a week would go by before the news filtered through, and Emma would probably have it with the public rather than from any private message, the like of which would go to Lady Nelson.

She was not, like Nelson's wife, in the charmed social circle that received news immediately from the Admiralty. Earl St Vincent, though he made polite and encouraging noises, thoroughly disapproved of her association with Nelson. Thomas Troubridge, very much the First Lord's protégé, felt that it was nothing short of disastrous to a man he considered a lifelong friend. So while Fanny Nelson was kept abreast of affairs in the Baltic, Emma was not. Rumours abounded of everything from defeat through victory to stalemate, but from exposure to the damage done by gossip she gave them little credence.

Emma had come to rely on James Perry. As the editor of the *Morning Chronicle*, even if he, too, was denied solid information, Perry was in a good position to ferret out news, so Emma knew that no battle had yet taken place, that Sir Hyde Parker had sent a despatch and that he had received a sharp reply, that her lover had, in his usual fashion, advised an aggressive course of action. What no one knew was what had resulted from all of that.

She also had Horatia to worry about. The child had fallen ill, probably due to an infection picked up from her wet nurse and, though she knew Nelson would worry, it was her duty to write and tell him so. What she did not tell him was that, having replaced the wet nurse, she had brought the baby into her own house rather than leaving it in the care of Mrs Gibson.

Emma was far from idle: as Sir William Hamilton's wife, she had to keep up the social engagements that position entailed. With his treasures sold, his government pension secured and a resumption of revenues from his estates, he was once more in funds. There were visits to the theatre, to the opera, to salons and houses where those people the court considered disreputable could gather to make jokes about their more pious brethren. They entertained at number twenty-three Piccadilly, and if occasionally a guest heard the cry of a small child, they were too polite to remark on it.

Sir William was determined to see nothing. He could enter his reception rooms when he had no guests and evince no surprise at seeing either Emma or her mother cradling a baby. He adhered to the fiction that the infant was a foundling, and while he knew that some ridiculed him as a booby and cuckold he was of an age and mode of behaviour that could ignore such jibes.

As host and hostess no visitor would see them as anything other than a contented pair. Privately they were mutually considerate and companions enough to laugh or shed tears at their shared memories: Naples in the good times and bad, friends and acquaintances from those happy days, an increasing number of whom, especially those of Sir William's generation, were dying off.

Not that Sir William spent much time at home. He had all his old friends to fill his days, the members of the Dilettante Club and the collectors of classical statuary and artefacts who saw him as one of their foremost experts. He was welcome in the superior coffee-houses of St James's and the auction rooms and galleries of London, either as a seller, a buyer, or an adviser. Sir William was welcomed in less salubrious establishments too, for he was genial company and a ribald storyteller.

He occasionally dined at home with Emma and her mother, although not if Nelson's relatives were there. Emma was determined to woo the family, but his sisters kept their distance and his father wrote but would not visit – he a partisan of Lady Nelson – for which Sir William was grateful. As a strict non-believer he found clerical company tiresome.

Emma's one success so far was a bore. William Nelson, Rector of Hilborough, was a black-clad leech with a silly, giggling, pudding of a wife. When it came to taking money off his brother, the man had no shame. He used the connection shamelessly in his pursuit of ecclesiastical preferment, for which Sir William thought him entirely unsuited.

They fed Emma's increasing loathing of Fanny Nelson, who had become, 'that woman,' and for reasons Sir William never fathomed, had been accorded the nickname, 'Tom tit', this despite the fact that they had received, in the past, many kindnesses from a person they now took every opportunity to revile.

Sir William recognised the type; they would eat at his board and that of Horatio Nelson and heap praise. But if anything caused them to feel that the grass was greener elsewhere, the Reverend William Nelson and his shrew of a wife would turn on the Hamiltons in the same way they had turned on Fanny Nelson. In the meantime, he would, as far as possible, avoid them.

Emma swung between feeling secure and the fear that separation would diminish Nelson's passion. She spent time in her Nelson Room, looking at his image and touching his trophies. She ached to have him close so that she could still her anxiety that he would come home from the Baltic to Fanny, having realised that for them to continue was impossible.

Her mother scoffed at this. Mary Cadogan had no worries about Horatio Nelson, she had seen the depth of his regard for Emma, although she still worried about their security. They were safe in Piccadilly for as long as Sir William kept his health. After that they would be prey to the whims of Charles Greville and he had such a tight fist with money that they would likely be out on their ear.

'Just as long as your papa don't do nothing daft and get his head carried away by a cannon ball.' The bright green eyes of Horatia Nelson were fixed on her grandmother's lips. 'For he be like that, always in the thick I'm told. If he goes we will be in a right pickle.'

Mary Cadogan was not one to see a problem without looking for a solution. She would have words with Emma's hero when he came home. Matters needed to be settled so that the comfort of his dependants was assured, the only other way being that he gave up fighting.

Mary Cadogan chucked the infant under the chin. 'We don't want to be traipsing around hunting for a place to lay our head, now do we? You wants a house you can call your own, that's what you want. And happen you want lots of family to come and visit.'

When Mary Cadogan thought of Nelson's family her actual opinion was only expressed in private. Brother William and his wife she saw as bloodsuckers and pious hypocrites, while Nelson's father was a pulpit groaner by the look of him. Maurice, the eldest, was said to be at death's door, having toiled away for thirty years in the Navy Office. He sounded like a decent cove, having lived for years with another man's wife, now blind, and he had shown kindness to his uncle's old black butler.

Mary Cadogan did not look forward to the happy family picture that Emma talked about, all the Nelson relatives reconciled to her and constant visitors. But if their presence was the price of peace of mind, then she would pay it.

Fanny Nelson knew she was being isolated from her in-laws, but was at a loss to know what to do about it. London held no charm for her so she moved to take rooms in Bath, where she could care for her husband's father.

The behaviour of the William Nelsons was particularly wounding, given what she had done for them. Fanny and Sarah Nelson had been close, while the schooling of both their children was paid for thanks to Fanny's gift for reminding her husband of his family responsibilities. Susanna and she had never got on. Sukey, as Nelson called her, had been a surrogate mother and no woman would ever be good enough for her little brother. Recently Susanna had written to remind her sister-in-law that her brother's happiness was her sole concern, almost a coded message that if Fanny Nelson was estranged, then she should look to herself for the cause.

Sitting over her embroidery, Fanny could not believe that her separation from Nelson would last. Despite the birth of a love-child this was still to her an infatuation, which must run its course before her husband came to his senses. The Hamilton woman could only open up the carnal side of him, whereas she had what 'the whore' lacked; refinement and respectability. In her mind she composed endless letters to him, and she imagined him reading them. One day something she wrote would act like thunderbolts to remind him of where his best interests lay.

Admiral Sir Hyde Parker was once more alone in the great cabin of HMS *London*, the masts of the Swedish fleet in their base at Carlscrona visible from his quarterdeck. The despatch that relieved him of his command was in his hand, and he was reflecting on the events of the previous weeks: the aftermath of the recent battle and the British fleet, now masters of the sea approaches to Copenhagen; the amount of work necessary to repair the damage to their ships; the number of dead and wounded on both sides, a heavy butcher's bill in which the Danes had paid the highest price in blood. And the way Nelson had behaved.

It was Nelson's truce that the Danes accepted. Had he been right to insist on staying aloof, leaving the bargaining to his junior admiral, even in the face of Nelson's protests that he was no negotiator? What had prompted it? The certainty that with his name and reputation, Nelson would do better than him, or the possibility that the Danes might not accept the terms, which would leave the victor of the battle with the opprobrium of failure?

Whatever, Nelson had succeeded. There had been a threat of course, because Nelson was no fool: he had warned the Crown Prince of Denmark that he would burn the Arsenal and reduce the Trekroner fort to rubble, leaving Copenhagen defenceless if his terms were not accepted. While negotiating he reminded his hosts that the very rooms they sat in, working on the protocols of a permanent peace, were within range of his mortars.

Parker had stayed in his ship, reassuring himself that in doing so he could repudiate anything that was agreed of which he did not approve, yet knowing, deep down, that matters were out of his hands. He had become a puppet, dancing to Nelson's tune, at the mercy of the man's luck, which even extended to the timely murder of the Tsar of Russia and his replacement by a ruler more disposed to make peace with England.

After this, Nelson was sure he was going home, and had even had his heavy luggage packed and stored in HMS *Blanche*. Not any more!

. . . You will relinquish your command with immediate effect, handing over to Vice Admiral, Viscount Nelson . . .

Not Baron Nelson anymore, but Viscount Nelson, and this in a letter pointedly addressed to Admiral SIR Hyde Parker. There would be nothing for him, no title, no fame, no commemorative swords or money grants from the City of London merchants. He was ordered home and would have to skulk into a London full of praise for a man he should despise but could not. A man who, at this moment, was on his way from his own ship to what, by the nature of things, must be a painful interview.

Sir Hyde Parker looked around his cabin, at the fine furnishings, thick carpets and valuable paintings with which it was adorned, all of the best, evidence of his great wealth. There was a fine portrait of his young wife: would it soon be replaced by that of the woman Nelson chose to call his Santa Emma?

They had celebrated her birthday just eight days before, with several glasses of champagne, all the old companions and members of the Crocodile Club and he, drinking toasts to the fair lady. This was done while each looked to see how the others reacted to Nelson's bright-eyed enthusiasm for the lady. Hardy's blank face, as usual, gave nothing away, nor did Tom Foley's enigmatic smile. Had Parker seen Freemantle shake his head? What did Dommet think of such a blatant affair? Parker would never know, because not one of the officers present would confide in him.

Did they talk to Nelson about him? Was he a butt of their jokes, seen as irrelevant? Faintly he heard the boatswain's whistles piping Nelson aboard. Did they have a more jaunty note, or was that imagination? Was the crash of that marine salute, the thud of their footwear on the planking and the clatter of the at-arms muskets more snappy than that which had been afforded to him?

'Sir Hyde,' said Nelson, as he was shown into the great cabin.

'Viscount Nelson,' replied Parker. Having been sitting silently his throat was full of phlegm, which made his voice sound croaked and weak. Hastily he cleared it, knowing as he did so that such coughing did nothing for the impression he was creating. 'I doubt I am the first to congratulate you on your elevation, but I do so sincerely none-theless.'

'You are most kind, sir.'

There was a moment then, when each tried surreptitiously to read in the other's expression what was going on in the opposing mind. Nelson was uncomfortable, in a situation he would have preferred to avoid. There was little doubt that before the Copenhagen battle, his former commanding officer had tried to avoid him, to ensure that anything in the way of glory remained his province.

It was also true that Nelson had been vexed by the thought that the man might receive a peerage for what he had done. But since the battle they had seen a great deal of each other, and Parker had reacted most graciously to whatever suggestions Nelson had made. While there was not much to love in the man, Nelson could not dislike him.

Sir Hyde Parker had faults both as a man and as a leader, not least his insensitivity to the feelings of others. His order to burn the Danish prizes, on the grounds that he still had two enemies to face, was the act of a man who had more than enough prize money in his pos-session and did not need more. Had Parker looked at the faces of the others present when he gave the order, men who could ill afford to see such valuable vessels go up in flames, he would have observed in them a look of deep antipathy. And he had failed utterly to under-stand why Nelson was so cast down by the death of Captain Riou, cut in half as a direct result of Parker's signal of recall. That was an act for which the commander-in-chief had proffered no explanation, in fact he had not made any mention of it at all, acting as though the signal had never been hoisted.

Parker was thinking that if he had not sent that signal this might not be happening. Or had he, by his delay in pressing home the attack, already burnt his boats at the Admiralty. How high his hopes had been when he set out, how low he was to be sunk now, forced to ask Viscount Nelson whether he might go home in his own ship and delay packing his furniture and stores until he reached an English port.

It gave Nelson no pleasure to reply, 'I fear I cannot oblige you, Sir Hyde. Until I have faced the Russians I cannot say that there will be no battle. But I will put at your disposal, as you did for me, HMS *Blanche*.'

What Parker did not know was that the despatches he would carry from Nelson would include a strongly worded request that he himself be relieved. To be a commander-in-chief was a very fine thing, a position to which Nelson had always aspired, but he disliked the Baltic, the cold northern sea did nothing for his health.

It was also a station on which he could expect to make nothing. The fleet had been forbidden to take prizes now that it looked as though peace was imminent – which was all very well for a wealthy man like Sir Hyde Parker, but not for Nelson who needed money. He had all the expense of a commanding officer's post without any of the concomitant income such employment generally provided. He had service and private responsibilities, his on-going legal case with St Vincent, numerous family dependents and, of course, Fanny.

HMS *Blanche* would also carry a letter to Davidson, requesting that his old friend inform his wife that she must accept their separation as permanent, although he would continue to provide for her. In planning the celebration of Emma's birthday, Nelson had been forced to look hard at the situation. He must take steps to ensure that he was spared the discomfort he had experienced before – the meeting in that hotel parlour, black looks and pained sighs, strained dinner parties and trips to the theatre, public arguments in front of people like his lawyer.

It had been a hard letter to write, not because of the words he used, which were genuine, but because he felt like a coward, unable to meet with Fanny and tell her to her face. How could he, a man who had never flinched from battle, be frightened of an encounter with a gentle creature like her? He had tried to think of her as an ogre, a shrew, a dried-up excuse for a spouse, only to fail abysmally.

The image of the woman he had so admired would not fade. He could not bring himself to hate Fanny, nor even to dislike her, and the thought of talking to her on such a matter reduced him to a perfect wreck. How could he stand to watch the pain his words would inflict? How could he face the tears that would inevitably follow? Might he not weaken at such a sight and say things that would only prolong the agony for both of them?

Parker coughed and returned Nelson to the present, to the fact that this was now his cabin. At this very moment Giddings was alongside the *Blanche* fetching his luggage from the holds, to be replaced by Sir Hyde's. Nelson didn't want to watch the man's face as his goods and chattels were packed and lowered over the side. It was his turn to cough and cover his embarrassment. 'I will, if you have no objection, call Captains Dommet and Otway to the latter's cabin. We have matters to discuss.'

'Of course,' Parker said, turning to look out through the casement windows at the cold, blue Baltic, 'though I hope I can count on your presence when I am piped over the side.'

'Certainly, sir,' Nelson replied, sad to hear the catch in the old man's voice.

Having seen the Swedes snug in harbour, Nelson was of the opinion that they would not come out this summer. At Helsingborg they had not fired on the fleet when they passed through the Sound and they would not now. Tepid allies, the rulers of Sweden would wait to see what happened. With the Danes out of the contest, let the Russians deal with Nelson.

Dommet had to bring him up to date with the state of all fifty-four ships in the fleet, their stores, personnel, fitness for whatever tasks Nelson had in mind. Beneath his feet Nelson was sure he could hear the sound of packing, and the slow tread of the heavy old Admiral himself. A couple of hours later Parker sent to tell him that he was ready to depart.

Nelson, Dommet and Otway made their way along the maindeck to the entry port to join every other officer on the ship. The marines were lined up, as smart as they had been when he came aboard and a knot of blue coats now stood silently waiting for the last rites. Parker appeared, walking between and saying farewell to men that he had brought to sea. Lieutenants and midshipmen, all sad, one or two of the youngsters with tears in their eyes. They knew they must seek a fresh sponsor if they were to progress in the navy.

Those who had come north with Admiral Sir Hyde Parker had had every reason, since they were serving in the flagship, to look forward to whatever promotion came about through action against the enemy. Now the connection on which they had relied to see them advanced was broken, and so comprehensively that even unemployed this admiral was of no use to them. Indeed a man under such a cloud, placing any appeal on their behalf, would as likely damage their cause as aid it. They had no idea even if they would stay on the flagship, because Nelson had his own mids and favoured officers whom he would bring aboard.

Then there was only his successor, and beyond him the waiting admiral's barge. Parker raised his hat in salute, which was returned by Nelson, who could not help but feel emotional to see a man, any man, so cast down. Then the pipes blew, the marines came to attention, and the retiring commander departed, holding his body stiffly to hide the fact that his spirit was broken. Above them his pennant came down, to be replaced by that of Vice-Admiral Viscount Nelson.

'Captain Dommet,' said Nelson, as soon as Parker was out of earshot, 'all launches to be hoisted inboard, and request the master to shape me a course for the coast of Russia.'

31

On Nelson's return from the Baltic, the landing at Yarmouth was very like the occasion of his return from Italy the year before; the same crowds, the same local worthies eager to sit with him in the same inn. The main difference was that Emma was not there to share it with; but he knew from her letters that she and their child were waiting for him impatiently. Thinking of them Nelson experienced an itch close to an ache, one that made even his missing arm tingle, a sensation that could not be scratched.

The local hospital was jammed with those wounded at the battle of Copenhagen, cases so serious that even after three months many were still bed-bound. Slowly Nelson went the rounds, talking with each man, asking about their ship and their part in the battle. He gave each of the nurses a guinea and told them they were saints as he did so, a scene that was captured by a local artist eager to sell his work to a national press besotted with anything pertaining to Nelson.

Over dinner he listened to the latest reports from France. Bonaparte, having forced peace on Britain's allies, was gathering troops, as many as forty thousand men, gunboats and flat boats to mount an invasion of southern England, a threat that had apparently denuded the seaside towns of Kent. Each worthy wanted to know if they should scoff at the pretensions of the Corsican or take them seriously. Viscount Nelson had advised caution, but not panic.

The locals had garlanded his coach and this time his escort of mounted Yeomanry had attired themselves as Jack Tars; striped trousers, kerseymere waistcoats, bandannas round their necks, and sennit hats with black bands embroidered with the name Nelson. But he travelled alone, Tom Allen, Giddings and Merry Ed Parker following behind him in a less salubrious coach with his luggage, leaving Nelson time to reflect that his time as commander-in-chief in the Baltic had been curious but largely ineffective.

Off Revel he had shown the Russians what they might face, the same fleet that had overcome the defences of Copenhagen and was well fitted to do the same to them. They were offended by his high-handed actions but by the time he was off Cronstat, within sight of the spires of St Petersburg itself, they had changed their tune. Now it was all peace and harmony, a terrible misunderstanding, the fault of the old Tsar, now replaced by his son, who knew well the value of peace with Great Britain.

The rest of his commission had been a fag: he had been plagued with an endless cold, suffered too many visits from too many of the self-important bodies that lined the shores of the Baltic. His ship was surrounded by boats every time he dropped anchor, with some count or duke petitioning for permission to come aboard to see the hero of the Nile and Copenhagen. The sight of the flag of Sir Charles Pole, an old friend and fellow admiral come to relieve him had the nature of a biblical deliverance and, with the shortest and friendliest of hand-overs, Nelson had taken ship for England.

When he saw Emma Nelson's heart nearly burst with joy. With the birth now months behind her she could appear in public undisguised, having gradually, and judiciously, shed the padding. She was more fulsome than before her pregnancy, both in the cheeks and in her figure, but the change pleased Nelson and made her, in his eyes, more beautiful than ever.

Emma saw a man, painfully thin, and worn out by his service, who needed feeding in body and soul. They greeted each other with excruciating restraint, given that Emma's husband and her mother were present. Forewarned of Nelson's imminent visit Sir William was waiting, as ever delighted to see his friend, but shrewd enough, once the pleasantries of welcome had been concluded, to make the excuses of a prior engagement and leave. Mary Cadogan stayed a little longer, taking mischievous pleasure in the way her presence, and inconsequential chatter, heightened the tension. Emma and Nelson were like two greyhounds straining at the leash. A woman of the world, she knew what would happen the minute she departed.

Here was a couple that had been split for four months, a pair who had not had any sex for a whole quarter before that due to the imminence of the birth of their child. Mary Cadogan was sure she could almost smell the musk of their mutual passion and finally, having run out of things to say, she stood to leave Nelson and Emma alone. As the door closed behind her there was a moment's pause before Emma flew to him.

'No one to go in the Nelson room,' Mary Cadogan said to the servants, thinking that if they disobeyed they might see more of the little admiral than they bargained for.

Almost before the latch on the door was securely home Emma was straddled across the chaise longue that sat under Nelson's Austrian portrait and they made love with a swift abandon that left no time for the removal of clothes. Emma felt as if she was being ravaged and Nelson was too fired to think at all, so it was over in what seemed like a minute. Nelson became aware of the sweat of his body and the thought occurred that this was the welcome home sailors dreamed of, and were so rarely gifted.

'You're frowning,' said Emma, running a finger along his forehead.

Nelson blushed, and mumbled that he had been thinking of Horatia, when in reality he was thinking of how different it would have been coming home to Fanny. Dry, cool skin, a polite and sexless welcome with no more than a chaste kiss on the cheek.

'Horatia is upstairs at this very moment.'

'You brought her here?'

'She lives here now,' Emma replied, adding swiftly, 'I could not chance another infection.'

Nelson's expression told Emma that he had a very good idea what she was risking; exposure as the mother of a child that was not her husband's, which would ruin her. 'You are so very brave, my love,' he said, stroking her cheek.

'Must I not match you, Nelson?' Emma replied. She had expected him to be angry, for the child would be disgraced as well as the mother, but instead he was showing her admiration.

Nelson smiled. 'Had you been there, Emma my love, Copenhagen would have fallen without a shot fired.'

'You must tell me all about it, every detail.'

'Horatia first,' said Nelson.'

Emma felt a flash of jealousy then, the unsettling feeling that she was no longer the sole centre of her lover's life. But the look in his eye was so innocent and beguiling that she banished the thought from her mind, got to her feet, rearranged and tidied her dress, then knelt to redo the buttons on Nelson's breeches. His words killed any lingering envy.

'Be gentle, Santa Emma,' he said, gruffly, 'or it will be a good hour before we get out of this room.'

Mary Cadogan had gone upstairs to attend to the child and get her ready for the visit that was bound to follow. She had expected the pair to sate their passion quickly, but even she was surprised at the speed with which they appeared. Horatia was on her back, dirty swaddling cloth at her grandmother's feet. Thus Nelson's first sight of his child was her with her feet in Mary Cadogan's hand while a wash cloth was being applied to her bottom, something Emma's mother reckoned untoward.

'If'n you wait outside just a moment, I'll be finished here and have her dressed again.'

'Pray, Mrs Cadogan, let me see my child like this.'

'I never knew a man to stand the smell.'

'Any man who has used the heads on a ship of war will not suffer to faint at such a tame odour.'

Emma watched from the doorway as Nelson took up station beside her mother, his attention divided between the child and the ritual: the washing, powdering and the replacement with a clean swaddling cloth, marvelling at the placing of the pins that held it in place. His daughter grasped a finger, tugging at it gently, and gurgling with pleasure.

'I fear little one, that your father would make a poor fist of changing you.'

'Tch!' spat Mary Cadogan. 'Whoever heard of a man tending to the needs of a bairn.'

'Did you not know Mother? Nelson is different from other men.'

Mary Cadogan was tempted to reply that the time they had spent downstairs lusting had led her to believe that he was much the same as any other men. Instead she said, 'Well, that's as maybe, Emma, but I don't fancy your wet-nurse, who is in the basement waiting to feed the child, will take to kindly to the Admiral watching her do her duty.'

Nelson was obliged to wait elsewhere while the child was fed and winded, then Horatia was brought to her parents to be billed and cooed over. Nelson knew he had never seen such perfection; the green eyes of her mother that wandered over his face with such trust, smooth and sweet smelling skin, the touch of tiny fingers, the occasional outbursts at a slight discomfort.

Eventually Horatia's Grandmother intervened to insist 'that it was time for the bairn to be put to bed.'

'There be a crowd outside getting bigger by the minute,' said Mary Cadogan when she returned, to find them sitting close together, holding hands. As if to underline her words the sound suddenly swelled as the front door was opened and shut, causing Nelson to move to another chair. Within less than a minute, Sir William entered the room. It was strange to look from Emma to Nelson and back and realise what they had been about. He reckoned that what he had become used to in Sicily, Naples, and on the journey home, had become unfamiliar through Nelson's absence. He also knew he would have to become used to it again, though that crowd outside worried him.

'You are now more than ever a public figure, my friend,' Sir William said with a smile, but the direct look he gave Nelson was intended to convey another meaning. 'The King himself would give his eye teeth to command such attention.'

Both Nelson and Emma got the message. He had called at the house hours ago, and some of those waiting outside had seen Sir William leave and also seen him return. It was not a good idea for Nelson even to contemplate staying the night under this roof. He had rooms in a hotel, which would fuel whatever gossip was prevalent regarding the state of his marriage, but at all costs what was here must not become a subject of public speculation.

'I have seen you for scarce a minute or two since my return, Sir William, It would grieve me not to have more time.'

'Then let us repair to my club, which is a mere walk away in St James's. There I can bask in your reflected glory, and I am sure we will find peace to share a glass of wine and a good blather.'

Nelson smiled. The sight of him and Sir William leaving together, arm in arm, would allay any suspicions that might lurk in an ill-disposed breast. Not even the most doubting soul would suspect that Sir William would cozen a man cuckolding him. Five minutes had Nelson in his cloak and hat, the distinctive *Chelenk* at the brim. His farewell to Emma was a promise in his eyes that he would see her on the morrow. Two old friends left to the cheers of a substantial crowd.

Nelson realised, over the next days and weeks, that what he had achieved at Copenhagen was not appreciated in the same way as his earlier victories. Certainly the public cheered and he was heaped with praise wherever he set foot. But there was none of the official response he had anticipated – no calls to attend city dinners, no medals struck or swords presented, thankfully no royal levee where he might be further insulted by his sovereign.

On his return from the Baltic Sir Hyde Parker had muddied the waters, not from any sense of malice, but in an attempt to restore his severely battered reputation in a country now longing for peace. His every action had been scrutinised in the press, not least his diplomatic efforts, some even questioning if a little more activity in that department might have avoided bloodshed. The mad Tsar Paul had been killed before the battle and the press chose either to forget or ignore that, given the time the news took to travel, neither he nor any man in his fleet could have known this.

Others insisted that he should have handed over to Nelson and come home of his own volition. Whatever, everything he had done, or not done, was castigated. In official circles he suffered even more, for the whole affair was seen as an embarrassing fiasco. Had Sir Hyde struck the Danes at once that would have answered: having delayed, he should perhaps have waited a few more days and peace would have come anyway. Nothing about the Baltic expedition had reflected well upon the Navy, except the success in a battle the provenance of which was doubtful.

The First Lord saw Sir Hyde Parker once, was gruff and refused to see him again. His fellow senior officers were cold: he had let them down by allowing himself to be ruled by his vainglorious subordinate. Stung by the reaction, Sir Hyde demanded a court martial, which was refused. That left behind it a deepening of the rancorous odour that surrounded the whole Baltic expedition.

However, what happened in the higher reaches of the populace was not replicated in the rest of the nation. Nelson had thumped the enemy, had shown three nations Britannia's fist, and reminded France that although she might rule the land, the sea was John Bull's province. Nelson soon came to realise that he could do nothing discreet in London. Everywhere he went, even if he could avoid a mob, reporters dogged his footsteps, and he cursed the very newspapers that had carried the stories of his exploits to the far corners of Britain and made him a public hero. He could visit Piccadilly, and have time alone with Emma and little Horatia, but he could not spend the night there.

He found the constraints intolerable, so when Mary Cadogan hinted that he needed a house of his own where he and Emma could get some peace, she was pushing at an open door. Emma was charged with the task of finding a furnished house for him to purchase, since neither he nor she had any furniture of their own, and there would be no time to have what they needed made. And much as he loved her daily company, Nelson insisted that Horatia would have to be put back into the care of Mrs Gibson to help to preserve both her reputation and that of her mother.

The immediate problem Nelson resolved by moving to an inn on the Portsmouth road, one where he was known. It was a place much used by travelling sea officers, offered good food, fine open country and a welcoming host. There he gathered around him the people he loved: Sir William and he spent happy days fishing together. Merry Ed Parker came too, fussing round his hero, always ready to oblige, too poor without a ship at present to pay for his own lodgings. At night Nelson shared Emma's bed without raising eyebrows. His brother William brought his wife, and his daughter Charlotte to stay, and arranged for their son, Horatio Junior, to visit from Eton. If it wasn't the whole family it was enough of one to make Nelson very happy.

His oldest brother Maurice had died while he had been in the Baltic and Emma had used the occasion of his funeral to ensnare Nelson's sisters, who were now occasional visitors and regular correspondents. Since the inn they were occupying was close by, Merry Ed was charged to make arrangements for the whole family party to visit Maurice's 'widow'. Nelson sat with the blind old lady and repeated the assurances he had given her in writing, that she and the house she occupied would always be a charge upon his conscience.

Fanny finally wrote and sent the letter she had composed so many times in her head. Any number of people had told her where and with whom her husband was staying, numerous tongues that hinted that she would dry any well of natural sympathy if she stood for such open effrontery. In truth, Fanny suspected she had dallied too long, that her letter should have been posted months before.

Nelson read it alone, by the sunlit window of his room. She congratulated him on his victory and insisted that her love for him was profound, an evident plea for reconciliation, not forgetting to add that she would still and always care for his father. The letter brought tears to his eyes, but did nothing to soften his resolve. But throughout the sunlit days of this interlude he would occasionally recall Fanny's words and it would sadden him.

A despatch and a summons from the Admiralty brought this idyll to an end. The country stood in danger and, with the citizenry fearful of invasion, St Vincent sent for their hero.

The interview with the First Lord had an undertone to it – apparent to Nelson in the way his old commanding officer failed to meet his eye. He surmised that, having become mired in politics, the Earl had lost the openness that had characterised their earlier relationship. Or perhaps it was the rum odour that still surrounded Copenhagen.

Troubridge was present, the most active member of the Admiralty Board and doing as much to run the Navy as his titular superior. Happy in the job, Tom was his old self: not that he succumbed to cheerfulness, being serious by nature. And he, too, seemed to have an agenda other than that they were discussing. Thus the meeting seemed chilly, and had an unreal quality for Nelson, who had come from the warmth and laughter of a family enjoying a holiday in a ramshackle inn to the formality of this, the First Lord's office.

St Vincent had been embarrassed since Nelson had entered wearing his hat in the athwart-ships manner, which seemed like excessive display. Worse, it was crowned with that damned silly Turkish bauble full of diamonds, while medals and stars festooned Nelson's neck and breast. The man he preferred to remember had worn a plain blue coat.

There was also the lack of natural conversational openings. He enquired first after Nelson's constitution, then for the health of family. That foundered on the impossibility of mentioning Lady Nelson, and a downright refusal to ask about Emma Hamilton. So St Vincent was obliged to execute several noisy coughs to cover his inability to let the talk take a natural course. And was Troubridge right, he wondered, that the way to rescue Nelson from his gross folly was to keep him occupied?

'Here is a list of ships both at Sheerness and in the Downs,' said Troubridge, passing over a paper that Nelson immediately began to study.

'Nothing over a 64-gun,' added St Vincent, 'but if you need bigger vessels we will look favourably on the request.'

'I cannot see them being of much use, sir. The French coast is too well defended and with all these soldiers present I would not want to take them on in a gunnery duel.'

'You will, however make your presence felt.'

'It is in my nature to do that, sir, as I hazard you already know.'

The late July sun was streaming through the tall windows of St Vincent's room and bouncing off the *Chelenk* pinned to Nelson's hat, which now lay on the table, and the reflection in his eyes made the First Lord growl.

'That is very much so,' he replied. Then, in what he saw as a witty way to register some of his disapproval at Nelson's gewgaws and the pleasure he was known to take from public adulation, he added, 'Mind, don't let what the wilder tongues say go to your head.'

'And what do they say?' Nelson asked innocently, his one good eye wide open, curious, and fixed on St Vincent.

The First Lord was sure Nelson had understood very well what he had been driving at, which made it difficult not to respond and tell Nelson he was, in his private life, acting like a fool. But that was outside St Vincent's bailiwick, so he took refuge by changing the nature of the point.

'Bonaparte,' he said. 'His reputation stands so high that his mere name strikes terror into a civilian heart. The Prince of Wales, who is at this moment drilling volunteers in Hyde Park, tells me at every turn that the man is a genius, not forgetting to add that he is a greater one and will defeat the Corsican as soon as he is given the chance.'

'If the Prince requires any advice on beating Napoleon I will be happy to oblige him,' said Nelson.

He didn't like the man, and had said so publicly, convinced that the heir to the throne had designs on Emma. And that thought affected the whole course of the discussion, in which Nelson seemed unable to concentrate. When he left, it was on a far from satisfactory note.

'I fear you are over-sanguine, Troubridge,' said St Vincent, as he resumed his seat. 'You think activity will cure him but he has been parted more than once from the arms of his trollop and run back to her.'

Troubridge was caught on the horns of a dilemma and it showed on his face. Regardless of what had transpired he could not forget that he liked and admired Emma Hamilton, something which would not trouble a First Lord who corresponded with but had never actually met the woman. But he loved Nelson, and could see that for him the liaison could lead only to disaster. Nothing on God's earth would make him air his suspicion of the birth of a love-child for the harm it would do his friend, but he suspected that it would not be long before the connection would be made by the newspaper-reading public. To these people, forty-shilling freeholders, provincial and metropolitan professionals, retired members of the armed services, the merchants of the city and the shires, and their wives, Nelson was Galahad, Lancelot and Arthur rolled into one. They clamoured for his presence at every point of danger, sure that their shining knight would vanquish whichever foe dared raise a threat to their peace and prosperity. Would these solid Christian folk still do so if they discovered that he had cast aside his wife for the charms of a married woman?

'And,' the First Lord added, 'the coast of Kent is a damn sight closer than the Skagerrak. What happens, with the eyes of the country upon him, when he comes home from there and within hours is closeted alone with her?'

He wanted to say, too, that Sir William was an old fool to have let such a situation come to pass, but feared because of the similarity of their ages that he might damn himself by association. John Jervis, Earl St Vincent had never married, indeed he was dead against such a thing for a naval officer, holding him lost to the service from the minute he tied the knot. Nelson had been doubly stupid, first in marrying a vapid creature like Lady Nelson, then by bedding the Hamilton woman. St Vincent corrected himself, the sin was in triplicate, given that the man had gone on from bedding her to damn near living with her. Troubridge interrupted a train of thought that had made his old wizened face look thunderous.

'That is true, sir, but idleness is certain to be fatal to his reputation. Employment at least has the virtue of distracting him.'

'He's a damn fool to be led by the breech,' spat St Vincent, 'and so is any man so smitten. Women are nought but fool's gold.'

St Vincent was confronted with his own dilemma. His position as First Lord being political he could not act as he otherwise would, and leave Nelson on the beach to teach him to behave. Addington's coalition government was as fragile as that which had preceded it, and Members of Parliament heard nothing but the Nelson name when they talked to those who had voted them in. To leave him unemployed in a time of crisis might affect the standing of the administration. He had to address the house this very day and reassure them. The name of Nelson, who had accepted the appointment to the Channel, would help.

'Have you decided what to say, sir?' asked Troubridge.

'I have.' Now the old man had a twinkle in his eye. 'I shall tell my fellow noble Lords that the Bonaparte threat is a serious one. But I shall also tell them that though the French can come, they cannot come by sea.'

32

Nelson, with Edward Parker and a new flag lieutenant, Frederick Langford, in tow, came to his new task by way of the Medway ports and Sheerness, coaching down the coast he was taxed to defend through Margate and Ramsgate to Deal. It was an odd command, gathered round a particular service, an aggressive posture in the Channel to face the threat of invasion that cut across the lines of responsibility of four other senior officers: the admirals of two fleets, the North Sea and the Channel, and two important shore stations, the Nore and the Downs. Thus the potential for irritation due to professional rivalry was high.

Much of the travelling time he used to recount his memories of sailing from these places as a boy and as a man, of his months spent taking soundings in the Thames estuary as a midshipman, so that to this day he knew and understood the currents. Then as captain of HMS *Boreas*, he had seen his frigate beached by a drunken pilot, so high and dry that the Sheppey islanders were able to walk round it and exchange caustic comments with an embarrassed crew and jeer at the blushing senior officer.

Both Langford and Parker knew that Nelson should have used the time to rest, but his temperament debarred him from that. When he was not reminiscing, he was planning and making his dispositions, studying reports of ships and their preparedness, the men who commanded them and their reputations, before calling them to meetings to expose them to his thinking. Then he had to face the volunteer soldiers raised to augment the too few regulars he had for coastal defence, to tell them not to fear the enemy should they land, and to fight the rascals wherever they found them.

It was Parker who informed him that the volunteers had never

331

taken seriously the threat of a French invasion, but that when they heard of his appointment, it had become clear to them that the danger was real.

'Then let us hope, Edward, that that scoundrel over the water learns that I am here, and thus supposes our response will be sincere.'

'Amen to that,' said Langford, who counted himself fortunate to be with Nelson in the position of flag lieutenant. If there were any plums going, then he would be first in line.

Nelson had been in Deal, where he would set up his headquarters, many times before, and he told his companions that it was the coldest place on earth. However, with France some thirty miles distant and the coast at Cap Gris Nez visible on a clear day, it was the anchorage he had to use if he was to confound Bonaparte. Pleasant enough now, on a warm July evening, he could recall it in winter, the biting winds that came from the east, scudding across the North Sea and the great barrier of the Goodwin Sands to chill a man to the marrow. He could see the sea now from the Sandwich road, azure blue where it reflected the evening sun, black where the shadow of a cloud fell.

To the north lay the stunning white cliffs of Ramsgate, then the great bight of Pegwell Bay, the mouth of the Stour, a place of shifting mud that had seen many a ship stuck fast until it became part of the landscape. Further south stood the first of the three castles built by Henry VIII, shaped like Tudor roses, but armed with cannon that could control the largest, safest anchorage in the country. It was here that the convoys were formed, ships from London and the eastern ports going deep in their hundreds, gathered inside the Goodwins to await their consorts and escorts. It was the landfall for vessels coming in from the Mediterranean and the East, the place where men were paid off and rehired by captains who did not need a full set of hands to get them into or out of the Pool of London.

And as always it was a crowded forest of masts. Nelson had come here as a boy, the last landfall before he departed on his first voyage to the West Indies. Would some of those he had sailed with on that journey, men who had come aboard at Deal, still be here, having just been paid off from a ship? Past Sandown Castle they came to the edge of the town, a strip of houses, a pair of streets that stood against the elements on the strip of rock that cut off the sea from the low-lying country behind.

Nelson knew Deal to be a den of iniquity. Most seaports, especially those favoured by the Navy, were places where the devil took precedence over the saints. But Deal was exceptional in its depravity;

a hotbed of smugglers so deadly that the Preventative Men of the Customs Service went in fear of their lives. A place where Billy Pitt had ordered every boat on the beach, several hundred in number, to be burned to try to cap their activities. It was also home to half-built barracks for a coastal defence force, soldiers who brought with them a tally of female camp-followers who, with their men, fought for precedence over the locals in the drinking dens and places of entertainment that prosperity supported.

The streets and narrow alleys of Deal were crowded yet still dangerous. It was a place of taverns and bawdy-houses, noisy, grasping whores, voracious ship's chandlers and greedy fisher-folk. Everything untaxed, from contraband silk to coffee, tea, brandy and fine wine, was readily available. Given that it was the first port of call to returning sailors with money to spend it had more than its fair share of crimps, false speculators, pickpockets and thieves.

And it was home to men who knew the French coast as well as their own back courtyard, who, in their specially designed swift-oared boats, could cross to the port of Gravelines, a place set aside by France as a haven for English smugglers, in less than three hours. They carried with them the gold that Britannia's enemies needed to fund their wars. It was plentiful in a nation engaged in vast international trade, but scarce for a blockaded continental power, and bought twice as much abroad as it purchased at home.

Past tall houses that backed on to the shingle beach Nelson could see the anchored vessels straining at their cables, one a frigate quite far out near the sands, which brought forth an unpleasant memory. He had been stuck out there aboard one ship for a fortnight, unable to get ashore because of the surf.

'Have I ever told you about the old *Albemarle*, Edward?' Nelson pointed down a slightly wider alley.

'No sir,' replied Parker eagerly. It was not true, he knew that Nelson had been anchored here with her for a whole month, but he could never hear enough tales from his hero and mentor. Langford, who knew him less well, seemed indifferent to his tale-telling.

'I would not have said it at the time but she was a dog of a ship, useless on a bowline, head forever falling off, only good for running away from the enemy not fighting, since her best point of sailing was right before the wind.'

When he had her Nelson had loved her, as he had every ship he had commanded. Only time could lead to disenchantment; and then only with a ship that had no saving graces whatsoever.

'*Albemarle* was converted from a merchantman and a French one

333

at that. Captain Locker, whom you will have heard me name as my sea daddy, advised me to refuse her as a command.'

He recalled William Locker's face, ruddy, smiling, stomping back and forth on his gammy leg, the man who had taught him everything he knew about the art of sailing ships and commanding men.

'I take it you ignored him, sir,' said Parker, fearful that Nelson might stop.

'The arrogance of youth Mr Parker! Take heed and guard against it. You, too, Mr Langford. It was in the year '82, which was a winter of storms, especially on this coast. This safe anchorage is hell in a north east wind, which drives through the northern shipping channel and lays a surf on the shore that is deadly. It is no friend to an anchor either. I was driven from one end of the Downs to the other more than once and kept the Deal hovellers in ale and smuggled brandy for the number of my best bower anchors they recovered from deep water. I had finally and gratefully been ordered to Portsmouth, and had come ashore on what I admit was a heavy swell to make my farewells to the senior officer here. Well, by the time we had shared a glass or two of wine and he had regaled me with the history of his life the wind had got up alarming again. I could see from the shore that *Albemarle* was far from sound, but it was another ship that dragged her anchor, a damned East Indiaman for all love, twice my draught, who went right athwart my hawse. Every captain spends time out of his ship, but God help him with the Admiralty if anything goes amiss when he is absent. So there I was watching my career being smashed with the same force as my bulwarks.'

'They would have regretted your loss, sir.'

Nelson looked at both Parker and Langford. 'They would not have known, and if by some miracle they had been gifted a sight of what I have done since they would not have apologised. The Admiralty, outside the serving sailors, is a home to placemen. And they, gentlemen, never admit to being wrong.'

'But you saved her, did you not?'

'Only by providence and bribery. Not a single boatman was willing to risk the sea and I had to empty my pockets of everything I possessed to persuade them.'

The coach had stopped before the Three Kings Hotel, which overlooked the beach and the calm blue waters beyond. But Nelson's mind was still on that grey, storm-filled day. 'Fifteen guineas, I calculated, when I had time to do so, and that is another piece of advice I will give you. When it comes to robbery in daylight, Edward, few can match the good folk of Deal.'

334

He stopped between carriage and doorway to add a valediction. 'Mind you, neither will you find better boatmen in a deadly rough sea.'

Then he entered the hotel, passing through the dark panelled hallway to ascend the stairs to a room where Tom Allen was already unpacking his sea chest. Giddings had found the kitchens, where food and warm company could always be guaranteed. Nelson sat down to write to Emma, and when his letter was finished and sent off, he returned to the making of plans. That evening he dined with Admiral Lutwidge, the man with whom he first went to sea as a King's sailor. He was no longer the tall, bright eyed officer he had been, but old, stooped and lined, yet still with a fine sense of humour.

They reminisced about the voyage to the North Pole in search of a clear water passage, of old shipmates and vessels, not forgetting the damage the crushing ice had done to their hulls. And Lutwidge joshed Nelson about that affair with the bear, when he and another boy had gone out trophy hunting only to find that the beast they intended to kill and skin was three times their size and deadly ferocious.

'I fear,' said Nelson, 'that some chronicler has spun that into a tale of heroism instead of foolishness.'

'The price of fame,' said Lutwidge, 'and of our expanding press. The editors see you as selling copy to a public eager for heroes, so I cannot see that will diminish.'

'And neither should it,' asserted the admiral's wife, a substantial motherly lady who was an avid reader of the news. 'Dark times, like those in which we live, require champions to shed light, and you, my dear Lord Nelson, do just that.'

There was a moment of silence, while both sailors let the discomfiture of such praise subside. Then they went back to their days in the ice-bound north or in tropical seas, to talk of glaciers, great whales, battles entered into and those missed, and of friends long dead.

Nelson hoisted his flag in HMS *Leyden*, a 64-gunner, the following morning, though he had no intention of using her for what he had to do first, which was reconnoitre the French coast. That was frigate work.

For Nelson the military problem was quite straightforward. An invasion force was gathering across the Channel from Flushing in the Netherlands to the Normandy coast: soldiers in encampments, naval personnel in gunboats reputed to be two hundred in number to protect the flat boats that would carry the army. To the south, a squadron of British warships blocked Brest and La Rochelle to prevent any French capital ships breaking out and entering the Channel.

An evening alarm had him at sea in HMS *Medusa* that night and the following day, the Nile anniversary, setting a course for the French coast. Behind him the captains of four bomb vessels struggled to get their ships to sea, then to find and keep up with their impassioned admiral. It was all in vain: the supposed French invasion fleet was nowhere to be seen.

Not one to pass up an opportunity Nelson made for Boulogne, the fishing fleet of that town fleeing ahead of him. It was supposedly the place Bonaparte had chosen as his headquarters. Its castle, as imposing as that at Dover, stood high on the hill behind the flat landscape of the tent-filled shoreline. The coast was lined with more than canvas: several batteries of guns and mortars had been mounted to protect the flank of the twenty or so gunboats strung out across the access to a harbour full of flat-bottomed barges designed for troop carrying.

'Well Merry Ed,' Nelson called to Parker, as he surveyed his enemy through a long telescope, 'shall we give them a bit of metal to chew on?'

Parker laughed. 'I think that would be very fitting, sir.'

With no plan laid, and the signalling system too poor for the task, Nelson called for a boat and personally went to each bomb ketch to appoint them their targets. Two were to play on the gunboats before the harbour, the others, supported by *Medusa*, to lay about the shore positions.

'And if you overshoot,' he told the captains, 'never fear, for your ball will land among the soldiery.'

It was a hot day's work, this improvised attack, with Nelson mostly in his boat being hauled back and forth, Giddings cursing and blaspheming under his breath as the enemy expended great effort to sink the man in command. At the same time he had to quell a trait in the boat crew from men who did not know of Nelson's dislike of swearing.

Balls came close, showering them with great founts of seawater, and the sea round them was peppered with case shot if they came too close. In the thwarts, often standing, the men saw a fellow with one bright eye, who wore his hat across his head not fore and aft so that the enemy could observe his rank from the thickness of the braid. He seemed to delight in the danger to a crew, under the command of a coxswain who reassured them that their admiral had luck in abundance. As the day wore on they came to believe him, because given what had been aimed at them, it was a miracle that nothing had struck a single man.

The water boiled around not only Nelson's boat, but the bomb ketches too. Occasionally something struck a hull, to send splinters flying across the decks. Aboard *Medusa* Parker could look aloft to see shot holes in the rigging, a spar blown out of its chains, and duck his head as blocks and the like showered the deck. The French, as was their custom, were firing high in the hope of striking the masts and rendering the ship unmanoeuvrable.

For all that Nelson was busy giving orders and altering targets, he was also storing in his mind the dispositions of the various batteries and other defences. This was an *ad hoc* attack, but it would precede a more planned one, because Nelson knew that the best way to prevent an invasion was to engage in endless disruption. The aim of this was twofold: to ensure no peace for a potential invading army, and to remind them that when they went on to the water, a powerful force was waiting to sink them.

The tally for the day was excellent. Half a dozen flat-bottomed boats sunk and another six severely damaged, an armed brig sent to the bottom, and another gunboat driven ashore, while the coastal batteries had much of their defensive revettes driven in. The enemy had been told that Nelson was on station, and that their serenity was no longer guaranteed. He broke off the attack in early evening and with a fair wind set off for the Downs, covering the thirty miles before dark.

Once back in his room at the Three Kings, with the surf gently breaking on the shingle outside his window, he could write to all and sundry, officials, superiors, friends and his lover, that he had done enough damage at Boulogne, especially to French morale, to lessen the chance of any invasion from there.

Emma was house hunting for a suitable gentleman's residence, not in London but close enough to make a daily journey possible. There was no shortage of possibilities, the continuing war, and the iniquitous new-fangled income tax to pay for it, had had a deleterious effect on prosperity. The trouble was furniture. She and Sir William had left hers to the mob in Naples, while Nelson had only enough to furnish the cabin of a flagship, and that was of little use in a domestic setting. Curtains and carpets were easy, as these could be purchased ready made or knocked up in days. But beds took months to manufacture, tables and chairs a year and anything heavier, like settles and wardrobes, up to half as much again.

London was surrounded by villages, and Emma looked at places in Harrow, Turnham Green, Richmond and Wimbledon. But anyone selling was moving to another house and taking their furniture with them, so it was on a house in Merton that she settled. The surveyor employed to look it over said it was the worst example of a supposed gentleman's residence that he had ever viewed.

He could not see what Emma could. It was not just that Merton was furnished, she liked it. All the house lacked was access to light in its interior spaces. The surveyor saw a tree-choked channel in the stream called the Wandle, Emma saw it cleared, flowing and stocked with fish. When the man saw rooms poorly decorated and dingy interior spaces, Emma saw that glass doors would light them, that a lawn full of weeds could be made like a carpet, an overgrown garden cleared and planted to taste. In her mind she saw a fine, arched bridge over that stream, though the statuary in the garden, an attempt at the classical that would offend a connoisseur like Sir William, would have to go.

She wrote to Nelson to tell him she loved it, and asked him to come and give his opinion. He replied that if she loved it, he would love it too, and as long as it was a suitable place for his family and Horatia to visit then he was content. Though he did add two asides, one humorous, the other less so. He, who was charged with defending Britain, at present owned no house in the country. And that to buy one, the nation's most successful sea officer would have to borrow two-thirds of the nine thousand-pound asking price.

But that money was forthcoming, from Davidson amongst others, and the process of purchase was put in train.

Nelson had two concerns, the first to plan his attack on Boulogne, the second to prepare for the visit Sir William and Emma had proposed to make when Sir William returned from his estates in Pembrokeshire. This involved Edward Parker in the discreet renting of a small cottage in the town, a place where Nelson and Emma could be alone, since the Three Kings was too busy a hostelry for anything of that nature to take place under its roof.

Nelson was obliged to spend a great deal of time at sea, looking at defences that ran the whole length of the coastline from beyond Hastings to the ports north of the Thames estuary. It was depressing to find that in his volunteer force, the Sea Fencibles, which numbered some twenty-six thousand, less than four hundred felt able to set foot in a man o' war. These men of Kent and Essex were prepared to defend their homes, but they could not see, as he did, that the best way to do that was to take ship and destroy the enemy on his own soil.

At least he had reasonable intelligence from the Deal smugglers, and in one of their number, Yawkins, nicknamed Yellow Jack, he found a pilot of rare skill. He had rowed and sailed into every inlet and harbour on the opposite coast and carried in his head a chart of all his junkets. A regular visitor at the Three Kings, he looked a real ruffian. He had a jutting forehead with thick grey eyebrows, bright blue, unblinking eyes, a hooked and battered nose, yet a ready toothless smile that did much to remove the sense of menace he engendered.

He was a Deal boatman to his fingertips, gnarled affairs that lay at the extremities of a huge pair of hands. His taproom company was mainly boys and Yawkins made no secret of where his preferences lay, but that was not an exception in any seaport, and after Giddings had squared up to him so that he would know the Navy was here, he was introduced to Nelson. The Admiral cared only for competence, and finding it, the two got on like a house on fire.

With Yawkins aboard Nelson had not only an exceptional pilot but a man who showed evidence of a brain and some tactical skill, able to advance a notion of what would happen if a course of action was decided on. Nelson wished that one or two of his captains had that capacity, as they were wont to seek glory or profit and have him up half the night on wild-goose chases after French ships that never materialised.

Meanwhile, he was asked his views on the possibility that the army might land a force at Flushing to destroy the part of the invasion flotilla based there. He passed on to the Admiralty the local opinion of such a venture – which was in fact that of Yawkins – who reckoned it was an operation fraught with peril.

One-armed, Nelson could not take part in an attack with boats – he would be a liability to the crew rather than an asset, and they would worry for him – so he stayed aboard the *Medusa* and sent off his four little squadrons to do the work without him.

His plan, outlined to his officers, sounded simple but was intricate: to attack the harbour, destroy the flat-bottomed vessels and sink, burn or bring out the gunboats, thus demolishing any hope that troops could either be embarked there or ever feel safe. To do this they carried materials to set fire to ships, picks and axes to knock out their keel timbers, as well as grappling irons to attach to those they could bring out. In addition, what shore defences had been erected should, if the opportunity arose, be broken down and the guns of the artillery spiked. The key to success was timing, and that meant that all four squadrons, fifty-seven boats in all, must attack simultaneously.

'Do not, gentlemen, be content with a single prize. There must be no cessation until the task is complete.'

Standing on deck he watched as the signal lanterns were lowered over the offshore side of *Medusa* to set his squadrons in motion. With muffled oars they rowed under his stern for a slow pull of what would be three hours to get them into position, the point at which his bomb ketches would open fire, lobbing mortar shells into the line of defence.

The first orange flashes erupted at the appointed hour, and Nelson stood on the quarterdeck in the dark, restless and nervous because that was all he could see, even when a raft of blue lights sailed into the air to illuminate what was happening. The pop of muskets was barely audible, and if men were engaged, yelling as they attacked, screaming if they were wounded or dying, he was too far off to hear or see.

He was left imagining what would be happening if things went well: terrified French seamen abandoning their boats and rushing ashore, leaving his men in peace to carry out their tasks. But what if it all went badly? What would the butcher's bill be for that? It was scant comfort to Nelson that he had taken as much care over this assault as he had at Copenhagen; at least there he had seen the effect of his instructions and altered his orders to cover eventualities.

On the return of the first boat he knew his attack had failed: half the crew were wounded and not one of them had set foot on an enemy plank. His four boat squadrons had arrived piecemeal, each attacking at a different time so that the enemy always had the numerical advantage. The French had set iron-tipped spikes pointing out to sea on the line of gunboats, with nettings hung in between which made getting close difficult and cutting through to the harbour impossible. Nor had the defenders panicked, as Nelson had hoped, when the mortars fell on them; they had stood fast and poured a withering fire into the attackers' boats.

Whoever was in command of the French had put soldiers on his gunboat decks, and they, with their disciplined rate of fire, had exacted a terrible price from Nelson's men. Parker, who had got there first with a crew of Medusas, had borne the very brunt of resistance: his thigh had been shattered by a ball, the whole boat crew only saved when they were taken in tow by another officer. Those coming behind Parker ran into an enemy wide awake and waiting, while one division of boats had got so lost that they never came into action at all.

The fire they faced as they tried to set light to the enemy gunboats was not just from the decks: enfilading fire came from the shore, from a French commanding officer who cared not if his musket balls hit his own men, and in the overhead light from the flares these shore-based soldiers picked off anyone with the temerity to stand up and try to carry out their duty.

Langford was badly wounded, as well as Parker. But forty-four were dead and another hundred and twenty-six wounded. Back in Deal Nelson set up Parker and Langford in the front parlour of the house he had rented to be with Emma. There they lay, with a doctor in attendance, while Nelson went off to see to the other wounded men who had been taken to the hospital. Then he went to his room to write a grim despatch to St Vincent.

33

Fretting over his losses, Nelson was even more concerned about the state of Merry Ed Parker. Langford was on the mend but Parker was sinking. His shattered leg would not mend and there was talk of an amputation. Nelson had spent hours between their beds, writing letters, hatching schemes to confound the French, and asking that he be relieved of what was not really a vice-admiral's command before the equinox came, and with it the cold north winds and heaving seas of the seasonal gales.

Nor could he see that an invasion was now possible. The period that might have seen it launched was fast passing, and the weather in the Channel, surely the most notorious sea in the world for a sudden, unheralded gale of wind, was bound to deteriorate as August passed into September. Bonaparte could not simply wake up one morning and launch his boats: it was far too large an enterprise – a week at least of preparation would be necessary to get everyone and everything in place for the final boarding.

He thought it a feint to apply pressure for peace, but he still had to act as if it was not, and it was unfortunate that the day Sir William and Emma chose to arrive he was off to Flushing. Here one of his officers, Captain Owen of HMS *Nemesis*, claimed a fleet of ships lay just waiting to be cut out. He took Yawkins as his pilot, gathered a squadron from Margate and set out for the Netherlands coast only to find that the supposed fleet consisted of a Dutch ship of the line, a couple of frigates and a smattering of gun brigs. They were well protected by sandbanks and could easily avoid action by retiring further upriver. He had the officer responsible in his cabin forthwith.

'Captain Owen.'

'Sir?'

'I require an explanation. I think you spoke of a large fleet of ships.'

'I saw more than appear to be here now, sir.'

Looking at him, Nelson reckoned he could see what Owen had espied, a chance for some glory. Small, rotund and with a pudding-like face and a waddle for a walk, he was not a very prepossessing specimen. He looked like a man unlikely to set the world on fire, one to indulge in a bit of wishful thinking. He was also probably of the type to think that Nelson would attack anything, regardless of the obstacles, and that to be there when he did would garner him some credit. Instead he received a rebuke.

'Thirty sail of ships, Captain Owen; pilots, Mr Yawkins among them, and he is not a man who likes to be trifled with. Bomb ketches and artillery officers, enough to confound an enemy fleet, which would be fine if we had found one.'

'Sir I . . .'

'Please do not tell me what was here, Captain Owen, and please in future investigate thoroughly what you see. Do not take me on futile chases to find vessels that can retire upriver at will. I should reprimand you in writing, but that would require a copy to the Admiralty. So I shall confine myself to a verbal warning, which will give you the chance to redeem yourself in my eyes. Now, be so good as to return to your ship.'

He was back in Deal within a day, to check that all was in order; that the rooms were suitable, that the bathing machine was in place, and that the man he had engaged to take Sir William sea fishing had made himself known. Langford – sitting with his leg up in the Three Kings parlour – informed him that Sir William was indeed afloat, and that Emma was with Captain Parker.

He entered the small pine-panelled room to find Emma holding one of Parker's hands, reading to him. She stopped as he slipped through the door. Nelson was taken aback at her beauty, and her smile seemed to wrap itself around him, spreading its warmth through his body. It was with some difficulty that he recalled the other reason for his visit.

Merry Ed lay back with his eyes closed, his face white, hair matted and unkempt, a shadow of his former self. The look in Nelson's eye, as he transferred from her to Parker, was familiar to Emma, though he bestowed it on few people.

It was one of his endearing traits, his concern for certain people, usually young men who had served with him as midshipmen then risen in the service. He cared not only about their health, but how they behaved and presented themselves and he was not to be gainsaid by difficulties. Hardy was a case in point, a ship's captain who should long ago have severed the umbilical cord that bound him to Nelson. Yet the Ghost hung on, partly, Emma suspected, from the fear of being without a guiding hand, but also because he had a regard for his admiral that transcended friendship. Parker was the same only more open in his affection. He adored his chief and made not the slightest effort to disguise it. Other officers shook their heads at what looked like grovelling, wondering why Nelson did not recoil from his homage.

'Milord,' croaked Parker, seeking to raise himself from his bed.

Nelson bade him lie still, seeing in the young man's eye not adoration, but his continuing debilitating fever. Knowing Emma to be ten times better than him with the sick, he listened as, book put aside, she recalled happier times, like the day so recently when they had visited the house of Nelson's late brother Maurice. They had played games in the garden, and amused the 'widow' with stories and listened to the tales of the old black butler that Maurice had taken in before he died, still there thanks to Nelson's support.

Parker had played the fool to perfection: he was good clown Merry Ed, jester at the Nelson court, always decent enough to be abashed at his inability to pay his way, always a willing messenger or organiser. Emma prattled happily until Parker slipped into sleep, then held out her hand to Nelson, who kissed it, though not taking his eyes off the invalid.

'I took this house for us, Emma, as a place we could be without being talked about.' He squeezed the hand he had kissed. 'You can have no notion of how I have missed you.'

If only Nelson knew how much they were talked about, but Emma was not going to tell him that. And she knew how much he missed her, since every note he sent told her so. She put her finger to her lips and led him out into the hallway and up the narrow stairs, to the only furnished bedroom.

Minutes later, below that room, Merry Ed Parker opened his eyes. It was an old dwelling, built in the time of Queen Anne, with creaking floorboards and oak beams that had seen much service. Those boards groaned now, gently but with increase, and Edward Parker managed, even through his pain, a knowing grin.

As soon as Emma described Merton in detail, Nelson named it 'The Farm'. For years he had wanted a country retreat that would be self-sufficient in everything, and as he and Emma lay side by side he talked of growing vegetables, flowers, fruit and meat for the board, and though Merton was nothing like that he insisted to Emma that he had plans to make it so. Laughing, they argued about that, since she had designs to make it a complete, if small, palazzo.

'You will not plough up my lawns for your turnips, Nelson, nor will I suffer to be woken by the crowing of the cock.'

What made Emma laugh then was not the *double entendre*, but the way Nelson blushed at the thought he had obviously formed but was too shy to voice. Emma had that wonderful gift of seeing two meanings in almost everything she said. Nelson was quick enough to cotton on, but too restrained by his upbringing to let on that he had. Quickly, he moved on to safer ground, by asking about Horatia, once more in the care of Mrs Gibson.

Emma knew the feeling she had when talking about her daughter was not envy, because she had suffered from that and knew how to recognise it, but the enthusiasm Nelson evinced when he talked of his daughter was so fulsome and open she felt disquieted, removed, as she was, from the centre of his thoughts.

Also troubling was that she spent a limited amount of time with Horatia, because propriety and social engagements did not allow for it. When she was quizzed about the child's behaviour it was with some difficulty that she answered, and was aware of borrowing incidents from her past that related to her elder daughter, Little Emma, now an adult nearing twenty, and not little Horatia.

There had been that day in Piccadilly when Nelson had called to find Little Emma there. She had been introduced as Emma Connors, and her mother had resisted the temptation to be open about her true birth. As far as Nelson knew, the girl was some kind of relative from Cheshire.

These thoughts filtered to Emma through Nelson's sermon on how his daughter should be raised; education both religious and mathematical, and she must be taught languages from an early age so she did not grow up as deficient as her father. How to walk, how to talk – on and on until Emma decided he sounded like his father.

Sir William, back from his fishing with a basket of mackerel, had changed into dry clothes. He was informed by Emma's Nubian maid, Fatima, that her mistress had gone to see Parker, and since he liked the young man, he decided to call himself on the invalid. It was Langford, still with his foot up in the parlour, who saved what might have been blushes by telling him that Nelson had gone there before

345

him. Sir William was obliged to root out Tom Allen, to go to the house and inform all there of his intention to call.

By the time he arrived Emma and Nelson were back at Parker's bedside, and Emma was again reading to him. But a canny soul like Sir William was a master of atmosphere, and had no trouble in deducing what had been going on. He could not resist a little gibe.

'Ah, my dear Emma, I swear that to see you baring your soul beside an invalid is to see you at your very best.'

Emma glared at him, while one-armed Horatio Nelson went bright red.

It remained their trysting place, with Merry Ed pleased at the time both Emma and his hero spent with him. He wanted more than anything for Nelson to be happy, and when an amputation was finally decided upon declared that he would lose ten limbs in the service of his admiral. Emma and Sir William, who had intended to stay two weeks, put off their departure for a few days. Nelson had written to Parker's family and greeted a father, penniless, he said, from having been robbed of his wallet on the way through London.

The operation, performed by Dr Baird, was a horrid occasion, made worse by the flickering candles that surrounded the operating table. Nelson had witnessed amputations many times but it was not something he had ever got used to. Dosed with both laudanum and rum, young Parker, strapped to the table, was in the rolling-eyed state of the drunk, babbling away and laughing at his own incomprehensible sallies. His eyes continued to dance merrily as Giddings placed the leather strap between Parker's teeth. At the same time Baird was busy with the ligature and wooden spike that, wound tight, would act as a tourniquet.

Baird sliced the flesh below where he would cut the bone, so that it could be folded over the stump and stitched. Watching, Nelson recalled his own amputation; the pain and the despair of knowing he would never be whole again. The knife went in deep further up, to dissect clean flesh above the corruption in the lower thigh. Pain seared through Parker's drunken brain and the smile changed to a rictus, the back arched, and it took Giddings and two of the brawniest members of Nelson's barge crew to keep the patient on the blood-drenched table.

Speed was all in these situations, so Baird worked quickly, ignoring Parker's stifled grunts and the mucus that shot out from his nose to mingle with the saliva at his mouth. The flesh surrendered to the blade in half a minute, and swiftly Baird took his saw from his assistant. If the pain of cut flesh was severe, that of the sinews of a bone was worse; the grinding sound of the saw sent a feeling of horror through Nelson. Parker was swearing to God and his mother through the muffling round his mouth as Baird, through the thighbone, tossed the leg aside and went to work with clean cloths to stem the blood enough for him to begin the work of repair.

One strip of hanging skin was folded under another, a third put in place before the suture, string attached, was sewn into the wound. When that string was pulled and caused no pain, when it came out easily and without a following of blood or pus, the doctor would know that the wound had healed.

It was over. Parker had passed out, and the barge crew, streaming with sweat, lifted the still comatose Parker back onto the bed.

At first Merry Ed seemed to rally, to recover some of his gaiety. But it didn't last and with the smell of corruption wafting up from the stump he began once more to sink. The Hamiltons were gone when he died, with Nelson sitting by the bed, praying with his equally distraught father.

He had never told Edward Parker that he saw him as a son. Happy as he was with his daughter, his desire for a male heir was strong, and Josiah Nisbet had been such a disappointment. He felt now as he imagined his own father had felt as his offspring had expired. The first Edmund and Horatio, gone before he was born, Maurice, his sister Anne, a second Edmund, Suckling, and his younger sibling George, who had lasted less than a year, dying before Nelson went off to school.

Edward Parker was laid to rest in the cemetery of St George's Church, so close to the sea that the faint sound of the surf on the shingle could just be heard through the narrow alleyways that led to Deal beach. And for what? The envoys had already crossed the Channel to discuss peace, and Nelson had been informed in a less than polite and public letter from Evan Nepean that any offensive action he contemplated must be put on hold. No French ship, no French port was to be touched.

Nepean represented the same Admiralty that had refused to pay for Parker's lodgings, his treatment or his funeral. In a rare public outburst, Nelson claimed that the young man could have stunk above ground or been thrown into a ditch for all they cared. The father had nothing, so Nelson paid for the interment and gave the fellow enough money to get back to his home.

It gave him no pleasure to find out that Parker *père* had touched half his officers for money, before proceeding to call upon a debt of Langford's that had still time to run, adding a premium that was not due. 'What to say, Hardy,' he sighed to the Ghost, fingering a silver gilt cup that he had had Emma buy as a gift to the surgeon who had looked after his Boulogne wounded. 'The man shames Merry Ed, but how can I complain when everyone knows Viscount Nelson is so very rich?'

Peace preliminaries were signed at Amiens at the beginning of October and, effectively, Nelson's service in the Channel was over, though it was weeks before he could take any leave since both St Vincent and Troubridge urged that his continued presence in Deal was necessary. Nelson had to suffer colds, seasickness and being tossed about in rough seas just to satisfy the fears of his superiors that the peace might not hold.

Nelson, himself, did not believe in this peace: it was too advantageous to Bonaparte, giving the Corsican menace time to regroup. And it had meant handing back to France and the Dutch many possessions that had been taken from them at some cost in British blood: the West Indian sugar islands, Ceylon, the Cape of Good Hope. Even Malta was returned to the Knights of St John.

The day he struck his flag was one of necessary visits: to William Pitt at Walmer Castle, his because he held the sinecure post of Lord Warden of the Cinque Ports, to old Admiral Lutwidge and his wife, and, most demanding of all, to the wounded sailors in Deal hospital. His pennant was lowered in the gloom of a late October evening and Nelson set off for Merton, a home he had never seen, travelling through the night with the intention of being there for breakfast.

Merton had been his for a month, and improvements had started, so the house and grounds were all ahoo with builders and gardeners when the master made his first entrance. Stopping his coach, Nelson got out at the gate and walked slowly up the drive, savouring the appearance of a residence that looked very fine in the early dawn light.

A stronger sun would show many things requiring attention, but in this light the place looked perfect: large but not awesome with a fine central block fronted by a classical porch, a perfect array of ten windows, the whole surmounted by a pediment roof that mirrored that of the porch. To one side the wing was square with a large window lighting what he assumed to be the main reception room. The other octagonal wing with windows on each face would no doubt hold the library on the ground floor and a withdrawing room on the upper, so shaped as to allow the windows on each face to catch whatever light there was at any time of day.

The front door, already painted navy blue, was open and the servants were about, raking and laying fires, lighting stoves, cleaning and polishing while their betters lay abed. Admiral Viscount Nelson, who knew none of them, was obliged to introduce himself. Behind him Tom Allen was unloading his sea chest, with his master having to ask where it should go.

His bedroom located, it was good to wander round the place while Emma was still asleep, touching the furniture he now owned, fingering books in the library that peace might give him time to read. He entered rooms in which shafts of sunlight were filled with motes of dust, others in which sat the decorator's trestles and pots of paint. He recalled how many times he had gone on board a ship that was still being readied, his cabin unpainted, his few pieces of furniture not yet arranged. Merton brought that to mind, and the thought was pleasing for being so familiar.

Then, as the clock in the hallway struck nine, he went to find Fatima, Emma's maid, so that she could tell her mistress Nelson was here, and that he intended to call. Fatima grinned, her full cheeks pushed out and her white teeth lighting up her face. Her eyes held the knowing look that said she was well aware of why Nelson would be calling.

Half an hour later, he and Emma were breakfasting together in her bedroom.

Having dreamed for so long of owning a comfortable residence Nelson was prepared to be disappointed. At one time, speculating with Fanny, he had hankered after a small cottage with roses round the door and children gambolling in the garden. Merton was much more than that, but it felt intimate. Over the following weeks rooms were put to rights, the roof repairs completed, and Emma put in her plate glass doors so that light was brought to the previously dim hallway. Plumbers plumbed, painters painted and carpenters sawed while a steady stream of visitors came and went.

James Perry, owner of the *Morning Chronicle*, and still a partisan of Emma, was a neighbour and welcome guest with whom both Sir William, who resided in the house at weekends, and Nelson, could happily converse. The adjoining property was owned by Mr Gold-shmid, a banker, who was a mine of good cheer and information regarding the progress of international affairs. The folk of the parish, under the pastoral care of the vicar, Mr Lancaster, were delighted to have the nation's hero in their midst and took pains to ensure that Nelson knew it.

Naturally the William Nelsons were early visitors. The Viscount was pleased to learn that his brother had been made a Prebendary at Canterbury. It pleased William less: he had sought higher ecclesiastical preferment using the Nelson name, and reckoned that with his bloodline he should be a bishop.

Christmas was celebrated in a house still full of dust and noise, but it fulfilled Nelson's hopes by being a place to which his family could come. The Boltons and the Matchams arrived with their large and noisy broods, all of whom were eager to play with and hold ten-month old Horatia.

The younger members of the family might be unaware of her parentage but the adults were not, and even if they had not suspected before they could be in no doubt now, seeing father and daughter together, of the blood connection. Horatia even looked like him and no man spent so much time playing with and talking about a foundling. And if Emma could carry off the lie of the connection, Nelson could not.

If they disapproved, no one hinted that it was so. Fanny Nelson, whom they had all related to in their own way in the past, was forgotten now and never mentioned. Indeed, if Nelson's father had not still been a supporter she might have been cut out of the family altogether. Emma headed Nelson's table, created the entertainments, oversaw the running of the house, ordered and supervised the improvements, and sat as the centre of attention in the evening when the family played cards or performed their party pieces.

Sir William, more frail than ever, but still with a sharp mind, was like an adopted grandfather. Like most men who had never had to suffer the behaviour of his own children he saw nothing but good in the breed. He was patient with them all, by the river teaching them to fish, in the library assisting them with their reading and their languages, or joining in with their noisy parlour games.

The person he was not patient with was Emma: since she was living here, and he used Merton as a weekend retreat, he felt a bounden duty to share in the expense of the upkeep. The strain that that put on his finances was considerable: he still had the rent in Piccadilly to pay, plus all the other costs, for carriages and the like, that were necessary to get him and his wife up to town and back again. And on top of that there was Emma's extravagance.

She could not be brought to see that the life they had lived in Naples could not be replicated in England: he did not have the means. She spent Nelson's money with the same prodigality, and Sir William had it on good authority from Alexander Davidson that the admiral was not wealthy. Successful warrior he might be, but when it came to prize money every other admiral outstripped him. Davidson was of the opinion that Nelson did the hard graft, while others, more assiduous in the stroking of their connections and the Admiralty, got the plums.

And Emma had made this very much Nelson's house. Portraits and trophies lined the walls, everything that Nelson had ever been given, won or sat for, even framed songs that had been composed in his honour. That was as it should be but Sir William felt that he was ever more set on the margin of Emma's life, for at Merton she never bothered to pretend that they were still a married couple. All he ever got was Nelson this and Nelson that, with no compensation in the article of consideration when they were together. As to Nelson himself, he was the same social misfit he had always been, never noticing, Sir William was sure, the way Emma treated him, so he was left out of any strictures Sir William felt he had to raise. Not that he got very far. Every time he taxed Emma with some slight it ended with his writing to make the peace.

Naval acquaintances called at the house they had named as Circe's Cave, especially the members of the Crocodile Club. There, his Nile captains, while often deprecating the way the place was a shrine to their hero, toasted the success of one of their number. Sir James Saumarez, just before the peace, had dished the Spaniards in Algeciras Bay. That occasioned bumper after bumper, but only after they had refought the battle on the dining room table. If many of them still held in doubt the whole association of Emma and their admiral, then they said nothing, for they were too attached to him to sour the atmosphere.

Winter turned to spring, and for a short time there were no builders present. Outside, those improvements he had discussed with Cribb, the gardener, began to show themselves; shrubs and plants budded nicely, early daffodils and tulips bloomed, the lawn was a mass of daisies, while bluebells spread like a carpet under the trees.

For the first time in nearly ten years, Nelson was not in uniform but in civilian clothes. He went to church on Sundays to occupy his own pew, and conversed outside with his fellow parishioners about the needs of the locality: improvements to roads, the provision of a canal, the next local Member of Parliament. He would walk home as Emma and Sir William coached, nodding to acquaintances, every inch the country squire, returning usually to a scene of domestic tranquillity.

The tributary of the river Wandle that cut through his property had been cleared and renamed the Nile by Emma. It had also been stocked with fish so that Sir William could while away his time with the rod. To Nelson, especially when Horatia was present, the weekends were bliss. There was always a guest and always a good dinner, and usually, in the evening, a performance of an attitude or two by Emma.

Walks would be taken on what Nelson liked to call his quarterdeck, the strip of gravel that fronted the house. There, with a friend or relative alongside, he liked to pace, converse and ruminate on the world beyond his front gate. His residence was no longer 'The Farm'. It was 'Paradise Merton' now, the place in which everything was contained that Nelson loved.

On Monday mornings, Viscount Nelson and Sir William Hamilton would take coach to join the throng of gentlemen heading for London to banks and law chambers, insurance brokerages and government offices. Or like Sir William, to Sotheby's or Christies for an auction. Nelson went to the Admiralty to discuss naval matters, often to the House of Lords, to listen to the debates and to work hard at the thing that he wished for most; that Lady Emma Hamilton should be accepted at court.

34

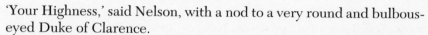

'Your Highness,' said Nelson, with a nod to a very round and bulbous-eyed Duke of Clarence.

Prince William Henry had been plump even as a boy when Nelson had first met him, although height had offset the worst effects. It was a family trait that had shown itself to a greater extent when he had made his cruise around the Caribbean. As a post captain the Prince had embarked on a voyage designed to bring closer to the House of Hanover the subjects of the sugar islands, and to show them that their royal family were employed and useful, not the rakish and idle spendthrifts of rumour. Thanks to him, it had done the opposite, reinforcing an image of boorish superiority. In the process it had put a blight on Nelson's career.

They had remained friendly, corresponding frequently. Clarence provided Nelson with a conduit to his father, however little it was appreciated, and the man who liked to be known as the 'Sailor Prince' had basked in his association with Nelson. At court, he could claim to know Nelson's mind, and had, at the time of the Nile, been a rock of optimism when all around him people had begun to despair.

'Damn good to see you Nelson,' he boomed, 'and looking so damned well. Life ashore surely suits you. Mind you, sir, no man's health was ever improved by being tossed about on the ocean.'

'I have Lady Hamilton to thank for that, sir. She has made for me a home at Merton that would restore the most jaded sailor.'

'Quite,' the duke replied, warily, 'and I know I have an invitation to visit you which I assure you I will take up soon.'

'I would be most obliged if you would, Your Highness.'

There was a pause, Nelson hoping that Clarence might name a day, his host wondering if he could change the subject. He had no intention of visiting Merton under present circumstances, for to do so would anger his father. Upsetting the man who held the family purse strings was not wise for a man whose debts always exceeded his income. One day he would go, but not yet.

'Saw Hardy the other day, Nelson. Ain't changed much, still the same dull fellow he ever was.'

'A capital seaman, though,' Nelson replied.

Clarence looked at him hard then, since he had heard from more than one source that Nelson had no high opinion of his abilities as a seaman. Fellow was wrong, of course. It was just one of the crosses he had to bear for being a member of the royal family. Nothing done was ever seen in a fair light. Why, not once on his quarterdeck had a single officer questioned his skill. Clarence checked himself then. There had been one in the Caribbean, a Lieutenant Schomberg, and from what the Prince recalled, Nelson had declined to remove the fellow. More than that, with Schomberg insisting on a court martial to clear his name, Nelson had obliged the fellow with a praiseworthy deposition.

Nelson interrupted these less than pleasant thoughts. 'We have known each other for a long time, Your Highness.'

'God, haven't we? Since the American war, Nelson, and that's, what, twenty-five years past.'

'I have always supposed you to be one of my partisans, sir.'

'Oh, that, Nelson, definitely that. From our days under Lord Hood. Every chance I got before the late war I would tell the Admiralty that you must be employed. I hope it helped you get *Agamemnon*, without which there would have been no Nile. Had a hand in the Baltic decision and your Channel service. Ever your partisan, Nelson.'

'Thank you for that,' Nelson replied, although he found it hard to believe. From what he knew of Clarence's relations with the Admiralty any suggestions he made tended to diminish opportunity rather than raise it. Prince he might be, but no great faith was reposed in his judgement.

'But I am, at present, looking for your support on a non-service matter.'

'Non-service?'

William Henry tried hard to make it sound as though such a notion was impossible, because he could guess what Nelson was seeking. He hoped it was on the subject of the Copenhagen battle, for which, much to Nelson's chagrin, no medals had been issued, but he feared otherwise.

'You know of my attachment to Lady Hamilton.'

'A fine woman,' replied Clarence, with a sinking heart.

'And a brave one, sir. I could list for you services that she has carried out for her country that would astound you.'

'I have heard of them,' Clarence said quickly, for fear that Nelson would indeed tell him.

'Then it seems to me that your father, the King, has not.'

'My father?'

Nelson was off, despite Clarence's best efforts, listing Emma's achievements in Naples on behalf of the fleet, her relations with the Neapolitan royal family, all with such conviction that the Prince was forced to listen. This was unusual; the protocol, brought over from Hanover by his great-grandfather, was that one only spoke to royalty when one was spoken to. They were never to be interrupted and certainly never lectured. Trouble was, Viscount Lord Nelson had known him as a boy and had taught him a great deal about how to handle a ship. Much as he would have liked to tell Nelson to shut up, he could not bring himself to do so.

'I feel that if these facts could be brought to your father by someone to whom he would listen, then he might soften his attitude to Lady Hamilton. She does not ask to be a court intimate, only to be received.'

'My father is a hard man to budge,' said Prince William. When it came to persons of questionable backgrounds, his mother was even worse.

'It seems to me, sir, given your own circumstances and the regard you say you have for me, that you would be well placed to advance her case.'

Clarence's eyes popped at the mention of his circumstances, the cause of much dispute with his father. He was living quite openly with a married woman who had borne him several children, yet he could not see how his visitor could possibly assume that his 'circumstances' had any bearing on the case. He was a Prince! What to say? To raise the man's hopes by agreeing then doing nothing? That might expose him to constant supplication, but an outright refusal would be too harsh. Obfuscation looked to be the best policy.

'You may have the right of it, Nelson, and you may not. But such things, if they are to happen must be thought out, not rushed at. Don't want to make matters worse, what! There are people I must talk to with wiser heads than mine. Should they advise that I should proceed we will talk again, and lay a plan of action.'

Long ago, watching his father and his brothers, Prince William Henry had perfected the meaningless smile – meaningless to him

355

that is. To those upon whom he chose to bestow it, it was meant to convey that they were no less than the person closest to his heart. That was the smile he employed now as he made a mental note to tell his servants that, should Viscount Nelson call in the next month or so, he would not be at home.

It was a red-letter day when Nelson's father finally consented to come to Merton. The old man had always liked Emma and even if he harboured doubts about her character he was a great man for forgiveness. His attachment to Fanny was strong and it was only the knowledge of his own failing health that forced him into a decision he would rather have avoided. He had attended too many deathbeds not to know his own was near, but he worked hard to hide this knowledge from his son.

Nelson saw a new gentleness in his father, a willingness to listen and communicate. It was as if he had finally acknowledged that his boy Horace had grown to manhood and could be treated as an equal. Over the weeks he stayed, Emma charmed him, and they spent many happy hours together, with Fanny never mentioned. Yet Nelson knew, for all his father's circumspection, that his wife had not given up hope of reconciliation.

He was right. Fanny knew, from hints and asides from her friends at the Admiralty, that had they still been together, had there been no risk of scandal, they would both have been out of London by now. Nelson would have been given a profitable command, one of the West Indian stations or the Far East. Should the war be renewed, as everyone expected it would, then Viscount Nelson, on such a station, could amass the same kind of fortune as the likes of Sir Hyde Parker, the kind of wealth that would allow him to live as his fame demanded. Surely, even as besotted as he seemed to be, Nelson could see the harm he was doing to his prospects with this adulterous liaison.

The Reverend Edmund Nelson being at Merton gave her a chance to communicate once more, so she wrote to him, repeating all the arguments for a reconciliation, and pointing out that she had, and was still behaving with dignified reticence. She had never traduced Emma Hamilton in public or in private, because to do so would be common.

The return of the letter, with the subscription added, 'opened but not read by Viscount Nelson' was a cruel blow to her hopes. In that, and a great deal of his previous behaviour, she could not recognise the man she had married. Where was the gentle kindness, the nature that saw good men where others saw base? That woman had changed him, stolen him away from her and the nation, the real Horatio Nelson.

She never knew how Nelson had felt as he wrote those words across her letter. He had been unable to read it from a fear that he might weaken. The same fear stopped him travelling to his father's funeral – Edmund Nelson passed away peacefully in Bath only weeks after his visit to Merton. The old man's suspicions about his health, never voiced in his son's house, had been correct. Although his relatives had warned Nelson that his father was fading, his death still came as a shock. It was purgatory not to attend the funeral, but if Fanny was there, Nelson would not be able ignore her. His greatest fear in meeting her face to face was that his resolve to separate from her totally might be tested.

Emma worked just as hard for her social acceptance as Nelson, using both the Piccadilly house and Merton to apply pressure on the well-connected guests she entertained. There was a long list of elderly sea officers, those who admired Nelson as numerous as those who did not, her husband's relatives and diplomatic contacts. The Marquis of Queensberry, who had the King's ear, came. He was one of the richest men in the Kingdom, a cousin of her husband, and eccentric enough to match King George himself. The Duke of Hamilton, one of England's premier peers and Sir William's brother, had visited Merton. There was Lord Minto, who had been Nelson's friend and adviser in Corsica. There were dukes, duchesses, former and serving ambassadors, bankers and courtiers aplenty, but all foundered on the rock of Hanoverian intransigence. As time went by, hope faded, and when she listened to Nelson insisting that all would be well, it was with a sinking heart, not a hopeful one.

Her faith was much restored when she, Nelson and Sir William, the *tria uno in juncto*, decided on a three-week journey to visit Sir William's estates near Milford Haven, stopping on the way so that Sir William and the admiral-hero could collect degrees from Oxford. Not for them the flight to Paris, which was, since the peace, the destination of most of British society. Nelson could not bring himself to love or visit a country that had been so recently an enemy, and one he suspected would soon be again.

Setting out from Merton, it was as if runners had been sent ahead to say they were coming. Just as when he had visited Windsor after the Nile, Nelson's name brought out the populace, leaving Sir William to reflect on the fact that King George, who disliked Nelson and would not receive Emma, often travelled in darkness for fear that his coach might be stoned.

The newspapers, and their dissemination throughout the country, had made something of Nelson the like of which he had never seen. Sir William Hamilton had grown up with royalty and had known many famous men, but not one had ever got more than polite admiration. The names of Drake, Anson, Boscawen and Blake paled beside Nelson's, and he was received wherever he went with adulation almost religious in its fervour.

The bridges at Maidenhead and Henley were so crowded it took an age to cross the Thames. Oxford turned out in vast numbers, and the hotel in which the party stayed was surrounded throughout the night while the most famous man in Britain played host to an endless stream of visitors. At Blenheim they looked at the palace the monarchy had built for John Churchill, first Duke of Marlborough. Emma stated that Nelson deserved one of twice the size, but he told her that Paradise Merton would suffice. No duke or duchess appeared to greet them: instead they sent out some cold food, which was rejected as smacking of condescension.

Continuing adoration soon displaced the cloud of that insult. A journey through the heart of England designed to take three weeks took six, with the freedoms of various towns offered wholesale and dozens of inns renamed along the route. Emma made sure that their reception should come to the royal ears. Let the King and Queen of England know that Nelson, the conqueror of the French, could probably, if he so chose, master them too. John Bull loved the Hero of the Nile and Copenhagen more than he loved Farmer George.

And everywhere there were seamen, officers and men who had sailed in a fleet or ship that Nelson had commanded. For him these were the happiest meetings, a chance to talk over old exploits and actions, to touch the heads of their offspring, the most recent of whom were often named Horatio.

By the time he reached Gloucester, Nelson had honed his speech, always made from some hotel balcony, and in it he praised his countrymen, male and female, and told them that they, of all the races in God's earthly kingdom, had the hand of the Lord on their side.

The only cloud on the horizon was Sir William, who appeared to be fading before the eyes of both his wife and his best friend. He seemed thinner week by week, his mind began to wander and he was wont to talk of things that had happened years before as if they were happening now, while he found it increasingly difficult to remember what had happened an hour before.

By the time the party had returned to Merton, what Nelson had thought would happen came to pass. Bonaparte was being bellicose again and the peace was threatened. Nelson's services were required and, as always, he was available.

Yet war was avoided, to many minds more by pusillanimous Britain than by French reticence. As he waited, the points of reference in Nelson's life acquired regularity. Naturally he called at the Admiralty, where St Vincent and Troubridge had assured him of the Mediterranean should war break out. Both, simultaneously, accepted invitations to Merton that neither had any intention of fulfilling. He spoke in the House of Lords, initial shyness giving way to an ease of speech and a command of subject that made him a draw. He had a list of friends and officers he felt duty bound to call on. Last, but far from least, he would call at Mrs Gibson to visit Horatia, often stopping at a toyshop on the way.

Horatia enchanted him; the way she smiled, watched his face, held his finger. She liked movement and noises, the most successful present being a watch with a tick so loud it could be heard on the other side of a door. This, waved before her on a chain, brought forth gales of childish laughter. On the rare occasions when Mrs Gibson entered her drawing room while the Admiral was present she would either find the pair surrounded by toys, playing happily on the carpet, or Lord Nelson sitting with his eyes closed, looking serene, with Horatia asleep on his breast.

It troubled him that Emma never called at Mrs Gibson's. She saw Horatia only when the child was brought to her, usually when the other children in the family were present. As a party-lover Emma always felt happier when a number of people were around, with her at the centre, planning games and outings, supervising races and contests, engaging Nelson with several children instead of just his own. But then she had other concerns; running and improving Merton, and looking after a husband who was wandering inexorably into his dotage.

Sir William made one more royal levee, determined to face his childhood friend, not sure what he would say, but certain that for Farmer George it would be uncomfortable.

'The country in which I grew to manhood is no more.' His servant realised that Sir William was talking to himself and did not respond. His job was to get the old man to Windsor and back again. If his charge rambled, which he was prone to do, that was none of his concern. 'Closed minds and closed legs surround the King, though that dull queen of his must have opened them often enough. After all, she has produced a string of fat idiots and twittering harpies.'

He was like that all the way, criticising his king and queen, the Prince of Wales and the dukes of York, Clarence, Kent, Sussex, and the princesses who were said to be too stupid to find themselves husbands. He made the levee, entering on the arms of old and trusted friends, and he mouthed words of reprimand to the man with whom he had shared a nursery. But he did not say them loud enough to be heard, his entire complaint taking place more in his head than his mouth. But when he returned to Piccadilly he was vehement about the manner in which he had told off his sovereign.

He was also feverish. Emma insisted he go to bed, and sent a message to Nelson to join her, since her husband's ramblings seemed to get worse, with an undertone of accusation.

'Greville dunned us both, Emma – and he will get everything. How are you going to live? You spend too much and save nothing. Nelson has no money, pray for war eh! What has it come to when we wish for that? You treated me shabbily Emma. I tried to hate you, and him, but every time I felt jealous I felt angry – with you, no, with myself.'

'My dear friend,' said Nelson, coming to the bedside.

'Nelson.'

'Yes.' Nelson took his hand.

'My true friend.' Sir William summoned the strength to squeeze, and Emma, who had moved to the other side of the bed, took his free hand.

'I hope so,' whispered Nelson.

Sir William gathered strength enough to pull. 'A *tria, uno in juncto*,' he said.

He repeated it over several days as he sunk towards death, only to come round again. He spoke of things in delirium that many would not have wanted to hear, of his hatred of the Church – all churches not just the papist one. Of the things he had seen on the walls of Pompeii and his certainty that the cult of Priapus was still practised by the superstitious peasantry of Calabria. Sir William fought to hang on to life with a naked tenacity the like of which he had never shown when up and doing. As his skin fell away from his face he came to look like some biblical prophet, foretelling a world where pagan gods would rule. The time came when his most frequent mantra was whispered not spoken, so that Nelson and Emma had to lean close to hear, 'A *tria uno in juncto*'.

'Always that,' said Emma, with a sob, as the blue eyes lost their sparkle and both she and Nelson began to pray for the soul of Sir William Hamilton. They were beside him for most of the night, not always praying or weeping, but discussing the practical matters attendant upon getting the body to Pembrokeshire, so that Sir William's wish to be buried beside his first wife, Catherine, could be fulfilled.

Before dawn Nelson left, and walked for an hour before taking lodgings a few streets away. He wrote to his sister-in-law Sarah to ask that she come and support Emma at this time of sorrow, heading the letter with the address of his lodgings. No longer could he write from twenty-three Piccadilly, the home of a friend happy to accommodate him. Emma was now a widow, which meant he could only cross her threshold when she had other guests.

Without the assistance Sir William had provided Nelson was forced to take a close look at his finances, and what he saw did little to lift his spirits. All the bills for Merton would now come to him, he had his brother Maurice's 'widow' to maintain, he had fees to pay for young Horatio at Eton, plus any number of requests from acquaintances and strangers who assumed that because he was successful he was rich. The opposite was the case; while not in penury he was hovering on the edge of discomfort, which could only get worse if he did not curtail the way Emma spent money on Merton, both the fabric of the place and the entertainment.

Emma saw debt as natural, he did not. Trades people had to be paid. As a young man he had lived too close to them to ever keep them waiting for their money. His father had dinned into him that to be in debt was a sin, but when he tried to discuss this with Emma she laughed at his fears.

Emma had lived so long with extravagance it had become a habit. Even, perhaps especially, the strictures of her mother were laughed off. Her debts had been paid by Sir William's legacy, and she had an annuity, albeit a small one, to sustain her. Everything would be fine, and to cap it all Emma was sure she was pregnant again.

Tom Allen shuffled as he spoke in a way that he had not for years, looking for all the world like a man in his first day of service. Nelson wondered where the fellow had gone who admonished him if he ate too little or drank too much, who insisted that instead of sitting at the dinner table yarning all night to his fellow officers he should take himself off to his bed?

Tom Allen wasn't hopeless as a servant, but on more than one

361

occasion Nelson had wondered if he was suitable to serve an admiral who often had in his cabin dignitaries and officers of other nations. What did they make of less than sleek Tom? He did not blunder about, but he was far from polished in the way he attended to his duties. When it came to Nelson's captains, who entertained him as much as he did them, he could not help but observe that they were better attended to than he.

Ever since he inherited Frank Lepée Nelson had known that he was not good with servants, inclined to let them tell him what he should do rather than the other way round. But he reckoned his needs were simple; honesty, discretion and no airs or graces. When it came to the last, Tom Allen was highly qualified: he had never lost the sound and manner of what he was, a Norfolk labourer. But he was familiar, a fixture in the day, and what was making him nervous was the fact that he wished this to be his last.

'Seems to me, your honour, that if'n I wait till war starts, then me getting out will be dependent on another peace.'

'There will be one, Tom, of that I am certain.'

Bonaparte had used the peace well; he had quelled his political troubles at home, managed to make his office of First Consul hereditary, reorganised the laws and customs of a country still stuck in the ways of the old regime, and reformed his army so that when it came to invasion he was an even more formidable foe than he had been eighteen months before. Only at sea would Nelson find if those improvements extended to his navy.

'Aye, but how long will it take? Eight years we've fought them buggers already, beggin' your pardon, an' who's to say it won't take as long again?'

'Is anything else prompting this Tom?'

There was a lot Tom might have said then, for he had little love of the set-up at Merton. Never as happy on land as he was at sea, he disliked Surrey even more than Naples or Palermo. He felt that what his master was about was sinful and that the gloss had long since been chipped off his lady. But all that would have sounded daft, given that his master was about to go aboard ship once more.

'There be a lady, a good girl, who lives not too far from Burnham. And I reckon with what you 'ave got saved for me, there be enough to make to her a proposal she might fancy.'

Nelson had his account book open in front of him, and he glanced at it, although he knew the figure he was about to quote, the sum in pay that Tom had never needed because practically everything he wanted was paid for.

'Ninety-six pounds Tom, which is not a fortune but a tidy sum none the less.'

'It would give me a start, and the lass I have my eye on is not without prospects.'

'Then so be it, Tom. I shall see you discharged and send you on your way with an addition to your pay.'

It stung Nelson that his sailor servant left that same day, in what looked like unseemly haste, but Tom knew that if he hung about, delaying his departure, he would see too much of the sadness his decision had caused. His determination might weaken and he would end up with another ten years of war. It was certain that whatever was happening his master would be in the thick of it, he always was. Yet it was hard for anyone to be in the company of Horatio Nelson and not want to stay.

Davidson found Nelson a replacement, a man named Chevalier who was a trained servant and knew how to serve at table and keep his masters' goods and chattels in proper order.

'For all love, have you found me a Frenchman?' Nelson asked anxiously.

'What I have found you, Nelson,' Davidson protested, 'is a gentleman's gentleman. It is to be hoped that exposure to him will make something of a gentleman of you.'

'A waste, Davidson,' said Nelson, taking his arm and walking him along the bank of his own little river Nile. 'I was ruined for that when I joined the Navy.'

Chevalier was a bit frightening, a tall lugubrious fellow, solemn in everything he did. He was so refined that Nelson was left to wonder if he could live up to his servant's high standards.

Everyone he needed was in place when the call came, a despatch from the Admiralty appointing him to immediate command in the Mediterranean. He had his new secretary called Scott, with Hardy as his flag captain, and he knew that when he went aboard his new flagship he would see before the mast many familiar faces.

The farewell to Emma had been tender and tearful, yet as they were in London he had had to leave her without spending the night. He rose at dawn in his own bed, and scribbled a hasty note to tell her not to fear for either his life or his love.

Portsmouth was all bustle, full of blue officer's coats, while the streets were a mass of carts, marching bands leading soldiers to their ships, whores offering a last chance to dip for men who might be going away to die. There was the usual street entertainment, fiddlers who would play an air of choice, jugglers looking for a penny, girls with trays of sweetmeats, peddlers with everything a tar might need on service, from ribbons to wedding rings that glistened enough, it was said, to fool some foreign troll. There were cattle and sheep on the hoof, chickens flapping in baskets, carts loaded with supplies for ship's captains containing wines, hams, cheeses, butter, plates to eat them off and cutlery to carve them.

And there were drunks too, many of them young men who, if they lived, would become captains themselves, the junior lieutenants and midshipmen. Now they were just boisterous youths, imbibing to excess, rollicking and joking, teasing the more sober citizens and eye-ing the ladies for a last carnal fling.

Chevalier struggled to accumulate all the things his new master needed, then to get them on to the right ship, a mammoth task which he carried out with quiet efficiency that never once interfered with his regular duties. Nelson was shaved, dressed, and sent on time to dine with other senior officers, and was woken at the right hour to go aboard his new flagship.

As they rowed out to the Spithead anchorage she stood out, high-sided and majestic, even among the rest of the three-deckers. Nelson had seen her many times since that first day in Chatham when, as a new midshipman, Lieutenant Frears had pointed her out. Expertly his barge crew took him alongside to the ladder that led up to the entry port. A hand was ready to ensure that he did not slip on the wet wood that was dipping in and out of the water, and that he had hold of the rope banister that would see him safe aboard.

Nelson stepped from grey daylight to near darkness, to the sound of crashing marine feet and high-pitched whistles, and Hardy said to him,

'Welcome aboard HMS *Victory*, sir.'

35

1805

When Nelson was piped off HMS *Victory* fifteen months later, to go ashore at Portsmouth, setting foot on land for the first time since he had embarked, he could honestly say that he was closing off the most frustrating chapter of his life. No battles, but long sea chases or an elusive enemy who did not want to meet him, and deliberate chicanery designed to cheat him out of a fortune in prize money.

The ships he had joined in the Mediterranean had had no news that hostilities had recommenced – that was brought to them by their new commander-in-chief. He had also found scurvy and low morale, both of which he had to deal with before any offensive action could be contemplated. The thought of that made Nelson smile. He had done everything possible to tempt out the Toulon fleet. Unlike most of his contemporaries he did not believe in close blockade, bottling enemy fleets in their harbours to render them ineffective.

The Nelson method, which gave them room to sail, took full advantage of the latest signalling system devised by Admiral Sir Home Popham, a truly alphabetical arrangement by which messages could be sent and understood if the weather was clear. He wanted the French at sea where they could be beaten. That was the best way to render them ineffective; by taking, burning or destroying them in battle. So he sailed all over the western Mediterranean, to Malta, the coast of Spain, Sardinia, even Naples, where his presence alarmed the court and a government who were determined this time to stay neutral in the new war.

The French popped their noses out once or twice. Under Admiral Latouche Tréville they ventured to leave Toulon when Nelson was a hundred miles away. On both occasions, having stayed at sea for twenty-four hours Tréville then dashed back, claiming to his First

Consul that he had chased the British blockading fleet off station. It would have been funny if it had not been credited by the Admiralty, who seemed to believe more of what *Le Moniteur* printed in Paris than Nelson related in his own despatches.

The French had humbugged him once, sending Nelson off to the east again for fear that, out of harbour, that was where they were headed. Still, there was a comeuppance: Latouche Tréville, reckoned France's best admiral, dropped dead of a heart attack soon after, it was said because he spent too much time climbing the mountain behind Toulon to look out for Nelson. He was replaced by another renegade aristocrat, a survivor of the Nile, Admiral Villeneuve.

Nelson was not at odds with his superiors in the same way that he had been with Lord Keith, yet he did argue, for they suffered from the same fears as the Scotsman. They dreaded that the French fleets should combine to achieve superiority in the English Channel, because the spectre of invasion still loomed large in their imaginations. And to make matters worse, Spain seemed to be drifting towards an alliance with France, which would give the enemy additional strength and ports all the way from northern Italy to the Scheldt.

Nelson's strategy was simple. Let them try to combine in the Channel. In the process the various units, Toulon, Brest, La Rochelle, would be vulnerable to attack and should they reach the southern coasts of England he had no doubt they would suffer the same fate as the Spanish Armada. If many misconstrued this as another example of risk-taking and glory-seeking, it was just a cross he had to bear.

Eventually Spain concluded an alliance with France. The government in London had known this was coming, so had Nelson. But with better access to intelligence they had had a more informed expectation than he of when this would happen. They used that knowledge to cheat him and his men out of a fortune by sending a detached squadron, not under his orders, to sit off Cadiz and catch the Spanish plate ships as they came in from South America. That capture ended Spanish procrastination, and catapulted them into the war on the French side.

Studying his immediate opponent, Villeneuve, Nelson suspected a timid fellow who, having seen what his adversary could do at the Nile, had no real desire to test his mettle again. Villeneuve's problem was Bonaparte, now Emperor of the French, and certain that at sea he enjoyed the same mastery of tactics that he held on land. Pushed repeatedly to get out to where he could be of use, Villeneuve finally sailed, eluded Nelson and got out into the Atlantic.

He sailed to the West Indies, no doubt intent on doing mischief there, but as soon as he found that Nelson had followed him, he upped anchor and skittled back east. One of Nelson's frigates managed to catch Villeneuve's tail, ascertained his strength and his course, and got the news back to England. The Admiralty alerted Admiral Sir Robert Calder, who had fifteen sail of the line covering Ferrol and Rochefort, to intercept, which he did, but the resulting action was inconclusive.

Nelson, unaware of this, had cracked on so hard that he got to Gibraltar before that action took place. Faced with combining British fleets, Villeneuve had run for Ferrol and Vigo on the northern shoulder of Spain to avoid battle. Now that he was back in harbour and blockaded, Nelson could go home.

On the way, thanks to newspapers given him by the Channel Fleet, Nelson had read the less than flattering newspaper reports of Calder's action, fought at long range and indecisive, with only two enemy ships taken and no real battle joined. John Bull was used to victory, and, if the newspapers were to be believed, he was not happy, the general opinion being that Lord Nelson would have done better. The man they flattered was not so sure; he knew Robert Calder as a dogged fighter. And John Bull, or at least those who wrote for him, was not a sailor. He knew nothing of wind, tide and circumstances at sea. Nelson was prepared to believe that Sir Robert Calder had done as well as he could until it was proved otherwise.

It seemed that dawn was the natural time for Nelson to appear at Merton, and when he arrived, it was to find, as he had the first time, all the servants and gardeners up and working. But it was different; the garden was looking mature and moss had begun to mellow the newest brickwork. It was gratifying to see a low wrought-iron fence along the edge of the Nile, put there on his instructions to prevent a drowning accident, for Horatia was finally living under his roof. It was to her room he went first, not Emma's.

The little girl was awake, still in her night-clothes, a bright-eyed four-year-old and talking. Books lay about the place and Emma's cousin, Sarah Connors, who was governess to the little girl, could report that she was a precocious reader, could already speak a bit of French as well as English, was of a good temperament and lively. The child had not seen her father for sixteen months, but she surveyed him without suspicion, and showed no hint of fear in her startling green eyes.

✽

'Nelson, you cunning dog', cried Emma. 'Why did you not alert me to your coming?'

She was out of bed in a flash, covering his face with kisses before trying to pull him back in to her still warm, rumpled bed.

'I travelled ahead of my own news, my love,' he replied.

Nelson was resisting her, refusing to be dragged into bed. Having looked forward to this moment he wanted to savour it, but he could see by the look in Emma's eyes that she thought him reluctant and he relented. Their love-making was swift and to Nelson, strangely unsatisfying. It was as if he had endowed the moment with too much and it could not meet his expectations.

Emma was conscious of this too, because she became sad, moaning that with her loss, and the resultant change of shape, she had forfeited his affection. Nelson soothed her as best he could because, truly, it was not her fault that the expected child had been stillborn, or that the difficult birth had affected her body. Indeed, there was more of Emma than there had been when he left: her waist had thickened and her breasts seemed a good third larger. Even her face was rounder, but her eyes were the same, as was her smile when he had comforted her fears. Her sunny nature could not abide gloom for long.

Nelson knew that for sailors who were away for months, sometimes years, change in those close to them was no gradual thing, it was sudden and could be shocking. It was commonplace to find a gross figure instead of the slim bride from whom they had parted, and grey hair that had been fair. Children as old as five might be looking at their father for the first time, and any child that had existed before a voyage was quite different on return. The sailor reunited was not the same fellow who had set out: men came back sick, and sometimes so changed by experience as to be unrecognisable.

He had come back to Emma expecting her to have changed, just as he expected her to see a difference in him. What he could not do, what she wanted he supposed, was to pretend he had not noticed. But parting was not all disadvantage: there was much to talk about, and usually ample time to do it. A good leave of several months saw marked differences mellow into mutual acceptance; the lover became familiar again and the sailor no longer looked for the person who had once been.

Letters had flown to the whole family, which caused them to gather post haste and fill his house with the sound he cherished; that of people he loved and who loved him chattering, eating, playing, drinking and gently arguing. Merton was truly paradise now. The adjoining fields had been bought and he had pasture for cows, sheep and horses, a vegetable garden that was flourishing under Cribb's careful hand, the beginning of an orchard and a hothouse in which to grow more exotic plants.

He had Emma and Horatia, who, with their guests, dined off china plates decorated with Nelson's armorial bearings, and silver cutlery to go with it. His long polished table was set with heavy candelabra and he, at the head and in civilian clothes, could imagine this life going on for ever, unchanging and very English.

That might have been the case had his service relationships remained unchanged, but they had not, which was obvious from his first interview with the new First Lord of the Admiralty. Admiral Lord Barham had replaced St Vincent when William Pitt had returned as Prime Minister the year before. He had commanded ships before Nelson was born, but had not been active at sea for thirty-five years. Yet Barham was held in high regard in the Navy as the man who had done much to improve the operations of the service.

In the 1780s, his reforms had ensured that when war threatened, Britain, rather than taking months, as they had for decades, could get a fleet to sea in weeks. Nelson had praised Barham in the past, and was prone to like him now, but two men who might have got on famously had a problem. They had to deal with the grit of that business of Sir John Orde and the Spanish plate fleet.

'You agree, sir, that the Cadiz station has hitherto been the province of the commander of the Mediterranean Fleet.'

'That is so, Lord Nelson,' said Barham. For an old man he was handsome, polished, with a warm, deep voice. What he was not, to Nelson's way of thinking, was entirely honest.

'Therefore,' Nelson continued, 'to send a squadron of ships to that place would, under normal circumstances, be seen as an addition to my strength.'

'It would, but the circumstances were not normal.'

'In what way?

'Well, Sir John Orde is too senior to be put under your command.'

'When I heard he had sailed I anticipated replacement.'

'Then the money he has from his Spanish captures would have gone to him anyway.'

'And to his fleet, Lord Barham,' said Nelson testily. 'You may feel that I am here remonstrating on my own behalf but I am not.'

Barham's blue eyes were hard, as was his jaw. 'I trust you are not so unwise as to remonstrate? I would remind you that I am your

369

superior officer and the person to whom the government has entrusted the good of the service.'

Nelson had argued with senior officers before, and the prospect held no terrors for him. 'We can argue about words, sir. What we cannot dispute is that Sir John Orde was given a squadron of ships, and was expressly gifted an independent command to the station on which huge amounts of prize money were there for the taking. We cannot dispute that the area in question was and should have been my responsibility, nor that the officers and men of the Mediterranean Fleet have been cheated out of a substantial sum of prize money.'

Barham agreed with Nelson, but his position debarred him from saying so. How could he tell the man that the affair was wrapped up in politics; that with Pitt and Addington jockeying to form a stable government Sir John Orde, who was not, as a sailor, much entitled to distinction, had been gifted that station because of his connections? In effect, a small party of wavering Members of Parliament had extracted his appointment as a price for their support of the Pitt ministry.

Sir John Orde stood to make half a million pounds out of his capture, while Nelson, who should have had half of that, would get nothing. He might claim that he was angry on behalf of his inferior officers and seamen, all of whom would have stood to gain, but he had every right to be furious on his own account.

'Has the prize money been paid out, sir?'

'No, it has not.'

'Then I demand that the Board look at the matter again.'

Barham the sailor would have said no, because there was no point. The Board would not budge to oblige Nelson unless extreme pressure was applied. Where would that come from? Not the King, who was now mad and disliked Nelson anyway; not the Prince Regent, who had taken the now wealthy Orde into his bosom as a companion, not Pitt, who needed the wavering vote to hold his government together.

But Barham the politician said, 'I think that is as it should be. Now I suggest we move on to other matters.'

Discussing naval tactics, the two men got on a lot better. Barham had a shrewd brain and agreed with Nelson that no good would come of pure blockade. It ruined the British Fleet to keep ships and men at sea all year round, and it was impossible to guarantee that the enemy would never get out, because at some time the wind must favour them by blowing their gaolers off station.

What Barham wanted was the same as Nelson: to draw the enemy to a place where they could be beaten and the spectre of invasion, so deleterious to the nation, lifted for good. He had spun a cunning web based on his own certainty that the only place where the French could safely combine was outside the sphere where Britain had control, namely the West Indies. He had it on good authority that Villeneuve had gone there in the expectation of meeting his fellow admirals from Brest and Rochefort. They had, however, failed to get to sea and make the rendezvous.

'Villeneuve, with the Dons, outnumbers any squadron we can put against them. Calder had a chance to scupper that but did not.'

If Barham was asking him to comment on the fighting competence of another officer, Nelson was not going to oblige, but when Barham asked who should take command of his squadron, he said, 'Admiral Collingwood, without a doubt.' 'Coll' Collingwood was an old West Indian friend, a man with whom he had shared a house as a lieutenant. He might not be the gayest of men, but he was a fighter and he had taken over from Calder when he had come home to demand a court martial. 'If Collingwood gets a crack at the enemy, you'll have your victory for certain.'

Barham lifted a silver eyebrow at that, and Nelson said, 'I have been sixteen months at sea, sir, and I would not be lying to you if I said that I am worried about the sight of my one good eye. My doctors have been invited to operate but I fear that there is no margin for error, no other good eye to take its place, so they hesitate.'

'That is wise of them, Lord Nelson, and I will take on board what you say about Collingwood. I think we should meet again in a day or two, when I am sure I will have more information regarding enemy dispositions.'

'Thank you, sir,' said Nelson, standing up. 'And you will put your mind to the matter of Orde's prize money?'

'Most assiduously.'

Barham stood to see his visitor out, certain that there was only one man to command the fleet of Cadiz, one man who would soothe the fearful voters of the cities and the shires, and that was Nelson himself.

When they met Pitt said the same thing. The Prime Minister was not so sure that Nelson's tactics were correct: he inclined to the notion of close blockade, 'For if they get together, Lord Nelson, they might amass a fleet we cannot contend with.'

'There is no such fleet, sir,' said Nelson, with utter conviction.

Two days later, while waiting to see Mulgrave, the Secretary of State for War, Nelson found himself sharing the anteroom with a hook-nosed army officer of quite staggering arrogance. The man, a general, sat ramrod stiff, and gave Nelson no more than a nod on entry, which got under his skin. After all, he was not hard to place with one eye, one arm and wearing his now famous *Chelenk*. Nelson was not prepared to be condescended to and initiated a conversation designed to rile the man.

'I think, don't you, sir, that the Navy stands in well with the country?'

'I'm sure it does.'

Nelson had met a few good soldiers in his time, but many more that to him were a disgrace to the uniform they wore. It was all about purchase, of course: with bought commissions the Army got the officers it could afford while the Navy had men it had trained from near childhood.

'With good reason, sir. The Glorious First, Camperdown, my own humble contributions at St Vincent, the Nile and Copenhagen.'

'Algeciras Bay, let us not forget that,' said the soldier quickly.

'The Army, however?' Nelson shrugged.

The general, who had been staring straight ahead, turned to look directly at Nelson, his eyes steady and penetrating. There was a faint glimmer of recognition in Nelson's mind, the feeling that he had seen that face somewhere before, yet he knew that the man had never served close to him.

'Perhaps, sir, if we were to flog our men more. I will not refer to the other practices for which the King's Navy is so rightly famous.'

Nelson flushed angrily, but instead of replying he stood up and left the room, enquiring of the clerk outside, 'Who is that officer in there?'

'General Sir Arthur Wellesley, milord.'

'Is he, by damn?' said Nelson, grinning. 'The victor of Assaye. I think I have just been put it in my place, and deservedly so.'

With that he re-entered the anteroom and, still standing, said, 'I fear I owe you an apology Sir Arthur.' Those unblinking eyes were upon him again. 'I must tell you that in my career I have met a lot of Army officers who leave a great deal to be desired in the article of application.'

There was just a trace of a smile at the edge of the mouth. 'I doubt Lord Nelson, that you have met as many as I.'

'Does that mean my apology is accepted?'

'Without reservation, sir.'

Nelson sat down again, facing Wellesley. 'I would be obliged to hear an account of your battle against Tipoo Sultan.'

Wellesley relaxed visibly. 'And I would appreciate a telling of how you fought at Copenhagen.'

'Not the Nile?' said Nelson, since that was the one usually requested.

'Copenhagen was a much more complex affair, and as a success, if you will permit me to say so, much more interesting to a military mind.'

Wellesley could not have said anything to please Nelson more. He, too, thought it a more complex battle. He also knew that it had gone unappreciated, a battle in which the Royal Navy had displayed qualities of raw courage and seamanship unparalleled in the annals of the nation.

'I do agree, Lord Nelson, for I see it, if you will forgive me, like a land battle. The outflanking manoeuvre, the taking of the enemy where their defence was weakest, the isolation to the point of futility of their main force.'

Nelson loved to talk of all naval battles, not just his own, and he was proud of Copenhagen. He employed the table and all the furbelows in the room to describe it, and Sir Arthur Wellesley asked some pretty pertinent questions, not least why the Danes had not done anything to respond to his movements.

'The command was too rigid. We found out afterwards that the Crown Prince had control over the orders all the way down to the rank of lieutenant.'

'With no military experience?' asked Wellesley.

'None.'

For the first time Sir Arthur grinned. 'Perhaps we should offer him a commission in the British Army.'

'Assaye,' said Nelson.

The clerk who came to fetch him to Lord Mulgrave found the two still at the table, Nelson wrapped up in the problem of fighting native armies on the Indian sub-continent, mentally astride an elephant riding into battle as the men of Hannibal had done two thousand years before. Now he had to stand: it was not possible to keep the Minister for War waiting.

'Sir Arthur, it has been a pleasure to meet you. Should I ever have to ask for a military officer to assist the Navy rest assured it will be you.'

'Hah!', exclaimed Wellesley. 'And wait till I tell my nephews and nieces that I spent time with Viscount Nelson. I shall be a hero to them for that alone. Assaye be damned!'

✸

'You say that you love me, Nelson, but as soon as an offer comes to go, you cannot fly from my side quick enough.' Emma said this gaily, her arm hooked through his as he walked in his garden, taking the last of the evening sun, but there was just a hint of anxiety behind it. How could he explain that Lord Barham had insisted, that with Villeneuve and the combined Spanish/French fleet now moved to Cadiz, tailed by Collingwood, the best chance of a battle lay there and the Admiralty wanted Nelson present? How could he say that he had accepted because he had formulated ideas that no other admiral would employ, not even those for whom he had the greatest regard?

The only way to stop French hopes was to destroy French ambition, and that meant the destruction of their fleet – not a ship or two taken and a withdrawal, but another Nile, this time in open sea. If he could do it he would have fulfilled the dream he had all those years ago, while suffering from malaria on the way back from Calcutta. He would be the greatest man in the nation, able to rise above the pettiness of those who refused to receive the woman he loved.

There was something else too: naked ambition and the residue of that daredevil boy who had gone to sea at thirteen. He craved success, and now he would have the means and the methods to achieve it. Like all good leaders he was prone to ask himself if he had the right to risk men's lives as a commanding officer. His answer was simple, better that he risk them than someone without his ability.

'Vanity,' he said, speaking without thinking.

'Vanity takes you to sea? Emma asked.

'No, I was thinking of something else.'

She stopped and pinched his ear. 'How dare you, Nelson, think of anything else when I am here?'

He smiled and kissed her cheek. 'It is a rare thing indeed when I do.'

It wasn't the first time Emma had teased him about his love of the sea, and he had long since tired of trying to manoeuvre for an acceptable answer. The truth was simple: he was a sailor, and lived in a strange half-world that was never complete. A few days at sea, and a sailor longed for the land: on shore too long and nothing could suppress the hankering to be away.

He was happy here at Merton, but not unreservedly so. Like any man, there were things that disturbed and perplexed him. He loved Emma deeply yet could not comprehend so many things about her. Why did she not share his deep need for the company of Horatia? He was wise enough to know that the child tended to take all his attention, which Emma disliked, and had long ago decided that the mother was as much a child in her way as their daughter. She had taken to gambling again, and he had also noticed since being home that she was drinking too much. Her extravagance had forced him to put Horatia's money beyond her control because he suspected that if she had it she would spend it. The recent loss of the child must have affected her, of course, and Sir William was not here to advise her.

But it was more than that he knew. Emma lived in a limbo of being neither wife nor lover, the latter because he was away at sea. The undertone of her correspondence these last eighteen months had hinted at an underlying unhappiness about her position, one that could not be regularised unless Fanny died, and Nelson had to admit that that was unlikely.

He had come home this time with half a mind to retire, but even that did not provide a solution, because Emma would still be subjected to malice. Some people would never accept her for what she was, would only see her past. Nelson reckoned that to be happy, to be a family in the sense that he desired, they could no longer live in an England where the association was frowned upon.

It was a problem that would only get worse as Horatia grew older. Emma was fecund; perhaps there would be another child. He wanted his daughter, and any other child, to have his name, to be acknowledged openly as his offspring, and to end this constant hiding away that had them living in separate lodgings when in London.

He had his estates still in Brontë, and though that gift from Ferdinand had been a drain on his finances rather than an asset, it was there to be exploited. The only barrier to that was that he had employed an agent to run it, and all the money it earned had gone on improvements. Perhaps with him there, and a new man of business to run the place, he could make it pay.

At least it would be warm, for Nelson had reached an age were he dreaded the English winter. The damp ate into him and he had to admit that his prospects for service at sea were rapidly diminishing. His eye worried him: he was not going blind yet, but he was approaching the point where for him to command a fleet would put his ships in more danger than any Frenchman could.

'This will be my last command, Emma.'

That stopped her. They were under a tree, out of the sunlight, and it was cold enough here to make him shiver. Emma was looking at him with those entrancing green eyes. He started to talk about his concerns, articulating things he had only up till then thought about.

'There will be a battle and, God willing I will be there, be it in a month or a year. But if not, I must come ashore. Another year at sea will be the death of me.'

Emma was not stupid – extravagant yes, flamboyant and mercurial, but underneath that ran a grain of sense. She knew that Nelson kept things from her, just as she knew that her behaviour sometimes annoyed him. He did not understand how insecure she felt. Sometimes at night, when he was at sea, especially after a letter that contained a modicum of criticism, she imagined him returning to his wife. If she had said that to him he would have laughed and called her foolish; but in the dark, alone, it frightened her.

Nelson had taken both her hands in his one. 'I wish to watch my child grow, and to be by your side, my love. You are, to me, my two beautiful girls, the most precious things on this earth.'

'How long do we have?'

'A day or two.'

36

It was a strange interlude, those remaining fourteen days, mostly spent in conference. Barham obliged him by letting him choose his own officers despite Nelson's assertion that any of the available captains would serve, that 'they were all of a one'. He sent a short note to Admiral Collingwood, telling him of his commission, with the hope that his old friend would stay as second in command.

In between, he was near to being hounded. It seemed once the news was out, everyone wanted to see him – the leader of the opposition Addington, now Lord Sidmouth, William Beckford, who came to Merton because Nelson had no time to accept a request to come Fonthill, among others. Invitations to dinner poured in, as well as appeals from various ministers to brief them on the situation. To all he said the same thing; that he hoped to be home by Christmas, with the combined fleets of the enemy well and truly trounced.

Emma was in limbo, keen to bolster Nelson's confidence, worried that his health might fail before he had had his battle, or that there would be no such thing, which would be an ignominious end to his career. Did he really mean to retire? Was she the cause of that or his health? Nelson was summoned to meet the Prince Regent at Carlton House, leaving Emma waiting for him in her London lodgings while he was called into the royal presence.

Prinny was fat, flabby and over-pomaded, sending out clouds of odour every time he moved. He tried to look regal and attempted to sound martial, but failed on both counts. He managed to imply that all good ideas flowed from him, perhaps even those of successful naval officers, which did nothing at all to endear him to the best of them. He caused even greater offence when he mentioned Emma, and asserted that she was still a damned handsome woman who had quite struck his fancy.

'Odd fellow, Nelson,' he said to his equerry, after the Admiral had left. 'I can quite see why my papa found him so tiresome. He has such vanity.'

His second meeting with the Prime Minister was of far more importance to Nelson, who was thankful that Pitt had come round to his way of thinking: Let us get the French out, then let us fight them. But he had another request to make, though when he spoke of his health he had to acknowledge that Pitt looked worse than he did.

'I will do everything in my power to bring our enemies to battle but the means I will employ will expose every commanding officer to a great danger.'

'I have heard a battle described Lord Nelson, and it sounded bloody enough, although I suspect words cannot do it justice.'

'You will have been told that in a fight the quarterdeck is the most dangerous place to be.'

Pitt looked grave. 'Which is where you will be, I take it.'

Nelson managed a smile, but in his mind he was thinking of how lucky he had been. Always he had imposed on the enemy, and it had been their commanders struck down, not him. But enough of his own companions had died in battle, and that piece of flying langridge that had hit him at the Nile, a bit lower, would have decapitated him. He was not worried for himself: the risk of death or injury was ever present to a serving officer in war, and did not signify because no one could be effective in a fight and worry about such things.

'You will be aware sir, that I am a partisan of Lady Emma Hamilton.'

The word partisan was odd to Pitt, who nodded. He would have called it something else.

'Then you may be aware that since the death of her husband she has become dependent on me.' Another nod. 'I also have responsibility for a child we have close to adopted, a sweet girl who, I hope, one day, might marry one of my nephews.'

Pitt was well versed in listening without responding, and it bothered him not at all that Nelson was being less than wholly truthful. He understood the need for discretion.

'I would venture to say that this child, should anything happen to me, would be too heavy a burden for Lady Hamilton to bear. It will not have escaped your attention that I have submitted on more than one occasion a memorandum detailing why she of all the people I know should be looked on favourably by the government for a pension.'

Pitt had read one, though he struggled to remember what Emma Hamilton had done.

'I believe she was in many ways the equal of her late husband in the execution of his office. Since the government over which you presided saw fit to grant Sir William a pension, it is my request that Lady Hamilton should have the continuation of that.'

'For services in Naples.'

'And Palermo.'

Pitt was good at silence too and he employed that now, this while Nelson recalled that the year before he had also petitioned Maria Carolina of Naples to do something for Emma. The reply, in which 'Dear Emma' was not mentioned, proved that royalty, both at home and abroad, had short memories.

Pitt knew what Nelson was saying. Should anything happen to him, he wanted Lady Hamilton and his daughter looked after. 'It is a matter to which I will give my most earnest consideration, Lord Nelson.'

The look in Pitt's eyes, plus the knowledge that he was a man who had a care about making commitments, was confirmation to Nelson that he was speaking the truth. 'Then I am content, sir.'

Pitt stood up, the interview over. 'Please be assured Admiral that I wish you all the speed and luck that God can muster. It is no exaggeration to say that you go forth with the fate of the nation upon your shoulders.'

'I merely carry that to the fleet, sir,' Nelson replied, standing also. 'There, what feels like a heavy weight now becomes tolerable by being shared amongst the best men in the kingdom.'

'Will you permit me to walk with you to your carriage?'

'I would be honoured,' replied Nelson, who doubted even the King was afforded that kind of courtesy from his First Lord of the Treasury.

No amount of partings can make them easier. He had left Emma a dozen or more times now, and always with feelings that had knotted his stomach. Emma was the same, anxious but working to hide it. There was little flaming passion, a slow and sweet love-making followed by a long night of talking about the future with the moon shining through the open curtains; his notion that they could not stay at Merton, that Brontë might be better for them. The possibility of death was not mentioned, and no decisions were made, but they

379

speculated on alternatives. Perhaps he could have that eye operation, perhaps something would change to make their life together better. Nelson killed in his mind the blasphemous thought that Fanny might expire; Emma did not.

'I love the life we have now, my dear, but I wish to see you acknowledged beside me. I want everyone to know how much you inspire me. How many times have I said that if there were more Emmas there would be more Nelsons?'

'Too many times, I fear. It makes people yawn with repetition.'

'Then they are fools who do not see sense when it stares at them. Do you remember the day we met, at the Palazzo Sessa?'

'How can I forget it, Nelson? My stomach still churns at the memory.'

'And that day when I fled from Naples?' He could see it now, the sunshine, the blue water, the shade under the awning, him close to Emma a little way off from everybody else, his blood racing. 'And to think I slung the King and Queen off dear *Agamemnon*.'

'Sir William was horrified at first,' said Emma, with the deep chuckle that Nelson loved to hear. 'But I recall he said to me how much you had impressed him by your zealous behaviour.'

'That makes me blush to the roots. If he had known the real reason.'

'Are you sure it was me?'

'It was not the French. I fled from you, and what I might do, not towards them. I wonder if anyone aboard suspected?'

'What about your servant, Lepée?'

'Too drunk to notice. He was four sheets to the wind before you ever came on to my deck.'

The conversation had been like this before when he was going to sea, a remembrance of the things that they had shared, the memories that Nelson insisted would bind them together into old age.

'There we will be, Nelson, you and I, doddering.'

'We shall never fail to make our bed.'

'Dowager me.'

'And I the country squire.'

'Having your wicked way with the milkmaid.'

'Emma!'

'You will have to do it by feel, of course,' Emma laughed, fondling him, 'you being blind, happen you'll end up milking instead of . . .'

'Emma.'

'Prude, Nelson.'

'I am, I admit it.'

'But still a man,' said Emma, her voice low and throaty. 'Every inch.'

'You should sleep, my love.'

'That I can do tomorrow.'

Nelson left in the cold dawn light with his servant, well wrapped up against the autumn morning chill. He had already visited Horatia's room to look at her and bestow a gentle kiss on her brow, to touch her small open hand and look into the sweet innocence of a sleeping child. Now he and Emma stood under the porch, he in his boat cloak, she in a dressing gown, trying and failing not to shiver.

'Come back to me soon.'

'Weeks, not months, I swear it.' He kissed her hand. 'To my most noble lady.'

There was mist over the river Nile, spilling on to the lawns, and the trees looked damp and forlorn in the grey light. Emma stood and waved until the sound of wheels on gravel was no more, then went back to bed to cry the tears she never let Nelson know of when he went to sea.

There was such a crowd at Portsmouth that he considered taking a boat from Southsea Beach to avoid them. But their faith in him obliged Nelson to leave by the sally-port, a way cleared for him by marines. The talk of the crowd, as he descended the steps to his waiting barge, was a mixture of 'Good lucks' and 'God Bless', and 'if you see my Arthur, your honour, tell him to stay sound.'

It was always a matter of pride to Nelson that he could look these people in the eye, the wives, sweethearts, brothers, sisters and sons of his sailors. On taking up his present command, he had found in the Mediterranean a fleet in some distress, not least in a band of sailors hankering for home, and suffering scurvy as well as all the ailments brought on by despondency. He had cured their bodies and their minds, and could boast how few of his men died on his commission. They had sailed to the West Indies in forty-six days, lopping a good ten off Admiral Villeneuve. And they had come home even quicker, in twenty-eight, showing what British tars could do in the article of ship-handling. And in six thousand round miles, not one man had been lost. Admiral Lord Nelson cared for their menfolk as much as they did themselves

He stood in his boat so that they could see him, not from vanity, but because there was fear in those breasts, not surprising in a naval town that mourned after every battle. *Victory* was out on the mother shoal of Spithead, securely anchored, having had few of the repairs he had hoped for after eighteen months at sea. He thought of the fleet he was about to take over, and that, allied to the sight of his flagship, yards crossed and ready in all respects for sea, lifted his heart.

They manned the yards when they saw him coming, the whole fleet cheering. Every ship saluted with thirteen guns, as was his right, the seascape full of puffs of smoke as all the vessels vied with each other to complete the honour first. Even stone-faced Hardy was amazed enough to comment. 'See how they love you, milord. They know with you here there will be a fight.'

'Damn it Hardy, I love them more than they love me. If Villeneuve could see this now he would scuttle.'

'I reckon you to be right there, sir.'

'Coll, you will not believe this but Hardy actually smiled,' Nelson said, to his old friend and second in command. Then he realised that Cuthbert Collingwood was no smiler either, and changed the subject. In fact, he was about to change a great many of his friend's orders. Collingwood took as his example men like St Vincent, who believed, when on blockade, in iron discipline: no inter-ship visiting, no buying of goods from the boats that carried fresh produce from the North African coast. And he of all people had to be persuaded to accept Nelson's plan.

'Do you agree, Coll, that no day is long enough to arrange a couple of fleets to fight a battle, certainly not according to the old system?'

'When, Nelson, have you ever paid heed to the old system?'

Collingwood had been behind him when he pulled out of the line at St Vincent, a total breach of the Fighting Instructions, an act that might have seen him shot after a court martial if things had gone wrong.

'Not often, I grant you. But it is even more pressing here, where dawn comes late and darkness early. We have no time for dispositions.'

He used the same words to his captains over two nights as they joined him for dinner. 'The fleet will sail in two divisions gentlemen, one under my command and one under Admiral Collingwood in *Royal Sovereign*. The order of sailing is the order of attack.

It was pleasant to pause then, to let it sink in just how much Nelson planned to deviate from the previous method of engaging an enemy. 'There will be no time to form a line of battle, and if we did so you must all realise we would be outnumbered. Our enemies have a third more ships than we do, and if we lay our ships in line to windward, as our still extant instructions tell us we should, we will never get close. That is what happened to Admiral Calder, and it will not happen to me. I want to go at them about a third from the head of their line, with the second division taking its point of attack ahead of the enemy's rear admiral. Thus we cut off the executive head and isolate what must be Villeneuve's best ships in such numbers that we can double up on them. I want no formality, gentlemen, but a pell-mell battle where our seamanship and gunnery will win the day.

Nelson waited, but no one spoke for a whole half minute. Then they started, voices full of excitement and approbation, men who were sure that they were at a point in history that had never before been seen; that the whole nature of naval warfare had just been turned on its head.

'Once the frigates have told us the enemy is out we will close with them. They will assume they have time to clear but our immediate approach will deny them the luxury. In line ahead we will break theirs. They have to be sailing on a wind, so their lead ships will struggle to come round and effectively be out of the battle. Thus the odds are redressed. The rear division will have to come up under the threat of our attacking ships dropping back from the point we breach the line to engage them.'

His one good eye ranged around the table, to be greeted with open enthusiasm and not a hint of dissent. No one wanted to say to him that he was taking a terrible risk because they wanted to take it with him. Not one captain or junior admiral wanted to point out that this was his first fleet action at sea: the Nile and Copenhagen had been static.

'Gentlemen, this is war, and no battle will follow some paper plan. If I am gifted the right, I will aim *Victory* ahead of Villeneuve's flag, to come down his windward side. What ship takes him on the other quarter is for its captain to decide, for nothing is certain in a sea fight. Shot will carry away masts and spars of friends as well as foes. I place my trust in my God, the arms of my country, and you.'

It was all anxiety from then on, waiting for action, seeing to his fleet, the need, since they were short of wood and water, to send six-of-the-line away under Admiral Louis, a less than happy old Crocodile who was sure he was going to miss the battle. Nelson moved his ships away from Cadiz, his heavier three deckers and the slower ships fifty miles off shore, behind a screen of fast sailing 74s, which were kept out of sight from the land, while inshore Captain Blackwood kept watch with his squadron of frigates, often right inshore.

Nelson was anxious, as always, for more frigates: they were the eyes of the fleet, the one thing that would ensure that Villeneuve could not slip out in a mist or foul weather and get away unobserved. If the combined fleet got into the Mediterranean, then the mischief they could make, with the addition of more ships from Cartagena, would be incalculable, while Viscount Nelson, forced to chase, would be made to look a fool.

Nelson received intelligence that the allies had got their soldiers on board, then that the combined fleet had been warped out of the inner harbour and were now bending on their topgallant yards. He could not know that in sending Louis away to revictual he had left Villeneuve thinking that his strength was diminished, that the opportunity had presented itself to bring overwhelming strength to bear on the British fleet.

On deck, during the day, he was pleased to see many of the ships being painted, trying to copy the buff and black chequer effect that had been achieved on the *Victory*, which would make them recognisable in a close-quarter fight. The day that rain came was one of deep frustration for them because the paint ran, and for Nelson, who feared that the closed-in weather would give his enemies a chance to do the same.

'Sail bearing nor, nor west, sir.'

It did not take much to get an anxious admiral on deck and he was up before the vessel, now actually two since she had a frigate in company, was identified as HMS *Agamemnon*.

'Berry by God,' he cried. 'There's always a fight where he is. Now we will have our battle.'

Five ships-of-the-line had joined, making up for Louis's absence. He was not equal to his foe, but Nelson reckoned the odds enough. More days went by, and he dealt as he had to with the problems attendant on being a commander-in-chief. And then it came, the signal he had been waiting for, that the enemy was at sea. Immediately he wrote to Emma and Horatia.

Nelson covered the mouth of the Straits of Gibraltar, that being Villeneuve's likely route, to break though there and make for Toulon, sailing to the north-west. Being a Sunday he agreed to divine service, but not in a way that interfered with preparations for battle.

With no sight of the enemy they ploughed on, eyes peeled. Blackwood had a line of four frigates repeating signals, through *Defence*, *Colossus* and on to *Victory*, thirty-three enemy capital ships under constant observation. The temptation to close with them was strong, but he wanted them well away from a safe harbour so forced himself to be patient. During the night, thinking he had drawn them far enough from Cadiz, Nelson altered course, preparatory to attack.

The state of the sea was worsening, with a heavy swell setting in from the west, but there was no excess of wind. As dawn broke they saw the enemy, a forest of masts ten miles to leeward. The signal was made to form two columns, with the Admiral cock a hoop. As soon as he sighted Nelson, Villeneuve bore away, turning back for Cadiz. Superior in ships, and even more in cannon, the Frenchman was running away.

'You are too late on this wind, my friend,' Nelson cried. 'I think I have you.'

His frigate captains came aboard, led by Captain Henry Black-wood, who Nelson recalled as a midshipman so timid on his first voyage that he had had to lead him to the masthead. He was not that now; he was a clear-sighted and fearless warrior. While they were aboard Nelson wrote a final letter, his last testament, just as he had done before every action. Everyone in the fleet who could write would do the same, while the illiterate would make other arrangements. Nelson's was to the point, naming Sir William and Lady Hamilton and the poor recompense they had had from their country for outstanding services. He had it witnessed by Hardy as the last of his goods were being struck below.

In full dress uniform, garlanded with his orders of chivalry, he went round the ship congratulating, encouraging, arguing about the number of prizes to be taken that day, making jokes, giving advice, wondering secretly how many of these men would be still there to laugh that night. Before departing, Blackwood suggested Nelson come aboard his ship *Euryalus*, but that invitation was declined for the poor example it would set.

'Farewell Blackwood, I will not speak with you again except by flags.'

Back on deck it was clear the wind was falling, which did not bode well. Both his divisions would be sailing bowsprit-on to a waiting enemy, which would leave them exposed to a withering fire before they could engage, so Nelson ordered Hardy to get up more sail.

Back in his cabin he had to kneel on the floor to write a personal letter to Emma, lifting his head as his lover's portrait was removed from the wall, telling his men to take care of his 'Guardian Angel'. Then he took up his pocketbook, left it on his writing desk, the only piece of furniture remaining, in which he would pen whatever took his fancy from now on. That, at this moment, was a prayer.

May the Great God, whom I worship, grant to me and my country, and for the benefit of Europe in general, a great and glorious victory; and may no misconduct in anyone tarnish it; and may humanity after victory be the predominant feature in the British fleet. For myself, individually, I commit my life to Him who made me, and may his blessing light upon my endeavours for serving my country faithfully. To Him I resign myself and the just cause which is entrusted to me to defend, Amen.

'Signal Admiral Collingwood that I intend to pass through the enemy van to prevent him getting into Cadiz.'

Slowly but surely the clouds were lifting and soon the first shafts of sunlight turned the gently heaving Atlantic waters blue. On various decks bands began to play and the sailors, with nothing to do but wait until action was joined, began to dance hornpipes below decks.

'Lieutenant Pasco,' he said.

'Sir,' replied the signal lieutenant, who was no less than that same pale-faced midshipman who had been a favourite of Emma.

'I think it time to amuse the fleet. I wish you to signal to all ships a message, that England confides that every man will do his duty, and be quick, because we must get up the signal for close action before we engage.'

'With respect, sir, might I suggest substituting "expects" for "confides". That word is in the signal book and will save seven hoists.'

'Make it so, Mr Pasco.'

It went up, and, once read out, the sound of cheers floated across the water. The ship astern, the *Téméraire*, was coming alongside, already her bowsprit was level with the front rail of the poop. Unbeknown to Nelson, his captains had decided that he was putting himself unnecessarily in danger by leading the division and they had evolved a plan to confound him. Seeing this Nelson picked up a speaking trumpet and called, 'Captain Harvey, you will oblige me by keeping your proper station, which is astern of the flag.'

He had looked over the side then, at the increase in the swell and how it might affect his ships. 'Another signal, Mr Pasco, to prepare to anchor after the action. I believe we have some foul weather on the way. And then Mr Pasco, number sixteen if, you please. Close action.'

'Aye aye, sir.'

'Captain Hardy, see how Admiral Collingwood carries his ship into action.' With a newly coppered bottom free of weed, *Royal Sovereign* was racing clear of her consorts, and Nelson, looking at Hardy, saw he had taken that as an admonition, and was gazing aloft to see if he could carry more sail.

'Poor Hardy,' Nelson said to himself. 'Ever the one to worry,'

'Sir,' Hardy said, 'your coat.'

'What of it, man?'

'It is too conspicuous, the stars and the like.'

'I have no time to change it.'

Hardy turned to a midshipman and ordered him below to fetch a plain coat for the Admiral. Suspecting they had all been struck below by Chevalier, Nelson belayed that order. 'Let the men see me, Hardy,' he cried.

Hardy came closer, so that he could speak in a lower voice. 'Sir, they will have men in the tops.'

'Then I hope they set their damn ships afire.'

Nelson disliked marines on the fighting caps, simply because as the attacking fleet he would always carry a greater press of sail than his foes. And to his mind they were in just the right place to set fire to the canvas with their flaming wads. One sail alight was all it took, if a man was not careful, to have the whole ship ablaze and going up like *L'Orient*.

It was silent below decks now; the bands and hornpipes had ceased. The cutlass blades and pikes were sharpened, the guns had all the powder and shot they could safely employ. Men stood poised on the sanded deck, occasionally dipping heads to look at the approaching enemy. Every twelve feet on the main deck had a cannon, and there was nothing else but those and what they needed to fight.

The smell was an odd one: human sweat, smouldering slowmatch, bilge, the tang of the sea coming through the ports. On the deck Nelson sensed this, the odour of anticipation which had no other expression but at times like these. He looked aloft and was surprised to see that the yards were clear of birds, another indication that a storm was approaching and that the sea birds had headed inland to avoid it.

His heart was near breaking with pride, for he knew that this day he had the enemy where he wanted them. He would have his battle and if it were successful he would have an indelible place in his country's pantheon. All his cares would end when the combined fleets of France and Spain were beaten. Everyone would have to accept his beloved Emma for what she was and his daughter would be a lady, the love-child of Britain's most famous peer.

Nelson was so happy he could have cried. He wanted at least

twenty prizes; he wanted to smash the power of Bonaparte's France. He recalled his mother then, and her words, 'For God must surely hate a Frenchman.'

Horatio Nelson did not hate them: he was too much of a Christian for that and no French survivor would want for anything in the way of charity from the British Royal Navy. But his nation had been at war with France for too many years out of the last five hundred. The ghosts of Edward of Crecy, the Black Prince, King Harry and a dozen admirals like Blake were with him now. He felt immortal.

The first cannons spoke, two ships opening up on the speedy Collingwood. He heard the Ghost say, 'Note the time.'

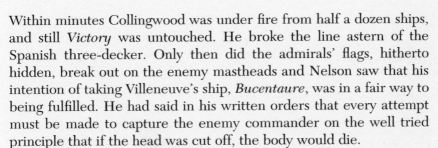

37

Within minutes Collingwood was under fire from half a dozen ships, and still *Victory* was untouched. He broke the line astern of the Spanish three-decker. Only then did the admirals' flags, hitherto hidden, break out on the enemy mastheads and Nelson saw that his intention of taking Villeneuve's ship, *Bucentaure*, was in a fair way to being fulfilled. He had said in his written orders that every attempt must be made to capture the enemy commander on the well tried principle that if the head was cut off, the body would die.

The ships ahead began firing broadsides, some high seeking to damage his rigging and slow him down, or carry away something so vital that *Victory* would become unmanageable. Those aimed at the hull were short but holes began to appear in the upper sails. Nelson heard them counted out, but stopped listening when the enumerator passed thirty.

The next broadsides were more deadly, sweeping across the upper deck, killing many including Nelson's secretary. A file of eight marines went down to another, like skittles at a fair, and Nelson heard Hardy curse as a splinter hit his foot.

'This is too warm work, Hardy, to last too long.'

Neither wound nor comment did anything to distract Hardy from the task at hand. He was steering to pass between the bowsprit of *Bucentaure* and the stern of the giant *Santissima Trinidad*, the 136-gun ship that Nelson well remembered from St Vincent.

'I long to have her, Hardy,' Nelson called, pointing at the towering Spaniard, 'for she is a beauty and would look very well with my flag at the masthead.'

Another shot hit the wheel, smashing both it and the men conning the ship and Hardy called for the party on the lower deck manning the relieving tackles to take over the steering. Another salvo more saw to the mizzen topmast which was blown out of its chains to come crashing down at the front of the quarterdeck. *Bucentaure* had hoisted more sail and achieved a bit more speed. This forced Hardy to put his helm down and steer astern of her, a slow business as the orders had to be relayed through the decks before the men hauling on the ropes that now controlled the rudder could oblige. That gap narrowed to as ship astern, *Redoutable*, sought to shut it off.

Nelson watched, not sure if his stratagem was about to succeed. It was very possible that all *Victory* would do was collide with one of the French ships. Hardy was looking at him, requesting instructions, which caused him to shake his head. 'I can do nothing about this, Hardy. Go on board where you please.'

Knowing it would take time to change course Hardy, given permission by Nelson to risk a collision, held his line. The Ghost only just made it, scraping *Redoutable*'s side on the way through the enemy line, before Hardy called for the helm to be put down and allow him to come up on the other side of Villeneuve's flagship. On the way through the gap the men in charge of the quarterdeck carronades, sixty-pound smashers deadly at close range, responding to no more than a series of nods, opened up on *Bucentaure*'s stern, paying her back wholesale for the damage she had inflicted on *Victory* during the approach. The stern lights went to matchwood as the great balls demolished them, before they carried on down the French maindeck, wreaking havoc in a space where the main obstacle to their deadly passage was human flesh.

HMS *Neptune* went after the *Santissima Trinidad*, while *Téméraire* and *Leviathan* followed Nelson through, the latter scraping past the stern of *Redoutable*. Hardy was ranging alongside *Bucentaure* now and the maindeck cannon fired their first devastating salvo, some demolishing the French bulwarks while others, aimed high, ripped through the topsails and the yards that held them. Now rate of fire would tell, as the well-trained British gunners overwhelmed their opposition by sheer weight of metal. Guns were dismounted, masts sundered into deadly splinters that shot in all directions, the fighting caps and the men who occupied them blown to perdition while the area around the wheel was an abattoir. *Bucentaure*'s rigging hung in shreds and she could neither steer nor sail.

Victory was not the only ship pounding Villeneuve. Truly the Nelson touch was apparent as his ships doubled up on the enemy to render their vessels useless. The return fire slackened as battery after battery on the gun decks was blown apart, trapping men under turned over cannon in a confined space that had become a charnel house.

Through smoke and sound Nelson could see that Admiral Dumanoir, in command of the van, had allowed clear water to open between himself and his commanding admiral, and from what he could observe, was making no attempt to come round and rejoin the battle. This changed the odds decisively in Nelson' favour: he had begun with twenty line-of-battle ships to face Villeneuve's twenty-three – now more than a half dozen were sailing away from danger.

A sudden burst of shot swept across *Victory*'s deck as she closed with her next opponent, *Redoutable*. Nelson could just make out a side lined with muskets and from the way gouges were being sliced out of the deck he knew there were men in the French tops as well. What was more telling was that the enemy, with whom Hardy had locked yardarms, had closed his ports and was refusing to take part in a gunnery duel – new tactics to Nelson.

The amount of shot sweeping the deck was lethal and forced Hardy to send the upper deck gunners below. With the sides of the two ships no more than yards apart, every time *Victory* fired she started a blaze that had to be doused by the men who had just discharged the cannon.

Hardy had got close to Nelson, and begged him to go below – even in the smoke he stood out like a lamp in the night, with his stars and decoration glittering. Nelson shook his head and walked a step away, staring straight ahead. Hardy prepared to follow, turning briefly to give more orders that would get his officers to safety as well.

On a heaving fighting cap, with a ship rocking on an increasing swell while firing at another moving deck, marksmanship was not of the highest. That was multiplied by the nature of the weapon, of a shorter barrel length than a standard infantry musket. That had a damaging effect on a gun whose accuracy at full length over a distance of a hundred yards was poor. So the ball that took Nelson was not aimed; it was fired by a fellow reloading and letting fly as quickly as he could in the general direction of *Victory*'s quarterdeck. But accidental musket balls do just as much damage as those that are aimed.

Nelson felt it enter the front of his shoulder, a searing red hot pain, and he could follow that pain as the ball lanced through muscle and sinew heading downwards and across. He felt it crash into his spine and imagined he heard the crack as it shattered. His legs gave way so suddenly that he was well aware of what had happened to him.

Hardy turned back to see him on his knees, his head forward, his face contorted, his weight supported by three extended fingers. There was a split second when time stopped and he could not register that Nelson had been hit, because if ever a man deserved immortality it was the Ghost's hero. Then he knelt over him

'My backbone is shot through,' groaned Nelson.

Hardy yelled for help, but nothing happened, because all those close to him were deafened by the blast of gunfire. He had to physically grab people before his wounded Admiral could be rolled into a sheet of canvas by a couple of marines, who ignored the agony they were inflicting as they carried Nelson below. Hardy had to put that out of his mind and concentrate on what to do next. For some reason his guns had stopped firing and he must rectify that, because it could not be that they were out of action; receiving no fire from the enemy and seeing his gunports staying closed they must suppose that he had struck his colours.

Nothing was further from the reality – *Victory* was in great danger. He felt certain that the captain of the French ship intended to board. If they could take the upper deck they could take the ship, so Hardy sent below for those marines manning cannon to come up and form a defence. The men who emerged, tumbling up the companionway as a trumpet sounded from *Redoutable*, looked nothing like marines: not a red jacket in sight, just check shirts and ears clothed in tight bandannas. But they carried muskets and soon began to employ them, firing at will.

With a crash a yard came down from the French tops, no doubt cut away to form a bridge between the ships and a stream of blue-coated soldiers emerged from below decks on the enemy ship. Their own discipline, the tight formation they adopted prior to an attack, counted against them as muskets from the *Victory*'s decks began to decimate them. From the foredeck, word was passed to Hardy by a written note that some Frenchmen were trying to use the anchor, catted to the side of the ship by the bows, as a means of getting aboard. That was a threat that had to be met without weakening the defence of any other part of the ship.

All over the upper deck men were fighting now, muskets blasting into bodies that were pressed against the end of the barrel, sailors jabbing with pikes or swinging cutlasses and axes that cut through flesh. Each sound, a scream of agony, a yell of effort, a shout for mercy, with no roaring gunfire to mask it, reached Hardy's ears, only muffled by the effect cannon fire had had on his own hearing.

And in a very short time he knew he was winning, with more and more men coming up from below who could not but outnumber the attackers. It was a three-decker 110-gun ship against a two-decked 74. With a complement of over eight hundred men Hardy had a third more crew to deploy than his French opponent. The crash of cannon sounded again, not from below decks but from the leeward side of *Redoutable*, taking those crowding the French bulwarks in the back, blasting over the side those that it did not kill. Hardy thought he recognised the *Téméraire* but she was so shot about herself that he could not be sure. All he did know was that a friend was firing broadsides and doing great damage to the ship with which they were both engaged. Some of the British marines had got aloft in the *Victory*'s tattered rigging and were trying to pick off targets on a deck no more than forty feet away, and *Redoutable* was stuck fast now between two British ships.

Through smashed bulwarks on both vessels Hardy could see the piles of dead on the French deck, could see that his fighting men had repelled the boarders and were now engaging the enemy on their own vessel. There were men too deaf to hear the mizzenmast begin to tear and tumble on the *Redoutable*. They had come up from below, where the great thirty-six-pounder guns blasting off in a confined space rendered hearing impossible for days after a battle.

Many of them were firing off or reloading muskets when they died under a ten-ton weight of falling French timber, or were swept overboard by rigging or a spar. Attached to that was the French ship's ensign, and Hardy and his officers were not the only ones to see it. Those French still engaged did too and, assuming that their captain had struck his colours, they began to surrender.

It took a while for the wind to clear the smoke, but all around him Hardy could see British ensigns still proudly flying beside ships that had no flag aloft even where they still had a standing mast. Boats were in the water and prizes were being taken, vessels that were expending running blood from their deck, through their scuppers, into the ocean, while messages poured aboard from Nelson's triumphant captains to tell their admiral the names of their captures. He wanted to go below but a warning cry alerted him to the fact that the leading ship in the French van was actually now tacking, coming round to rejoin the battle, and he must assume that the rest would follow. He must get *Victory* into shape for another fight. Only when he was sure his ship was once more ready to fight could he go below.

It was three decks down to the cockpit, a confined space lit by a single lantern. Nelson lay in the arms of two of the ship's supernumeraries, one holding a pillow. He was ashen, even for a man whose face was reckoned pale, and his good eye told of great pain, but he managed a smile for Hardy and a strong-voiced question as his flag captain knelt beside him. 'Well Hardy, how do we fare?'

'What did he say?' the flag captain asked, because his hearing was still fuzzy from combat. One of Nelson's supporters repeated it close to his ear.

'Tolerable well, milord. Twelve or fourteen of the enemy ships are in our possession, but the five of the van have tacked and show every intention of bearing down on us. I have called for some of our fresher ships to come about and assist, so no doubt we will give them a drubbing.'

'I pray none of our ships have been struck, Hardy?'

That, too, required to be repeated, so Hardy got very close to Nelson as he replied. 'No, no sir. There is no fear of that.'

'Pray ensure Lady Hamilton has everything belonging to me.'

The bustle of people shifting made Hardy look. Beatty, the surgeon-general of the fleet moved closer and he crouched to examine the patient. Nelson heard the Ghost insist that something could be done, and thought, 'Poor Hardy, who will he look to now?'

The pain in his upper body was intense, but he could feel nothing below his waist; no pain, no feeling at all. Around him he could hear voices, though they were not making much sense. As Nelson contemplated death, he felt the need to add up the sum of his life because he suspected expiry was going to be a slow affair – although, thank God, not the kind of lingering demise that might go on for days.

Mentally he addressed his Maker in the knowledge that he had been no saint but neither had his sins been great. If Emma was a sin he was not prepared to repent, because he could not bring himself to believe that his God would ever condemn such a true affection as he felt for her.

'There must be some chance, surely,' Hardy moaned, in a cracking voice.

'Oh, no. Has not Mister Beatty told you, Hardy? My back is quite shot through. It will not be long now.'

Nelson's mind was wandering: faces of those he had loved or perhaps wronged swam in and out of focus behind closed eyelids. He did not know that Hardy had gone back to the deck to fight the ship. Beatty's low drone, as he talked to those holding Nelson's body, brought him back to full wakefulness and he spoke, only to find that he was repeating himself, telling the surgeon he was paralysed, which was annoying. 'I feel something rising in my breast. I think it is a sign to tell me that I am going.'

'I must confess, milord, that I can do nothing more for you. If the pain is too great we have laudanum to relieve it.'

'It is so great, Beatty, that I wish I were already dead.'

That caused a mental prayer, a plea for forgiveness. No man had the right to interfere with the good Lord's prerogatives. 'Yet I would live a little longer if I can. God be praised, I have done my duty.'

Would that count in his judgement? Would his actions in the face of the blasphemous tyranny of the Revolution be laid in the credit column of his celestial account? God must be on his side. He could not be with men who had denied him, committed regicide, pillaged France and made her a pariah among nations.

'It is good that dear Emma cannot see me now.'

The whole ship shook and rumbled as Hardy fired off a broadside. Coming through the timbers on which he lay, the shock passed through his body, bringing renewed agony, and Nelson whispered. 'Oh, *Victory*. Even you cause me pain.'

That was the last shot Hardy fired in the battle, because the last two ships in Nelson's column had steered to engage the leading French vessel. Soon he was downstairs again, holding his chief's hand and congratulating him on a great victory, leaning close to hear the dying man's low voice.

'How many?'

'I can only swear to fourteen or fifteen taken, but there may be more.'

'I had hoped for twenty.'

Suddenly Nelson was above deck again, whole and back in command, and he recalled his signal before the battle and the swell that had prompted it. The way Nelson cried for Hardy to anchor sounded like a twice-repeated howl.

'I can trust Admiral Collingwood to do that, milord.'

That produced a sudden burst of strength, and an assurance that went with command. 'Not while I live. Anchor, Hardy!'

'Milord.'

Nelson clutched the Ghost's arm. 'You won't throw me overboard, Hardy?'

Having moved his head away, that had to be repeated, and Hardy understood it well. Nelson had had a dread of such a fate ever since he had seen his first burial at sea. It was a fear that he had voiced many times, and one that he had been reassured about just as often, but Hardy repeated the promise to him nonetheless.

'Then take care of poor Lady Hamilton.' The voice came with a renewal of strength, as he added, 'You know what to do.'

The pain increased in intensity, and Nelson, who nearly passed out, found his vision had become blurred. Hardy's face so close to his, lost focus and so did his hold on reality. There was a murmuring voice that sounded low and sweet like Emma's. Her smiling face, her laughing green eyes, filled his mind, like a vision.

'Kiss me Emma.'

He felt a cool pair of lips on his forehead and asked, 'Who is that?'

The strong voice of the Ghost broke his reverie. 'It is me, milord.'

'God bless you, Hardy.'

He sank into a dream, and it was as if his whole life floated before him: the flotsam filled Thames that had delivered him to the sea as a boy, the face of John Judd, the man who had taught him seamanship, midshipmen, lieutenants, captains, admirals, his father, brothers and sisters, living and dead, and Fanny. But they all lost out to the faces he loved most, first Horatia, and then Emma.

His supporters saw his lips move but the words were too faint to hear, as Nelson told his wife that he held her in great affection, but he *LOVED* Emma. The last words anyone heard were, 'Thank God I have done my duty.'

They laid him out and covered his face, for even an admiral would have to wait till all was secure before he was taken to his cabin. The sheet that he had been wound in to bring him below was used to cover his face and, after a last look, Surgeon Beatty went back to the cockpit, to the hell of the other wounded. He stopped beneath a lantern and looked at the cribbed notes he had been taking. Beatty knew that he had witnessed history being made as he watched the death of Nelson. He examined what he had written, and went to a shelf on which rested a quill and ink. Ignoring the cries of the men being operated on by his assistants he looked at the words, 'Kiss me, Emma.'

With a bold stroke he cut through Emma, and put in its place, 'Hardy'.

William Nelson called every member of his family to his house near Canterbury two weeks after the great funeral at which, it seemed, the entire nation had mourned. Every serving admiral in the country had attended and there was not a single one who did not want to assure him that his brother had been the best of men, and that they had been, in the face of the mistrust of others, his strongest supporter.

The Prince of Wales had claimed Horatio as an extra brother, so close had they been, and did William know that the scheme for defeating the French at Trafalgar had come from an idea he proposed when supping with the Admiral? Why they had even planned the battle on his table, with the great sailor astounded by the prince's perspicacity.

He was also under instructions to say that even through the confusion of his affliction the King was distraught at the loss of his favourite sailor. Mr Pitt, the Prime Minister, had offered deep condolences, and mentioned the conversation regarding a pension for Emma, inviting William Nelson to come and see him about it.

The family obeyed the summons because William was now its head. He was Reverend the Earl Nelson now, with a grant of ten thousand pounds from a grateful government to help him buy an estate, and an annual pension for him and his heirs of five thousand per annum. Fanny had a pension too, as the lawful wife of the nation's greatest hero.

'It falls to us to protect out dear brother's memory,' said William, having struck, standing before them, what he thought was a suitably noble pose.

This earned him a hearty nod from his plump wife Sarah. Several of the others were thinking that he had grown even more pompous, if that was possible.

'It falls to a family connected to a peerage to behave in a certain way. With this in mind I have written to Lady Nelson to ask her why she sees a breach between her and ourselves, and to request that steps be taken to overcome what can only be called a misunderstanding.'

'Quite,' said Lady Sarah Nelson. 'Everyone knows we have always held her in the highest regard.'

'It may also have come to your attention that I was obliged to take on and diminish the pretensions of Lady Hamilton in the matter of our dear brother's untimely demise. She lays certain claims to inherit parts of his estate that I cannot find it within myself to entertain.'

What William really meant was that he and Emma had had a flaming row, with much cat calling, more accurate from her, that he was a snake in the grass, than from him, who was too pious to utter the word whore.

'It is my intention, while visiting upon the lady no unkindness, to detach the name of my brother and the title he bequeathed me from that association. I would take it very amiss if any one in the family sought to thwart that aim.'

The warning was plain; take sides by all means, but if you want to share the largesse of Trafalgar, ensure that you choose with care. And they also knew that if William, Earl Nelson, was not going to mention

Horatia, was not going to acknowledge what they all knew in their hearts, that she was their late brother's true daughter, then they would be wise to follow his course.

Emma heard the words and recalled enough Italian to suspect they were Latin. Outside the grubby window the good people of Calais were going about their business, with no thought to the woman who had a strong suspicion that she was dying in the alcove bed in which she lay.

Her world had collapsed in the ten years since Trafalgar: Merton, too expensive, had been sold; Sir William's annuity was too slight to support her tastes; the Nelson family were either actively hostile or too afraid to help; and William Pitt, who had almost promised an admiral going on service a pension for her, had died.

She had never been good with money, and her choice of friends had not been of the best. But as she lay there she could reflect on a life that had had more excitement and pleasure than most.

Horatia was a good child, dutiful, and to Emma dull for that reason. She had inherited the dour ecclesiastical side of the Nelson bloodline, but Emma had kept her by her side through thick and thin, even through the darkest days spent in debtor's gaol. Horatia was her link to Nelson, and for all the airs and graces of the earl, there was only one.

She could see his face now, the half smile which wrapped everyone exposed to it in some kind of magic spell. Perhaps disapproving that the only person who would care for her was a papist priest. But no, Nelson had not been like that. He could love a scoundrel as well as a prince. Who could ever live up to his example? Not she.

The priest droned on as Emma slipped away. The face of the man she loved seeming to beckon her to a brighter place, a land of sunshine and warmth, of tarantellas and songs. She was hardly aware that his daughter was holding her hand

THE MORNING CHRONICLE, 16 JANUARY 1815.

It is with great sadness that we report the death yesterday, in Calais, of Lady Emma Hamilton, wife of the former Ambassador to the Court of the Two Sicilies.'

James Perry, editor and owner of the paper, read the obituary he had written, saying to himself, 'you have gone under your last bridge now, fair Emma.'

AUTHOR'S NOTE

This book, like the first volume, *On a Making Tide*, is fiction based on the facts surrounding two remarkable people. While it is historical it is not meant to be a history. There are hundreds, if not thousands of books on Nelson and Emma Hamilton. Nothing would please me more than that the reader should become so enamoured of the subject as to take a deep interest in the mass of biographical information available.

Allied to the reading of original sources, I too, have consumed numerous books. The best biography of Horatio Nelson is still *Nelson* by Carola Oman, first published in 1947. Someone should reissue that for the 200th anniversary of Trafalgar in 2005. Likewise *Beloved Emma*, by Flora Fraser, ranks equally when it comes to the life, loves and tribulations of Emma Hamilton. For the battle of Copenhagen, Dudley Pope's *The Great Gamble*, just reissued, is unsurpassed.

If Emma is less an actor in this drama than Nelson, it is not because of the part she had in his life. It may displease those so partisan of Nelson that they often dismiss her from his story, but she was the centre of his life, more to him than fame and even naval success. And of those who gathered to mourn Nelson at his funeral, a goodly number were outright hypocrites. Nelson was a hero to the nation before Trafalgar. He only became a hero to the court and to society after his death. It is sad to reflect that some of that same hypocrisy is still around two hundred years after Nelson's death.

If there is a certain indication of the truth of their feelings, it lies in society's treatment of Emma, and even more, of their child, Horatia, who was not wholly acknowledged as her father's child until fifty years after his death. She resided with both the Matcham and Bolton branches of the family and eventually married a clergyman.

The title, given to his worthless brother, was passed to Thomas Bolton when William Nelson died, his own children having pre-deceased him. Thus, one of the greatest warrior titles of British history and all the benefits that flowed from it: money, social position and until very recently an automatic seat in the House of Lords, passed down through the heirs of Nelson's sister, not through that of his own child.

It is true that Emma behaved unwisely in the years between 1802 and her death, but she was forced to live on her wits and the little she had from the memory of the man she loved. But she was not the ogre she has been portrayed. She was warm, gifted, beautiful when young and touched something in Nelson that no other woman could. Perhaps, as well as a Nelson Society dedicated to his memory, we should have an Emma Hamilton Society to celebrate the life of the woman who captured the heart of Britain's greatest naval hero.

David Donachie
Deal, Kent, 2001